Michelle Smart's love affair with books started when she was a baby and would cuddle them in her cot. A voracious reader of all genres, she found her love of romance established when she stumbled across her first Mills & Boon book at the age of twelve. She's been reading them—and writing them—ever since. Michelle lives in Northamptonshire, England, with her husband and two young Smarties.

Cathy Williams can remember reading Mills & Boon books as a teenager, and now that she's writing them she remains an avid fan. For her, there is nothing like creating romantic stories and engaging plots, and each and every book is a new adventure. Cathy lives in London. Her three daughters—Charlotte, Olivia and Emma—have always been, and continue to be, the greatest inspirations in her life.

THE SECRET BEHIND THE GREEK'S RETURN

MICHELLE SMART

CLAIMING HIS CINDERELLA SECRETARY

CATHY WILLIAMS

MILLS & BOON

First Published in Great Britain 2021
by Mills & Boon, an imprint of HarperCollins*Publishers* Ltd,
1 London Bridge Street, London, SE1 9GF

www.harpercollins.co.uk

HarperCollins*Publishers*
1st Floor, Watermarque Building,
Ringsend Road, Dublin 4, Ireland

The Secret Behind the Greek's Return © 2021 Michelle Smart

Claiming His Cinderella Secretary © 2021 Cathy Williams

ISBN: 978-0-263-28253-5

This book

For mo

THE SECRET BEHIND THE GREEK'S RETURN

MICHELLE SMART

MILLS & BOON

CHAPTER ONE

NIKOS MANOLAS SAT in his car shaded beneath the orange trees lining the quiet Valencian suburban street, elbow resting against the window, fist tucked under his chin. On the other side of the road ran an imposingly high fence the length of the pavement and beyond. Small intermittent signs warned trespassers against breaching it.

Nikos's narrowed gaze rested on the gate ten metres away that admitted people onto the land behind the fence. He'd watched the gate for two minutes and knew he should move on before he attracted the attention of the armed guards on the other side of it.

He'd wanted one last look. He'd had it. Time to go.

He switched the engine on and put the car into gear. Before he could make his intended U-turn, the gates opened.

He put the gearstick back into neutral. A Mercedes built like a tank slowly nosed its way through the gates and pulled onto the road. He held his breath as it passed him. The tinting of the car's windows made it impossible to identify the driver.

In his rear-view mirror he watched the Mercedes shrink into the distance and take a right at the end of the street.

Nikos rubbed his chin and then, with a burst of adrenaline, put his foot on the accelerator and spun his Porsche around.

The road the Mercedes had joined was quiet this hot mid-morning, making it easy to keep tabs. When it joined the V-21, he made sure to keep three cars between them. The deeper into the city they drove, the thicker the traffic.

It had been over eighteen months since Nikos had been in the heart of Valencia. Much of the architecture was medieval, the roads and streets narrow, but modern developments had their place too, and as he drove past the majestic Palau de les Arts Reina Sofia with its sweeping roof like a feather plume, he blinked away memories of the evening he'd taken Marisa there to watch *Tristan and Isolde.* If he'd known the so-called 'Most revolutionary opera' had been, in its essence, a romance, he'd have made his excuses and begged off. Nikos liked his entertainment to be like his affairs; frenetic and forgettable.

Not that he'd enjoyed any form of entertainment in recent times. For the past year and a half he'd lived the life of a hermit in the Alaskan wilderness, residing in a log cabin accessible only by small plane.

Readjusting to society was proving harder than he'd envisaged. He'd imagined himself returning to civilisation with a bang and throwing himself back into the old party lifestyle but in the two weeks since he'd emerged from his self-imposed exile, he'd found himself reluctant to return to the spotlight. He supposed he'd become used to isolation.

When the Mercedes indicated to turn into the huge shopping complex, his chest tightened. This had been the place Marisa liked to shop. She knew its layout better than he knew the layout of his Mykonos home.

By the time the automatic sensors had read his licence

plate and he'd waved his bank card in front of the scanner, he'd lost sight of her.

It was for the best, he thought, grimacing. It had been a strange burst of sentimentality that had found him outside the Lopez estate in the first place and curiosity that found him wasting precious time tailing an old lover to an underground car park. Time to follow his original plan, to drive to the airport and resume the life he'd been forced to hide from. His plane had been refuelled, his crew ready to fly him home.

As he followed the exit signs, he caught sight of the tank-like Mercedes parked ahead. It was only as he approached it that he realised it was in a row of spaces reserved for parents and children.

He slammed his foot on the brake. The car behind him sounded its horn in protest.

Why the hell would Marisa park there?

Pulse suddenly surging, he cast his gaze around for a free space and, cursing under his breath, drove straight to the closest one, which was still a good distance away.

The distance didn't matter. Out of the car, he could see clearly enough.

What he saw made his blood freeze. Marisa, curly golden-red hair bouncing in all directions, was scooping a small infant from the back of her car.

The blood in his head defrosted into a burn in an instant.

She carefully placed the child in a buggy, strapped it in, then reached back into the car and removed a large bag which she slung on the back of the buggy.

The elevators into the complex were directly opposite where Nikos had parked. In silent horror, he watched her stride towards them. He needed to hide. One slight turn of her head and she would see him.

But he couldn't move. Couldn't wrench his gaze from the lover he'd vanished from and the child—baby—he'd had no idea existed.

Marisa Lopez scrunched a face at her appearance. Should she leave her hair down or pin it up? Yes, to the former and yes to some under-eye concealer. Her light golden skin had become so pale and the rings under her eyes so dark she resembled a corpse. The black dress she'd chosen to wear only enhanced the effect, a point reinforced when her sister, Elsa, walked into her dressing room and burst into laughter. 'I suppose funeral chic beats aubergine chic.'

'Don't,' Marisa muttered. Only vanity had made her return the aubergine-coloured dress. It had clashed horribly with her red hair. This black dress, though horrendously unstylish, was marginally more flattering colour-wise.

Elsa stood behind her, wrapped her arms around Marisa's waist, groped for her hands and rested her chin on her shoulder. Their eyes met in the mirror. The contrast between them had never been so stark. Elsa shone with good health and happiness. Her eyes, though, brimmed with concern. 'Are you okay? You don't look well.'

Marisa opened her mouth to assure her sister all was well but the lie refused to form.

'I can't do this.' The words expelled in a puff.

A line cleaved Elsa's brow.

'I can't marry Raul,' Marisa whispered, and squeezed her sister's hand tightly for support as the truth of her feelings, which had swirled inside her like steadily thickening soup for so long, suddenly solidified into truth. In a stronger voice, she repeated, 'I can't marry Raul.'

There. She'd said it. Finally admitted it.

'You were right.' Her spine straightened and her lungs inflated as she spoke. 'I keep thinking about what you said the other day about not trusting him and you're right. He lied to me. Raul doesn't want to be a father to Niki. He only wants the business.'

Marisa's relationship with Raul was very much one of convenience brought about by the circumstances that had seen her world implode when a vicious cartel had targeted her family's shipping company to smuggle their drugs around the world. Her parents' refusal to comply with their demands had resulted in her father's murder.

This had come only a few short months after Marisa's lover had drowned and she'd discovered she was pregnant.

Up against a network of brutal crooks with her father dead, the multinational family business passing into her hands, a fatherless newborn baby to love and nurture, her sister in a different country and her mother a wounded soul, Marisa's desperation for help had found her arranging a marriage with Raul Torres, a man she knew socially who ran a business of a similar kind to Lopez Shipping.

She'd been upfront about what she wanted: a father for her son and help running the badly neglected family business.

She'd chosen Raul because she'd believed he was one of the good guys. Believed they had what it took to make a good team. Believed he would make a good father to her fatherless son.

Belief had differed greatly from reality.

A month ago, the cartel had discovered the Lopezes were working with international authorities against them and hatched a plot to kidnap Elsa from her home in Austria. Santi, a man who'd been practically raised a Lopez, had taken Elsa into hiding. Marisa, her son and her mother had stayed in their heavily guarded estate, terrified for Elsa and essentially under siege. Then, two weeks ago and after fifteen months of hell, the cartel were finally defeated. It took a huge international effort to bring them down; private security forces teaming up with worldwide security organisations and culminated in a co-ordinated swoop of arrests across twelve countries.

'I keep thinking about what you said about the cartel and you were right about that too,' Marisa said. 'Raul offered us no protection at all. He abandoned the baby he swore he loved to his fate.'

And that, along with his increasingly obvious indifference to her son, was unforgiveable.

Slipping her hand from Elsa's, she rubbed her forehead. 'What am I going to do?'

'End it.'

'I know that. I mean *how* am I going to end it?' She stepped closer to the mirror and stared at her reflection, stared at the ugly dress her subconscious had chosen for her. Her gut had known before she did that she couldn't marry Raul.

'Call him. Do it now,' Elsa urged.

She found a smile. 'I can't break up with him an hour before our engagement party. That would be like poking a hornets' nest. This family doesn't need more enemies.'

Raul wouldn't tamper with the brakes of her car like the cartel had done to her father, or drown her dog, or plot to kidnap her sister, but Marisa had learned in their time together that the man she'd chosen to marry out of desperation had a strong streak of narcissism and an unlimited capacity for grudge-holding. He knew enough secrets about Lopez Shipping to ruin them.

'Well, don't wait too long,' Elsa warned.

'I won't,' she promised. Now her mind was made up, she'd do it as soon as possible. She managed another small smile. 'Although, with luck, this dress might make *him* decide to end it.'

Leaving the dressing room, Marisa walked through her bedroom then tiptoed into the dark adjoining nursery.

Her heart swelled as she peered into the cot. Her son, her heart, her life, was fast asleep, his little chest and podgy belly rising and falling. She kissed her fingers then gently placed them to his silky-soft cheek.

How could anyone look at this child and not feel the compulsion to love and protect him?

She picked up the photo on the cabinet beside the cot, the swelling of her heart sharpening as she gazed at the wry smile of her son's father. Nikos. The love of her life.

Dead.

Hot tears stung the back of her eyes and she hurriedly blinked them back before kissing Nikos's face and placing the photo back on the cabinet.

His memory lived as an ache in every beat of her heart. Only by nestling her love and grief deep inside her and holding it tight until darkness fell and she was alone to purge the anguish of his loss, had she learned to get through the days. The pain never seemed to lessen.

After taking a moment to compose herself, she left the nursery through the main door and knocked on the door opposite. Estrella, their housekeeper, opened it. Estrella had worked for the Lopezes since Marisa was eight and had happily agreed to babysit for the night.

'We're leaving now,' Marisa said, wringing her fingers together. 'Can you check the baby monitor's working for you?'

The room she'd put Estrella in was so close to the

nursery she'd hear him sneeze before the monitor picked it up.

Marisa hated being parted from her son. Since his birth, she'd only left him for a handful of evenings, and a few hours here and there when it had been absolutely necessary for her to attend work in person. This would be the first time she'd left him alone with anyone but her mother and the first time she'd left him for a whole night.

'It's working fine.' Estrella held the baby monitor to her ear. 'I can hear his breathing.'

Marisa resisted the impulse to yank the monitor from her hand and listen for herself. She knew she was a paranoid first-time mother but she defied anyone to walk in her shoes and not be the same.

'You promise to call if there's any problems?'

'There won't be any problems but I promise.'

'I'll be back by ten in the morning, at the latest.'

'There's no rush, so take your time.' Estrella gave a wide, sympathetic smile. 'Enjoy having a lie-in.'

The thought alone made the nausea in her belly bubble afresh. Marisa *liked* the early-morning closeness with her baby while the rest of the household slept.

It was just for one night, she reminded herself. In the morning she'd be back home with her son and would cuddle up with him and plan how to end her engagement without provoking Raul's vengeance.

The exclusive hotel's staff had done a fabulous job of turning its function room into a glittering party pad. The two hundred guests chatting and dancing had a constant flow of champagne and canapés, the bar at the far end plentifully staffed so no one had to wait long to be served. The world-famous DJ played a medley of tunes to suit all ages and tastes and judging by the smiles, everyone seemed to be enjoying themselves. Everyone except Marisa.

Her gaze kept falling on Elsa and Santi, glued to each other's sides. They'd finally admitted their love for each other two days ago. Marisa had known for years that the two of them were meant for each other but suspecting something and seeing that love bloom before her eyes had been both heart-warming and heart-wrenching.

She had loved like that once. Loved with the whole of her heart.

Swallowing the ache, she let Raul drag her around the room to welcome their guests together and tried to curb her irritation at his annoyance every time she checked her phone for messages from Estrella.

How had she ever thought he would make a suitable husband for her and a good father for her son? She must have been mad.

No. Not mad. Frightened. Overwhelmed. Likely suffering from postnatal depression.

Once he started chatting with a group of his golfing friends, Marisa escaped his clutches and found her own friends, a bunch she'd been to school with and remained close to.

Her respite lasted only until the end of the DJ's first set.

Raul took her by the arm and steered her to the raised dais. He wanted to make a speech. Of *course* he wanted to make a speech.

Knowing she had no choice but to go along with it, she snatched another flute of champagne from the tray of a passing waiter and climbed the steps.

The music stopped. Raul took the prepared microphone and called for everyone's attention. The dance floor filled, their guests eager to hear what he had to say.

He held her hand tightly. The feel of his skin on hers made her flesh crawl.

'Thank you all for coming tonight and for your understanding at the postponement,' he said. Their party should have been held two weeks before but the takedown of the cartel and the danger it had put Marisa and her family in had forced them to postpone. 'It certainly wasn't through choice but as you know, recent events took the decision out of our hands. This has been a difficult time for me and my future wife, and your support has been appreciated.'

Marisa almost choked on her champagne. Luckily Raul was too busy basking in the applause to notice. She loved how he made it sound as if it had been a difficult time for them as a couple when the truth was the coward had hidden away until it was all over.

'I ask you all to raise a glass to my fiancée. To Marisa.'

But the crowd had fallen silent. Their attention had been taken by something that parted them like Moses and the Red Sea.

Marisa followed the open-mouthed stares. In the newly created gangway stood a tall, solitary figure. He was looking directly at her.

Heart suddenly racing, prickles ran up her spine and over her skin.

Certain she was hallucinating, she blinked hard and tried to catch her breath, fought to keep her shaking legs from collapsing beneath her.

It couldn't be.

The prickles infected her brain, reduced it to fuzzy mush. The room began to spin. Something distant smashed. She had only the faintest awareness it was the glass she'd been holding before the world went black.

* * *

Nikos cut through the stunned silence to bound up to the dais where that idiot Raul hovered over the prone Marisa, doing absolutely nothing.

The complete shock at Nikos's appearance meant no one was capable of stopping him from checking her pulse, satisfying himself that she was alive, then scooping her into his arms.

'Excuse me,' he said as he carried her through the still-frozen crowd. 'She needs air.'

Her large brown eyes opened. Fixed on him. Widened. Blinked. Blinked again. She whimpered.

A waitress opened the double doors so he could sweep a now struggling Marisa out of the room. Her hand pushed at his chest but her movements were too sluggish to be effective. The whimpering was growing. It cut through him. It was the sound a wounded puppy made.

A member of the hotel's concierge team hurried to them. 'Can I call a doctor for you, sir?'

'Not necessary. She fainted—a shock, nothing serious. Can you get the elevator for me?'

'Certainly.'

The concierge pressed the button and the elevator door opened.

'Top floor,' he commanded, stepping inside with her. Marisa had stopped struggling and gone limp. Her eyes were screwed tight like a child trying to make itself invisible to a monster.

He'd never meant to scare her and neither had he intended to make such a grand entrance.

When the birth certificate of his son had been presented to him earlier that day, Nikos had been collected and analytical in his response. The mental preparations he'd made for a positive result greatly aided this mind-set. Remaining dead to Marisa was no longer an option. Allowing her engagement party to go ahead was not an option either, and he'd set off to Valencia immediately. He'd called the hotel on the drive to the airfield, certain all the rooms would be taken, and had been surprised to find the penthouse still available. Surely the happy couple would be spending the night in it?

How happy were they? How happy was *Marisa*?

He'd done his research on Marisa's fiancé during the flight back to Valencia. A few phone calls with mutual acquaintances—explaining his return from the dead had been dealt with by giving promises that he would explain in person when he next saw them—and he'd learned Raul's only attribute was that he was rich. One friend quoted him as 'an untrustworthy snake'. That had been the most positive of the opinions.

At the top floor he shifted her position to free a hand and pressed his thumb to the security box. Inside the suite he laid her loose body carefully on the sofa and took a step back to look at her properly for the first time in eighteen months.

What on earth had possessed her to wear such an unflattering dress to her own engagement party? The Marisa he'd dated had a love of fashion. This dress was something the old women of Mykonos would wear. And where was the make-up she loved to wear? Whenever he'd told her she didn't need it, she'd laugh, thank him, then trowel it on until every freckle was masked and her eyes, lips and cheeks shone with unnatural colour. Now, all her freckles, faint though they were, were on display, and his chest tightened to remember how he'd adored waking to this bare face.

She didn't move a muscle under his scrutiny. He suspected she was playing possum.

Shock at his resurrection he'd learned in recent days meant varied extreme emotions. He'd give her a minute to compose herself.

Truth was, he could do with a moment of composure too, and his suite's bar was fully stocked.

He selected an eighteen-year-old single malt, unscrewed the lid and poured a hefty measure into a crystal glass. As he took his first sip, he sensed movement behind him.

Turning, he found Marisa only a foot from him.

He took another, larger drink to burn through the lump that had formed in his throat and held her silent stare.

Her head tilted slowly from side to side as she gazed at him through wild, wide brown eyes. Her plump lips were pulled in a straight line. She was breathing heavily through her pretty nose. With her golden-red tangled mass of frizzy curls—another curious thing: the Marisa he'd dated had used every product known to humanity to prevent frizz from forming—she had the look of someone sizing him up, someone…

The word 'rabid' flashed through his mind.

Marisa stared at the ghost before her, too scared to blink for fear he'd disappear.

Since she'd woken from her faint, secure but so *frightened* in his arms, the only thought in her pounding head was that this couldn't be real.

Nikos was dead.

Dead.

She'd mourned and cried herself to sleep every night for eighteen months. She'd woken every morning with a throbbing ache in her heart that time hadn't even begun to heal. She'd carried his child, given birth to his child, loved and raised his child without him.

And all the time he'd been alive.

Alive and so incredibly *vital*.

That really was Nikos in front of her, a wary expression on the face that had lived as nothing but a memory for an agony of time.

The emotions that flooded her were too hot and overwhelming to be contained a moment longer and they overflowed with a howl she had no control over as she leapt at him.

CHAPTER TWO

NIKOS DIDN'T MOVE away or attempt to defend himself from the fists beating against his chest and the screamed indecipherable words. He kept his composure, his gaze fixed above her head, determined to remain dispassionate against the onslaught of Marisa's rage.

She'd always been his temperamental opposite. Where he was cool and analytical, she was warm and passionate. Even her fury, he was now discovering, was passionately delivered.

But when the impact of her beating fists weakened and he sensed her purge was over, he looked down and his guts twisted.

It wasn't fury that had contorted her beautiful face and turned it into something red and swollen. And it wasn't fury that dropped her to the floor with a thud, made her fall onto her side, pull her knees to her chin and weep in a rocking ball.

Unprepared for such an emotional display, he rubbed his cheek and swallowed air through rapidly tightening lungs.

A box of tissues sat on the suite's bureau and, needing to do something, he strolled over and picked it up then placed it on the floor beside her before finishing his drink.

Theos, he needed another one, and poured himself an even heftier measure, which he downed in one. His next measure was more sedate and he poured an equal amount in another glass before taking it to Marisa.

Her sobs and the racking of her frame seemed to be lessening but he kept a cautious distance as he crouched down. 'Here,' he said quietly, speaking in English, a language they were both fluent in. 'Drink this. It will help.'

Marisa wanted to cover her ears and drown out his voice. *Nikos*'s voice. This was simply too much to take in.

All those long nights she had dreamed of this, Nikos alive, the time that had passed since his death nothing but a vivid nightmare.

Oh, God, *he was alive.*

Dragging her trembling hands over her face and trying her hardest to catch a breath in a chest so bruised, she sat up. Not yet ready to look at him again, she took a handful of tissues and blew her nose.

A glass was thrust in front of her face. Fine dark hairs poked out beneath the sleeve of his shirt around his wrist. It was enough to make fresh tears fall and she grabbed more tissues to wipe them away before taking the drink. She threw the liquid down her throat. Unused to neat spirits, she didn't expect the fiery burn that followed but it helped, cutting through the fog of her brain and sharpening her senses.

'Another?' he asked.

Still unable to look at him, she nodded.

When the refilled glass held by the long, tapered fingers appeared before her again, she snatched it off him and downed it.

'Better?'

She blew out a short breath before daring to meet his stare.

He was crouched on his haunches, light brown eyes studying her. 'Ready to talk?'

But her throat was too constricted to speak. Rising to her knees, overwhelmed with the need to touch him and assure herself that she hadn't hallucinated him into life, that Nikos truly was here, mortal, breathing, she reached out a hand and pressed it to his cheek.

Gazing into his intense eyes, she rubbed her thumb over his strong jaw, felt the unshaven dark bristles tickle against it, then gently skimmed it down to his mouth. The heat of his breath warmed her skin before she reached her other hand to his face and traced her fingers over it. The furrowed brow, the lines around his eyes, the long nose that bent a little to the left, the cleft in his chin, not a millimetre of skin left unexplored.

He didn't blink, not even when she brushed her fingers up to the widow's peak of his hairline and dived them through the cropped dark brown hair to trace the contours of his head and down to his neck. Only when she felt the beat of the pulse beneath his ear and felt her own pulse beat in response did she drop her hands and sag back on her bottom.

A beat of charged silence passed before he rose and walked his long, lean frame to the armchair.

Nikos sat heavily and watched Marisa shuffle until her back rested against the base of the sofa opposite him. She hugged her knees to her chest and rested her chin on them.

He tried to gather his thoughts, a task made harder by the sensation dancing over his skin where her fingers had caressed. *Theos*, hers was the first real human touch he'd felt in eighteen months.

Gritting his teeth, he forced himself back to the matter at hand. He'd composed what he would say to her on the flight over, had run over it many times in his head, had known much of the delivery would depend on her reaction to him. He'd guessed emotions would be involved—this was Marisa after all—but he'd never imagined those emotions would be so raw. So hard to witness.

Their affair had lasted much longer than his previous relationships but it had never been serious. Nikos didn't do serious, never had, never would. He liked the bachelor life and greatly disliked being answerable to anyone, a hangover from his teenage years. As he liked to tell people, if you want to watch an innate rebellious streak bloom in real time, send a wilful fourteen-year-old to a strict foreign boarding school.

He'd lasted two terms before being expelled. He'd lasted a whole four months at the next one. He'd only avoided expulsion at the third because his grandfather had bribed him. If Nikos could survive the school year without as much as a sanction *and* pass his exams, he could finish his education and have fifty thousand from his trust fund. There had been other conditions attached but they'd been ignored the minute the money had hit his bank account. He'd been sixteen years old.

Nineteen years later and Nikos still lived his life on *his* terms. Until his forced exile, life had been great. He'd loved making money and he'd loved spending money. He'd loved having the wealth that meant the world's most beautiful women gravitated to him and allowed him to take his pick of the crop.

Marisa had been the first woman he'd actively pursued. She'd been in the VIP section of his Ibiza nightclub when they'd met. Instantly attracted to her, he'd nonetheless assumed she was another vacuous socialite. His assumption that she'd willingly come to his villa for a night of no-strings fun had been swiftly disabused.

Unused to female rejection, he'd gone all out to woo her. She'd agreed to meet him the next day for lunch by the pool at his villa…and had turned up with a gaggle of friends. It had taken a week of messages and calls for her to agree to a date. It had taken another month to get her into bed and then had come the next surprise—she'd been a virgin.

He supposed that's why their affair had lasted as long as it did. It had been impossible to get bored with someone who refused to play the usual games and constantly kept him on his toes. Marisa had her own life, one she'd been unable and unwilling to revolve around him. Her parents had been grooming her to take over the running of the family shipping business, something she'd taken very seriously.

As he'd had more flexibility with his working hours, Nikos had found himself in the strange realm of being the one to make all the running. It had been worth it. Marisa had taken work seriously but outside office hours she had been excellent company; passionate, funny and witty, open-minded, as happy dining in a cheap café as she was in a Michelin-starred restaurant. That she was as sexy as sin had been the icing on the cake.

She was also naturally affectionate. She would end a short phone call with a good friend saying she loved them. She told *everyone* she loved them. She'd told Nikos she loved him hundreds of times but for Marisa, they were just words, so to have witnessed such naked distress at his resurrection sat heavily in his guts.

He didn't see how it could be real. Even his grandfather hadn't been this emotional at Nikos's return.

He was pretty sure his father hadn't known he'd been missing. Even if he had, Nikos doubted he'd suffered more than a solitary pang. His father hadn't cared for him as a child and cared even less for him as an adult.

Swirling the remaining single malt in his glass he went straight to the subject that had brought him here. 'You have a son.'

Her brown eyes flickered. He read the surprise in them. He'd often thought how their eyes were mirrors of their personalities; Marisa's dark and warm, his light and cold.

'I saw you with him. Two days ago,' he added when her mouth dropped open.

Tears filled her eyes. He held his breath and warily waited for them to spill over and for her to fall to pieces again.

It didn't happen. She swallowed rapidly and nodded. 'He's mine?'

She brushed a falling tear and nodded again.

He took a large sip of his drink. He'd known it in his heart but having it confirmed still came as a rush.

'You named him for me?' He asked the question though he already knew the answer. He'd seen the birth certificate.

Nikos Marco Lopez. Born eleven months ago weighing three kilograms. Born seven months after he'd faked his own death.

She let go of the hold around her knees and rested her head back against the base of the sofa. 'Why…?' Her husky voice broke.

The sound of her anguish cut straight through him, and he filled the void of silence before she could find her voice again.

'You must have many questions,' he stated. 'Let me explain as best I can. Anything I miss, ask when I'm finished. And then I will ask questions of you. Fair?'

Her gaze searched his before she closed her eyes and inclined her head in agreement.

He took a moment to put his thoughts in order. 'As you must have guessed, I faked my death. It was not a decision I made lightly. An international drug cartel wanted to use my clubs to sell their goods.' Her already ashen face paled even more and he leaned forward. 'Yes. The same cartel.'

She brought her knees back to her chest.

'They would not accept no as an answer. You remember the firebomb in my London nightclub? That was them. What you don't know is they made a bomb threat against my club in Ibiza. It was fake but I have no doubt they were capable and willing to do it for real. In the space of eight days, my French lawyer, the head of my Santorini security and my club manager in Madrid disappeared. I received a package that contained photos of my missing lawyer. I won't describe them to you but it showed the depraved lengths they were willing to go to in order to force my hand. Among those pictures was a photo of you.'

A whimper came from her tightly compressed lips. He ignored it, just as he ignored the violent churn in his stomach to remember his reaction to finding her photo nestled amid evidence of such cruel barbarity.

'It was clear that no one associated with me would be safe until I gave in. But I would not submit. Drugs are an evil in this world and I will have nothing to do with them.'

Nikos understood too well the inherent wickedness of drugs. His parents had been addicts with the unfortunate blessing of a substantial monthly allowance from a trust fund on his half-English mother's side to feed it. One of his earliest memories was of going into the living room one morning and finding her semi-conscious on the sofa with a needle stuck in her arm.

'I employed an international security firm and with their help, I faked my death and disappeared. My business partners could legally take care of the businesses. My "death" meant the cartel had no reason to go after you or anyone else associated with me.'

There had been no debate in his mind about confiding his plans to Marisa. Safer for her to believe he was dead.

But he couldn't switch off the horror of those photos and for his own peace of mind and to satisfy himself of her safety, he'd employed the same security force to keep watch over her.

'Drowning gave a plausible reason for me to vanish. I was smuggled to Alaska and spent the months of my death alone in a cabin in the Alaska Mountain Range. Without a body, a death certificate can't be issued for a number of years, which meant I could resume my life when it was over.' He raised his shoulders. 'And now it's over.'

Over but with the wreckage still to be cleared.

Despite his best efforts, the Lopezes had still got caught in the cartel's snare. He knew perfectly well it had been incidental to his own dealings with them—the cartel had needed to increase its distribution processes so they could get their evil goods into the nightclubs and other places it was sold—but it had still come as a blow when he'd learned via the daily report he'd received of Marco Lopez's murder a year ago. A devastating blow made harder by being eight thousand kilometres away and helpless to do anything about it.

Marco had been a good man who'd welcomed Nikos into his family, and Nikos's guilt that he'd only had Marisa watched sat like poison in his guts.

That had been the lowest point of his exile. It had also been the moment he'd understood why Felipe Lorenzi, the man who ran the security operation, had insisted on sending him to such a remote part of the world. Sitting idle while the world burned was not Nikos's style but placing him one hundred and twenty kilometres away from the nearest road had gone some way to curbing his impulsive take-charge tendencies.

He didn't like to remember how close he'd come to packing a rucksack and taking his chances in the Alaskan wilderness when he'd learned the devastating news. If Felipe hadn't called to tell him the Lopezes had also hired him to run their personal security in the wake of Marco's death, he would have made that hike.

And if a single one of the daily reports had mentioned Marisa's pregnancy or the birth of her child...*his* child... he dreaded to think what he would have done.

Marisa tried to process what she'd just been told but there was so much to wrap her head around. Too much. Nikos had made a clear and conscious decision to fake his own death. He'd willingly allowed her to believe he was dead.

She met his stare and hugged her knees tighter. 'Why didn't you tell me?'

He raised a shoulder before having another drink. 'My death had to be convincing. Believable.'

'I understand that... Can I have some more Scotch?' She would get it for herself but didn't trust her legs to keep her upright. Everything inside her felt jellified.

He got to his feet and strolled to the bar. She couldn't stop herself watching his every move, afraid that if she took her eyes off him for a second he would disappear again. None of this felt real.

She clasped the refilled glass tightly while he settled

back on the armchair and she tried her hardest to get her scrambled thoughts in order. 'I think I understand why you did it—faked your death. That cartel...' she squeezed her eyes shut as memories flashed through her: her father's coffin; gentle Rocco's dead body floating in the swimming pool '...were evil. But I don't understand why you didn't tell me, why you were happy for me to believe you were dead.'

'I wasn't *happy* about any of it,' he retorted bitingly.

'You could have confided in me. Prepared me. I can keep my mouth shut, especially about something as serious as that.'

'Secrets don't stay secrets if they're shared. And if I had told you, who else should I have told? My grandfather? My business partners?'

His indifference, both in his choice of words and his tone, pummelled through her. When she looked at him and found the indifference there in his stare too, her battered heart withered. 'I would have confided in you,' she whispered.

'You don't know that. Until you're in a situation, you don't know how you would react.'

'There is no way I would have let the man I love think I was dead. I wouldn't have put you through that pain.'

She caught a tiny flinch in his features before he said, 'Not even if you knew the pain would be temporary and that the alternative would mean actual, physical danger?'

Temporary? Marisa had a large sip of the Scotch and let it burn down her throat. 'The cartel was taken down two weeks ago,' she said slowly.

He inclined his head in agreement.

'Why are you only telling me now? Why not then, as soon as the danger was over?'

He took another drink of his own.

'Are you only telling me now because you've learned about Niki?'

His light brown eyes flickered. 'You call him Niki?'

She nodded. She'd named him for his father but the first time she'd said the name aloud she'd burst into tears. It had got easier hearing others say it over time but those tears and the fact that she'd wanted him to have his own identity without the burden of a dead father to live up to had found her developing her own variant of the name.

'What's he like?'

'A baby. He's beautiful. He has your colouring—I think he'll be tall like you too. He's crawling and tries to stand himself up, and he cut his first tooth two weeks ago...' Her words trailed off as she was reminded, again, that Nikos could have safely knocked on her door two weeks ago and put her out of her misery. He'd chosen not to. 'Tell me the truth, Nikos, are you only here now because of Niki?'

'I can't ignore the fact I have a child.'

'No,' she agreed. 'You can't. But what I want to know is would you have told me you were alive if you hadn't found out about him?'

'What would have been the point? You've moved on with your life. You didn't need a ghost from your past showing up.'

She tilted her head back and breathed through the tightening in her chest. 'So that's a no, then.'

'I did what I thought was best.'

'For who? You or me? You can't think I wouldn't have found out eventually. You always intended to resume your life—we have friends in common. Someone would have seen you and told me. Sooner or later the media will pick up on it.' She downed the rest of her Scotch in an effort to drown her growing anger. 'Is that what you wanted for me? To get a call or read an article telling me the man I'd mourned for eighteen months was alive and kicking? Or was it that you didn't care enough to tell me? That rather than it being *me* who'd moved on, it was you and this was one conversation you simply couldn't be bothered to have?'

'I didn't imagine you'd moved on. This is your engagement party.'

'And what, you made assumptions about my state of mind? Stop making excuses and be honest with me. You've had two weeks to tell me you're alive and the only reason you're here telling me now is because of Niki.'

Resting his elbows on his thighs he leaned forward. His features were expressionless as he said the cutting words, 'So what?'

CHAPTER THREE

MARISA HAD TROUBLE closing her jaw enough to speak. Were her ears deceiving her or had Nikos really just said that? '"*So what*"?'

He shrugged, his expression now nonchalant. 'Yes. So what? We were lovers but you knew the score. I don't do long term and I never pretended differently. I'm not here to resurrect an affair that would have soon died a natural death. You've moved on and I've moved on but that doesn't stop me wanting to know my child and being a father to him.' He swirled the last of the Scotch in his glass and then tipped it down his throat.

Marisa hadn't thought the evening could produce a bigger shock than Nikos being alive but this revelation landed even harder, filling her brain with the dizzying heat that had made her faint only an hour or so before.

It felt like she'd fallen through a trapdoor and had hurtled down and down to land with a thump that left her entire body bruised.

She knew the score? What score? She had a vague recollection of a date together when they'd talked about dreams for their respective futures and Nikos saying something about never wanting to be tied down, but that had been in their early days, before they'd slept together, before things had intensified so much that being parted had become a physical ache. The nights they couldn't be together had still been spent together, laptops open, catching up on their day and making dirty talk through video calls before wishing each other goodnight.

Did none of that mean anything to him?

And what about all the times she'd told him she loved him? Didn't that mean anything either? He'd never said the words back to her but every time she'd said it, he would either kiss her if they were together in person or blow her a kiss if they were speaking through their laptops or phones.

He was very different from her. She'd known that from the outset. His refusal to say the three magic words would have affected her far more deeply if she hadn't intuited from the little he'd told her of his background that love as a word held no meaning for him. Nikos showed his feelings by deeds and in the six months they'd been together his actions had been those of a man infatuated.

Or was that what she'd wanted to think? Had she seen what she'd wanted to see? Believed what she'd wanted to believe?

She stared into the face that was giving so little away and fought to keep the tears burning the back of her eyes from falling. 'Don't you even care about Raul?'

If Nikos had ever felt anything for her then *surely* he would feel something at her being engaged to another man, and it was taking all the control she had not to fling herself at his feet and beg him to snap out of this horrid ice-cool persona and tell her she wasn't alone in feeling overwhelmed at being in the same room together again, that she wasn't the only one having to control hands that yearned to touch and lips that yearned to caress, an entire body that yearned to wrap around him and feel his warm skin against hers.

The growing desperation for his touch fought with what her eyes were telling her. This icy Nikos was a facet of his personality she'd seen only fleetingly before and never directed at her.

Nikos strove not to let the rancid burn at the mention of Marisa's fiancé show on his face. When he'd learned two months ago during a wet afternoon spent trawling the internet that she'd become engaged, he'd shrugged it off. See? He'd been right that her affection and words of love had been nothing special. She'd picked herself up and found a replacement for him. Good luck to her.

When, later that same night of discovery, he'd found his fingers typing the name of her fiancé into his search engine, he'd been so disturbed at his actions that he'd hurled his phone at the wall. It had been unfortunate that he'd used enough force to crack the screen. His strength had been surprising too, considering how drunk he'd been that night.

He would not accept that his online search of Raul Torres's name earlier that day and all the calls he'd made about him had been like lancing a boil. He'd only done it because her fiancé would be a huge part of his son's life. Any father would do the same.

Theos. Him, a father.

'I don't know the man,' he answered evenly, swallowing his anger to stare directly into her eyes. 'But I don't care for what I've heard. Does Nikos think of Raul as his father?'

Her head dropped. She rubbed her hands over her face before answering. 'He hardly knows him and he's too young to think in terms like that.'

'Good.' The relief he felt made his body sag but he ignored it to inject a warning tone into his voice. 'I don't want to make trouble for you, Marisa, but I don't want my son to think of anyone as his father but me.'

But the sickly pallor her skin had turned told him her mind had wandered away from him and his stomach clenched to think it was that man it had wandered to.

'What's wrong?' he asked.

'Where's my handbag?'

'I assume it's where you left it.'

She staggered to her feet. 'My phone's in it. I need to get it.'

'You want to go back to the snake pit for your phone?'

'If there's a problem at home, Estrella won't be able to get hold of me. She's looking after Niki for the night.' Just thinking it was enough for icy shards to stab at Marisa's chest and pierce into her brain. How long had she been uncontactable in this suite?

'She must have your mother and sister's numbers?'

'Yes….'

'Then stop panicking.' He reached into his pocket and pulled out his phone. 'What does your bag look like?'

'Small and silver… Can I borrow that to call Elsa? I know her number by heart.'

He unlocked it and handed it to her. 'If she doesn't answer, we'll call the concierge service. They'll find it.'

Thankfully her sister answered, assured her she was looking after the bag, and promised to bring it to the suite straight away. From the tone of her voice, Marisa could tell she was dying to bombard her with questions but, for once, Elsa restrained herself.

When the call was over, she dragged her feet to the bar where Nikos had moved to, pushed his phone to him, and helped herself to another Scotch.

Marisa had avoided alcohol during the pregnancy and in the weeks she'd unsuccessfully tried to breastfeed, and had barely touched it since. She'd never been a heavy drinker but any tolerance she'd developed would surely have been lost. With the amount of Scotch and the earlier champagne she'd had that night, she should be drunk but the only effect it was having on her was a slight numbing of all the mounting shocks and adrenaline surges.

How could she have forgotten about her phone? It didn't matter that Nikos was right and that the housekeeper could easily get hold of her mother and sister. Niki was her responsibility.

But, dear God, this was all so overwhelming. Impossible. Nikos standing close enough that she could reach out and touch him.

Her grief for him had left her bedbound for weeks. Only the positive pregnancy test had got her out of bed, some maternal instinct kicking in that demanded she take care of herself for the sake of her growing foetus. Her baby had been the spur she'd needed to fight through the despair. His birth and the responsibility that came with it had forced her to nestle Nikos away into the hidden reaches of her heart. Though time had never even begun to heal the pain, it had dulled her memories of how deeply her need for him had consumed her. She'd been like a schoolgirl, daydreaming constantly about him, aching for him, her mind on him wherever she was and whatever she was doing.

To stand beside his towering body now, to watch him breathe, drink, the movements of his mouth and throat when he spoke, the movements of his muscles, flesh and blood, *alive*…

It was too much. Every cell in her body ached to throw itself at him, to rip his black shirt off and press her cheek to his chest and feel the steady beat of his heart in her ear.

And then she caught his baleful stare and nausea roiled in her belly. He wasn't here for *her*. He didn't want her any more. Nikos had moved on in every way imaginable.

Holding her glass tightly, she filled her mouth with the fiery liquid and willed her eyes not to leak again.

He leaned his back against the bar and breathed heavily before saying, 'I meant what I said. I don't want to cause trouble for you, Marisa, but Raul Torres is bad news. From everything I've been told about him, the man's a snake, in business *and* love.'

She swallowed the Scotch and willed even harder for the tears to stay hidden, tried to breathe through the crushing weight in her chest and stomach. 'What business is it of yours?'

Nikos had watched her fall apart at his feet with an indifference that bordered on clinical. He'd just admitted he wouldn't have cared if she'd spent the rest of her life believing he was still dead. He'd never had any intention of seeing her again.

'If you marry him then he has influence over my son,' he said roughly.

'He's not going to have any influence because I'm not marrying him.' She drank more of the Scotch and gave a tiny spurt of near-hysterical laughter. 'It's almost funny. I only went ahead with the party tonight because I didn't want to humiliate him but he's been humiliated in the most public way imaginable. God knows what he'll do now.'

Nikos stared at her. The anger that had pulsed and churned at the mention of her fiancé reduced fractionally. 'You were already planning to end the engagement?'

'Yes. I thought he was a good choice but I was wrong. He let me believe he'd love Niki as his own but it was a lie. If he cared about Niki he would have been there when we needed help but he abandoned us. It's the business he wants.' She finished her Scotch, placed the glass on the bar and wiped her plump mouth with the back of her hand.

'If he abandoned you,' he said slowly, 'why go ahead with the party? Why care if you humiliate him?'

'Because he's got a vengeful side. He's expecting to take over the running of Lopez Shipping—we were going to align our two businesses. He's already learned too much about how we run ours. He can undermine us and undercut us and steal our contracts and do God knows what other damage. I need to end things amicably. After everything my family's been through these last eighteen months, the last thing I want is another fight.'

'What on earth were you thinking when you agreed to marry him?'

'Actually, he agreed to marry *me*.'

'Marriage was y*our* idea?'

'Yes.'

'What the hell…?' The woman who'd made Nikos do all the running in their relationship had been the one to propose? The notion landed like a white-hot slap.

She spun to face him, eyes narrowed dangerously. 'Have you forgotten that my father was murdered?' she ground out. 'Our dog drowned! Can you imagine what it was like for me to have a newborn baby and a business to run under those circumstances when the cartel was still out there circling my family like sharks? I was juggling a thousand balls on my own and the people who should have helped wouldn't or couldn't.'

'So you went running to Raul Torres?' he accused. 'I learned in one hour of research that he's a snake and you chose *him* as a father to my child?' And a husband for herself.

'I was trying to protect us!'

'You *had* protection!'

'Paid protection! Niki had no father or grandfather. All he had was me and Mama.' She put the bottle of Scotch to her lips but before she could take a swig lowered it again. 'Don't you think that if my son's father hadn't decided to fake his own death without telling me, then things might have been different?' Her face contorted as she swigged the Scotch. 'If you'd confided in me and had the courage to tell me we were over—and, let's be honest, you used the faking of your death as an excuse to dump me without the bother of having to tell me—I would have been hurt but at least I would have known you were out there and that one day you'd come back and be Niki's father. I would have had something to hold onto.'

'Don't blame your lack of judgement on me,' he snarled. Her insinuation that he'd been too cowardly to end things had hit the intended target.

It was true that he'd had no intention of seeing her again but that was because he'd reasoned they'd had their time together. It would have come to an end anyway. He'd given Marisa more than he'd given any other lover. Given her all he was capable of.

If he'd known there was the smallest chance that she could be pregnant then of course he would have acted differently but he hadn't had the faintest idea and for her to try and put some of the blame for *her* actions on his shoulders was enraging. When he'd made the decision to fake his death, her family had been nowhere near the cartel's radar. He'd never dreamed they could have created a life together either, but he knew it now and he was here, ready to take responsibility and step up to the mark. If he was the coward she implied he'd still be in Mykonos. He would be like his father, happy to leave the burden of an unwanted child on someone else's shoulders. 'I get that it's been a difficult time for you…'

'*Difficult*?' she screamed. 'I gave birth to my son with my father fresh in his grave and thinking the man I loved was fish food!' And with that, she hurled the almost empty bottle of Scotch across the suite. It landed on the dining table and smashed into pieces.

Nikos surveyed the damage, from the shattered mess of glass on and around the table to the woman who was staring at him frozen in white-faced horror.

He was saved from deciding which mess to prioritise by the knock on the door.

Trying to get a grip on the fetid emotions burning his guts, he rubbed the back of his neck. 'That will be your sister.'

'I'll get it.'

He watched her stumble to the door then turned away. He didn't like the way his heart tugged to see her trying to hold her head up, as if she were fighting to regain her dignity.

Swallowing hard in a throat that had inexplicably thickened, he began collecting the larger shards of glass. By the time he'd put them in a bin and called the concierge service to send someone to the suite to clear the rest of it, Marisa and Elsa had finished their murmured conversation and they were alone again.

She stood with her back to the closed door hugging her silver bag to her chest.

'Has Estrella been in touch?' he asked.

'Just to put my mind at ease that Niki's fine.'

'You don't leave him much?' He observed her reaction carefully. Not until he watched Marisa interact with their son would he be able to judge her as a mother but it was necessary to be prepared.

Her shoulders hunched in on themselves as she stepped wearily to the sofa. 'Very rarely.'

She sat heavily and clutched at her head. After a long

moment, she met his stare. 'I'm sorry,' she whispered, throat moving and chin wobbling. 'I didn't mean to throw it.'

A spike of guilt sliced through him.

'I'm sorry too. I shouldn't have passed judgement.' And he had no right to feel any kind of jealousy that she'd moved on with her life. It was irrational and no doubt caused by spending eighteen months with only his tortured thoughts for company.

Marisa rubbed her pounding forehead and tried to control the trembles fighting to break out through her.

Since Niki's birth, she'd spent each and every day using all her strength to keep a lid on her emotions. Nikos's return had sprung the lid free and it was terrifying how easily the emotions were taking control of her.

'I know I made a mistake with Raul,' she said, the compulsion to explain too strong to keep contained. 'But, Nikos, I was desperate. All I could think was that Niki deserved a father and that I needed help. My head was all over the place. Grief...' She swallowed and rubbed her forehead even harder, choosing her words carefully. 'I'd lost my father and protector. I didn't want to marry anyone but I thought I needed to, for Niki's sake and for the business's sake.'

'What about for your sake?'

'Those reasons *were* for my sake. I was trying to find some kind of peace of mind. Protecting my son and getting help for the business was the only way for me to have that.'

'Yes, but you can't deny that Raul's a handsome man,' he observed casually. 'Waking up to that face must have made it an easier pill to swallow.'

She clutched her cheeks, immediately understanding his implication. 'God, no, that had no part in it. We didn't... We never...'

His brow rose sceptically. *'Never?'*

'No!' Marisa dropped her gaze to the carpet between her feet in a futile attempt to hide the flame of colour scorching her face. 'I wasn't ready.'

She would never have been ready, something Raul, with a ready-made mistress tucked away, had been happy to accept, but there was no way she would admit that to Nikos. Her pride would not allow him to know how desperate her grief for him had been or that the thought of another man touching her left her cold inside, not now that she knew how little she'd meant to him.

To her great relief, their conversation was interrupted by another knock on the door.

This time it was the concierge service. The splinters of glass were vacuumed in short order but the noise was enough to make the pounding in her head feel like a dozen hammers were knocking inside it.

'Headache?' Nikos asked when they were alone again, observing the way she was now clutching her whole head. The colour he hadn't noticed return to her cheeks had drained from her again.

'I don't feel so good.' She didn't sound so good either. Her words had a definite slur to them. 'I think my body's telling me off for all the Scotch…and the champagne.'

'I'll get you some painkillers.'

He found some in his toiletry bag, took a bottle of water from the fridge and handed them to her.

She gave a grateful, wan smile and swallowed the painkillers down with half the water.

'Lie down and rest for a while,' he said.

'I need to speak to Raul.'

'Out of the question.' He wasn't letting her out of his sight.

'Nikos—'

'No,' he cut in firmly. 'You're not in any state to deal with him. Rest, sober up...'

'I'm not drunk.'

'You should be.'

'I know.'

He couldn't help but smile. 'You're not drunk but you *are* feeling the effects. Your body's telling you to rest, so rest. Have my bed if you want.'

She shook her head, the action making her wince. 'I should go home.'

'Is your housekeeper expecting you back?'

'Not until morning.'

'Then rest for a while. I'll get my driver to take us to your home when you're feeling better.'

'Us?'

'I want to see my son, Marisa.' And see with his own eyes what kind of a mother she was. From everything she'd said, he doubted she was as lousy and indifferent a mother as his own had been but he needed to be certain. Words were cheap. If he sensed for a second that she treated their son as an encumbrance or neglected him in any way, he would sue for custody. He hoped it wouldn't come to that.

'Okay,' Marisa whispered, resting her head back. Her head was *killing* her. 'You can see him but you'll have to wait until morning to meet him properly. He's grouchy like his father when he doesn't get enough sleep.'

Nikos's faint chuckle was the last thing she remembered before she fell asleep.

CHAPTER FOUR

NIKOS, ARMS FOLDED across his chest, gazed at Marisa fast asleep on the sofa in exactly the same position she'd been when he'd left the suite an hour ago. He should wake her. That couldn't be a comfortable position to sleep in.

He whispered her name. No response.

Swallowing back the lump in his throat, he placed a finger to her shoulder and carefully prodded. No response.

He stepped back and considered his options. He could leave her as she was or carry her to his bed. When he'd lifted her into his arms earlier after her faint it had been an automatic reaction, something he'd done without any forethought.

A small part of him acknowledged he'd swept her out of the party room before Raul regained his wits enough to try and bring her round himself.

He could hardly believe the rush of exultation that had swept through him at Marisa's admission that she hadn't slept with her fiancé.

Marisa was the only woman Nikos had been with whose sexual appetite matched his own. His shock at her virginity had quickly been forgotten as her inhibitions had disappeared. In the bedroom, she'd blossomed, gained a voracious appetite that had blown his mind and fed his own hunger into a heady lust that had kept him with her far longer than he usually stayed with a lover. As bad as it had been to imagine her enjoying those same heady, sensual appetites with that vile man, he wouldn't have thought any less of her for it. Humans were carnal creatures, Marisa especially so.

What had stopped her enjoying them with Raul? Did motherhood reduce a woman's libido?

He took another step back and cursed himself for speculating and exulting over something that was none of his business. It was natural that he would still feel stirrings for her. There hadn't been anyone since her, no one for him to transfer his lust to. He would rectify that as soon as possible.

Spinning on his heel, he strode to the suite's bedroom and looked in the wardrobe. There, he found spare bedding. He grabbed some and carried it back to the living area.

Working swiftly, he put the pillow on the edge of the sofa and then gently coaxed her flat so her head rested on it.

She stirred and mumbled something that made him freeze and sent his pulses soaring.

It sounded like she'd said his name.

For a passage of time that lasted an age, he stared at her beautiful face, hardly able to breathe, the thuds of his heart echoing in his ears.

She stirred again and pulled her knees up to the foetal position. The familiarity of it wrenched something in his chest.

He gritted his teeth and forced air into his lungs.

It was late. It had been a far more emotional evening than he'd anticipated and he too had drunk more Scotch than was good for him. It was no wonder his reactions were all over the place. A few hours' sleep would put him back on his usual even keel.

In one burst of action, he pulled her shoes off, draped the blanket over her and strode to the suite's bedroom, closing the door behind him.

Marisa opened her eyes, going from heavy sleep to full alertness in an instant.

Nikos.

He was alive.

Or had she dreamt it?

A look at her watch told her it was four in the morning.

She threw the soft blanket off—where had that come from? Had he put it on her?—and her stockinged feet sank into thick carpet.

Rubbing her eyes, she stared at the sofa. At some point while she'd slept, Nikos had put a pillow under her head, laid her flat on her side and covered her.

She hadn't dreamt him.

Heart in her throat, she found herself in the adjoining room before she even knew she'd opened the door and walked into it.

The light in there was incredibly faint, the little illumination coming from the lamp Nikos had left on for her in the living area. It was enough for her to see the shape of his body nestled under the covers, breathing deeply.

She definitely hadn't dreamt him.

Nikos was alive.

The relief was almost as overwhelming as it had been the first time, and, eyes glued to his sleeping shadowed face, she stretched out a trembling hand and lightly pressed her fingers against his cheek. The warmth of his skin made her sag with fresh relief and assailed her with memories of the joy she'd felt to wrap herself against him at night and bask in the heat that had radiated from his body. After their first night together, any nights spent alone had always felt so cold. From the nightmare day she'd been told he was missing, the coldness had lived in her constantly.

The relief was short-lived. A hand twice the size of her own flew like a rocket from under the sheet and wrapped around hers.

'What are you doing?'

Her heart jumped into her throat, the beats vibrating through her suddenly frozen body.

Nikos raised his head and blinked the sleep from his eyes, trying to clear the thickness from his just awoken brain, and stared at the motionless form standing beside him.

'Marisa?' His voice sounded thick to his own ears too. Was he really awake? Or dreaming?

As his eyes adjusted he saw the shock in her wide eyes before his gaze drifted down to notice the buttons of her dress around her bust had popped open in her sleep to show the swell of her breast in the black lace bra she wore.

Arousal coiled its seductive way through his bloodstream to remember the taste of her skin on his tongue and the heady scent of her musk. He tugged her closer to him, suddenly filled with the need to taste it again, taste *her* again, to hear the throaty moans of her pleasure and feel the burn of their flesh pressed together. It was a burn he'd never felt with anyone but her.

Her lips parted. Her breath hitched. Her face lowered to his...

His mouth filled with moisture, lips tingling with anticipation. He put his other hand to her neck and his arousal accelerated.

It had been so long…

Then, with her mouth hovering just inches from his, she jerked back and snatched her hand away. It fluttered to her rising chest.

'I'm sorry for waking you,' she whispered, backing away some more. 'I was just checking I hadn't dreamt you.'

And then she disappeared from his room as silently as she'd entered it, leaving him blinking at the empty space she'd filled only seconds before.

Nikos put his fingers to his cheek. If he couldn't still feel the burn from the mark of her touch, he would believe he'd just dreamt the whole thing.

Marisa unlocked the door and stepped inside the reception room. She removed her shoes and waited for Nikos to do likewise. In silence, they headed for the stairs. It was only six thirty. She'd messaged Estrella to tell her she was coming home. Her mother would still be in the suite she'd expected to share with Marisa at the hotel but the rest of household would be sleeping. There was one member of it, though, that she was confident would be awake. Her son.

The silence between her and Nikos had been almost total since he'd appeared in the suite's living area, freshly showered and ready to meet his son.

Neither of them had mentioned her visit to his bedroom. If she had her way it would never be spoken of. It had been a foolish, impulsive thing to do. She tried not to beat herself up about it but it was hard. It seemed like everything she did lately was wrong.

But when she opened her son's bedroom door and found him lying on his back, kicking his plump legs in the air, she allowed herself the credit of knowing that when it came to him, she mostly got things right. He was a happy, healthy baby. What mother could ask for more?

As soon as he saw her, his legs kicked even more frantically and he held his arms out to her.

She leaned over to scoop him up. 'Good morning, baby boy,' she murmured, kissing his cheek.

Wide awake, he grabbed at her hair and jiggled in her arms. And then he caught sight of the stranger in the midst and stared at his father with frank curiosity.

Nikos found himself holding his breath, his stare totally and utterly captivated by the chunky bundle in Marisa's arms. Eyes of a colour he couldn't determine were fixed on him, cute little mouth making funny blowing noises. He had a cleft in his chin Nikos recognised from his own baby photos.

His heart swelled. For a moment he felt light-headed.

That was his son.

He blinked and caught Marisa's cautious stare.

'Do you want to hold him?' she asked.

He'd never held a baby in his life. 'How breakable is he?'

'If you don't drop him, we won't find out.' Then she smiled. 'You won't drop him, so don't worry. Here.' She passed the happy, curious child to him.

Baby Nikos, completely unperturbed to be handed to a stranger, immediately grabbed at Nikos's nose.

Having expected something light and noticeably fragile, it was a relief to feel his son's solidity, even if it did come with additional bounce.

He laughed and met Marisa's stare again. 'He's *beautiful*,' he said, awestruck.

'Yes. He is.' She sighed but her expression was as enchanted as he knew his must be. It was an expression that put to rest his fears that she could be anything like his own mother. Then her expression changed into something wistful. 'Let me change his nappy and then we'll get him some breakfast.'

The hours that passed were the most surreal of Nikos's life. As someone who'd never wanted to be tied down by anything so had never considered having a child, even as some distant future thing, the depth of feelings for his son were like nothing he'd felt before. And they were immediate. One look and he'd been spellbound.

But that wasn't the most surreal aspect. Marisa's willingness to show him the ropes and to answer all his questions about their child—and there were many, he had almost a year of his son's life to catch up on—was astounding. Considering how his resurrection had affected her, he'd braced himself for a fight, had half expected her to make a quick introduction and then boot him out of her home.

He'd also braced himself for her mother's appearance but Rosaria had surprised him too. She'd returned from the hotel and joined them for brunch in the dining room, much thinner than he remembered but as impeccably made up, her demeanour curious but with only a little of the frostiness he'd expected.

Not until Marisa announced she was going to put their son down for a nap and would take a shower, leaving him and Rosaria alone together, did she bring up the elephant in the room. Namely, his faked death.

He explained it as he'd done to Marisa the night before. She listened carefully and asked many questions, only little tells of emotions flickering on her face. He'd just finished his narration when Marisa returned.

When she'd left the dining room she'd still been wearing the ugly party dress she'd slept in and her hair had turned into something that had resembled a rat's nest.

The transformation was remarkable. Her slim body was wrapped in a summery patterned teal chiffon off-the-shoulder dress that fell just below the knees, her hair damp and already drying into its natural curl with no frizz in sight. She'd applied a little make-up and, as she strode to the table, he found himself straightening when he caught a waft of her perfume. She smelled amazing.

She sat next to her mother opposite him and poured herself a coffee before turning her dark brown stare on him. 'You've been filling Mama in on your death?'

Nerve endings stirring, he clenched his hands and shifted in his seat as he inclined his head. 'Is Niki sleeping?' Nikos couldn't believe how easily the diminutive of his son's name had come to him.

'Yes.' She put the baby monitor on the table.

'Good. I have a proposition to discuss with you both.'

His lips twitched to see their heads tilt in unison.

'I want to buy into your business.'

The time spent alone after putting Niki down for his nap had given Marisa time to collect herself. She'd been certain Nikos would want to discuss access and custody and all the things he, as a father, had a right to discuss, and she had wanted to be cool, calm and collected enough to deal with it.

The traumas of the last eighteen months had aged her inside and out. She'd carried a child. Her previously flat stomach was now rounded with silvery scars across her abdomen. Permanent exhaustion meant her skin no longer glowed with health and vitality, but the simple acts of showering and changing into non-horrible clothes had calmed her and made her feel better in herself, and she'd entered the room confident she was now in the right mental space to handle him.

But her confidence had been a delusion. One look at Nikos breathing and talking was enough to make her poise wobble. His comment that he wanted to buy into the business shattered it.

Nikos's stare flickered to her mother before his light brown eyes settled on her. 'If you're in agreement, we'll have the business independently audited and I will pay the recommended value for a third share of it. We will draft an agreement where the three of us each own a third or, if you prefer, the two of you and Elsa own two-thirds between you. Marisa retains overall control but we appoint someone—I have someone in mind—to manage the day-to-day running of it.' He nodded his head at her. 'That person will report directly to you.'

Marisa was too dumbfounded to speak. Nikos owned a chain of nightclubs across Europe. He invested in tech companies. His business interests were diverse but the common theme amongst them was that they were 'hip'. The Lopezes' shipping company was far too old-school and traditional to ever be called hip. In their six months together he'd been interested in the work she did but had never shown the slightest interest in the business as an entity, so for him to make this proposition...

It was left to her mother to pull herself together and ask the pertinent question. 'You want to buy into the business...but *why*?'

'To dissuade Raul Torres from starting a war against you.' He turned his gaze back to Marisa. 'I spoke to him last night, after you fell asleep. You were right about him wanting revenge for ending your engagement.'

Her head felt light. Fuzzy. Since waking, she'd been so wrapped up in Nikos and their son that she'd forgotten all about Raul. 'You spoke to him? About our engagement?' While she'd been zonked out on his sofa?

He shrugged. 'He called your phone. I didn't want to wake you so I answered it. We met in the lobby.'

Marisa clutched at her cheeks, digging her nails into the skin to sharpen her wits. 'What did you talk about?'

'It wasn't a long conversation. I told him the engagement was off and that your businesses would no longer be aligning. He wants the ring returned,' he added indifferently.

She touched the finger it should have been on. She'd stopped wearing the ring within weeks of the engagement, only slipping it on when she saw Raul. It had never felt right there.

It had been little over half a day since Nikos had appeared like a ghost at her engagement party. He'd lobbed one shock after another at her, all without breaking a sweat. Look at him now, announcing the termination of her engagement and the business deal she'd arranged with the nonchalance of someone announcing what they'd be having for their dinner.

She inhaled deeply through her nose and said through gritted teeth, 'What gave you the right to do that?'

'Can someone tell me what's going on?' her mother interjected. 'You're ending your engagement to Raul?'

Glaring at Nikos for revealing something she hadn't got round to telling her mother about, she braced herself. 'Yes.'

'Thank God for that.'

Marisa faced her mother, open-mouthed with shock.

Her mother smiled wanly and shrugged. 'I never thought he was right for you.'

'Then why didn't you say anything?'

'I did try,' she reminded her gently, her eyes conveying a reminder of a conversation between them that she would never repeat in front of Nikos. That she'd thought it was too soon for her. That Marisa shouldn't commit to another man when her heart still belonged to Nikos.

Marisa had batted her mother's doubts away. Giving her heart wasn't part of the deal with Raul. She had no choice when it came to loving her son, that was something primal and ferocious, but her love for Nikos had been too strong, the pain of his loss too much to ever risk feeling like that about anyone again.

Turning back to Nikos, she glared at him even as her heart cried. 'I want you to explain why you took it on yourself to end my engagement when I have a voice of my own.'

Her eighteen months spent mourning him had allowed her to put rose-tinted glasses on some of the less savoury aspects of his personality, namely his take-charge attitude. She wouldn't go so far as to call him a control freak but when given a problem, he would immediately see a solution and implement it, which was great if you'd asked for a solution, not so great if you hadn't.

She remembered them speaking via their personal laptops once when her screen had kept turning itself off. In the morning, a package had arrived before she'd set off for work. A brand new laptop from Nikos. It hadn't occurred to him that she would prefer to fix her current laptop and that if it wasn't fixable, choose a new one for herself. She'd been touched at the gesture but irritated that he'd gone ahead and sorted it without any consultation with her.

'You were worried he'd turn nasty,' he said with a shrug. 'And you were right to be. But he will only pick a fight he knows he can win. He'll think twice about starting a war against you if I'm part of the business.'

Her jaw would snap if she ground her teeth any harder. 'Is that because only a man can save us?'

His eyes flashed. 'No, because I'm someone who's dealt with bullies like him before and know how to handle them.'

'What do you think we've spent the past year doing against the cartel?' she snapped back. 'My mother met with their representatives *on her own* with a secret recording device to get evidence against them. Hers was the only non-circumstantial evidence that allowed their arrests. Without her *you'd* still be playing dead.'

Nikos dug the tips of his fingers on the table and leaned forward, glowering into the furious wide brown eyes.

He knew exactly the danger Rosaria had put herself in, knew too that she'd done it out of the protective mothering instinct his own mother had been born without. The united front and open defiance the whole Lopez family, Marisa included, had shown the cartel in the face of their intimidation tactics and violence had been astounding, but her insinuation that he'd hidden away like a coward until it was all over was beyond insulting.

That it was also close to how he'd felt during those impossibly long months only added fuel to his fury.

Having to stay hidden, far from civilisation, thousands of kilometres from the action, reliant on emailed reports for news of what the hell was going on, unable to influence *anything*, his only contribution the millions of his own money he'd thrown into it, had been torture. If the cabin he'd been given to bunker down in hadn't needed constant maintenance, he would have gone stir crazy.

He'd given up his life to bring those bastards down. He'd lived as a recluse in an alien landscape. He'd done all that in part to protect *her*. To neutralise the cartel's interest in her as a means to get to *him*.

'What you two did to help defeat the cartel was incredible,' he said, keeping a tight hold on his anger. 'But Raul is a different kind of danger. You said so yourself. During my talk with him last night, I made it clear that if he attempts any kind of sabotage, I'll come after him.'

Mimicking his pose, she put her own fingers on the table and leaned towards him. 'For all we know, your threats might have made it more likely that he'll try to sabotage us.'

'My buying into the company puts my presence front and centre for him, and if he's got any sense and searches my history, he'll learn I'm not a man who makes threats—I make promises.' There was a big part of him that hoped Raul *did* try some sabotage. It would give him the excuse he needed to destroy the man who'd abandoned his son and his son's mother when they'd most needed him.

Never had he felt such loathing for another human being, different even from his hatred for the cartel who'd wreaked such evil damage. Every second of their chat had been spent fighting the urge to ram his fist in his face. Not even spelling out in graphic detail exactly what he would do should Raul attempt any retribution against the Lopezes and witnessing the Spaniard's smug exterior crack had sated the urge.

'You didn't even consult me about it!' she raged. 'You took it on yourself to end my engagement and threaten, promise, whatever you want to call it, a man I categorically told you I did *not* want to start a war with!'

'My chat with him last night was to prevent a war,' he bit back.

Her dark brown eyes were ablaze and locked on his, the sparks shooting from them landing on his skin and penetrating into his bloodstream. The angry colour heightening her cheeks brought to mind so clearly the exact shade on her skin when he brought her to orgasm that he pressed his fingers even harder on the table to stop them snatching her to him. *Theos*, she aroused him, every part of him.

'And I don't know why you're directing your anger at me when I'm trying to help you,' he continued. 'You proposed to Raul because you wanted a father for Niki and help in running the business—*I'm* his father and I'm offering you that help. I'm also offering an investment in it and giving you the opportunity that *you* wanted to have someone help you so you can take a step back without losing control. My offer gives you everything you wanted with added protection *and* your family retains majority control.'

The babbling that suddenly came through the baby monitor cut through the tense atmosphere like a grenade.

CHAPTER FIVE

MARISA LOOKED FROM the baby monitor to Nikos, blinking rapidly as she got to her feet. 'I'll get him,' she said tightly. 'Mama, don't agree to anything without me.'

Her exit did nothing to lessen the tension permeating the air, which had tautened Nikos's muscles.

Rosaria had dropped her attempt at friendliness, her demeanour now cool and scrutinising. She studied him for a long time before speaking. 'Why do you really want to buy into our business?'

'For the reasons I've already said. Your family has been through enough—it doesn't need a war with Raul Torres.'

'I was never happy about that relationship. There's something about him I never trusted. I offered to stay on and help her with the business but my role was so limited there was little help I could give.' Her tone softened, eyes turning misty. 'Marisa inherited her business brain from her father.'

The business had always been her father's domain, Nikos remembered. Rosaria had been involved too but to a much lesser extent. Both Marco and Rosaria had looked forward to handing the reins to Marisa and retiring together. And Marisa had looked forward to it too. He'd admired her dedication, her insistence in learning every single aspect of the business before she took over, her determination to run it as well and as profitably as her father had.

It was supposed to happen when she turned twenty-five. She'd turned that age two months ago. The business had been hers a year before she would have considered herself ready to take it on.

Suddenly it hit him fully what a torrid time she'd had. The responsibility that had been cast onto her young shoulders. All that while grieving, juggling the threat of the cartel and the demands of a newborn baby.

The angry tension in his muscles loosened as he imagined the strength it must have taken her to get through all that.

'But Marisa is headstrong,' Rosaria continued in a stronger voice. 'You tell her not to do something, she's twice as likely to do it. She inherited that from me. But what I don't understand is why *you* would want to help us in this way.'

'For my son. Taking the pressure off Marisa can only benefit him, and I'm not being entirely altruistic—it's a good investment.'

'I know it's a good investment.' Her gaze did not waver. 'What I'm wondering is if your intention is to invest in my daughter too.'

Invest in a bed to take her in, he thought before he could stop himself. His blood still hummed from the fire that had blazed between them only minutes ago.

Theos, he needed to find himself a new lover.

Keeping his tone even, he said, 'My only interest in your daughter now is as the mother of my son.'

Rosaria leaned across the table and covered his hand, forcing him to keep their stares locked together. 'Marisa has been to hell. If you ever had any feelings for her, do not put her back there. And don't look at me like that,' she continued when he raised a brow. 'Marisa is as strong a woman as I've ever known but she's only human. I won't have her hurt again. If you don't see yourself having a future with her then…'

'I've already made that clear to her,' he interrupted, removing his hand. Then, reminding himself that this was a woman whose husband had been killed and whose youngest daughter had been targeted for kidnap, he modulated his tone. 'I'm not here to rekindle our old relationship. We've both moved on but we do need to form an amicable relationship for our son's sake.' He knew better than anyone how children could suffer from parents at war who put their own needs and desires first.

'You don't need to worry about me, Mama. Nikos and I are history.'

The buzz in his veins flared up again.

Carrying their son in her arms, Marisa strode back to her seat. She threw a saccharine sweet smile at him before speaking to her mother. 'Tell me you haven't agreed to anything yet.'

'I'm going to respect your judgement on this one,' her mother said before slipping into Spanish. 'If you do agree to it, make sure you have it written into any contract that he's forbidden from killing himself again.'

Marisa's gaze landed on him as she replied, also in Spanish, 'I'd kill him myself if he did that again.'

A surprising bubble of mirth rose up his throat, a welcome antidote to the bile that had lodged in it at Marisa's chirpily delivered announcement that they were history.

Shouldn't he be relieved that she considered them over, the same way he did?

When he'd faked his death it had been with the full knowledge that the fake termination of his life was the real termination of his relationship. His gallows humour had made him wryly acknowledge that at least he wouldn't have to deal with the histrionics that always came with ending a relationship, even those that had lasted only a fraction of the time spent with Marisa.

When Rosaria left the room and they were left alone with their son, Marisa's eyes narrowed. 'Did you understand that?'

'Yes.'

'Since when do you speak my language?'

'Boredom's a killer when you're dead,' he quipped to counteract the needles prickling over his skin to remember the endless, lonely evenings spent listening to online Spanish tutorials. He'd figured that seeing as he had hours of time on his hands, he might as well use it productively. He would listen to it in bed too, drifting into sleep with the rhythm of the Spanish language playing like music into his ears.

'You taught yourself?' If she was impressed, she was doing an excellent job of hiding it.

'I now understand it perfectly. It's speaking it I need practice with.'

'Then you'll soon get plenty of practice—the majority of our staff speak only a little English and I doubt any of them speak Greek.'

His pulse quickened and he leaned forward. 'Does that mean you accept my proposal?'

She studied him in the same impervious manner her mother had done only minutes before. 'With conditions.'

He was the one doing her a favour. His offer was more than generous. And she had the nerve to impose conditions on him?

He'd forgotten how magnificent she could be.

'Name them.'

* * *

Marisa peered closely into the mirror to check her makeup hadn't smudged, then added more lip gloss. She'd always taken pride in her appearance—her deliberate attempt to sabotage her own engagement notwithstanding—but there were occasions when it mattered more than others and seeing Nikos came into that category. Her pride wouldn't let him see her at anything less than her best. She needed all the confidence she could muster to handle being in the same room as him.

In the two weeks since his return from the dead, she'd had to dress and present herself at her best every single day because Nikos was always around, visiting Niki every evening and dining with them as a family. Then there had been the numerous visits to the business headquarters and the docks and the many meetings with their respective lawyers to thrash out their business agreement. She literally couldn't get rid of him. He gave every impression of someone planning to hang around Valencia for the rest of his life.

But he wasn't hanging around Valencia for her. He was hanging around for their son. If not for Niki, she still might not yet know that Nikos was alive. He wouldn't have cared if she'd learned about his resurrection by social media or through her social circle's grapevine.

He wasn't worth an ounce of the pain he'd put her through.

She never dropped her guard around him and worked religiously to maintain a serene if aloof front. She made sure to always keep her tone amiable and whenever their hands brushed when passing their son between them, she gave no reaction at all. Most importantly, she made sure not to stare at him. The times their eyes locked she would deliberately un-focus hers, so as not to feel the effect of his.

When they'd been together she'd seen what she'd wanted to see. Now she only let him see what she wanted him to see because if he could see the truth, he'd see she was holding on by her fingertips.

This was the man she'd been besotted with, the man whose death had come close to breaking her. To get through the days of her grief without him, she'd had to nestle her love and pain deep in her heart. Now, to get through the days with him, she had to bury those old feelings and never, ever let them out. Let emptiness swathe her and replace the fear and pain.

It was the hardest fight of her life.

There was a light knock on her bedroom door before her mother appeared. 'Are you ready?'

Marisa took a deep breath and nodded.

Rosaria stood behind her and together they stared at their reflections.

'I'm proud of you, darling.' Her mother captured one of Marisa's curls in her fingers. 'Your father would be too.'

She closed her eyes and willed back the burn of tears. It was because of her father that she'd agreed to Nikos's business proposition. The contracts cementing the deal would be signed in an hour.

How badly she'd wanted to throw his offer back in his face, but that would have been her pride talking and acting for her.

Her father had inherited the shipping business from his own father and had taken such pride in running it to the same high standards that Marisa had always wanted to do the same for him. He'd worked his backside off to give his family a good life and his daughters the best education money could buy and had still managed to be a wonderful, present father *and* taken their dead housekeeper's orphaned son under his wing and mentored him from a screwed-up rebellious teenager into a billionaire businessman.

Nikos's deal meant her family's legacy would live on and all the pressure she'd been under would be lifted. The structures they were putting in place for the business meant she could take a back seat for as long as she wanted and devote her time and attention solely to her son.

Best of all, her son had a father. Not just *a* father but *his* father, and Nikos was proving himself an attentive and loving one. Everything she'd wanted her son to have.

She would just have to learn to live her life with the man she'd once imagined her future with, as a part of her future. But not for her sake. Loving her son but not loving her.

'Come on,' she said, taking her mother's hand and squeezing it. 'Let's get this done.'

'Have you decided what you're having?' Nikos asked. Marisa's face had been hidden behind the leather-bound lunch menu ever since they'd been shown to their table, dropping it only to thank the waiter for her glass of wine.

She lowered it an inch for her eyes to peer over. 'I think so.'

He nodded at the hovering waiter, who was at their table in a flash, and gave his order.

Marisa's face appeared in its entirety and she followed suit.

'See,' he teased when they were alone again and she didn't have a menu to hide behind any more. 'That wasn't so hard.'

'I was trying to decide what to eat.' She sipped at her wine, eyes flickering from him to the artwork on the restaurant's walls. It was something she often did, a subtle refusal to engage with him unless it was about their son or the business. Infuriatingly, her behaviour only made him want to engage with her more, to provoke a reaction, to feel the weight of those large brown eyes on him as she hung on his every word.

He knew this was contrary to everything he'd told her *and* himself because, doubly infuriating, he was constantly having to clamp down on the thickening of his blood and loins whenever she was within fifty feet of him and having to stop himself goading her into arguments just for the pleasure of seeing her cheeks saturate with colour and her eyes blaze with the passion that always roused him.

He wanted to goad her now, tear her attention from the abstract painting she was studying and force her attention on *him*. He supposed it was like when a child was denied something—it only made them want it more.

Other than that first night when she'd fallen apart and couldn't tear her eyes from his face, Marisa acted not only as if the previous eighteen months hadn't happened but as if their time together had never happened either. She accepted him as part of their son's life while carefully keeping herself at arm's length. It had become obvious that though she'd behaved rashly in her proposal to Raul, she really had moved on with her life without Nikos. Whatever pain his 'death' had caused her had been fleeting. Her reaction to his return had been nothing more than a large dose of shock, and he'd come to the conclusion Rosaria's warning about not hurting Marisa were the words of an overprotective mother.

In the two weeks he'd spent in Valencia, he'd learned Marisa was as overprotective of their son as Rosaria was of her. Marisa rarely let Nikos out of her sight, her home office more of a crèche than a place of work.

She was still studying that damned painting. How could it hold her interest so thoroughly? It looked like something a child would paint.

'Can we talk business?' he asked, and instantly regretted his rough tone. Not only was he thinking like a child denied attention but now he was acting like one.

Strangely, as a child, he'd never acted in such a way. He'd learned at too young an age that begging for attention only provoked greater indifference. Only when he'd been taken into his grandfather's custody and given a window into how other families lived had he started to understand their neglect and to ask questions.

The biggest question had been what was so damn wrong with him that his parents couldn't love him and had willingly given him up?

Marisa's large brown eyes locked on his, her expression open, almost serene. 'What's on your mind?'

How infuriating that he should be frustrated by *her* indifference.

It just proved he'd been right all along that whatever feelings she'd once had for him had been fleeting. Unsustainable.

But her love for their son was neither fleeting nor unsustainable. She would never give Niki up like Nikos's parents had given him up.

A chill ran up his spine.

What if one day she were to look at Nikos and see what his parents had seen? What if she saw in him whatever it was they'd seen and decided Niki was better kept from him?

He took a sharp breath to counter the disquiet racing through him and curved his mouth into a cool smile.

That scenario would never happen. He would never allow it.

'I brought you here to celebrate so let's celebrate.' He raised his wine glass. 'To a successful business collaboration.'

She clinked hers to it. 'I'll drink to that.'

He drank and raised his glass again. 'And to the successful end of your engagement.'

Her eyes narrowed but she clinked her glass to his. 'Let's hope there aren't any consequences.'

'If there are, he'll pay for them. I'll see to it personally. The business will be protected.'

'I'm counting on it. It's the only reason I agreed to your buy-in. *Salud.*' She tilted half her wine into her mouth. The act was neither salacious nor provocative but the awareness that always thrummed under his skin when he was with her intensified.

Marisa looked at the giant langoustines placed before her and laughed. It sounded natural, she was sure of it.

This celebratory meal was the first time they'd been alone together since Nikos's return and she found herself working twice as hard to maintain a cool front and fight her eyes desire to fall onto his gorgeous face. She had to avoid too much eye contact with him. She'd become lost in his light brown gaze too many times before.

'If the main course is as big as the starters, I'll have to tell Santi not to cook too much for us tonight,' she said lightly.

'You're going to your sister's?'

'She wants to show off Santi's cooking. I meant to tell you earlier. Don't worry, you're invited.'

'That's good of them to include me but I'm flying to Ibiza later.'

At this, her heart juddered and her composure cracked. Her hand spasmed against her wine glass, sending the pale liquid flying.

Cheeks flaming instantly, she was saved from the weight of Nikos's suddenly piercing stare by a passing waiter hurrying to clean it up and refill her glass.

Nikos was leaving? That should be something to celebrate, not something that made her chest feel like icy shards were penetrating it.

'It's not like you to be clumsy,' he commented when they were left alone again, thoughtful eyes fixed on hers, forehead indented with the contemplative lines she recognised.

'It was an accident.' She tried to speak dismissively but there was a tremor in her voice. Her bones felt like they'd become jellified again.

His right eyebrow rose sardonically.

She had a large drink of her fresh wine and willed her heart to settle.

'What are you going to Ibiza for?' she asked, and was relieved that this time her voice had mostly returned to the casual tone she'd spent two weeks perfecting.

There was a slight narrowing of his light brown eyes before they glittered and a knowing smile played on his lips. 'I need to check in with the club.' A flash of white teeth. 'Let them see in person that I'm not dead.'

'Do your staff know?'

Nikos put a scallop in his mouth and nodded slowly, not taking his eyes from her beautiful face.

Marisa's reaction to the news about him leaving had his heart pumping hard with triumph.

In one beat of a moment, the self-possessed, collected woman who'd treated him with an almost brittle cordiality had lost control. Just one brief second, enough to be a clumsy insignificance were it not for the effects of it still showing, there in the flush of her cheeks, in the quiver in her voice, in the unsteadiness of her hands.

When he'd swallowed the scallop, he said, 'Everyone who needs to be notified has been but it's time for me to show my face again and see for myself that everything's running as it should be in all the various clubs and businesses. It's something I'd planned to do before but learning about our son and sorting out everything with your business changed that.'

A host of emotions played on the face he could see straining not to give anything else away. 'I imagine it will take you a while to get through them.'

He added more food to his fork. 'My PA has arranged for me to visit them and sit down with each management team over a week.'

'Sounds like you're going to be busy.'

'It will be non-stop. It should have been spread over two weeks but I wanted it condensed to get it done as quickly as possible.' Limiting the time he had to spend apart from his son.

'Will we see you in that time?' she asked with a casualness that would have been convincing if her cheeks weren't still flaming and her eyes darting everywhere but at him.

'I hope to make a couple of visits back to Valencia when time allows... If that's agreeable to you?'

'Of course,' she said brightly. 'Niki's become very attached to you.'

What about his mother? he wondered idly. 'And I've become very attached to him too.'

'I had noticed,' she said with a dry nonchalance that might have passed as natural if he wasn't watching her so closely.

'And it's with that attachment in mind that I have a request to make of you.'

Having just popped some more langoustine into her mouth, she arched an eyebrow in query.

He leaned forward. 'When I have finished checking in with all my management teams, I want to take Niki home.'

The colour drained from her face and the fork in her hand dropped onto her plate. Her eyes widened and her shoulders hunched as she placed a hand to her chest. She cleared her throat. 'You want to take him to Mykonos?'

'And you,' he clarified.

'Me?' The sudden dread that had clutched Marisa vanished under the surge of her racing pulse and she found herself arching towards him. 'You want me to come too?'

His speculative stare held hers. 'He's still getting to know me and he's too young to leave you yet.'

The brief rush of adrenaline flatlined. She didn't even know why she'd experienced it. This was the man who'd faked his own death with no thought or concern about her and, even if she could forgive that—not his reasons for faking his death which she understood, but his complete dismissal of her in his planning and execution of it—she couldn't forgive or forget his failure to let her know he was alive once it was all over. If he hadn't spotted Niki, he'd have been happy never seeing her again. She meant nothing to him. He didn't want her. She was welcome in his home only as the mother of his son.

Well, she didn't want him either. He was welcome in her home only as the father of her son. If he got down on his knees and begged for them to start over, she would laugh in his face.

She just wished she didn't wake every morning with panic in her heart that she'd dreamt his resurrection and that every minute spent with him didn't make her feel so jittery and flushed inside. It was there now, the heat that had lived in her the entire time they'd been together, the cells of her body straining towards him, her pulse never settling into a steady rhythm.

'Let our son visit my home, *agapi mou*,' he said, light brown eyes boring into her. 'My heritage is his heritage. He deserves to know about it, do you not agree? And one day, everything I have will be his.'

Her cheeks flamed at the endearment that had slipped off his tongue so smoothly she was sure he hadn't noticed. 'When you put it like that, how can I say no?'

She couldn't. She knew that. Not unless she wanted to be actively cruel.

It astounded her how quickly the bond between father and son had formed but it was there and it was real and it was a *good* thing. All children deserved to have the best relationship possible with both their parents and she would never deny her son that, no matter the personal cost to herself.

And it was costing her a lot.

'So you'll come?'

She strained every muscle in her face to form a smile. She'd spent weekends with Nikos at his homes in Ibiza, Barcelona, Rome and London, while work commitments had forced her to turn down invitations for weekends at his homes in Mallorca and Athens, but the one home she'd longed for an invite to had never come. His real home. The island where he'd been born and raised. The island his family lived on. Mykonos.

'Sure. We'll come.'

His face widened into a grin, eyes glittering. 'Excellent. I will make the arrangements.'

CHAPTER SIX

NIKOS FOLDED HIS arms across his chest and eyeballed his club manager. 'Did I, or did I not make it clear when I employed you that my clubs have a zero-tolerance policy on drugs?'

Toni's face was a classic mixture of fear and wounded pride. 'We do our best. We can't be held responsible for everyone who comes in.'

Nikos leaned across his desk. He'd deliberately not invited Toni to sit. 'And that's where we disagree. You have let the issue slip in my absence.'

'I didn't—'

'Do not interrupt me. Whatever our clients take before they enter our premises is nothing to do with us unless they are visibly wasted but the rules of the club are simple. Each guest is searched upon entry. All drugs are confiscated and destroyed. Those who refuse are themselves refused entry whether they're an office worker or a rock star. Those who don't like the rules are welcome to party in other establishments.' He held up the bag he'd swiped from a young lad on the dance floor. 'There must be a hundred pills in this. Let in on *your* watch. You're fired.'

'It was one mistake,' Toni protested.

'I've been in touch with the authorities. In my absence there has been a steady increase of drug-related incidents linked with this club. It's clear to me that you've been running a policy of turning a blind eye. Those days are over. The buck stops with you. Now get out.'

Toni's jaw clenched. For a moment Nikos wondered if he would have to physically remove him but then he turned on his heel and stormed out, slamming the door behind him.

Toni was the second club manager he'd fired in five days. Both for the same reason. Nikos hadn't spent eighteen months 'dead' to bring down a drug cartel and stop them poisoning his guests with their evil substances for his own staff to allow those same substances onto his premises.

Dear God, it had been men like Toni the cartel had targeted and put under threat, men like Toni that Nikos had given up eighteen months of his life to protect. When his Madrid club manager had gone missing days after his London club had been set fire to, he'd immediately quadrupled security at his clubs and employed bodyguards for high-profile employees like Toni. *Including* Toni. He'd conference-called them to spell out the danger they were in and all he was doing to mitigate it. Which had been everything. He'd been too sickened with fear for his employees' lives to do anything less than everything.

And then he'd found the photo of Marisa and the sickening fear had turned to icy terror. For as long as he resisted the cartel's demands, no one connected to him would be safe.

Shaking off the memories that still felt too fresh for comfort, Nikos rose, straightened the sleeves of his shirt from beneath his suit jacket and left his office.

When he'd opened his first club, the one in Ibiza, other club owners had called him mad for refusing to turn a blind eye to drugs. Club-goers wouldn't set foot in a club where they couldn't take the fuel that allowed them to party all night long!

He'd proved them wrong. Lure in the best DJs, provide top facilities and an exclusive, hedonistic atmosphere and the club-goers would flock to you.

That night, as usual, his Barcelona club was heaving with clubbers.

Nikos entered the VIP section and gestured for a drink as he joined the old friends waiting to celebrate his resurrection with him. This was something he'd done during all the club visits so far; get the business side sorted first and then party hard. After eighteen months of solitude, he had a lot of partying to make up for.

Champagne and raucous conversation flowed. Beautiful women displaying their wares fluttered their eyes at him and drank flirtatiously through straws. He could take his pick of them. Hadn't he been looking forward to taking his pick and to the familiarity of the chase that had been missing for eighteen months? Two years if you counted the six months he'd been with Marisa. Not just with her but faithful to her.

But, just as when he'd sat in the VIP sections of his other clubs that week, Nikos had to actively force himself to have a good time. Despite all his best efforts, nothing worked. Instead of feeling a part of things, he felt like an observer on the outside looking in. It all just seemed so damned superficial. It was at times like this he found himself missing the physical aspect of life in the Alaskan mountains. There had been a purpose to felling a tree, stripping it and chopping it into firewood. Cathartic too. A means to release the demons that had plagued him in those long, long lonely months.

After all that solitude he should be ravenous for female company but, yet again, he felt absolutely nothing. Not one woman captured his interest. Not as much as a flicker of attraction.

Here he was reclaiming his life and all he could see when the scantily clad beauties paraded before him was Marisa.

Two more nights and she would be in Mykonos with him. The thought alone tightened his sinews and thickened his blood more than a whole nightclub of scantily clad women could do.

Their relationship hadn't come to a natural end, he now realised. The flame of desire between them hadn't been allowed to burn itself out and, until the flame extinguished itself naturally, he was stuck. He couldn't move on.

To hell with the complications of another, much shorter affair. To hell with never going back. Nikos wanted his *life* back and that couldn't happen while Marisa remained unfinished business.

Marisa held Niki securely as she disembarked from Nikos's private plane, grateful her son hadn't suffered on the flight. He'd flown for the first time only a month ago and had hated every minute of it. This time she'd been prepared and he'd spent the flight content.

A large black car was parked a short distance from them and her already erratic heart ballooned painfully to see the long, lean figure standing against it.

Nikos's presence in her life these last seven days had been reduced to two snatched, fleeting visits to see their son. His near absence had brought no relief. It shattered her that far from his distance giving her space to properly get her head around their situation, she still woke every morning having to assure herself that he *was* alive.

She had to stop her hands grabbing her phone to call him just to hear his voice.

Worse was the way her heart had thrummed for the entirety of those short visits. Worse still was the way it leapt whenever he fixed his gleaming eyes on her. The way her pulse thrummed when his gaze lingered too long on her... *Dios*, it was a sensation she hadn't felt in so long and it was terrifying how pleasurable a sensation it was. No matter how hard she tried to find it again, the control she'd mastered around him and that had cracked in the restaurant seemed far out of reach.

He strode towards them, shades on, a wide smile on his stubbly face, dressed in faded jeans, a grey V-neck T-shirt and a battered leather jacket. She'd forgotten how good Nikos looked in jeans and she frantically beat away memories of the washboard stomach and snake hips beneath them.

She forgot to hold her breath when he pressed a hand to her hip and leaned in to brush his cheek to hers. A flash of warmth against her skin and an enticing dose of spicy cologne hit her senses at the same moment he scooped Niki from her arms and set about planting huge kisses over his face.

She had just enough sense to be grateful he'd taken their son from her. From that moment of bodily contact, her limbs had weakened into mush.

'Comfortable trip?' he asked casually.

She semi-successfully curved her lips into a smile. 'Thanks for sending your plane for us.'

Holding Niki securely around his belly, he lifted him above his head. 'Only the best for my son and his mama.'

Their luggage had already been whisked into the boot of the car. A baby car seat had been installed in the back and Nikos strapped him in as if he'd done it a thousand times. The seat was so large it shrank the spacious interior.

The minute the door of the car enclosed them all inside she regretted not sitting up front beside the driver. Nikos's cologne filled the cabin, the bulk of his body, which was placed between her and their son, taking up almost as much space as the car seat. From the corner of her eye she saw him remove his jacket. For the first time since his return, she could see his arms and the contours of his body, and she pressed herself closer to the door and fought her greedy eyes' attempts to stare at him.

Was she imagining that, without a suit to hide most of his spectacular body, he was more muscular than she remembered?

She crossed her legs away from him and breathed through her mouth.

Soon they were driving through narrow streets in pretty towns with thick white walls and colourful roofs. She focused her attention on the nearing Aegean Sea, glimmering brightly under the setting sun, and tried to tune out the man who sat beside her.

'He's asleep.'

Nikos sounded so put out by this that she found herself smothering an unexpected giggle. 'He always falls asleep in cars.'

'There is still much for me to learn about him.'

'You know all the important things. Everything else is just window dressing.'

There was a long pause.

'Thank you.'

She turned her face to him before she could stop herself. 'For what?'

'For bringing him here.' His smile was wry but there was a softness in his eyes. 'I know it can't be easy for you to accept me into your lives when you spent all that time thinking I was dead. The way you've handled things has been incredible. When I think of everything you've been through, with the cartel and losing your father the way you did… I know how close you were to him.'

A lump formed in her throat and she had to swallow hard to speak past it. Losing her father on the heels of losing Nikos had ripped at the fabric of her sanity. 'It hasn't been easy. If not for Niki…'

'If not for Niki…?' he prompted when she stopped her words from running away from her.

The weight of his stare pressed on her chest.

'He pulled us together,' she said quietly. 'Getting through the rest of the pregnancy and preparing for his birth gave us focus. Mama…' She shook her head and looked back out of the window, trying her hardest to keep control of the words falling from her lips. 'Grief is like swimming through a black cloud and when it's someone you loved with all your heart and who you'd imagined yourself growing old with, it's a physical bruise that hurts with every breath you take. But having a child forces you to be strong, whether the child's an unborn baby or an adult. The primal urge to protect them is too powerful and so you pack away the pain and grief just to get through the days. You pack away *all* feelings. Bury them.'

And never let them out again.

Suddenly afraid her control had failed and she'd revealed too much about herself, she added as temperately as she could manage, 'That's how Mama got through it… how she *gets* through it. The only emotions she allowed herself were maternal ones. She was like a tiger roaring to keep her cubs safe.'

It had been like that for both of them. Two bereaved

souls trying desperately to keep their heads above water enough to stop their children drowning with them.

Her skin prickled at the intensity of Nikos's probing stare that she could sense was trying to penetrate her skull to read her mind but the next time he spoke was as they approached a small village and he casually mentioned they'd reached his land.

Not until the car stopped in front of a sprawling three-storey, square-roofed villa did she realise the village was one huge interlinked complex. She counted ten properties surrounding the main villa in a horseshoe formation, all a pristine white.

She got out and felt a sigh of pleasure form in her throat. Surrounded by gentle rolling hills with the sea lapping to the rear, Nikos had made himself a home in paradise.

Hot tears stabbed the back of her eyes and her pleasure soured. How she'd longed to come here in the months when she'd been head over heels in love with him. She'd dropped enough hints but they must have been too subtle because he'd never picked up on them. Always he'd had a reasonable excuse not to invite her to accompany him on his visits home. She'd swallowed it every time and suppressed the nagging doubts that if he was as serious about her as she believed, he would want to show his main home off to her.

Deep down she'd known he didn't want her here. If she hadn't she would have gone further than drop hints. She would have asked him outright.

By not doing that she hadn't had to deal with his certain rejection. She could continue believing they were meant to be together.

She'd opened her home to him. Her family had opened their hearts to him. He'd failed to reciprocate and she'd ignored it. How had she been so wilfully blind?

* * *

Nikos carried his son from the back of the car. Marisa was staring at his home with her arms tightly folded. The last of the sun's rays poured on her, turning her hair into a curly golden halo. Her beauty was something that never failed to dazzle him and now that he was resolved on the path he intended to take with her, he welcomed the fizz her presence put in his veins.

'What do you think of my home?' he asked when he joined her.

She dropped her arms and blinked, but before she could answer, Niki decided the time was right to throw himself into his mother's arms. Like a slippery eel, he dived out of Niko's hold to her. If Nikos hadn't had such a good grip on him and if Marisa's reflexives weren't so honed, their son would have hurtled head-first to the ground. In the blink of an eye, the pair of them were holding their son sandwiched between, Marisa's breasts crushed against their interlinked arms.

For the briefest moment, time stood still.

Nikos found his gaze locked onto her wide eyes. Her face tilted, lips parted in frozen shock. And then he saw the colour creep over her cheeks and her throat move, and the compulsion to cover her parted lips and kiss her so thoroughly that she couldn't stand sent a rush of heat flooding through him.

Because, in that brief moment of triumph, Nikos's strong suspicions were confirmed.

His mouth curled into a slow smile.

Marisa's attraction to him was still there. He could practically taste it.

A warm beat echoed in Marisa's head. She didn't know if it was shock at her son's daredevil antics or being trapped in Nikos's stare that was causing it. At that moment, all she knew was that he was gazing at her as if he wanted to eat her whole.

She was brought back to her senses by her son, merrily jiggling between his parents' crushed bodies, oblivious that he'd been nanoseconds from a fractured skull, waving his arms around and smacking her in the face.

'Niki,' she chided, disentangling an arm from Nikos's hold to gently take her son's wrist. Niki grabbed her hair with his other hand. Before she could remove it, Nikos took the offending hand.

'Leave Mama's hair alone.' He pressed even closer to her to unpluck the little fingers clutching her hair.

Sensation brushed from the tips of her hair and danced into her skin. Her already thrashing heart went into overdrive and she held her breath, trying her hardest not to inhale his scent.

He smoothed her hair back into place and looked down at her. His eyes glimmered, a smile spreading over his face before he finally stepped away from her with a murmured, 'That was close.'

She breathed deeply and swallowed, jiggling Niki on her hip, trying her best to look serene, trying her best to appear oblivious to the current of heat that had just passed between them.

But she couldn't deny the expression in Nikos's eyes, not when she'd seen it so many times before, right before he would crush his lips to hers and make passionate love to her.

She tightened her hold on Niki and willed her heartbeats to stop crashing against her chest.

It was a look he must have given to hundreds of women in his time. If she hadn't been a naive virgin finally ready to fall in love, she would have known she was nothing special to him a long time ago and better protected herself.

Romance and love had never been on her radar. From her earliest days Marisa had wanted to join the family business and had taken seriously her father's decree that she must work hard and earn her place in it. Unlike her sister and most of her friends, she'd studied hard at school and had rarely bothered with boys. School holidays in her teenage years had been spent shadowing her father as he'd gone about his business.

She'd studied at Valencia University so she could continue learning everything about the business while she completed her business degree. She hadn't been entirely single-minded but she had been very focused, and when she'd graduated and taken her place at her father's side, she'd had the best of all worlds—a great career and a wonderful circle of friends. She hadn't wanted or needed more.

And then she'd met Nikos and fallen head over heels in love.

He'd turned to the smartly dressed man who'd appeared from the house. Nikos introduced him as Angelos, his butler, and then they were swept inside where a handful of staff waited for introductions in the large reception area.

Marisa tried to pay attention to their names but was too taken with the villa's interior. Even Niki stopped wriggling in her arms to gawp. Where her home in Valencia was traditionally Spanish with plenty of colour, this was almost exclusively white, from the thick, high walls to much of the furniture. Only the hard floor beneath her feet differed in being a pale, warm grey. And yet there was nothing cold about it.

Where her home had defined rooms with doors leading from one to the other, this had defined spaces reached through open arches, and she followed Nikos through one into a huge living space with four separate sofa areas. Through another arch in the far distance she could see the sea...

No longer waiting for Nikos to guide her, she shifted Niki in her arms and headed for the arch. Stepping through it, she found herself in a vast living space that extended seamlessly to an equally vast terrace. Open-mouthed, she slowly craned her neck from left to right, taking in the long infinity pool that lapped inside and then seemed to stretch out to the Aegean itself.

The hairs on the nape of her neck rose before Nikos's voice rumbled in her ear. 'What do you think?'

'It's stunning.'

He grinned and stepped onto the terrace, beckoning for her to follow. 'Let me show you the grounds.'

Marisa tried her best to pay attention to the tour itself rather than her tour guide, but her attention grew increasingly fractured. Not only did she have to concentrate on holding a bored baby in her arms but Nikos kept close enough to her that her senses threatened to go into overdrive. At one point he even rested a hand on her back when showing her the playground he'd had installed for their son and then, when he took Niki from her, his eyes held hers with the gleam in them that never failed to make her belly melt.

She could only manage appreciative murmurs at the spa and business centre situated in two of the smaller villas, the open-air cinema, the soft play room for Niki near the shallow end of another swimming pool so large a holiday resort would be proud to have it.

When they returned to the villa, a matronly figure stood with the butler waiting for them with a small suit-case at her side.

Nikos shook her hand, spoke to her in Greek then

made the introductions. 'Marisa, this is Seema. I've employed her as Niki's nanny for your stay here.'

Nikos watched Marisa's dark brown eyes widen before her gaze darted from him to Seema then back again.

'Pleased to meet you,' she murmured, extending a hand.

'Pleasure to meet you too,' Seema replied shaking the offered hand. Then she spoke to their son. 'You must be Niki.'

To his surprise, Niki shied away from her and buried his face in Nikos's shoulder. No amount of coaxing would get him to look at her.

'This isn't like him,' he said to Marisa. 'Usually he's so sociable.'

She shook her head tightly. 'He always needs time to get used to new people.'

'He took to me straight away,' he pointed out.

She shrugged. 'You're the only one. Maybe it's because on some weird baby level he recognised you as his father.' Then, as Nikos was puffing up with pride at her observation, she addressed the nanny. 'Don't worry, he'll be comfortable with you very soon but he's in a new country in a home that is strange to him. I'll take care of him tonight and then tomorrow we'll introduce the two of you again.'

Seema looked to Nikos for approval. His orders to her had been clear—she would be responsible for his son's routine that week, especially with regard to evenings and nights. As he could also feel Marisa's laser stare piercing through him, he nodded. 'Angelos will show you to your room and make you familiar with everything. If we need you this evening we'll page you.'

She bowed her head and disappeared with his butler.

There was a moment of silence before Marisa said,

'You've employed a nanny?' Her low tone did not disguise the underlying menace in it.

He met her flinty stare. 'Obviously.'

Her eyes narrowed and glinted. 'You had no right.'

He bristled. 'I had every right. I'm his father.'

'And I'm his mother and I'm only here *because* I'm his mother.'

'Seema has impeccable references. She was nanny to the King of Agon's children.'

'I wouldn't care if she came gold-plated! You had no right to go over my head like that, no right at all, and don't quote the "I'm his father" line at me again; you don't know Niki well enough yet to know what's in his best interests.'

'*Whose* best interests?' he disputed coolly. Nikos had been prepared for Marisa's annoyance about the nanny but her line of attack on the matter was out of order. 'His or yours?'

Angry colour stained her cheeks. 'How dare—'

'You hardly let him out of your sight. Even when we were organising the business partnership you brought him along to all the meetings. You do everything for him. When it comes to our son, you're a control freak.'

The dark circles under her eyes proved how much she needed a break but a break would never happen if she had to get up at the crack of dawn each day to care for their son. He'd spent enough time with Mother Marisa to know she wouldn't trust him to care for Niki on his own. Not yet. She'd get up and hover between them.

That employing a nanny to care for their son left more time and opportunity for seduction was only secondary…

The baring of her teeth made him quite sure that she would have slapped him if he didn't have Niki in his arms.

'Caring for Niki is *my* job,' she snarled.

'You never relax or take time for yourself.'

'I'm a mother. It comes with the territory.'

His chest tightened as the image of his own mother floated in his mind and before he could stop himself he said, 'Not for all mothers.'

Not all mothers were tigers who roared to keep their cubs safe, like Marisa and her mother. Not all mothers had a primal urge to protect. Some mothers looked at their children and felt nothing.

Marisa's angry stare tempered, became contemplative. The piercing of the laser burn lessened as the composure he'd had so much fun cracking since her arrival visibly reset itself.

In a much calmer tone, she said, 'In future, please consult me before making any decision about our son's care.'

'Does that work for me too?' he challenged. 'Only it seems that you're the one who gets to make all the decisions for him.'

'That's because I'm the one who raised him without his father for eleven months. I earned that right.' Then she looked at their son and her features softened. 'But I take your point. If you disagree with my judgements then we should discuss it.'

'Who gets the final say?'

'Logic does. Failing that, *me*.'

Nikos had to control every muscle in his mouth to stop it from opening and biting back some home truths to her. He was acutely aware that, though their son couldn't understand what they were saying, he would undoubtedly be picking up on the tense atmosphere between them. He would not allow Niki to witness any kind of war between his parents.

Swallowing back the rancid taste on his tongue, he indicated the winding staircase. 'I'll show you to your rooms.'

CHAPTER SEVEN

MARISA HELD NIKI close as she stepped over the threshold of the door Nikos opened for her in the wide corridor, using his solid little body as a shield to protect herself from the emotions thrashing and crashing inside her.

She'd known it would happen one day soon, that Nikos would assert his authority as a father, but she'd surprised herself at the strength of her feelings about it. Until that moment, every single decision about Niki had been made by her and her alone. Nikos had been dead! The times when she'd been uncertain about something she'd sought her mother's advice but the ultimate decision had always been hers. His sudden assertion of parental authority while she was fighting the effect his nearness was having on her had made her angrier about it than she should have been... And his reasons for it.

Why would he employ a nanny for her benefit? Why would he care if she took time for herself? She *knew* he didn't care a jot for her...

But he still wanted her. Hadn't she known that since their meal together? And hadn't she sensed it before that?

His desire was there in every gleam of his eyes, a sensual promise that lived as a hum in her veins.

He didn't care for her but he still desired her as a woman, and, as she gazed around the room that would be hers for the week, she caught a glimpse of her reflection in a full-length mirror. For a moment she stared at the woman with the child in her arms.

A mother. A daughter. A sister.

A woman.

And then she caught Nikos's eye in the reflection. The icy steel she'd seen during their brief, heated argument had melted. What she saw in his light brown gaze now...

Her abdomen turned to liquid.

Marisa quickly looked away and forced her attention back to the room. It was as vast and white as the rest of the place but there were colourful feminine touches in the soft furnishings. The splashes of colour were the reds and oranges she adored, colours she hadn't seen in any other part of his home. Had these colourful touches been added for *her*...?

She couldn't stop her eyes darting back to Nikos. He stood by the glass door in the centre of the far wall, which had floor-to-ceiling windows, watching her.

'What do you think?' he asked.

She had to swallow hard to get her throat moving. 'It's perfect, thank you.'

The returning gleam had her tightening her hold around their son, who, oblivious to the undercurrents happening around him, was merrily babbling away as he took in the newness of his surroundings.

Suddenly desperate to escape the intimate confines, she backed to the door. 'Where's Niki sleeping?'

He stepped away from the wall, a knowing half-smile playing on his lips. 'The room opposite. It's been turned into a nursery for him. I'll show you.'

If she didn't have Niki in her arms, she'd have run out of the room.

The nursery was a big hit with Niki, who immediately went crawling to the building blocks set out on the floor for him. The adjoining dressing room had been filled with brand new clothing and all the toys a baby on the cusp of his first birthday could wish for. As dinner would soon be ready, Marisa decided a change of clothes for him was needed. All the travelling had made their son grubby. It might have proved a great distraction from Nikos if he hadn't stood next to her at the baby changing table so he could make funny faces at their son while she put a new outfit on him.

He stood so close—deliberately, she was sure of it—that her lungs contracted. She could feel the heat of his skin vibrating against hers and a job that should have taken two minutes doubled because her brain forgot how to work her fingers and thumbs.

As she fumbled to get socks onto her son's plump feet, Nikos's phone vibrated and he stepped away from her.

She met her son's bright happy eyes and blew out all the air she'd been holding in one long puff, trying to make it into a joke for fear that if she didn't, she would burst into tears. They wouldn't be sad tears. They would be frustrated tears. Frustration at herself for still hungering and responding so desperately to the man who'd treated her so abominably.

'My grandfather's back,' Nikos announced. 'Is Niki ready?'

She pasted a smile to her lips, nodded and stepped aside to let Nikos pick him up.

Following them out of the room, she vowed to get a grip on herself. With this firmly in mind, she said, 'When you say he's back, does your grandfather live here?'

'He lives in the villa next to the spa. He could have had a wing in here but he likes privacy to entertain his lady friends.'

'I didn't realise,' she said evenly, descending the stairs in step with him. He'd never mentioned his grandfather living with him.

'What, that my grandfather still has an active sex life? It's something I try not to think about.'

A welcome kernel of laughter tickled her throat at his deadpan comment. 'No, that he lives with you. Is that a recent thing?'

'He moved in when I finished the renovations eight years ago.'

'What made you buy it? Was it the views?'

There was a tightness to his smile. 'I inherited it from my mother.'

She was instantly confused. 'I thought you grew up in Chora?' Chora was Mykonos's capital and she distinctly remembered him saying it was the part of the island he was from.

'This was my home until I was six.'

'That must have been quite a change for you.' Nikos's beachside villa was incredibly remote. 'Did you move for school?'

'No. My grandfather took custody of me,' Nikos replied shortly. 'He took care of me as a child and now I take care of him.'

Shock had her tightening her grip on the bannister. *Custody?*

But there was no time to ask what he meant by this for he increased his pace to greet the elderly gentleman waiting for them.

Nikos's grandfather, Stratos, was a man of, Marisa guessed, around eighty. He had a shock of white hair, a weather-beaten face, twinkling blue eyes and, from the way he bounded to them, the energy of a man half his age.

When Nikos made the introductions, she was taken aback to see the blue eyes turn to ice as they landed on her. His kiss to her cheek came with a definite coolness that immediately put her on edge. She was old enough to know that everyone couldn't like each other but this was the first time since her school days she'd detected such an instant and noticeable dislike of her.

What on earth had she done to cause it? Could it be something as simple as Stratos being prejudiced against the Spanish or redheads?

If it was prejudice causing his frostiness to her, she was relieved to find his attitude didn't extend to her son.

Stratos couldn't speak Spanish or English. Marisa understood Greek far better than she spoke it—teaching herself Nikos's language so she could teach it to her son had been her greatest joy during her pregnancy—so that meant any ice-breaking conversation was out, but he didn't need verbal conversation to communicate with his great-grandson.

At first, Niki was as shy with him as he'd been with the nanny Nikos had hired. Stratos was undeterred, parking himself on the hard floor where he waited patiently for Niki's confidence around him to grow and was soon rewarded by his great-grandson using him as a human climbing frame.

Not once during this did he look at or attempt to communicate with Marisa.

Nikos did, though. Though she kept her stare on the two generations playing on the floor, she could feel his gaze burning into her. She wished the burn didn't feel like buzzing velvet in her veins. Wished her skin didn't shiver with awareness of his presence. She'd been wishing these things since he'd come back into her life.

Her mind kept going over his throwaway comment

about his grandfather having custody of him. How had she spent six months of her life loving someone without knowing something so fundamental about them? The few things he'd revealed about his past had been delivered matter-of-factly before he'd turned the conversations around to her. It had been done in such a subtle way that at the time she'd preened under the weight of his thirst for knowledge about every aspect of her life. Now she realised it had been a deflection to stop her asking questions about him.

But these were thoughts that had to be put on the backburner when dinner was served and they all headed out to the table on the terrace to sit beneath the warm night sky.

Stratos took the seat next to the highchair and insisted on feeding Niki the specially prepared mush. The utter disgust on her son's face as the concoction hit his tastebuds was photo-worthy. He spat it out, globules of green goo landing on Stratos's white shirt.

For the first time since their introduction, the elderly man met her eye. He burst into loud, gravelly laughter that set her off too.

'Has that got courgette in it?' she asked when they'd all stopped laughing and Niki had been pacified with a bread roll and a banana and Stratos had gone back to ignoring her.

Nikos grinned. This was his first shared meal with his son in his own home. He would never have imagined a month ago that something so simple and ordinary could provoke such huge enjoyment.

He'd shared plenty of meals in Valencia with his son but they'd all been with Marisa and her family. As outwardly welcoming and obliging as her mother and sister—on the occasions she'd joined them—had been to him, he'd known perfectly well that both of them would have cheerfully stabbed him with their forks if they'd thought they could get away with it. Strangely, he'd never had that vibe from Marisa, but then he remembered that in those first weeks she'd worn her indifference like armour.

He wondered if she was aware how greatly that armour had been stripped away. Or if she realised that every time she spoke to him, her fingers captured one of the ringlets splayed over her shoulders?

Seated diagonally from her, the pleasure of the evening was intensified by the enjoyment of her lovely face as his vista throughout the meal. Marisa was a beautiful woman but under the rising moonlight, her beauty turned into something other-worldly.

'I've no idea what the chef made him,' he answered after a drink of his wine. 'I should have warned him not to put courgette in his food.'

'You can add peppers and aubergine to the list,' she said without looking at him, fingers tugging on a ringlet. 'I made a batch of baby-friendly ratatouille a few days ago and you'd have thought I was trying to poison him.'

'I'm still amazed you can cook.'

'Only baby food,' she hastened to remind him, eyes darting to his before quickly looking away again.

Yet another example of her devotion to their son.

His own mother had never, to Nikos's recollection, cooked him a meal. She'd generally been too busy cooking her drugs to worry about feeding her son, and it rolled like poison in his guts to imagine his own son, belly cramping with hunger, teetering on a kitchen stool to reach a cupboard for food.

Theos, what was it about fatherhood that made the past feel more vivid and present than it had in decades?

Not just fatherhood. Marisa. The diametric opposite

of his own mother but with the same power over her son in her hands.

He swallowed the poison away with more wine, determined not to ruin this evening by allowing thoughts about his mother and the past to intrude.

The main course over, staff cleared their dishes away. Marisa got to her feet. 'I need to put Niki to bed.'

'Stay for dessert?' he coaxed.

She shook her head while unclasping the highchair straps keeping their son contained. 'It's way past his bedtime.'

Loving the way her silhouette played under the moonlight, Nikos looked her up and down. 'Seema can put him to bed tomorrow night and you can stay with the grown-ups.'

She didn't rise to the bait, lifting Niki from the highchair. 'I like to put him to bed myself.'

'You like to do everything yourself.'

'Only when it comes to this little one.' She leaned Niki towards Stratos so he could kiss his great-grandson goodnight then placed a polite kiss of her own to his wrinkled cheek.

Nikos watched her subtly brace herself before she carried their son to him. He took full advantage of her nearness, slipping an arm loosely around her back to keep her close. 'Goodnight, *moro mou*,' he said to his son as he smacked kisses over his face. When Marisa attempted to step away from him he trailed his fingers to her hips and slipped a finger into the pocket of her snug linen trousers. 'Don't *I* get a goodnight kiss, *agapi mou*?'

Her features tightened as her face made the tiniest of jerks before she found her composure and turned her flashing eyes on him. 'Of course.'

He heard the breath she took before she lowered her

face, their son in her arms making her movements careful. As her plump lips made light contact with his cheek he turned his face and their lips brushed. The moment of contact was fleeting but enough for him to taste the heat from her mouth. Heady warmth unfurled in him and coiled through his bloodstream.

Face bathed with colour, blinking rapidly, holding their son like a shield, she stepped away from him. When her eyes met his again there was dazed accusation in them.

'Goodnight, *agapi mou*,' he murmured, holding the stare. 'Sleep well.'

She took another step back then inclined her head and turned. Moments later, she disappeared inside.

It took a few more moments for Nikos to pull himself together.

Shifting in his seat, Nikos topped up his and his grandfather's wine glasses.

'Your son is going to be a real character,' his grandfather said with a chuckle.

Nikos smiled in response and took a large drink of his wine. His blood still pumped unexpectedly hard from the effects of the fleeting kiss.

'I never thought I would live to meet a great-grandchild, least of all from you.'

Nikos was an only child but had a dozen cousins he'd run amok around Chora with. He kept in touch with a few of them and the rest he saw at the usual family events of christenings, weddings and funerals. 'It was as big a surprise to me as to you.'

His grandfather's gaze became serious. 'You need to marry her.'

Nikos's good mood ended with those five words. 'That isn't necessary.'

'You won't think that if she stops you seeing him.'

'Marisa wouldn't do that,' he refuted automatically.

'You don't know that for sure. I raised you but she didn't tell me about him, and don't tell me she didn't know how to, she had the means and money to contact me if she'd wanted, and she has the means and money to fight you if she decides to stop you seeing him.'

'She loves him too much to do anything but what's best for him.' But his grandfather's cynical words had set off a pounding in his head. Hadn't similar thoughts already occurred to him?

'Her opinion on what's best might mean keeping him from you. What *is* best for him—and you—is having parents who are married.'

'My parents were married. That was hardly best for me.'

His grandfather winced. 'That wasn't marriage's fault. That was the drugs' fault.'

'They hated each other with or without the drugs.' And neither had cared a jot for him, he thought with a stab.

'They loved each other once. It was the drugs that ruined them.'

Nikos bit back his temper. He wasn't prepared to fall into another argument about it. His grandfather had a more sympathetic view of the past. Nikos supposed that was Stratos's love for his son still wanting to see the best in him despite all the evidence to the contrary.

'I only remember them as being at war with each other. I'm not going to put Niki through that. We'll formalise a custody arrangement when he's old enough to be parted from her for periods of time.'

'And when will that be?' his grandfather challenged. 'Do you see the way she is with him? She watches him like a hawk. It will be years before she allows you to have him without her.'

The ring of truth in his grandfather's words reminded him of how the colour had drained from her face when he'd asked if Niki could come to Mykonos. The colour had only returned when he'd clarified he meant for her to come too. He remembered, too, her earlier reaction to him employing a nanny. By her own admission, Marisa liked to do everything for their son. She did not like her judgement on his welfare to be challenged.

But marriage?

'You will have to hope she's amenable to a formal arrangement,' his grandfather added into the silence.

'She will be.' But Nikos's words sounded unconvincing to himself.

'I know you hate the idea of marriage but, remember, it doesn't have to last for ever.'

He flickered his eyes to his grandfather. His marriage to Nikos's grandmother, had been tragically cut short by her death from ovarian cancer four decades ago. Stratos had never said it in words but from the little he *had* said, Nikos had intuited the marriage had not been a happy one. His grandfather had enjoyed many lady friends since his wife's death but had never remarried or lived with another woman.

By the time his grandfather retired to bed, the doubts Stratos's words had sown had solidified his own fears into weights in his guts.

Too uptight to sleep, Marisa, baby monitor in hand, opened the glass door in her room and stepped out onto the balcony.

Putting the monitor on the wrought-iron table, she stepped to the balustrade and breathed deeply as she gazed out at the Aegean lapping on Nikos's private beach in the near distance. If she inhaled hard enough the faint salty tang might clear her mouth of the taste of Nikos that no amount of minty toothpaste could eradicate.

A throb of heat pulsed in her abdomen. Their lips had connected for barely a second but that second had been long enough for their breath to meld together and for any hope of control to be shattered.

She wriggled her shoulders to fight the shiver lacing her spine as she replayed the sensual tone of his voice when he'd bidden her goodnight, and forced her attention on her surroundings rather than the melting mess she was in danger of turning into. Look at the stars! See how they reflected off the black sea. See how they shone so brightly. The Valencian suburb the Lopez estate was located in was renowned for its wealth and beauty but it had nothing on Nikos's home. This had everything, beauty *and* peace.

What secrets were contained within its boundaries?

Many secrets. She was certain of it.

She'd intuited his childhood had been very different from the happy idyll of her own, but never had she guessed it had been bad enough that his grandfather had taken custody of him. He'd never even hinted at it. All she'd really learned about his childhood was that he'd lived and gone to school in Chora until he was fourteen, when he was sent *by his family*, as he'd put it to her, to boarding school in England, and the names of his childhood friends, many of whom he was still in contact with.

She squeezed her eyes shut in an attempt to drive Nikos's image away. She'd come out here to clear her mind, not think about him even more.

But not thinking about him was impossible when she could feel his presence in the buzz of her veins and when so many old familiar feelings were blossoming and singing and anticipation quivered low in her pelvis.

When she opened her eyes, she noticed for the first time that the long, wide balcony stretched further than the limits of her room. Tightening the sash of her satin robe, she followed her curiosity to the end of it and discovered the balcony was shared with the room next to hers. The curtains running the length of the glass wall were drawn but that didn't stop her taking a step back and then quickly padding back to her own half.

Tingles danced over her skin as instinct told her the adjoining room was Nikos's.

CHAPTER EIGHT

IT WAS LATE when Nikos carefully opened the nursery door and tiptoed to the cot. Staring down at the innocent sleeping form, he lightly stroked his son's soft cheek as his mind ran through the myriad ways Marisa could keep them parted if she so chose. It was all he'd thought about since his grandfather had vocalised the unease that had been steadily building inside him about Marisa's power.

She did have the money and the means to make life as difficult as she wanted it to be for him to see his son. She loved their son in a way his mother had never loved him, and if his own mother could turn her back on him, what was there to stop Marisa from doing the same? Her wealth didn't compare to his but when coupled with her protectiveness of their son and the imperious majesty she could turn on like a tap, it would make her a formidable opponent if she chose to fight him.

Nikos had never backed down from a fight in his life but those fights had never had a flesh and blood child at its centre. His own childhood had been wrecked by neglectful, warring parents and, though this situation was very different, he would do everything in his power to stop his son going through anything remotely the same.

However much the concept of marriage turned his stomach, it would give him greater authority and legal protection, and make the custody issue smoother when they eventually divorced. More civilised.

He bent over and kissed his son's forehead. 'Sleep well,' he whispered.

Niki had been a part of his life for such a short time but already he knew that, for his child, he would do anything. Even marry his mother. And in the process stop her ever having the opportunity to take his son from him.

Now all he had to do was convince Marisa, and as he closed the nursery door behind him, his lips curved into a smile and his skin prickled with arousal as he imagined the most effective way of getting her agreement.

Marisa sat back on the plush heart-shaped seat in the corner of her balcony and took a deep breath to calm herself. Her heart had leapt into her mouth when the baby monitor's green light had flashed to indicate movement in the nursery. She'd been on the verge of charging into the room when Nikos's whispered voice had sounded through the monitor.

The cartel was defeated but the paranoia that had dogged her the last year lived on.

The semblance of peace she'd found on the balcony was further disturbed moments later when the door at the far end slid open and a shadow fell over the moonlit marble flooring.

Heart immediately striding into a canter, she hugged the satin robe she'd slipped over her short silk pyjamas tighter around herself and strove for nonchalance at Nikos's approach. The canter became a ragged thrum when she spotted the bottle of white wine and two glasses in his hands.

'I thought you were tired.' A smile played on his handsome face. A smile that made her belly turn to goo.

'I couldn't sleep.'

'This should help you.' He pulled up a chair by the table, positioned it close to her, opened the bottle and poured them both a glass. Gaze holding hers, he held one out to her. 'Here.'

She shouldn't. Definitely not. What she should do is wish him goodnight—again—and go back to her room and lock the door behind her.

They hadn't been alone together, not properly, not just the two of them, since the night of his return.

She absolutely should not allow herself to be alone with him under the moonlight.

She took the glass from him with murmured thanks and put it to her lips. It was crisp and delicious. Much like the man her eyes were locked on.

He gave another stomach melting smile and relaxed into his chair. He was sitting so close to her his knees were inches from her feet. 'What's on your mind?'

'Nothing important.' Seeing his eyebrow rise lazily at her obvious lie, she added, 'We share this balcony?'

'Yes. My room's next to yours.'

'Oh.'

'But you had already guessed that,' he said knowingly. 'You were waiting for me.'

The rush of heat to her cheeks was so excruciating she couldn't find the words to deny it.

Because his words were the truth.

She'd hurried away from his end of the balcony back to hers and sat on this very seat with a cocktail of emotions racing through her blood. The strongest had been anticipation. She just hadn't realised it until Nikos had vocalised it.

'Don't be embarrassed, *agapi mou*.' He put his glass on the table and leaned forward to take her bare foot in his hand and gently pull it onto his lap. 'I know it will be impossible for me to sleep knowing only a wall separates me from you.'

'I…' She tried to breathe. Tried to find the will to pull her foot away and drag her stare from his face.

Ever since Nikos had returned she'd done everything in her power to avoid his gaze. And this was why. Once caught in the depths of his light brown eyes there was no escape.

His fingers made feather-light circular motions over her toes.

Why wasn't she resisting?

'There's no shame in wanting someone,' he whispered. His circling movements reached her ankle. Flaming shivers licked her skin. 'Or shame in admitting defeat.'

She tried to snatch air in.

'We have both tried to fight the inevitable,' he continued with that same sensual huskiness in his voice. A finger slowly traced up the inside swell of her calf. 'It is like the tide fighting the moon.'

She wanted to deny it. Loudly. Scream that he was wrong.

But that would be her wounded pride screaming. Nikos had broken her heart then stamped on the shattered pieces for good measure. There was nothing left of her heart for him to damage.

Nikos saw the emotions play out over Marisa's face. He noticed every pulse in her eyes, every ragged movement of her chest. He saw the flush of colour on her cheeks and the way her breasts strained towards him and the outline of her nipples pressed against the fabric of her nightwear. And he saw the fight she was waging against herself.

His fingers crept to the sensitive flesh of her inner thigh. 'Do you still have feelings for me?'

Her throat moved but still she didn't speak.

He inched his seat a little closer, nudging her thighs apart with his knees as he swirled his fingers even higher. 'I still have feelings for you.' His fingers reached the hem of her silk pyjama shorts. 'I try to forget you but there has been no one since you.'

Her breaths were coming in short, ragged bursts. When he slowly slipped a finger under the fabric of her shorts, her body trembled. He could feel the heat coming from the heart of her femininity and inched his thumb closer to the core.

She jolted, eyes widening.

'I've imagined us together so many times,' he whispered. He could see her trying to bring herself back into focus, and ran his thumb up the lips of her pleasure until he reached her swollen nub. Her back arched, breaths now coming in pants.

'I remember your scent.'

Keeping the pressure on her nub, he slid a finger inside her. Her head fell back. A soft moan escaped her lips.

'I remember your taste. I remember how good we were together.'

With a trembling hand she pulled the sash of her robe apart and then unbuttoned her pyjama top, exposing the breasts he'd once carelessly thought had been designed especially for him.

Then, breasts swaying with the motion, using her elbows as support, she lifted herself upright until she had a hand clutching the collar of his shirt and her molten brown eyes met his.

'Nikos…?' His name sounded like it had been dragged out from deep inside her.

Nikos was so turned on that now he was the one struggling to speak. 'Yes, *agapi mou*?'

She pressed her pelvis tighter against his hand and covered his free hand, lifting it and placing it on her breast. 'Stop talking and take me to bed.'

And then, still holding tightly to his shirt, her head fell back and she shuddered violently.

The tattoo of Marisa's heart drummed loudly in her ears as she fought for breath.

Her hand clutched Nikos's shirt like a vice. The strength of the orgasm that had just erupted within her should have drained the arousal from her but the ache in her core still throbbed.

Leaning closer to her, he moved his hand out from under her shorts and slowly wound it around her back.

She met the hooded stare with a frankness she had denied them both these past weeks. His lips were tightly set, nostrils flaring as he breathed in and out. His body had gone rigid.

She inched her face closer to his until she felt the heat of his skin against her own and the musky scent of his skin and the faint scent of his cologne soaked into her senses. She rubbed her nose against his cheekbone and breathed him in some more, releasing his shirt to bury her fingers into the soft dark hair and dig the tips into the back of his skull.

The fight was over. She had lost.

But she had won too. The incredible feelings ravaging her were proof of that.

For the first time since Nikos's death, she felt like Marisa again. A woman with desires and needs, not just a mother, a daughter, a sister.

The sensual side of her nature—a side only Nikos had seen—had been locked in hibernation since the day of his death and now he'd awoken it, unleashing the burn that had once seen her beg for his touch.

He couldn't hurt her again. She knew that now. The damage he'd caused was irreparable.

But he could give her pleasure. Pleasure like nothing else on this earth.

Nikos stared into the molten eyes still pulsing with the effects of her climax. Her body still trembled, her sweet breaths still ragged.

Arousal bit him so fiercely that the scrape of Marisa's nails against his skull was as effective as if she'd taken his excitement in her hand. It was a struggle to draw in the air he needed to temper it, a task made harder when every inhalation drew her scent into his lungs.

He needed to get hold of himself before he...

He sucked in a sharp breath as she pressed her cheek to his and dragged the hand not kneading his skull down to his hand and placed it back against her breast. The shallowness of her breaths whispering against his skin was as erotic as the feel of the plump weightiness in the palm of his hand.

Theos...

He gritted his teeth and closed his eyes against the deep throbbing in his loins.

Nineteen months of celibacy and the effect was to make him feel like an overly excited teenager about to bed a woman for the first time.

He hadn't felt such desire even then. The closest he'd come to feeling like that was the first time with Marisa. It had been the headiest, most erotic moment of his life. Her virginity and the length of time she'd forced him to wait for consummation had heightened the effects. That's what he'd thought. But it had only got better. And better. And better.

Nineteen months of celibacy but his body remembered. Every cell in his body pulsated in anticipation.

Eyes wide open and burning into his, her lips dragged slowly to his mouth and hovered, lips parted but only a whisper of connection between them. The sweet taste of her breath danced onto his tongue. Her fingers dug deeper into his skull.

The last thread holding him to the earth snapped and with a groan he had no control over, Nikos captured her beautiful lips in a kiss of pure, hedonistic savagery.

Tongues entwined, teeth grazed, fingers bit into flesh. There was little comprehension that she'd shifted her body until she was straddling his lap and their bodies were crushed together.

Clasping her bottom, he rose to his feet, lifting her with him. Her legs wound around his waist as he carried her through the open door to the turned-down bed.

In seconds he was lying on top of her, kissing and nipping, their hands working together in a frenzy to strip away the barrier of clothing. Shrugging his shirt off, he covered a breast with his mouth and greedily sucked and licked, hands wrenching at the silk shorts she'd dragged down to her hips, then worshipped her other breast as he worked the shorts to her knees. She kicked them off while her hands tugged at his unbuttoned trousers, sitting up to get a better grip before she yanked them down with his underwear until they were kneeling before each other, naked and panting with lust. For no more than a second they stared into each other's eyes. Nikos's arousal reached boiling point to see the unashamed desire in hers and the colour slashing her face.

He pounced. She pounced.

Their mouths locked together as he fell back on top of her.

Marisa's thighs parted with no thought from her brain. There were no thoughts. Only sensation. Such glorious, heavenly, mind-blowing sensations. The weight of Nikos on her, the feel of his skin against hers, his taste and scent on her tongue and infused in all her other senses…

The heat burning between her legs was almost too much to bear and when she felt the heavy weight of his erection right where she needed it to be, she moaned, '*Please*, Nikos. Please. Now.'

He drove inside her in one long, hard thrust.

The relief was so great that she cried out.

Arms wrapped tightly around his neck, legs hooked around his waist, mouth buried in his shoulder, Marisa closed her eyes and fell into the saturating pleasure.

Deeply he thrust into her, in and out, a fusion of heat and flesh driving each other on until she felt the thickening between her legs and clung even tighter as the pulsating ripples broke free and carried her to a peak that left her limp and boneless.

A breeze came through the opened door. Nikos closed his eyes and welcomed its cooling touch. Marisa lay on her back beside him, the sheets pulled up to her shoulders. When he'd rolled off her she'd wriggled away from him. She'd made no effort to touch him since.

They hadn't exchanged a word since their explosion of lust. He didn't know about her but the thumps of his heart had been impossible to speak through. It was yet to settle back into a normal beat.

It had never beat normally around her…

He took a deep breath. That kind of thought was what had made him glad to end their relationship. Too many strange thoughts in the minutes and hours after making love.

In the aftermath of lovemaking back then, Marisa would always cuddle up to him. She would put her ear to his chest and, though it had gone unspoken, he'd known she'd been listening to his heartbeat. It had been the strangest feeling, unsettling and yet somehow comforting, the way she'd taken such pleasure from the beating of a heart. His heart. She would stroke his skin too. Nuzzle her nose against his chest. Stretch against him and tilt her head to smile at him. Whisper that she loved him. He'd never believed those words but to hear them had always filled his chest with so much emotion it had hurt his heart to breathe through it.

Now she might as well be a corpse for all the life he detected from her.

But she was awake. Marisa was too deep a sleeper to fake it. When sleep came for her, she rolled onto her side and curled into a ball. He'd always hated the loss of her warmth when she did that. Often he would wake and find he'd curled into her as if his sleeping body had subconsciously sought her out. He'd never done that with anyone else either.

'What are you thinking?' he asked.

There was a long period of silence before she answered. 'Why?'

'It's not like you to lie quietly after sex.'

'It's been a long time since we shared a bed, Nikos.' She sighed and turned her face to his. 'Shouldn't you go back to your own room?'

'Do you want me to?'

She looked back to the ceiling. 'I think it's best.'

'Why?'

'Sometimes Niki wakes early. I bring him back to bed with me.'

'Can't you do that with me here?'

'It would only confuse him.'

'Why?'

'It just would. I don't want him to think you and I are like other mamas and papas.'

'Isn't he too young to think like that?'

'I don't know what he thinks. He might have lots of fully formed thoughts in his head.'

'He might,' Nikos conceded. 'And one of those thoughts might be a wish for his mama and papa to live together.'

'Don't speak like that.' She rolled to the edge of the bed and slipped her robe on.

'Why not?' he challenged. 'Is that not a normal wish for a child?'

She tightened the sash and got to her feet. 'Nobody's normal is the same as anyone else's.' She stepped out onto the balcony. A moment later, the outside light was turned off and she came back in, closing the door behind her.

Using the dim light of the moon and stars to illuminate the way, she carried the baby monitor to her bedside table and sat on the bed with her back to him. 'I mean it, Nikos. I don't want to confuse him.'

'Neither do I.'

'Good.'

'I only want to do what's best for him, as I know you do.'

Her head dipped forward.

'Which is why I think we should consider marrying.'

The stiffening of her back, the slow turn of her body to face him, the wide eyes and open mouth were almost comical but the situation was too serious for him to find amusement in it. Now that the idea of marriage had rooted in his head, he knew he had an uphill battle to get Marisa's agreement but was confident he would succeed. All he had to do was pull the right strings.

As difficult as the task would be, there was already relief that the decision had been made. Nikos's feelings for his son grew by the day. He wanted to be a real father to him, with autonomy, not someone for Niki to visit a few times a year. He wanted the security of knowing his son could never be taken from him.

He could manage a year of marriage and then separate from Marisa knowing he had the right of being a father in the law's eyes on his side. Sure, she'd named him as the father on Niki's birth certificate but marriage gave him much greater protection. She wouldn't be able to deny his demand for equal access.

A year of marriage also meant a year of having Marisa in his bed and that brought relief of a different hue. Such a short time since they'd made love but already fresh awareness was coiling through him.

It had been like this before. His desire for her had intoxicated him. Almost driven him to madness.

A year of marriage would be long enough to spend his passion for her and allow them to reach the natural end his fake death had denied them.

Now all he needed to do was persuade Marisa to say yes.

CHAPTER NINE

MARISA SHOOK HER head as if expelling water from her ears. She'd been holding onto herself by the skin of her teeth, desperately fighting the craving to lie in Nikos's arms and recapture the closeness she'd always adored after making love when he'd dropped his bombshell on her. He thought they should marry?

How was she supposed to process something like that? It would have been less of a shock if he'd told her he wanted fly to Jupiter and colonise it.

She stared at his dimly lit face, looking for a sign that he was joking. He lay stretched out on the bed, arms folded above his head, his gorgeous face expressionless, but she sensed him soaking in her shock, waiting for her to get herself together. It was an expression that made her hackles rise.

Shifting her entire body round to face him, she folded her arms tightly around her chest, afraid he would see the ferocious thudding of her heart. 'You think we should marry?'

'Yes.'

She shook her head again. 'What on earth for?'

'For Niki. For all of us.' He rolled onto his side and propped himself up on his elbow. 'Being away from you this week made me realise how much I need you both in my life. I want us to be a family, *agapi mou*.'

How she wished the strings of her heart didn't tug so hard at this. 'You've changed your tune.'

'I didn't know how much being a father would change my perspective on life. You had an idyllic childhood with a mother and father who were together and I want that for our son. Don't you want that for him too?'

She'd wanted that once, she thought with a deep wrench. She'd ached for it. Her early pregnancy had been spent clinging to the futile hope that Nikos was still alive, cast away on a desert island sending smoke signals and creating a giant SOS on a beach. He would be found. She would tell him of the pregnancy and he would drop to one knee, declare his love for her and they would live happily ever after.

But that hope had always been in vain, and she'd known it. He'd fallen overboard in the Mediterranean. His crew had discovered him missing the morning after a night anchored at sea in bad weather. The last person to see him alive reported he'd been standing on deck, watching the surrounding storm. The hunt for him had been one of the largest undertakings the region had ever seen. All the small uninhabited islands in the Balearics, the area in which he'd disappeared, were thoroughly searched numerous times. No body had been found.

The sea had swallowed Nikos up. Eventually, her heart had accepted this, as well as the knowledge that her son would never know his father. When her own father was subsequently murdered, she'd had to deal with the unimaginable pain of his death and the aching realisation her son would have no father figure in his life. Once, she'd hoped Raul might be the father figure Niki would come to need. Blind desperation for help with the business, and safety and protection for her son had seen her propose to him.

And now Nikos was offering her the one thing she'd always longed for from him and all she could think was that he hadn't cared to tell her he was alive and well until he'd learned about their son.

'Since when do you need me in your life?' she asked.

'Since I came back into it.' His gaze didn't falter. 'I thought we'd both moved on but what we've shared tonight is proof that what we had is still alive.'

Her pelvis clenched and blood thickened to remember exactly what they'd just shared and she pressed her thighs tightly together, doing everything she could not to allow all the internal sensations show on her face. 'Is that what tonight was about?' she asked as evenly as she could. 'A seduction to remind me how good we are together? To soften me up with sex so I'm more open to the idea of marriage?'

'Partly.'

She closed her eyes at the sting of his admission and turned away from him.

'But you can't deny the chemistry between us has been getting stronger,' he added into the silence. 'What we just shared was going to happen and it will happen again whether you agree to marry me or not.'

'Your ego is as big as ever,' she said shakily.

The mattress dipped. Tingles raced up her spine, breath catching as she felt him close the gap between them. When he placed his hands on her shoulders and pressed a kiss on the arch of her neck she had to clench her teeth to stop a moan escaping.

'Not my ego,' he murmured into her hair, pressing his chest into her back. 'The truth. And I know you feel it too.'

Nikos cupped a weighty breast and rubbed his thumb over a nipple that hardened at his touch.

'See?' he whispered. 'Already you want me again. There is not a minute when I'm with you when I don't fantasise about us being together like this.'

She caught hold of the hand manipulating flesh that had always been so sensitive to his touch. Her fingers dug into his skin and stilled as if in hesitation before lacing through his.

'This is just sex,' she said with a sigh.

'Good sex. Great sex. Just as we had before. Remember how good we were together? We can have that again.'

She yanked his hand off her breast and shuffled away from him. 'If we were so good together, why didn't you come back to *me*?'

He chose his words carefully, regretting his honesty in those hours after his return. If he'd known then what he knew now—if he'd *felt* then what he felt now—he would have handled things differently.

'You'd moved on. You were engaged to another man. I thought I'd moved on too but no one compares to you.' He closed the gap she'd created and put his hands on her hips. 'There has been no one but you since the day we met, and I know we can make it work. We can be a real family and give Niki the love and stability I never had.'

She was silent for a long time but he took comfort that she didn't pull away from him again.

'Tell me about it,' she said.

'What?'

Now she did pull away, stretching across the bed to put the bedside light on. Then she turned round to face him. 'Tell me about your childhood.'

'It's history,' he dismissed.

'*Your* history. If you want to marry me so Niki has the love and stability you never had, then I want you to tell me why. Explain it to me. Make me understand. Otherwise my answer is no.'

Nikos could see from the set of her jaw and her unwavering stare that Marisa wasn't bluffing. He cursed himself for unwittingly opening the goal for her to shoot into.

He'd never brought Marisa to Mykonos when they'd been dating because he'd needed to keep a separation between them. He'd never discussed his childhood, had always made it clear from the outset in any relationship that it was an off-limits subject. But Marisa was not like his other lovers. On the surface, she'd been of the same breed as the others. Glossy. Immaculate. But surfaces were deceptive and hers was more deceptive and far deeper than most.

The first obvious difference between her and his other lovers had been her refusal to go home with him that first evening. It hadn't been the refusal that had marked her as different but that she had meant it. Marisa hadn't been playing a game of hunt and chase. She'd had self-respect and he'd quickly come to respect her hugely for it. She'd got closer to him than anyone ever had, and it had been a battle to fight through the intoxication of their lovemaking to resist letting her get any closer.

He'd resisted bringing her to the home of his early childhood because he'd sensed she had the capacity to dig beneath the villa's glossy, immaculate exterior and bring the ugly truth into the light.

To bring Marisa here would have meant answering questions about a part of his life he preferred to forget.

His instincts back then had been right.

But his past had been pushing for air, swirling into his thoughts during his time in exile, the memories strengthening and blindsiding him ever since his son had come into his life.

Stomach churning, he leaned back to rest against the headboard. 'What do you want to know?'

'Everything. But we can start with your parents and why your grandfather took custody of you.'

He wanted to rip his gaze from her stare. Instead, he straightened his spine and met it head on. 'My parents were drug addicts.'

There was a flickering in her eyes.

'You sure you want to hear this? It isn't pretty.'

'I'm sure.'

He shrugged. So be it. Maybe giving the memories the oxygen they wanted and Marisa wanted would be enough to silence them for ever.

'Don't misunderstand me—I don't want you to imagine a scene of squalor like the junkies that are portrayed in films. I mean, they *were* junkies, but they were high functioning. They were both clever, high maintenance individuals who needed a steady fix of narcotics to help them function.'

'You keep saying *were*? Are they both dead?'

'My father's alive but I haven't seen him in a long time. Fifteen years, maybe. My mother died ten years ago. She came from a wealthy family...' he waved his hand around to indicate the villa he'd inherited from her '... and was what in today's terms would be a socialite. My father was a musician. I'm told he was once an excellent one. They were both mild drug users when they got together but their influence on each other was destructive. They supposedly loved each other once but all I remember is them hating each other. They had many all-night parties here and would just erupt in front of everyone.' He laughed grimly. 'Everyone acted as if it was normal, two grown people throwing ornaments and threatening each other with knives…'

'What?' She interrupted, her set face suddenly cracking with horror. 'You *saw* this?'

'I witnessed a lot of violence and drug taking. I was put in my grandfather's custody when my mother smashed a glass over my father's head. He wasn't seriously injured but there was enough blood that one of their friends called for a doctor.'

He blinked away the memories of the blood pouring over his father's shocked face that moments before had been twisted in a goading snarl. Nikos had been playing with his stuffed elephant, making it ride his toy truck, and he remembered the sickening thuds of his heart as he'd pretended not to see or hear, just kept the elephant and truck circling and circling.

'The doctor saw me playing on the floor surrounded by vast quantities of drugs and felt duty-bound to call the authorities. They took me away and gave me to my grandfather.'

'And you were *six*?' she asked faintly. Her face had turned ashen.

'Yes. It was agreed my parents' lifestyle wasn't conducive to raising a child and my grandfather agreed. I didn't know it then but he'd been fighting for custody of me for years. He'd never approved of what he thought of as their champagne lifestyle but his suspicions of drug use had been just that—suspicions. He had no hard evidence and my mother had the wealth and contacts to ban him from their home and put a stop to his interfering. Those were the days I presume she had some form of maternal feelings for me.' Those maternal feelings hadn't lasted long enough for Nikos to remember any sign of them.

'So overnight you were taken from your parents and

given to your grandfather?' She shook her head. 'I can't even begin to understand how that must have felt.'

'You know what you just said about everyone's normal being different? Drug addicted parents who hated the sight of each other was my normal. It took a long time for me to understand and accept I would never live with them again.'

Months and months of nightmares.

His parents had been his world and he'd loved them. His life had centred round pleasing them. A smile from his mother or an absent pat on the head from his father had been enough to fill his childish heart with joy that would last for days.

His mute terror at the violence he'd witnessed between them and the ache in his heart when another night would roll around without a goodnight kiss had been nothing to his terror at being taken from them.

Marisa brought her knees up to her chin and tried to take it all in as dispassionately as Nikos had narrated it. It was impossible. All she could see in her mind's eye was a little dark-haired boy playing on the floor surrounded by stoned adults, drugs and blood. She saw faceless authority figures swooping in and leading him out of the only home he'd known by his hand, the little boy not knowing his world was on the cusp of changing for ever. Or that *he* was on the cusp of changing for ever.

'And when you did accept it…how did you find living with your grandfather?'

He pulled a face. 'Difficult. We both did. I'd had no discipline at all and was used to fending for myself. We clashed very badly, especially as I got older. He sent me to boarding school in England when I was fourteen. English boarding schools have a reputation for strictness. My mother paid for it.' His face twisted bitterly. 'She could have used her wealth to fight to keep me, paid others to care for me, all kinds of things she could have done to keep me under her roof, but she chose not to—turns out she found it preferable to live without the bother of a child. But she was more than happy to pay for me to move countries.'

Nausea churned in her belly. Nikos's observation that Marisa's childhood had been idyllic was true and something she'd always been aware of and thankful for. Compared to what Nikos had been through it had been served to her on a bed of rose petals carried by winged cherubs. Not for a single second had she wondered whether her parents loved her. Their love had been so deeply imbedded in her that there had never been a need to question it.

Struggling to speak, she whispered, 'What about your father?'

'Within months of me being taken from them, they split up and he left for the mainland. He's still there now, in Athens, I think, playing his guitar in restaurants. He snorted and smoked most of the money he got off my mother in the divorce.' A pulse throbbed on his jawline. 'You know, I grew to hate them. I mean, *really* hate them. Especially my mother. She had the money to fight for me. I had a small inheritance of my own from her parents. It was put under my grandfather's control.

'He gave me a sum of it when I turned sixteen. I lived independently off that money and turned it into a fortune while having the time of my life, and didn't return to Mykonos until I was twenty-three. I hadn't seen her in six, seven years and the change I saw in her was enormous. She'd had so much work done to her face that it looked plastic but it didn't hide the damage from her addictions and lifestyle. I still hated her but seeing her like that…' His lips tightened. 'I began to feel a responsibility to her.'

He laughed morosely. 'It is strange how we change, isn't it? I never thought I would feel that. A responsibility for that woman. But I did.'

'Maybe it was seeing her with adult eyes,' she suggested softly. 'You could see her vulnerabilities.'

'Maybe.' He shrugged. 'I got into the habit of calling her every few days. One day she didn't answer. I tried a number of times. I was in London and called the Mykonos authorities. They found her dead on her bedroom floor.'

Cold horror sliced through her heart.

'She'd overdosed.'

Marisa rubbed her mouth against her knee and closed her eyes to stop the threatening tears from falling. He didn't want her sympathy.

In the end, all she could think to say was the honest, simple truth. 'I'm sorry.'

Nikos swung his legs off the bed and opened the door to step onto the balcony.

He needed air.

Fingers tight around the balustrade, he rolled the tension from his neck.

For so many years he'd wished his mother dead. It had been a wish he'd hated himself for but one he'd been unable to block. Not until he'd learned she'd been dead for four days before her body had been found had he recognised the miserable loneliness of her death had been a mirror to the miserable loneliness of her life.

The grief he'd felt at her death had knocked him for six. How had Marisa described grief? Like swimming through a black cloud?

His had been a grief he'd never expected to feel and he'd hated himself for it. She'd never grieved for the loss of him so why should he grieve for the loss of her?

He'd smothered the grief quickly and locked it away. Forgotten.

Until now.

He waited until the tight knots deep in his guts had loosened before returning to Marisa's room.

The knots loosened some more to see his son sitting on the bed, wide awake. A huge beam spread over Niki's face to see him.

Nikos met Marisa's eyes.

She shrugged ruefully. 'He's not used to sleeping in new places. This is only the second time he's not slept in his own cot. We spent a night in Geneva when the cartel was being taken down—I think he woke up four times.'

Niki held his arms out for him. Nikos slid under the bedsheets and pulled his son to him. If Marisa still wanted him to leave she'd have to ask again.

But she didn't ask. She slipped under the sheets next to him and smiled to see their son bouncing on Nikos's chest.

'He loves you,' she observed, her wistful gaze alternating between his face and their son's.

'I like to think so.'

'He does.' Lightly—so lightly it felt like a feather brushing against him—she ran a finger over his forehead then turned her attention to their son, whose cheek she kissed. Her shoulders rose before she let out a long sigh and lay down.

Pulling the covers over her shoulders, she said, 'If you snore, you go back to your own room.'

His chest had filled with too much emotion for him to protest at this slight with anything stronger than, 'I don't snore.'

The sad amusement in her eyes filled his chest even

more. 'Don't let him stay awake too long otherwise we'll have a grumpy baby tomorrow.'

He swallowed the boulder lodged in his throat and nodded. 'Understood.'

Her eyes held his for the blink of a moment before she turned her back to him and turned the light out.

Struggling to breathe, Nikos held his son's wrists to steady him as he merrily bounced away on his chest and watched his happy, babbling face in the starlight.

'Nikos?' Marisa's sleepy voice broke quietly through the darkness. 'We'll talk more about your suggestion tomorrow. Okay?'

CHAPTER TEN

NEVER IN HIS life had Nikos woken with such a weight pressing on his chest. But this was a good weight. An excellent weight. He opened his eyes and found his son straddling his neck, his face hovering over his with the look of an archaeologist examining an important find. The sun had risen but Nikos was quite sure it was earlier than he'd woken since his own childhood.

Grinning, he lifted Niki into the air and sat up, shushing him as he went so he didn't wake Marisa, who was curled up like a hedgehog under the sheets beside him.

He stared at the golden-red curls poking out and felt his heart catch. On the verge of leaning over and capturing one of those curls, he was prevented by a miniature finger being inserted up his nose.

He held onto his laughter until he'd closed the nursery door. His amusement soon turned to head-scratching as he tasked himself with cleaning and changing his son's nappy and pyjamas. Just as he was debating whether or not to wake the nanny, a sleepy Marisa entered the room, smothering a yawn. Even with her hair shooting up in all directions and puffy eyed, she looked beautiful, and Nikos felt an immediate stab of longing pierce him.

He'd hardly slept himself. While his son and son's mother had slept deeply with him on the huge emperor-sized bed, he'd been alert to every move they'd both made, the few lulls into sleep filled with vivid dreams that had merged into reality when he'd opened his eyes.

Had his mother ever brought him into her bed when he'd been a baby? Had his father? Had they ever shared the same room? All he'd ever known was that each had had their own room that the other was expressly forbidden from entering. He'd been forbidden from entering either of them too. He remembered mornings, his stomach hurting from hunger, creeping around the vast kitchen in search of food, dragging a stool around to climb on to reach the taller cupboards, too frightened of their anger to go into their rooms to wake either of them for help. Neither had minded him making a mess in the kitchen— his mess only added to theirs—but woe betide him if he woke them up. Those were the only rules in the Manolas household: no entering his parents' bedrooms and no making a noise that could wake them from their sleep.

When he'd first been taken from them he'd thought it was because he'd made too much early morning noise. It had taken a long time to realise that, though he'd been forcibly taken, they'd willingly let him go. They'd given him up.

What had been so wrong with him that they could do that? Give him up? It was a question he'd asked himself many times through the years but it took on an even greater significance now.

What had been so wrong with him that they'd denied him the affection Marisa lavished on Niki? Look at her now, standing beside him at the changing table, pressing kisses on the face of their naked son, who was making bicycle motions with his legs. He didn't imagine his mother had ever done that to him.

'Why didn't you wake me?' she asked.

'When did you last sleep in?' he challenged.

'What's sleeping in?'

'See?' He gave her his sternest look. 'Go back to bed. I've got this.'

Ignoring his directive, she tickled their son's belly. 'You're changing him?'

'Obviously.'

'If it's that obvious, where's his clean clothes?'

He hadn't thought of that. From the look on her face, she knew it too. She smiled. 'I'll get some for you. Shall I get you a clean nappy too?'

He hadn't thought about that either.

He had a lot to learn. From the look on Marisa's face she was happy and willing to teach him.

He just had to hope she was happy and willing to teach him as his wife.

The first full day in Mykonos passed slowly for Marisa. Spent lazing around the pool with the nanny and Stratos, who still seemed to be cold towards her, it gave her plenty of thinking time. All her thoughts were wrapped around Nikos...

The lovemaking they'd shared. That was something she didn't so much think about but shimmered in her veins as a constant reminder. Her pride wanted to be angry that his seduction had been planned but she'd waited for him on that balcony. She'd wanted it as much as he had and from the ache in her pelvis, she knew that if he came to her room tonight, she would open the door to him without hesitation.

Making love had been a physical act she'd abandoned herself to without fear of losing her heart. The feelings that had erupted within her when he'd spoken so dispassionately about his childhood were far more frightening.

She'd felt the pieces of her damaged heart knit themselves back together so they could cry with sympathy for the damaged little boy he'd been. The Nikos he was today was not the six-year-old child he'd once been, and it was imperative she separate those two Nikoses, however difficult it would be, especially if she agreed to his proposal.

That, more than anything, had played on her mind all day, tying all the other issues together and making the strings of her heart play a concerto.

Terrifyingly, she had slept more soundly with him sharing her bed than she had since the day he'd gone missing from his yacht. Today was the first morning since his return that she hadn't woken with panicked ice stabbing her heart.

She genuinely didn't know what to do for the best. Could she really deny her son the opportunity to have the blessed childhood she'd had for the sake of her pride? And could she deny Nikos that experience? Didn't he deserve the chance to be a real father, to share in all the joys of watching their baby reach all those important milestones and all the day-to-day joys she took for granted? The joy of beaming early morning smiles? The joy of feeding him something that wasn't immediately spat out? The joy of baths and getting drenched by manically kicking legs connecting to water?

She had to wait until mid-afternoon before the opportunity came to ask Nikos the questions that had been steadily forming in her jumbled mind as the day had gone on. His grandfather had gone to his chess club and the nanny had taken Niki to the nursery for his nap.

Nikos joined her on the terrace, a smile on his gorgeous face and two glasses of fruity cocktails in his hands.

'Here,' he said, handing her one. 'Don't worry, it's not too strong.'

The strings of her heart were plucked again. How well he was getting to know her as a mother, anticipating her thoughts and worries.

There was something incredible in how he could make the separation of her as a mother and her as a woman and cater for the needs of both. More incredible still that it had taken his return for her needs as a woman to reawaken.

He'd roused so many buried feelings and impulses. Feelings and impulses he'd been the one to bring to life in the first place...

'Thank you,' she murmured. This was the first time they'd been alone together all day and, from the safety of her shades, she let her greedy eyes soak in the glory of his body, only a pair of brief black swim shorts covering any flesh. She'd always loved his body. Its muscular leanness. The olive hue of his skin. The dark hair that covered his chest and made a tapering line down to his groin. The snake hips. The tight buttocks. The long, toned legs. The whole package.

From the smirk on his face and the way he brushed his fingers against hers as he released the cocktail glass, Nikos knew exactly what she was doing. She didn't care that she'd been caught ogling him. After the night they'd shared and the confidences he'd entrusted to her, she was beyond denying her desire for him. It was too late for denial. Much too late.

Propping herself on an elbow to face him, she had a sip of the cocktail while he stretched out on the sunbed placed inches from hers, and felt heat crawl over her face as his eyes, also hidden by shades, swept over the length of *her* swimsuit-clad form.

'Your body's changed,' she said. 'You're more muscular.'
He grinned. 'I lived in a log cabin in the Alaskan

Mountains for eighteen months. If I wanted heat, I had to chop trees for firewood. Trust me, in the winter months it gets *very* cold.'

About to ask about his time in exile, her words were stolen when he extended a hand and encircled one of her breasts. 'Your body's changed too.'

She shivered at his touch and put her glass on the table at the top of the adjoining sunbeds. 'Having a baby does that to a woman.'

He smiled knowingly and rubbed his thumb over a nipple. 'Having a baby has only made you more beautiful.'

She couldn't help her snort of derision at this.

He caught a curl in his fingers. 'Why do you find that funny?'

'You haven't seen me naked in the light yet.'

'Yet?' He quirked his eyebrows. 'Then I have something to look forward to?'

'Maybe.'

He put his head in the crook of his elbow and inched his face closer to her. 'There is no one here now…'

She put a finger to his lips without thinking. He kissed it.

'Nikos…' She sighed.

He rubbed the tip of his nose to hers. 'Yes, *agapi mou*?'

The warmth of his breath seeped into her pores and it took more effort than she would have believed possible to keep her thoughts on track. 'What we were talking about last night… Your idea of marriage.'

He rubbed his nose against her cheek. 'Have you decided it's an excellent idea?'

She moved away a little and rolled onto her back but that attempt at distance did nothing to stop his hands roaming over her body. Pressing her thighs tightly together, she tried to tune out the sensations skipping over her skin at his touch. 'If I'm going to agree to it, we would have to live in Valencia.'

'I know.'

'I know Mykonos is your home but it's too far from the business and too far from my family. My mama loves Niki. She's been the most wonderful support to me. I can't take him from her.'

He made slow circles around a hard nipple with his finger. 'I've already agreed to that, *agapi mou*.'

'Oh.' She swallowed. She should slap his hand away but it felt too good. 'So you have. Sorry.' She had to swallow the moisture filling her mouth again. 'I was so prepared and ready with arguments that I didn't listen properly to your answer.'

His fingers dragged down her belly. 'I would want us to spend a good amount of time here too,' he told her as he gently cupped her pubis. 'I want Niki to know this as his home too. But I agree, it is more practical for us to make Valencia our main home.'

His fingers drifted away from her as he rose to his feet. He pinched the sides of his shorts and fixed his hooded eyes on her. She hadn't even noticed him remove his shades. 'Anything else?'

He tugged his shorts down. His enormous erection sprang free.

She could hardly think, never mind speak through the lust rampaging through her. 'I want Niki to go to school in Valencia.'

He sat on the edge of her sunbed and pulled the straps of her swimsuit down. 'He is too young for us to worry about school yet. We can decide that nearer the time.'

'And...' He'd pulled the top of her swimsuit past her

breasts and immediately taken one in his mouth while he slowly pulled the rest of the suit down.

'Yes, *agapi mou*?'

'No...taking...' She squeezed her eyes shut and tried to concentrate, even though he'd tugged the swimsuit down past her thighs. Only dimly did she realise she'd actively helped him in removing it and that it was her kicking the suit away.

He climbed between her legs and gazed down at her. 'No taking...?'

'Charge,' she breathed.

'Like this?' He slid inside her, long, deep, all the way to the hilt. Then, before she could really savour the sensation, immediately pulled out. 'No taking charge like that?'

'Nikos...' His name sounded like a moan from her lips.

He plunged inside her again. 'Is that what you meant?'

He made to pull out of her again. She grabbed hold of his buttocks with both hands to keep him in place.

'You win,' she breathed, wrapping her legs tightly around him. 'Take charge.'

'And you'll marry me?'

'*Yes.*' At that moment she would have agreed to anything to stop him pulling out of her again.

'Then I take charge with pleasure.'

'Time to get up.'

Marisa opened a bleary eye and found Nikos perched on the edge of the bed beside her. 'What time is it?'

'Nine.'

She lifted her head. A cup of coffee had been placed on her bedside table beside the baby monitor. 'Why didn't you wake me?'

'Because you're adorable when you sleep.' He placed

his lips to her ear and whispered, 'If our son hadn't woken so early, I would have woken you in a much more pleasurable manner.'

She found it incredible that she'd slept so late *and* slept through the early morning babbling she'd always been so attuned to. Either she'd been exhausted from making love until the early hours or her subconscious had let her sleep soundly, knowing Nikos was taking care of their son. The latter, she decided as she tilted her head for a kiss and breathed in his freshly showered and shaved scent.

'Where is he?'

'With Seema in the nursery. And you need to get up. We have an appointment to attend.'

'Have we?'

He kissed her mouth. 'Yes, *agapi mou*. An appointment to register our intention to marry. We can book the wedding too. Get everything in hand.'

The last of her sleepiness flew away. Sitting upright, she stared at him. 'Since when are we getting married?'

'You agreed to it yesterday.'

So she had. Under sexual duress. After she'd said yes, they'd made love hard and fast on the sunbed then gone to bed and made love at a much more leisurely pace until Niki had woken from his nap. The early evening had been spent with their son and then, the minute he was asleep, they'd gone straight back to bed.

Truth was, they'd been far too busy talking with their bodies to speak verbally.

Truth was, she'd happily shoved her agreement to marry him to the back of her mind rather than confront the magnitude of what she'd done, and now that she was confronted with it, darts of panic were making their way through her.

'I didn't agree to marry you immediately.'

'The decision has been made so why wait?'

Because you don't love me!

Love? Since when had she started thinking about Nikos along those lines again? She didn't love *him*. She loved their son and she wanted him to have the same happy childhood she'd had, and Nikos deserved to be a father to him every bit as much as she was a mother to him. He'd hurt her badly, something she would never forget, but now she understood him better, she was prepared to move on from that hurt for their son's sake. Hadn't Nikos proved he deserved that chance? He'd swiftly bought into the business, installed his top people to assist her and take the load off her—she wouldn't be here in Mykonos now if he hadn't done that—and he'd proved his devotion to their son. *Those* were the reasons she'd agreed to marry him. She'd been prepared to marry Raul for the business and Niki's sake, so why not marry Niki's actual father? The damage he'd inflicted had been too great for him to hurt her again but the passion between them was every bit as strong as it had always been. At least marrying Nikos meant marrying a man she was happy to share a bed with!

What she must not do, under any circumstance, was think about Nikos as a child in desperate need of someone to love and care for him, and think she could be the woman to do that.

'I agreed on the proviso you didn't take charge,' she said.

He raised a brow, the look in his eyes as he brought his face to hers making her pelvis contract. 'Really? Because I seem to remember you *begging* me to take charge.'

She leaned into him, her lips tingling from the whispered heat of his breath…

'You're not doing this again.' She darted away from him and jumped off the bed, hurrying to the far wall.

'Doing what again?'

'Using your magic penis to stop me thinking properly.'

The look he gave her was one of incredulousness. And then his gorgeous face broke into a grin and he burst into a deep rumble of laughter.

Nikos laughed so long and so hard his chest hurt. 'I have a magic penis?' He chortled, wiping mirth-induced tears from his eyes.

Eyes alight with amusement, she sniggered. 'Why else do you think I agreed to marry you?'

He got to his feet.

She shot a hand out in warning. 'Stay back. Do not touch me until we've discussed this.'

He loved a challenge. Especially when given by a sexy, sleep-tousled redhead who thought he had a magic penis.

'I want to marry in Spain.'

Locking his gaze on her, he took a step towards her. 'Why?'

'That's where my family are.'

He took another step. 'They can fly here. I want to marry here on Mykonos.'

'Why?'

Because I can marry you quickly here, and the sooner I marry you, the sooner I know my rights as a father are protected. The less time I give you to think about it, the less time you have to change your mind.

He took her extended hand and pinned it above her head, staring deep into the lust-riven dark eyes. 'We have better beaches.'

He cut her protest away with a kiss.

CHAPTER ELEVEN

MARISA WAS ADDING blusher to her cheeks when Nikos walked into her bedroom. Her heart thumped to see him and she had to concentrate hard to affect nonchalance at his appearance and stop her hand from reacting to the thump and splodging blusher over her nose.

After they'd made the wedding arrangements that morning, Nikos had casually mentioned they would be going to his nightclub on the island that night to celebrate their engagement.

She'd been unable to think of one good reason to refuse.

Not having bothered to pack any going-out clothes, she'd got him to drop her at the main shopping district in Chora so she could buy herself an outfit to party in. She'd wandered through designer boutiques and more touristy shops with no idea why the thought of celebrating made her feel so bereft.

She'd agreed to marry him. She'd agreed it would happen in Mykonos. She'd agreed it would happen this coming weekend. She didn't have a clue how he'd got the officials to agree for it to happen so quickly, but here she was, a day after she'd told him one of her terms for agreeing to marriage was that he had to stop taking charge, just five days from actually doing the deed.

To make the day extra special, they would be marrying on their son's first birthday. She thought this fitting. The stars were aligning to approve her decision.

On top of all that, Nikos had agreed to her stipulation about them living in Spain. So what did she have to feel bereft about?

And why had she found herself wandering away from the shops and into the more residential areas with the strings of her heart tugging manically to imagine a small Nikos playing on the uneven cobbled streets?

He walked over to where she sat at the dressing table, lifted her hair and placed a kiss to the nape of her neck. Sensation quivered deliciously over her skin.

'You smell gorgeous,' he murmured, 'and look spectacular.'

She met his reflection in the mirror and smiled through the ache growing in her chest. He looked pretty spectacular himself. Dressed in black chinos, dark grey shirt unbuttoned at the throat and a charcoal blazer, he managed to look smart, casual, elegant and devilishly handsome all at once.

'Did you get hold of your mother?' he asked.

She nodded as she opened her palate of eyeshadow.

'And?'

'She said to tell you that if you hurt me, she'll personally see that you never father another child.'

There was a flickering in his eyes but his tone remained casual. 'And what did you say to that?'

'That I'm not stupid enough to let you hurt me again.' She picked up a brush and dabbed it into the glittering deep brown colour and met his gaze again before applying it to her eyelids. 'Our marriage is for Niki's sake. We both know that. And now she knows that.'

'But is she supportive of it?'

'Yes.'

'And your sister?'

'She thinks I'm mad, but she's coming to the wedding.'

'Why does she think you're mad?'

She shrugged, taking a fresh brush and dabbing it into the glittering gold colour. She wouldn't repeat her sister's furious rant about Marisa throwing her life away on a man who'd happily discarded her like unwanted trash. But Elsa wasn't a mother with a child who would thrive much better with his father a permanent part of his life. 'Elsa's in love. She thinks only people in love should marry.'

'And what do you think?'

'That love marriages are, historically speaking, a recent thing.' She reached for her mascara. 'History is littered with successful marriages built without love.' And she'd spent an hour sitting on the beach terrace of his nightclub, which was a café by day, searching her phone for examples of them while waiting for Nikos to collect her.

'I bet those successful marriages had great sex at their core.'

'But only with each other.' She held his gaze a moment longer before applying her mascara, trying her hardest to keep her hand steady so she didn't poke herself in the eye at the lie she'd just uttered.

Most of the successful non-love marriages she'd read about had only been successful because both spouses had either turned a blind eye to other lovers or explicitly agreed to them.

She knew there was no way she could tolerate or accept infidelity—just the thought of Nikos in the arms of another woman made her stomach churn violently—and had searched even harder for the faithful marriages.

But those had brought no comfort either. They had been successful because the couples had fallen in love with each other.

Nikos heard the unspoken warning and put his hands on her shoulders to drop a kiss into her hair. 'Then I am ahead of you on this one,' he said silkily. 'There has been only you since the day we met and while you wear this, there will be only you.'

She twisted to face him.

He dug into his back pocket and pulled out a black velvet box. He flicked the lid open and held it out to her. 'Your engagement ring.'

She stared at it for the longest time. He wondered if she was waiting for him to drop to one knee. That, of course, would be ludicrous.

Strangely, when he'd found the ring—and he'd scoured every jewellery shop in Chora before finding his gaze drawn to this one—he'd examined it closely with an unbidden fantasy playing out in his mind. In that fantasy he'd dropped to one knee. In that fantasy, Marisa had cupped her cheeks in delight then thrown her arms around him. In that fantasy, she'd said she loved him.

He'd pulled himself out of the fantasy with his guts twisting. They twisted now to remember it. It had to be fatherhood causing this unseemly sentimentality. Nikos's love for his son was like a garden of drab weeds suddenly filled with beautifully scented colourful flowers. It was not unreasonable to suppose his subconscious would try to extend that love to the mother of his son.

'Are you going to try it on?' he asked when she made no move to touch the ring.

She plucked it from the box and slid it on her wedding finger. Then she got to her feet and held it out to him. 'It's perfect.'

For a moment he was too taken with the whole effect to respond. Wearing a short black sequined wrap-around dress that hugged her curves and exposed just the right amount of cleavage, she glittered; an exotic shimmering mirage. She must have sprayed something in her hair too for, under the ceiling light, it glimmered too.

At that moment, all he could think was that *she* was perfect.

Stratos, who'd taken his lady friend out to dinner, was getting out of his car as Marisa slipped into the back of Nikos's. She waved. The lady friend waved back. Stratos pretended not to see her.

'Why does your grandfather hate me?' she asked Nikos when his driver set off.

'He doesn't hate you.'

'Haven't you noticed? He barely acknowledges my existence.'

After a moment, he sighed. 'He is angry you didn't tell him about Niki.'

She tried to keep her composure but his unexpected answer pierced straight through her.

'Why didn't you tell him?' The question was asked amiably enough but she could see the curiosity in the light brown eyes.

'Nikos...' About to tell him how she'd fallen to pieces when he'd been presumed dead, she stopped herself. 'Your death... I was grieving you when I learned I was pregnant.' It had suddenly struck her, the only moment of clarity in two weeks of desolation and anguish, that her daily bouts of nausea might have a different cause to grief: The food poisoning she'd suffered the month before his disappearance and the realisation it could have affected the contraceptive pill she took faithfully.

Had she blocked out the effects it could have on the pill because she'd subconsciously *wanted* a baby...?

Shaking off the ridiculous thought, she said, 'The pregnancy came as a shock...' The biggest shock but also the most miraculous. 'But a good shock.' Good enough to pull her out of the pit of despair and give her focus.

His eyes bored into her. 'You were glad to be carrying my child?'

She touched the tips of her fingers to his warm cheek. 'Knowing I had your child growing inside me gave me more comfort than you can imagine. I never intended to keep it a secret, I just wanted to get past the three-month mark before I told anyone other than my immediate family. I guess I was being superstitious about it but the fear of miscarrying was very real to me.' Terrifying.

Even now she dreaded to think what she would have done if she'd lost her baby, lost that last link to Nikos in those dark times.

'But then, when I reached the safe three-month mark, all the stuff with the cartel started. I found Rocco dead...' She closed her eyes to clear the image of her beautiful dog, drowned in the pool. 'I cannot tell you how frightened I was. I was terrified they'd learn about the pregnancy. By the time Niki was born, I'd lost my father to the cartel too and my life had turned into a nightmare. All I cared about—and I do mean *all*—was keeping him safe and protected from them. We turned the estate into a fortress that I hid our son and myself in as much as I could.'

Marisa watched Nikos as she spoke, watched as his face slowly tightened into stillness, his only reaction an almost imperceptible movement of his Adam's apple.

'I'm sorry I didn't reach out to your grandfather,' she

whispered. 'I should have done. I should have thought of him, and if I'd known how close you were and just how much he meant to you, I would have done. Please, tell him it wasn't deliberate malice on my part and that I'm really sorry I hurt him.'

Lips taut, he bowed his head. 'I will explain everything to him.'

'Thank you.'

Nikos rested his head back and blew out a long breath of air, fighting the cauldron of emotions battering his guts at all she'd had to deal with.

He should have been there.

'You remember the day you first saw me with Niki?' she said, breaking through his thoughts.

He pinched the bridge of his nose and nodded.

'That was the first time he'd left the estate since he was born. I had him at home,' she added.

'That explains why he's so shy with strangers,' he said, attempting a smile.

'Probably.' She covered his hand with hers and gently squeezed.

'I did wonder why you hid yourself away even before your father's death,' he mused aloud, returning the caress.

Her face jerked. 'What are you talking about?'

'I had you watched,' he admitted.

Her eyes widened in shock.

'The cartel sent me a photo of you,' he reminded her, speaking evenly to fight the bile that always rose whenever he remembered the moment Marisa's picture had suddenly appeared amongst the photos of his lawyer's desecrated body.

Nikos had already been fighting a roll of nausea but that picture of Marisa, clearly taken using a long-range lens, had pushed him over the edge and he'd vomited for the first time in his adult life.

'Felipe Lorenzi's team helped me fake my death and protect my people, and I paid them to put a team together to watch over you too.'

Even beneath the make-up she wore, colour stained her face.

'I had them keep watch over the estate and follow you closely but discreetly every time you left it, and report to me daily by email. I did the same with my grandfather.' He managed a smile. 'Wi-Fi was practically the only modern convenience that log cabin had. I needed to assure myself that you were safe. My biggest regret is that I didn't ask them to watch your whole family as well when they left the estate.' He swallowed back another wave of nausea. 'I didn't know your family had been dealing with the cartel too, not until after your father's death.'

She continued to stare at him. He could see her thinking, putting all the pieces of the puzzle together. When she spoke, a tremor rang through her voice. 'So, when we employed Felipe to fortify our home with his men and to work with us and the international security services to bring the cartel down, they were already working for you on the same thing?'

He inclined his head.

'Then how did you not know about our son?'

'For reasons of confidentiality.' Nikos had confronted Felipe about his failure to mention in a single one of his staff's reports about Marisa, the pregnancy or subsequent birth of Niki. 'My instructions were to keep a watchful eye on you and to take action at any sign of danger. When your family then came to employ his team too, they were bound under strict privacy contracts. Would you have welcomed them into your home and entrusted your physical safety to them if you'd thought they would discuss your private lives with others?'

Lips clamped together, she hesitated then shook her head.

'If the pregnancy or Niki's birth had been relevant to any of the reports, I would have been told, but the subject never came up. God knows, I wish it had...'

'Would it have changed things if you had known about him?' she asked.

'I don't know.' He clamped his jaws together. 'Maybe it was for the best that I didn't know. If I'd reappeared before they were taken down you would have been an even bigger target for them. But those months... Marisa, they were the hardest of my life. Physically. Mentally. When I learned the cartel had targeted your family, I thought I was going mad. The only thing that stopped me—'

He cut himself off, thrown back again to the sheer terror that had clutched his heart and how close he'd come to hiking through the mountains to get to civilisation and back to her.

He took a deep breath and continued. 'Once I knew Felipe had taken responsibility for your family's safety I could think a little straighter but it was still hard. I hate to think I would have endangered you or our son for the sake of my ego.'

'It must have been hard for you being so far from the action and for all that time,' Marisa intuited. Nikos was such a take-charge man she could imagine nothing more excruciating for him than being stuck thousands of kilometres away, unable to influence anything.

'It was horrendous. Felipe must have known I would struggle to be so far from you...from everything...and that's why I was given a log cabin in the middle of nowhere that needed constant maintenance.' He managed a grin. 'It's hard to spend your days brooding when there's trees to fell and water to collect if you want to drink or clean yourself.'

Oh, God, tears were forming. Marisa could feel them stabbing into her eyes and she blinked rapidly to stop them falling, using her hand as a fan to dry them.

'What's wrong?' he asked.

She smiled to assure him she was fine but didn't dare open her mouth, not until she had control of herself.

The deprivation he'd put himself through. The isolation.

Eighteen months of his life.

She'd never thought of it in those terms before or considered how tough it must have been for such a gregarious man to give up everything that made life a joy and hide in the shadows, or considered how selfless his actions had been.

He'd done all that, in part, for her. And he'd paid for her to be watched over. He hadn't just faked his death and forgotten about her, as she'd thought, he'd paid a crack team of ex-special forces to watch over her and keep her safe, long before she'd even known the murderous cartel existed.

Did that mean that he *had* cared for her?

But if he had, then why had he, before he'd discovered their son's existence, been happy for her to learn of his resurrection on the grapevine? If you cared for someone, you didn't treat them like that.

Could things be any more confusing?

As she fanned her hand in front of her face, her engagement ring glinted. It was an art deco style, pear-cut champagne diamond set in rose-gold. When he'd produced it, she'd had to work so hard not to let the joy burst out of her.

Marisa absolutely adored champagne diamonds. Loved the colours and the way they changed under the light. And she loved rose-gold over normal gold. And she loved anything art deco.

The man who wanted to marry her so he could always be a part of their son's life had given her the engagement ring of her dreams.

The driver stopped outside a typical Mykonos building; whitewashed Cycladic style, set along a narrow cobbled street but which differed from the other bustling streets they'd driven through by the sheer number of people queuing like overdressed bunches of grapes for admission. It was all very different from when she'd waited for him earlier, drinking coffee on the club's beach terrace.

When she stepped out of the car, the flash of cameras in Marisa's face announced the paparazzi's presence.

In an instant, Nikos was at her side, taking her hand and sweeping her past the enormous bouncers, who parted in surprisingly nimble fashion to admit them.

Inside, the feel and vibe of the place were exactly what she expected from her experiences at his other nightclubs. Bodies packed like sardines, drinks in hand, swaying under multi-coloured strobe lights to the pumping beat. A Manolas nightclub was not somewhere you went for conversation. It was a place you went to dance the night away to the best DJs in the world.

The VIP section of his Mykonos club was reached by a set of wide stairs that formed a semi-circle around the main dance floor. More bouncers guarded the entrance to it. One unhooked the red tasselled rope barrier and nodded a respectful greeting as they slipped past them.

The inner sanctum was far less crowded than the ground floor and she recognised many of the faces in it even if she didn't know them personally. They all seemed to know her, though, or *of* her, and as she sipped champagne, flashed her engagement ring at anyone who asked, and had shouted conversation with one of Nikos's cousins, she relaxed.

She'd always relaxed in Nikos's clubs. In her university years she'd often gone on girls' weekends away to Ibiza and always they had dressed up and hit Manolas. They'd all agreed it was their favourite club because they felt safe there. Plentiful bouncers and more discreet undercover security in the crowds had stopped drunken wandering hands going too far, and then there had been the freedom of knowing your drink wouldn't get spiked thanks to the strict no-drugs policy. Having your bags searched and having to empty your pockets at the entrance was a small price to pay for that kind of safety.

It had never occurred to her to question why Nikos enforced such a tough policy on drugs, not even when they'd formed a relationship, and, as she cast her gaze around the heaving dance floor, she thought again of everything it had cost him to stop the cartel from filling this place and all his other clubs with their narcotics and help stop anyone else falling into the kind of addiction that had turned his parents into monsters and ultimately killed his mother.

'What are you thinking?' he asked, speaking into her ear to be heard.

She smiled and rose up on her toes to plant a kiss to his mouth. That was something he often asked. If he didn't care for her, why would he want to know?

As the night went on and the partying got more raucous and Nikos stayed glued to her side, she found herself asking the same questions—if Nikos really only wanted to marry her for their son's sake, why did he care so much about what she thought? Why had he gone out of his way to choose the perfect engagement ring for her?

And, if he didn't care for her, why had he gone to so much effort to keep her safe even before he'd known their son existed?

'Let's get some air,' she shouted after the midnight hour had struck.

Hands clasped, they headed out to the huge VIP terrace.

Avoiding the smoking section, they settled on a secluded sweetheart seat and let the sea breeze cool their skin. Outside, the noise levels were far more favourable for conversation but Marisa was content to listen to the laughter from the revellers on the ground floor beach terrace and the snatched chatter of others partying on their own.

Fingers playing absently with the buttons of his shirt, she only realised she'd undone one and had slipped her hand under it to encircle a nipple when he huskily said, 'What are you doing?'

'Touching you.' She tilted her head to stare into his eyes. 'Do you want me to stop?'

His eyes gleamed. 'No.'

'Good.' She stretched her leg and then casually hooked it over his lap. A large hand rested on her thigh, right at the hem that had ruched up to skim her bottom. Marisa leaned into him and pressed her face into his neck. 'You smell amazing.'

Moving her hand from his nipple, she pulled it out from beneath his shirt and slowly trailed her fingers down his stomach to his belt.

When her fingers gently traced over the length of his erection, straining beneath the confines of his chinos, Nikos tightened the grip on his glass of bourbon. There was something incredibly seductive about her touch and the way she kept nuzzling her nose into his neck, arousing him despite the revellers spilling out in all directions.

How far was she prepared to take this?

How far was he prepared to let her take it?

She lifted her face to lick the lobe of his ear. 'I haven't thanked you properly for my ring, have I?'

She gently cupped his erection again before her fingers crept back up his chest. He didn't know if he was relieved or disappointed, then found himself swallowing as she moved her thigh just enough that her knee pressed against his excitement.

'When we get back, I'll thank you properly,' she breathed, rubbing her nose over his cheek then capturing his bottom lip with her teeth. She nipped it gently at the same moment she encircled his other nipple.

He tightened his grip on her thigh, fighting the heady urge to slip his fingers beneath the material.

Just at the moment lust was about to override propriety, she unhooked her leg, jumped to her feet and tugged at his hand. 'That's enough air. Let's dance.'

Stunned at the change of pace, he stared at the beautiful face alive with more delight than he had seen in... since he'd come back to her.

'You want to dance?' he managed to croak.

She pulled her lips together before another wide smile lit her face, and she leaned over to speak in his ear, giving him a wonderful view of her naked breasts in the dip made in the material. 'Not really. I want you to take me home.'

He just stared at her. Somehow, her smile widened even more.

'Have I stopped you thinking, *mi amado*?' Wickedness flashed in her eyes before she slipped her hand over his buttocks and ran her tongue over his lips. 'Now you know how you make *me* feel.'

Then she stepped back again and waved the phone he hadn't even felt her filch from his back pocket at him.

Nikos snatched it from her and called his driver.

CHAPTER TWELVE

THE MOMENT THEY were alone in the private cabin of his car, Nikos turned off the microphone connecting them to the driver and pulled Marisa in for a kiss he'd thought he might explode from waiting for.

Whatever burning arousal her teasing had done to him, it had had the same effect on her. In a medley of tongues and ferociously moving lips, she straddled him, her hands going straight to the buttons of his shirt and practically ripping them apart. At his waist, she yanked on his belt and then, with a grace that was almost poetic, she dropped to her knees on the cabin's spacious floor. Undoing his chinos, she grasped the sides and tugged them down past his hips and then, finally, freed him from the torturous confines.

There was no hesitation. Her head dipped and she took him in her mouth.

Theos, but the sensations were incredible. Mind-blowing. The way she ran her tongue the length of it, the way she squeezed…

He groaned and closed his eyes, reaching for her hair to thread his fingers through.

What was it about this woman he reacted to so viscerally? How did her touch burn him in a way that no one else's did?

When she danced back up his body to straddle him again, he clasped the back of her head and kissed her deeply, a kiss broken as he moaned into her mouth at the encompassing pleasure that filled him as she sank down on him.

The relief of having Nikos inside her was so great that Marisa held onto it for as long as she could. Already there was a quickening building inside her and she tried her hardest to fight it, wanting to savour the pleasure.

Then, as she finally began to ride him, throwing her head back in ecstasy when his mouth closed over an aching nipple, she realised this was a pleasure she would enjoy for the rest of her life and, bucking onto him, she cried out the rapture erupting through her every pore.

Marisa lay with her head on Nikos's chest, listening to his heartbeat. She loved the solid thump it made against her cheek, the way it seemed to sink through her skin and become a part of her.

'Are you awake?' she whispered.

It had to be at least three in the morning. After their frantic drive home, they'd rushed through the villa to his bedroom and done it all again. She should be shattered but she was still buzzing from the adrenaline of the best night out she'd had in possibly for ever.

'That depends on what you want,' he murmured sleepily, tightening his hold around her.

'Nothing. Well, nothing for a few more minutes,' she teased.

Stroking her back, he laughed. 'I think I might need a few more minutes too, *agapi mou*.'

She gently nipped at a flat, brown nipple.

'You're sex mad.' There was admiration in his voice.

'Sex mad for *you*,' she corrected.

'As long as it's only for me then carry on.'

She dragged herself over his chest so her breasts crushed against it and she could look at his gorgeous face. 'You do know it is only you, don't you?'

A furrow formed in his brow.

She kissed him lightly and ran her fingers through his hair, then sighed dreamily. 'You're the only man I've ever wanted, the only man I've ever been with and the only man I'll ever be with.'

Suddenly she was flat on her back, Nikos pinning her to the mattress as he stared into her eyes, the expression on his face unreadable before he suddenly crushed his mouth to hers in a kiss so passionately violent that arousal flared for them both again and soon Marisa was moaning in his arms and clinging to him as he drove their mutual passion to glorious heights.

The next few days managed to pass both crazily fast and crazily slow. On the one hand was their forthcoming wedding, the reception of which was doubling as a birthday party for their son. Everything had been booked and guests confirmed. Nikos had employed the most efficient wedding planner and given her all the funds needed to grease any palms that needed it. The day seemed to be approaching with the speed of a freight train.

The crazily slow side came from the joy of just being alive. Nikos's grandfather had gone away on a trip for a few days with his lady friend, which helped Marisa relax around the villa. Many happy hours were spent with Nikos and their son, just the three of them. In the evenings they would put Niki to bed and when Marisa was satisfied he was fast asleep, they would lock the bedroom door and make love until they were so spent that sleep claimed them, whether they wanted it to or not.

After three days of this bliss, Nikos went to his business centre to catch up on neglected work. With her own business being taken care of and nothing of any urgency needing her attention, Marisa left Niki napping under the watchful eye of his nanny and set off with the butler to decide where to house her family and the other guests who would be staying with them for the wedding.

The guest villas, she decided, were the best place for her friends, who could be as loud as they liked without disturbing anyone, and she pointed to their names on Angelos's clipboard, trying out a little Greek on him. He beamed and congratulated her efforts, which in turn made her beam with pride. She'd asked Seema to speak to her in Greek when they were alone in an effort to speed up her understanding of the language. Soon, she hoped to surprise Nikos by conversing with him in his native tongue.

With the guest villas allocated, they returned to the main villa.

Marisa had never been on the second floor before and she found the rooms as spacious and richly furnished as those on the first floor, all except for one room. That room had only a large, battered ottoman in it.

Once the rest of the guests had been assigned their rooms and Angelos had gone back downstairs, curiosity took her back to the unfurnished room.

It was just an ordinary room with white walls, duck egg blue drapes and a soft grey carpet. All the same, she found herself hesitating before entering it and walking to the ottoman.

She crouched down and lifted the lid. Her nose wrinkled at the stale, musty scent that was released. Within the ottoman's confines was a jumble of toys.

Her heart lurched. These were the last things she'd expected to find.

Cautiously, she picked up a ragged stuffed elephant and ran her finger over the indentation made by a missing eye. There were more stuffed toys, plastic army figures, children's jigsaws, plastic trucks and other assorted toys crammed inside. Everything looked old. Faded. Forgotten.

She turned at the sound of approaching footsteps and then Nikos appeared with Niki in his arms.

There was the strangest expression on his face, one that immediately made her think she'd done something wrong.

'Sorry. I was being curious.' She dropped the elephant back in the ottoman.

Recognising her sudden wariness, Nikos forced a smile and made himself step over the threshold.

He hadn't set foot in this room in ten years.

He joined Marisa at the ottoman and peered down at the long-forgotten contents with a chest so tight it was like someone had trapped it in a vice. Niki took one look and started jiggling with excitement and making grabbing motions with his hands.

'Can he…?'

'No.' He curtly cut Marisa's question off before she could finish it.

She took Niki from him, her wariness more pronounced.

He grimaced and took a deep breath. The tightness and emotions bubbling in his guts were not Marisa's doing. In a more moderate tone, he said, 'This was my bedroom. This is the only thing of my childhood my mother kept.'

He'd discovered his childhood ottoman in the days after her death when sentimentality had compelled him to enter his old bedroom for the first time since he'd been taken from his parents. The rest of the room had been stripped bare. The ottoman and its contents had been the only proof in the entire villa that a child had once lived and breathed within its walls.

Nikos remembered the clear instruction he'd given the design team when he'd made the decision to renovate the place. Get rid of every piece of furniture in the villa but keep the ottoman. Keep that exactly where it is. And then he'd closed the door on his childhood bedroom and never opened it again. Not until now.

He picked up the elephant Marisa had been holding when he'd entered the room. 'This went everywhere with me.' He gave a sharp laugh and opened the dressing room door. 'Sometimes we would hide in here together when my parents were trying to kill each other.'

He looked at Marisa, rocking Niki on her hip. He turned away from the empathy shining in her eyes and looked out of the window at the guest villas in the near distance. He'd had them built over the patchwork of land that had once been his daily view.

Within a year of inheriting the place, he'd eradicated every inch of his parents' presence and his childhood from it. Apart from the ottoman.

As if reading his thoughts, she quietly asked, 'Why did you move back here?'

A pale blue sports car was approaching. His grandfather returning from his jaunt. Nikos watched it get closer while answering, 'Why would I not? It's the perfect location with all the land I could ever need.'

'But the memories...'

He faced her again and, injecting light into his voice,

said, 'Memories are the past. If we allow the past to hold onto us, we can never move to the future.' To prove his point, he headed for the door, waiting for Marisa to join him so he could close it and leave the past behind, where it should be.

They walked in silence. When they reached the stairs, he caught one of her curls in his fingers. 'My grandfather is back. I'm going to talk to him about what you told me the other night. Do you want to join us?'

She shook her head. 'You go ahead. I'm going to take Niki for a swim.'

'Okay.' He cupped her cheek and placed a tender kiss to her lips before kissing their son's head. 'I'll join you when we're done.'

Marisa carried Niki to the nursery armchair and sat him on her lap. Rubbing her cheek over his soft head, she tried to swallow the choking lump in her throat.

She didn't understand why she was close to tears over an ottoman full of Nikos's old toys. Why should it affect her so deeply when it didn't matter to him?

But, if it didn't matter to him, why had he kept it? And why was that room the only unfurnished room in the whole villa?

Every time she thought she'd unlocked the mystery that was Nikos, she found another lock that needed a key.

Niki stood himself up on her lap and bounced, gurgling away happily. Wiping away a stray tear, she laughed.

'What would I do without you?' she said, putting her mouth to his cheek and blowing on it, making him laugh manically. She blew another raspberry on his cheek and savoured the musical sound of his laughter.

Had Nikos's mother ever blown raspberries on his cheek? Had his father ever bounced him on his lap?

Surely, *surely*, they had given him affection as a baby. Hadn't Nikos said his mother had used her wealth to stop his grandfather getting custody of him when he was a baby? That had to mean something.

The alternative was just too unbearable to contemplate. That Nikos could have spent his most formative years without any of the love and affection she'd been lucky enough to take for granted.

Niki stopped bouncing and rested his face in the crook of her neck. Stroking his back, she squeezed her eyes shut to stop any more tears from leaking.

Whatever love Nikos had been denied in his life, she would make up for it. Because there was no point in denying any more that she loved him. She had always loved him. And, though he might not recognise it as love and might never say the words, he loved her too. She knew it in her heart.

Sniffing back more tears, she shifted Niki higher. His head drooped. She kissed his sleeping face and gently laid him in his cot. Their swim could wait while he napped.

Making sure the baby monitor was working, Marisa crept out of the nursery and went in search of the man she loved.

'They killed her father?'

Nikos swirled the last of his coffee in his mouth before swallowing it and answering his grandfather. They were sitting side by side on the terrace facing the sea, the afternoon sun beaming down on them incongruous against the darkness of their conversation. 'Yes. They tampered with the brakes of his car.'

'Why didn't you tell me this before?'

'I told you her family had suffered at the hands of the cartel.'

'But not like this.' Stratos shook his head in disbelief. 'You didn't tell me the poor child lost her father while she was pregnant with *your* child and thinking you were dead.'

The churning and twisting that had plagued Nikos's guts since he'd walked into his childhood bedroom earlier cranked up. His skin felt as if insects were crawling over it.

That damned ottoman.

Stratos continued shaking his head. 'For such a good man you have a real problem with empathy.' And then he sighed. 'I know, I know, it's something you can't help but I worry for you.'

'Your worry is misplaced,' Nikos said curtly. 'So, you will stop pretending she doesn't exist?'

'I will apologise to her... Where is she?'

'Taking Niki for a swim.' He'd intended to join them but the way he felt he would be better served taking a long swim in the sea his gaze was fixed on. Thrashing his way through the waves would pound all these damned feelings out of him.

That damned ottoman of toys. Opening its lid had been his personal equivalent to opening Pandora's Box.

After his mother's death a decade ago, he'd closed both the door to his childhood bedroom and the door in his mind. The past was the past. What purpose did it serve to dwell on something to which he would never get any answers?

But the past had been closing in on him since his isolation and now it filled his head, cramming him with emotions and thoughts that flooded through him as if a tap had been turned on.

Why had his mother kept the ottoman when she'd got rid of all his other possessions?

Had she had latent feelings for him? A small residue of love in her heart for him?

And why had *he* kept the damn thing?

'Are you okay?' Stratos asked.

He breathed heavily and poured himself another coffee. Why was he thinking like this?

His mother and father had allowed him to be taken from them without a fight when they'd had the money and means to get him back. It was that simple. Why feel futile pangs of sentimentality over it? It was the best thing that had happened to him. If they'd wanted him back, he would have returned to a home that had bordered on a drugs den where his only love and companionship had come from a stuffed elephant.

Before his grandfather had saved him and welcomed him into his home, that stuffed elephant had been his best friend. His *only* friend. Nikos hadn't played with a single child until he was six years old. Cousins he'd had no idea existed became his playmates. *Real* playmates.

The stuffed elephant had been left behind and forgotten along with everything else.

So why the hell was he allowing it to be remembered?

The only emotion he would allow himself to feel was love for his son. In two days he would marry Marisa and he'd know that, whatever happened, his son would always have his love and protection.

He had a drink of his coffee. In no mood to hear another lecture about how his parents' neglect of him was all down to their addictions, he said, 'I was thinking about the wedding.'

'Everything is in hand?'

Nikos nodded.

'Good. I'm glad you came around to my way of

thinking. When I remember the battles I had with your mother...'

Battles that had ended when Nikos passed babyhood and lost his cloak of protective cuteness, making him unlovable.

But she had kept his toys...

'Marriage will protect you and protect your son. Remember that. But take it from a man who knows—a miserable wife makes for a very miserable life.'

'We won't be married long enough for me to make her miserable.' The hackles of his crawling skin rose at the look on his grandfather's face. 'A temporary marriage was *your* idea.'

'I know.' Stratos sighed. 'But that was when I thought selfishness had stopped her telling me about your son. I didn't know—'

'The decision has been made,' he interrupted curtly. An image of Marisa's beautiful face shining up at him with that softness in her eyes...

He banished it swiftly. *Theos*, his guts were cramping. His heart felt like it was tearing. 'A year of marriage is the most I can live with.'

This was what sentimentality did to you. Made you doubt yourself. Made you imagine feelings that didn't exist.

The cramping in his guts was a form of guilt, and unnecessary guilt at that.

He hadn't promised Marisa for ever. That was one lie he'd never told her.

'Time might change your mind,' Stratos said, his expression sad.

'*No*. One year and then I file for divorce.'

If time was going to change anyone's mind it would be Marisa's when she'd spent long enough with him to

see whatever it was that had turned his parents away
from him.

He swallowed the burn of nausea rising up his throat
and again banished the image of her beautiful face from
his mind…and that softness he so often saw in her eyes
that, if he'd been a man who inspired love, he could almost believe was the look of love.

CHAPTER THIRTEEN

MARISA BACKED SLOWLY to the stairs, covering her mouth tightly to stop the scream from escaping.

When she reached the top of the stairs she flew down the corridor to Seema's room and rapped loudly on it.

'Are you okay?' the nanny asked when she opened the door.

'What is the word for divorce?'

'It's *diazýgio*.'

She closed her eyes and pulled in a breath. She hadn't misunderstood. 'Thank you.'

Checking Niki was still sleeping, she hurried to her bedroom, grabbed her phone and called her sister.

Elsa answered on the third ring. 'Hi, big sister! How's Mykonos?'

'Is Santi there?'

'Yes... What's wrong?'

'Can you put him on, please? It's important.'

Seconds later, the man she'd grown up thinking of as a big brother figure was on the phone. 'What do you need?'

She swallowed her relief that he'd got straight to the point. 'Can you send one of your planes to get me?' Santi owned a fleet of planes that delivered freight across the world. He also had his own private jet.

'Are you in Mykonos?'

'Yes.'

'When do you want to be collected?'

'As soon as you can get here.'

'I will send a plane to you now. Keep your phone on you for instructions... Marisa?'

'Yes?'

'Are you okay?'

'No. But I will be. Please hurry.'

'Hold on a minute. I have a better idea. Speak to your sister while I make some calls.'

'Marisa?' This time there was panic in Elsa's voice. 'What's happened?'

'Nothing.' Yet. 'But the wedding's off. I can't marry him.'

'What's *happened*?'

'I'll tell you when I get home.' Her real home. A home filled with people who loved her. 'Do me a favour and don't tell Mama. I don't want her to worry. I'll tell her when I get back.'

'You're scaring me.'

'I promise it's nothing to scare you. He's not hurt me, I swear.' Not physically.

'You promise?'

'I promise.'

'Okay... Santi wants to talk to you again.'

There was no preamble. 'I've spoken to a contact. He's on Santorini. He's sending his jet to you now. All being well, it should land in an hour. Shall I send a car to get you to the airport?'

'Yes, please.'

'Hold tight. I'll call you when the driver's ten minutes from you. It won't be long. Hold tight,' he repeated, and then the line went dead.

Marisa didn't waste any time. Forget packing. Clothes were replaceable. Chucking her passport and Niki's into her handbag, she secured the bag over her shoulder then hurried to the nursery to pack a change-bag for Niki.

Thankfully, the ground floor was empty of people and she was able to carry Niki and their bags to the underground garage without being seen. The keys for Nikos's showroom of cars were hanging up and she pressed them all until the one with the baby seat in it flashed. She strapped a still-sleeping Niki into it before unclipping and carefully removing the seat. Rather than go back up into the house, she pressed the button to open the garage's sliding doors and waited for rescue in the shade of the terrace that ran along the side of the villa.

Her hope of being miles away before Nikos noticed they were missing was foiled a minute later when footsteps crunched behind her.

'Where are you going?'

Almost jumping out of her skin, Marisa spun around to find Nikos walking towards her.

Nikos scanned her slowly, taking in the guilt blazing on her face to the protective way she stood before their sleeping son. She couldn't have known the garage was alarmed. The moment she'd set foot in it, an alert had gone to his phone. He'd watched her every move.

'Where are you going?' he repeated icily.

She just stared at him, her face now the colour of an overripe tomato.

The faint sound of a phone buzzing broke the tense silence that developed.

'Are you not going to answer that?'

Throat moving, she slowly pulled her phone out of her handbag and put it to her ear. *'Hola.'*

The one-sided conversation in which she was required

only to make the odd noise of acknowledgement was over in less than a minute. She kept her eyes on his face the entire time. He didn't think she blinked once throughout it.

Nikos folded his arms across his chest and clenched his jaw. 'Speak to me. Tell me what's going on.'

Her eyes closed. When she snapped them back open, she said in a tone that turned his blood to ice, 'I'm going home.'

Now he was the one to stare without blinking. Every part of his body tightened, his lungs squeezing into balls.

She was leaving him. He could see it in her eyes.

He'd sensed it while watching her hurried movements in the garage.

Marisa was leaving him. Her flustered guilt had been replaced with a calm defiance he recognised from the weeks following his return. Her controlled demeanour was at complete odds with the turbulence Nikos now found himself fighting.

Hadn't he always known this day would come?

'And when were you planning to tell me?'

'I was going to send you a message.'

'A message?' Red-hot rage pulsed through him, burning through his brain. He fought to stop it echoing in his voice, speaking through gritted teeth. 'You were going to leave without a single word of warning?'

'Yes.'

She would have let him worry. Let him put out a search for her. Let him imagine the worst.

Clamping down on the rising rage that swirled with something else, something indefinable but which felt like a weight was pressing against his heart, he said, 'You have a reason?'

Contempt flashed in her eyes. 'Oh, yes.'

'Do you want to share it with me?'

She looked at her watch. 'Not really. I have a car coming.'

'A car...' He gave a quick, humourless laugh. 'You have been busy.'

'Not me. Santi. He's arranged a plane to get me home, so if you're thinking of trying to stop me leaving, you'll have him to deal with.'

'I wouldn't stop *you* leaving, *agapi mou*.' He let his gaze fall to the car seat and the child sleeping in it she was shielding with her body. 'Our son, though, is a different matter...'

She showed not the slightest hint of intimidation at the menacing words he'd deliberately left hanging.

Stepping slowly to him, she folded her arms across her chest, mimicking his stance.

Her words were delivered quietly but with absolute precision. 'I'm taking Niki home. To Valencia. To his family. To the people who have loved him since he was in my belly. And if you think you can stop me then you will learn just how dirty I'm prepared to fight.' Her face tilted. 'But I think you know that—after all, isn't that your reason for marrying me? To guarantee your access and rights to our son?'

To see the colour drain from Nikos's face stoked the fire in Marisa's belly. So her instincts *had* been right. Her Greek wasn't good enough to understand everything Nikos and his granddad had said but she'd caught enough to get the gist of it. Their body language had told her the rest.

She'd understood his reasons immediately. Understood every little part of it.

And she also understood he'd lied to her. His proposal had never been about giving Niki a stable family.

It had been all about Nikos, the dirty, cruel, unconscionable *bastard*.

Moving her face as close to his as she could get without actually touching him, she summoned every muscle in her face to form a smile. 'I heard everything... Did I forget to tell you I taught myself Greek while you were playing dead? Oh, yes, I did forget...deliberately forgot... You see, the truth is I wasn't prepared to give you the satisfaction of knowing just how desperately I grieved for you, or that my grief was so strong I had to listen to recordings of your language at night to get any sleep. That's how I found comfort. Because it was that strong.' She nodded for emphasis. 'My grief for you. I wanted to die.'

Nikos's guts fisted. The punch it made rippled straight through him.

Still speaking in that same, calm, quiet, matter-of-fact tone, she continued, 'I'm sure I would have got through that naturally with time, but the one thing that helped me cope with the grief was discovering I was pregnant.' She patted her stomach and widened her smile.

His already cold body chilled to the marrow.

'It's a real shame you missed out on the pregnancy. You never got to see my belly move or feel him kick. You missed out on the morning sickness too but I'm willing to bet you're glad about missing that part. It's funny, but only this morning I was thinking how much I would love us to have another baby and thinking that this time you could share in all of it. Not yet—I was thinking in around a year's time.' She lifted her shoulders and pulled an 'oops' face. 'That was a bit silly of me, wasn't it, what with you planning to serve me divorce papers then?'

She took a step back and shook her head in the fashion of a disappointed teacher.

'I assume you decided a year of marriage was long enough for the law to be on your side if I refused to play ball over custody arrangements? How clever you are, *mi amado*. You think of everything. I congratulate you on your deviousness.

'If only I was a poor woman, you could have gone straight for the jugular and used your wealth to get full custody without a fight. But I'm not going to fight you...' Her nostrils flared. 'Not unless you force me.' Eyes like lasers, she hissed, 'I will never stop you seeing our son but you will have to kill me before I let you take him from me. Now please excuse me, I hear a car—that will be my driver.'

She turned her back to him and leaned down to pick up the car seat.

'Are you not going to give me the courtesy of hearing me out?' Nikos asked in as modulated a tone as he could manage when he could barely hear his own voice over the roar of the heartbeats drumming in his ears. But the car coming to drive her away...he could hear that. Hear it closing in on them.

Her back to him, she retorted, 'I heard everything I needed to hear when you were talking to your grandfather.'

'So you've appointed yourself judge *and* jury?' Hooking his hands to her shoulders, he spun her round. 'This is the very reason I wanted us to marry. You think you are entitled to decide everything but you do *not* get to decide everything when it comes to our child. I'm his father.'

'You're a *liar*,' she snarled in his face. Any pretence at calm had gone. The façade she'd been wearing had dissolved like a block of salt hitting hot water. 'You said you wanted us to be a family and give Niki stability and I believed you. I swallowed my pride and did what was best for our son when all the time you were doing only what was best for yourself.'

'I was protecting my interests. How do I know you will always do what's best for him?' he demanded, his anger flaring back to life. 'Things change and people change, and I know all too well how money and power can be weaponised against a child's best interests. I was fully aware that if you decided to kick me out of our son's life, I would have an uphill battle to fight you so, yes, I lied to you, but what would you have me do? Would you have me on the fringe of our son's life waiting for the day you decide even that is too much? Without marriage, any agreement we made about access and custody would be on *your* terms. *Everything* has to be on your terms. You don't trust anyone with him. You're scared to let him out of your sight.'

'And why do you think that is?' she screamed, eyes wild. 'My life turned to hell! *I* went to hell! Your death almost killed me! Loving him saved me—he was my saving grace because he was the only part of you I had left, and I will not apologise for being overprotective, not when I spent the first eleven months of his life terrified I would lose him like I lost you and my father.'

All the fight and fury in him dissolved at the same speed hers had risen. Staring at her furiously stricken face sent the punches rippling through him harder and faster than they'd ever punched through him before.

But the fight had left her too. Tears broke through her rage and she swiped them away furiously.

'Damn you, Nikos,' she sobbed. 'Why couldn't you just leave me alone? Why did you have to do this? I never denied you any part of him. I swallowed my pride and my hate for all you'd done to me and welcomed you into our lives for Niki's sake and I made my family welcome you too, and still you think I'm just waiting for an excuse to kick you. You still see me in the same way you see everyone else—as potential hurt to be pushed aside before they can get close enough to reject you like your parents did. You think there's something wrong with you but it was never you, it was *them*. They were wrong, not you, but until you can believe that you're doomed to hurt everyone who loves you.

'I don't care how badly you were hurt as a child—you're a fully grown man who knows better than to treat people worse than dogs, but that's how you've treated *me*. How could you do this to me? Knit my heart back together and then willingly rip it apart again? Did you *ever* have feelings for me?' But then she covered her ears and staggered back. 'No. I don't want to hear it. I can't. You've broken me enough.'

The car had pulled alongside them. The driver had got out and was watching them.

Pulling her shoulders up, Marisa carried the car seat to him. 'Can you strap it in for me, please?' Her hands were shaking too much to do it herself.

About to get into the car, she turned to stare at Nikos one last time.

He hadn't moved. His features were unreadable.

Raising her chin, she swallowed and said, 'I will instruct my lawyers to draft a custody agreement when I get home. It will be as fair as it can be to all three of us.'

And then she closed the door, turned her face away from him and gazed at her son.

Niki's eyes were open. He looked at her and gave a beaming smile that melted her broken heart.

Nikos watched the car until it was no longer in sight. He couldn't make his legs move to return inside.

He sank down on the top step of the terrace and waited for the cold fog that had enveloped him to pass.

Clasping his pounding head, he swallowed hard. Everything inside him felt bruised and tight. Deep in the pit of his stomach, sickness churned, rising up his throat to leave a bitter, metallic taste in his mouth.

Time slipped away. The fog didn't clear… Not until he caught the sound of a distant car nearing. His heart thumped then everything in him slumped to realise the sound was coming from the wrong direction. A moment later, his grandfather's sports car appeared, the top down.

Stratos parked in front of Nikos and put his elbow on the lowered window. 'Everything okay?'

He managed to jerk a nod.

'You're sure?'

Another nod. He cleared his throat. 'Where are you going?'

'Poker night at Stelios'. We're having food first. I tried to find Marisa to apologise but I couldn't find her. I'll talk to her tomorrow.' He put the car back into gear. 'Got to go—I'm already late. Don't wait up,' he added with a cackle, then drove off in the same direction Marisa had not long travelled.

For an octogenarian, his grandfather had a remarkable social life. A string of women. Raucous nights out with good company. The kind of social life Nikos had looked forward to resuming after his resurrection. The kind he would have if he hadn't learned about his son.

He blinked. What was he thinking?

Hadn't he stayed out of the spotlight and avoided any kind of socialising until he'd seen Marisa again? Hadn't he embedded himself back into her life?

The only times he'd enjoyed himself after his return

from the dead had been with her because the vacuous social scene he'd once revelled in no longer meant anything to him. His isolation had changed him. Marisa had changed him. His son had changed him.

And how had he learned about his son? By following the mother. Why had he followed the mother? Because the compulsion to see her one last time had been too strong to resist...

Fighting the direction of his thoughts and unable to look a moment longer at the road on which she'd travelled away from him, Nikos dragged himself to his feet and walked back into his home.

The emptiness was stark.

The silence was deafening.

He held tight to the bannister and climbed both flights of stairs without any thought of where he was heading.

Shuffling along the corridor on the second floor, the nausea in his stomach rose up like a wave. He doubled over, pressing his hands to the sill of the window he was passing to support himself, and closed his eyes.

When the sickness passed, he opened his eyes and found his gaze drawn back to the winding road in the distance. His grandfather's car had disappeared.

He straightened sharply as clarity exploded into his thoughts.

His grandfather wasn't the one who needed to apologise to Marisa. His antipathy had been a direct consequence of Nikos's actions. If he'd opened up to Marisa all that time ago about his life, she would have understood what his grandfather meant to him and reached out to Stratos, however deep her despair had been.

But he hadn't opened up. He couldn't change that. Couldn't change who he was. Couldn't change that he never opened up to anyone...

But hadn't he opened up to Marisa? It had been forced on him but he *had* opened up to her, about virtually everything.

She knew him better than anyone else. When he'd given her his blasé reason for moving into this villa the look in her eyes had told him she understood the real reason behind it, even if it was one he'd never acknowledged to himself, that he'd moved back here to prove to himself that the past didn't affect him when the ottoman's very existence proved otherwise. Marisa had seen that. And still she'd given him that same soft smile of love.

Yes, love.

Whatever it was that had stopped his parents loving him hadn't stopped Marisa placing her cheek to his chest and listening to the beats of his heart…

The beats of his heart picked up speed and he looked at his old bedroom door. That's where he'd been heading, he now realised, but what he'd intended to do in there he didn't know, just knew it no longer mattered. If he wanted a future then he had to free himself from the shackles of the past. Free himself properly. In his heart.

Having his child growing inside Marisa had given her comfort. When she'd described grief as being a bruise that hurts with every breath you take, she'd been speaking about her grief for *him*. How had he not seen that?

Because he'd never thought for a second that he could inspire such feelings in anyone.

When he'd hidden in the shadows for eighteen months, hers had been the face he'd seen before falling asleep. Hadn't he done the same as she'd done in those long months apart? Listened to recordings of *her* language to help him sleep?

Theos, he saw it so clearly now. *Understood* so clearly. Marisa had been the reason he'd taken the extreme action of faking his own death. To protect her. Because, even then, the thought of anyone or anything harming her in any way had been unbearable and he'd preferred to die himself than expose her to any danger.

Patting his pockets, he found his phone and, fighting the panic threatening to overwhelm him, quickly scrolled through the contacts.

'Thodoris?' he said when his call was answered. 'It's Nikos Manolas. I need your help.'

CHAPTER FOURTEEN

NIKI HAD BEEN amazingly well behaved on the flight over to Mykonos. Unfortunately, the return journey was yet to go so smoothly. He'd taken one look at the plane at the private airfield they were flying from and started bawling. He was still bawling and the plane hadn't even taken off. Marisa soothed him as much as she could but all her bribes of food and drink—she kept emergency ready-made baby food and baby milk in the change-bag—went to waste.

Picking him up and pacing the cabin while rubbing his back, she asked the cabin crew the reason for the delay. They'd been ready to take off for twenty minutes. None of the crew knew or, if they did, weren't sharing the reasons with her.

She sat down again and made another attempt at giving Niki milk. This time he accepted it and quietened.

Marisa soon wished he would become fractious again. Resting her head back against the leather seat, she squeezed her eyes shut and tried to banish Nikos's face from her mind. Tried to ignore the unbearable pain in her heart. Tried to banish the tempest of emotions swelling inside her. Tried to stop the force of the painful ragged rise and fall of her chest from pushing out the tears forming behind her eyes. It would have been easier to stop the sun from rising. They fell down her face like a burning stream.

Her hands full with feeding Niki, she couldn't wipe the tears away, and she turned her face to the window to stop them falling onto him and tried her hardest to get control of herself. She didn't want her devastation to feed into Niki's developing emotions. She *must* keep hold of herself until she was in the security of her home and the privacy of her bedroom. She could fall apart then, just as she'd done during those desolate months and months spent believing Nikos to be dead. Pack her emotions back inside her.

'Are you okay?' One of the cabin crew was hovering beside her, clearly concerned.

She gave a jerky nod, and something she hoped was a smile, but couldn't open her mouth for fear the anguish would pour out of it.

Turning back to look out of the window, she saw through the film of tears clouding her vision something large and black approaching.

She blinked vigorously then found herself freezing when her vision cleared enough to recognise the object. It was a car. One of Nikos's cars.

She blinked again to see him jump out of the front passenger seat before the car had even come to a stop.

His long legs sped in a blur towards the plane.

Moments later and he was in the cabin and striding over to her.

His eyes locked straight onto hers. His Adam's apple moved up and down his throat repeatedly before his lips finally parted.

'Don't leave me,' he said in a hoarse voice.

She could only stare at him. Was this really Nikos?

Was this wild-eyed, dishevelled man the same perfectly groomed and contained man she'd left only an hour ago?

His frantic eyes held hers. There was a sheen in them...

And then she remembered what an excellent actor he'd already proved himself to be and turned her face away. 'Go home, Nikos. I've already said we can make an agreement for custody that's fair to all of us. You've nothing to worry about. I won't stop you seeing Niki.'

'This is nothing to do with our son. Please, Marisa, I am begging you... Don't go.'

'Why?' she asked tonelessly.

'Because I can't live without you.'

Thinking she might be sick at the new lows he'd just plumbed, she snapped her face back to him. 'You sick, lying bastard.'

Nikos winced but accepted the deserved blow. 'I am a bastard. I've treated you appallingly but I'm...' He took a deep breath and pulled viciously at his hair. 'Can you give Niki to one of the crew? There are things I need to say that I don't want him to hear.'

Her red eyes—*Theos*, his cruelty had caused that— narrowed but after a moment she rose from her seat and carried Niki to the door behind which the cabin crew stayed.

Nikos sank into the seat opposite the one she'd been sitting in and bowed his head, scraping his nails over the back of his skull, trying to gather his thoughts before she returned.

His thoughts were still splintered when she sat down again.

He lifted his head.

Her legs were crossed, spine straight, an imperious expression on her blotchy, tear-stained face. He recognised that expression. It was the one she'd used in the weeks after he'd broken her heart when he'd brazenly confessed to having had no intention of telling her to her face that he was alive. Why hadn't he recognised her stance as a protective shield?

'My grandfather told me earlier that I lack empathy,' he said slowly, the answer to his own question coming to him.

'He is not wrong.'

'He is. To a degree.'

She arched a brow in response.

'I learned at a young age to block feelings.'

'I've already guessed that. And you have my sympathy for the reasons behind it.'

'I don't want your sympathy.'

'I know that too.'

'I can stop my heart from feeling. Turn it to stone.'

'To stop yourself from being hurt again. You don't need to be Freud to understand that, Nikos.'

He nodded his agreement. 'It stops me being hurt but it also stops me being able to recognise other people's pain.' He grimaced and corrected himself. 'Rather, it enables me to *ignore* their pain, even the pain of those who are close to me.' He gave a grunt of gloomy laughter. 'Not that I have let anyone get close to me, not even my grandfather—even from him I can separate my heart. I lived in England for seven years and barely thought of him. Can you believe that? That man saved me, put up with all my rebellions and I treated him like that?'

'You've made up for it with him.'

He felt a tiny release of the pressure on his chest at this slight softening.

'And then I met you.'

She stiffened.

'Marisa… You…' He pinched the bridge of his nose and swallowed. 'I don't know why it was different with you but there is something about you I reacted to more strongly than I have ever reacted to anyone before. I have never craved someone's company before and it was never just about the sex, even if I did try to kid myself that that's all it was. I told myself your words of love to me were just words. How could you love me, someone so inherently unlovable his parents let him go without a fight?

'But you would put your cheek to my chest and I'd know you were listening to my heartbeat. You wanted to feel *my* heartbeat. No one had ever done that before. No one had ever got close enough to. And I would feel your heartbeat against my skin too and the warmth of your body and just want to stay there and never let you go.'

The imperious expression on Marisa's face had gone.

'I think I fell in love with you a long time ago and didn't know it. But even if I had, I would have fought it and the outcome would have been the same. I would have still faked my death without telling you and with no intention of resuming our affair because it was safer for me. You'd got too close… Every day of our affair lived in me the fear that you would see whatever was rotten in me that my parents had seen and push me aside without another thought.

'When I found that photograph of you in the pile of photos of my lawyer's dead body…' He closed his eyes and sucked in a breath. 'That was the first time I'd felt real terror since I was taken from my parents and it was a thousand times worse. That was the thing that pushed me over the edge into faking my death. I needed to protect you. I insisted on daily reports about you. I could only sleep at night if I knew you were safe. When I learned what had happened to your father... *Theos*, my terror for you...'

Her eyes glistened. Her chin was wobbling, throat moving.

'Once it was all over, I never wanted to see you again. You'd made me feel things, *agapi mou*, and that terrified me. Feelings leave you vulnerable. It's perverse logic, I know, but subconsciously I knew if I pushed you away first then you couldn't leave me. You couldn't hurt me.'

A tear rolled down her cheek. He wanted so badly to press his thumb to her cheek and brush the tear away.

'I tried to stay away from you. I even told myself the day I waited outside your estate that all I wanted was one last glimpse as a private goodbye. If it hadn't been for Niki, you wouldn't have seen me again but he was the excuse I needed to justify throwing myself back into your life and even then I fought it. I fell in love with our son and I could accept that love because he was an innocent child who could never hurt me, whereas you... Marisa, you have no idea of the power you have over me. You have no idea how much it tortured me to imagine you with Raul. I thought you'd moved on—how could you not? How could I be special enough for anyone to grieve?'

'But I never moved on from you. It was impossible.'

The beats of Marisa's heart were so strong the echoes thrashed in her dazed, barely comprehending head. The desperation with which she wanted to believe him...

But the *fear*.

She shrank back as he slid onto the floor to kneel before her and shrank into herself when he took her hand. She tried to block her ears to his words, deny them their power.

'There is only you,' he said quietly. 'And I can't fight it any more or deny it to myself. I love you. You have turned my stone-cold heart into something that beats freely with love for you. It's *you* I need to be with. *You* I need to spend my nights with. *You* I trust with my life, my soul and my heart. Please, give me one more chance, let me prove myself to be the man you deserve, I beg you, and not for our son's sake but for mine because I can't live without you. I've tried and every road leads back to you. Let me earn your love and your trust. I swear on our son's life that I will never betray it again. I swear.'

Marisa barely noticed her fingers had laced into his. The seams of her ripped, damaged heart were threading hesitantly back together and, finally, she dared to look at him. 'When I agreed to marry you, it was for Niki's sake.'

He breathed deeply. 'I know.'

'Everything I've done since I learned I was pregnant has been for him.'

His voice became a hoarse whisper. 'I know.'

'But you...' She leaned forward, closer to him. 'You brought me back to life. You made me remember that I'm not just a mother but a woman with needs of her own. And that woman loves you,' she whispered. 'She's always loved you.'

His throat moved. 'I never deserved it. But I will. If you'll let me.'

Hands shaking, she cupped his cheeks and stared deeper into his eyes. The look she saw in them sewed the last piece of her heart back into place.

'Yes.' Unable to contain the feelings a moment longer, she brought her face to his and kissed him. 'Oh, Nikos, yes.'

He made a sound like a prayer and then his arms wrapped tightly around her and she was enveloped in his arms so tenderly and lovingly that her mended heart soared into song.

Nikos stared into Marisa's eyes, filled to the brim with emotions. And when she smiled and said, 'Let's get our son and go home,' he knew he would spend the rest of his life worshipping her and thanking God every day for bringing her into his life and setting him free to love. To love her.

[faint bleed-through text from previous page, illegible]

EPILOGUE

NIKOS STOOD BACK and admired his handiwork. He'd spent the weekend in his 'man cave', as his wife called it, sanding and repainting his childhood ottoman. It looked brand new. He liked to think his son would be thrilled with it but knowing Niki, he would think of it only as an excellent new space for when he played hide-and-seek with his sister. And that was okay. More than okay.

Childhood was precious and his children would one day grow into adulthood with the happiest of memories to look back on, and this ottoman that had witnessed so much trauma would now be nestled in a home filled with love. It had been reborn, just as he had been.

The man cave door opened and Marisa appeared. She slipped an arm around his waist and pressed herself close to him. 'You've done an amazing job,' she said softly. 'Are you pleased with it?'

He kissed the top of her head and pressed his cheek into her hair. 'Yes. Thank you for not letting me set fire to it.'

She squeezed her arms around him. No further words were needed.

He remembered how she'd found him months after their wedding, about to place it on the fire-pit, thinking it needed to be done to set the past free in its entirety. How she'd wrapped her arms around him, much as she was holding him now, and quietly asked if he was sure he wanted to burn the only solid reminder of his mother's love for him.

'For all her sins and neglect, she did love you, Nikos,' she'd said. 'And if you ever still doubt that, look at this ottoman and remember that deep in her heart, whether she acknowledged it to herself or not, she couldn't bear to lose all of you. She kept a part of you with her. Now it's for you to keep a part of her with you.'

It had taken a further four years for him to set to work on it. Four years of unconditional love from the woman he would give his life for. Four years of happiness that had flushed the pain of his childhood from him until all that was left was a rare kernel of melancholy.

For a long time they stood in silence, doing nothing but stare at the object of his past brought into their present to be a part of their lives for ever.

'Mama, Mama!'

The voice of their son carried through the air and they left the man cave to find five-year-old Niki racing to them. His three-year-old sister, Rose, ran after him, cheeks puffing, arms pumping as she tried valiantly to keep pace with her adored big brother.

Niki's light brown eyes were alight as he breathlessly said, 'Aunty Elsa and Uncle Santi are here.'

Golden-haired Rose threw her arms around Nikos's knees and stared up at him with the same bright-eyed excitement. 'Baby Marco here too!'

Holding their children's hands, they headed off to welcome their house guests and fill their home with even more love and laughter.

* * * * *

CLAIMING HIS CINDERELLA SECRETARY

CATHY WILLIAMS

MILLS & BOON

CHAPTER ONE

WHERE IN GOD'S name was she?

James pushed his chair back, swivelled it at an angle so that he could relax back, feet up on his desk, folded his hands behind his head and scowled darkly at his office door, which had been slammed shut just a few minutes ago.

Actually, *slammed* risked being an understatement. He was surprised the thing was still on its hinges. Naomi, his now ex-girlfriend, had stormed out of his office, blazingly angry, only just managing to resist the temptation to hurl one of her designer Jimmy Choos at his head.

Her raised voice had been loud enough to shatter glass. Certainly, his entire office must have stopped dead in their tracks. He suspected they might well have downed tools completely so that they could huddle and dissect what they had heard, and doubtless he would be peppered with questions the second he stepped foot out of his office.

There were distinct disadvantages to being a boss with an 'open door, feel free to speak your mind' policy, he decided. A hub filled with young computer geniuses who thrived on the encouragement he gave them to enjoy the informality of his state-of-the-art workspace in order to nurture their creativity had spawned, he glumly thought now, a team of outspoken employees who wouldn't think twice about a formal inquisition into Naomi's noisy departure. Who could resist a full-blown gossip-fest about a woman whose parting shot had been that 'he hadn't heard the last of this'?

Right now, he needed his cool, level-headed secretary to return some semblance of normality to what remained of the day, but where the heck was she in his hour of need?

Next to him, his mobile phone buzzed. He looked at it, saw it was Naomi, and decided that any further conversations would be futile—although he knew she wasn't the type to take things lying down. He had no interest in picking up where they had left off. What more could there be to shout about? And neither was he interested in any kind of reconciliation. The relationship was dead in the water and he had to acknowledge that he had sleepwalked his way into that one.

He'd thought what they had was fun. He'd assumed she was on the same page as him. She'd talked about her career as a catwalk model and how it would be the perfect springboard for her to branch out into fashion design. She'd claimed to be a career woman with no time for anything permanent. She had shown him drawings she had done for a collection of casual wear, and hadn't batted an eyelid when he had accidentally held up the first sketch the wrong way. She'd been the epitome of easy going, so who could have blamed him when he'd casually asked her if she would like to accompany him to his brother's wedding in Hawaii?

They were to spend a few days in the Caribbean, because he'd wanted to seal a deal with a promising start-up company in Barbados. She had been given free rein to choose whatever five-star hotel she wanted, no expense spared. There would be luxury on tap, she would be able to do as she pleased during the day while he worked and they would have the nights to themselves. Of course, he would only get through the preliminaries. Pinning down the final deal would require his trusty PA, so he would have to conclude business in London, but he would have been able to kick-start the process. Then they were to have a leisurely tour of the various Hawaiian islands before the wedding.

It had all made perfect sense and would have spared him the headache of going to Max's wedding on his own. Personally, he had nothing against people getting married, even though he'd only just recovered from the shock of his die-hard bachelor brother waxing lyrical about the joys of tying the knot.

As a result of his own experiences, however—and from the experiences of some of his friends, who had flung themselves headlong into wedlock at way too young and tender an age, only to regret the impulse a couple of years down the road—commitment and everything it entailed was a game he had no intention of playing any time soon. Hence the prospect of being the best man and bachelor-in-residence at his brother's wedding had filled him with a certain amount of dread. He had been to five weddings in the past six years. And, was it his imagination or were all the unattached females at weddings sprinkled with some kind of weird fairy dust that suddenly made them want to fall in love and rush down the aisle? Having Naomi on his arm, he had concluded, would be the speediest route to making sure he wasn't targeted by anyone with stars in their eyes. Naomi, like him, knew just what relationships were all about. Fun. No strings attached. Just two adults enjoying one another.

Except he'd been wrong.

James snorted at his own idiocy in thinking that she had been as casual about their affair as he had, but was spared the frustration of dwelling further on the hissy fit to which he had just been subjected by one firm knock followed by the soft push of his office door opening.

'About time.' He swept his feet off the desk and briskly sat forward as Ellie leaned round to hand him a mug of coffee—strong, sugarless and black. Just the thing he needed. The woman was a mind reader.

'About time?'

Ellie looked at her charismatic, wildly sexy boss and suppressed the usual shiver of unwelcome awareness that rippled through her every time she saw him.

She'd been working for James Stowe for three years and he still managed to have an annoying effect on her, although she had always been adept at concealing it under a calm, professional exterior. She wasn't a fool. She knew that an inconvenient attraction was just an annoying blip, easily swatted away, and it was easy enough to swat away because Ellie was sensible enough to conclude that what attracted her was the pull of the opposite. Her stupidly sexy boss was brilliant, utterly unafraid of taking risks and enjoyed the sort of sybaritic, revolving door love life that privately made her shudder. Never mind the more prosaic fact that she'd seen some of the women he dated, and the possibility of him being attracted to her was as far-fetched as a lion being drawn to a mouse.

It was an environment where the dress code was 'anything goes', and the excess energy of the young, talented thirty-strong staff was burnt off at the ping pong table, the darts board or in one of the 'debating rooms', where they could exchange their ideas as forcefully as they wanted. But Ellie always dressed in a uniform of sober suits and flats and, whatever energy she wanted to burn off, she did it at the local swimming pool once a week.

Where her boss was stupidly clever and outspoken in

a way that sometimes made her feel faint, Ellie was just the opposite, and she privately maintained that that was the reason why they worked so harmoniously together.

'Where have you been?'

Ellie calmly swerved to sit at the leather chair in front of his desk. She glanced down at her tablet, which she had brought in as she always did, to make notes about whatever mountain of urgent emails he needed her to deal with. When she looked at him, it was to find him glaring at her.

'To the dentist,' she said briskly. Disgruntled blue eyes met her calm grey ones and she fought not to flush.

He was so beautiful, it was almost a sin. His hair was chestnut-brown, thick and straight. His features were chiselled to perfection, his nose straight, his mouth full of sensuous, wicked promise. Sometimes in the early hours of the morning, when her thoughts were prone to drifting, an image of him would pop into her head and she would savour the taboo pleasure of thinking about the six-foot-two alpha male with the kind of loose limbed, careless grace that made heads turn.

Of course in the cold light of day such thoughts never intruded, and if they did it was easy to dampen them because any woman in the presence of a guy like him could be excused for feeling a bit tingly now and again.

'Did you tell me that you weren't going to be in until…?' he made a show of consulting his Rolex '…*two-thirty in the afternoon?*'

'Of course I did. I also emailed you to remind you a couple of days ago. If you'd like, I can have the email printed off—'

'Not necessary,' James growled, waving down the suggestion dismissively. 'I suppose you've heard what's happened?' He didn't wait for her to answer. 'This office is a hotbed of gossip. It's impossible to have any kind of private life here! I expect you were grabbed the second you came through that door? Treated to every tiresome detail of the drama that unfolded in your absence? Which, incidentally, would not have happened if you'd been at your desk instead of in a dentist's chair! How's the tooth, anyway?'

'The tooth is fine. Thank you for asking.'

'So…?'

'Trish *did* mention that there was something of…er… an incident with…your girlfriend,' Ellie admitted.

'An incident?'

'It's none of my business,' Ellie said diplomatically in an attempt to divert her boss from the looming onslaught of thunderous rage.

Darling of the gossip pages as he was, and photographed on practically a weekly basis with one of his women glued to his side, he was fiercely protective of his space in the office. Girlfriends were not allowed within the hallowed walls of the converted factory in Shoreditch which housed some of the sharpest computer brains in the country, and their counterparts with business acumen.

Ellie shuddered to think of the reception Naomi would have had, and knew the ensuing drama would have made his blood boil.

His staff all knew that he was a guy who didn't believe in longevity when it came to relationships with women. Although nearly every member of staff felt free to quiz him about whatever latest hot model happened to be gracing his bed, he was actually remarkably tight-lipped when it came to discussing his private life. He threw out just enough by way of answers to satisfy curiosity, but who really knew what motivated a man who seemed so averse to settling down?

Ellie, who never asked questions, wondered whether

she was the only one to notice that reticence—the way he never really shared anything meaningful about himself.

Did he do so with anyone?

She realised that she was bursting with curiosity about the blow-up with Naomi but she impatiently put a lid on it. Curiosity about her boss would end up being ruinous for their working relationship, and way too challenging for her peace of mind.

'The whole thing could have been avoided,' he growled, ignoring her lack of input with the sweeping nonchalance of someone accustomed to a rapt audience. 'Naomi should have known better than to show up where I work. I've always made it very clear to the women I date that play is one thing, but work is quite another, and the two don't overlap. Stop staring at that tablet as though it's going to rescue you from sitting here.'

Ellie looked up. 'I thought you wanted the business with Neco Systems sorted at the speed of light in case someone else came along and snapped them up. I spent the morning compiling the contract. I thought we could run through it before I emailed it to you.'

'If you'd been at your desk, you could have escorted her out. Tactfully.'

'It's not my job to deal with your girlfriends, and why would I have escorted her out?'

'Because you know I don't indulge women here unless they work for me.'

Ellie gave up on any prospect of her tablet rescuing her from a conversation she both did and didn't want to have. Somehow indulging in any kind of personal conversation with her boss felt all wrong. It almost felt *threatening*. But what really scared her was the element of *excitement* that went hand in hand with that. He was so clever, so restless, so intrinsically edge-of-seat, addictively commanding.

Part of her wondered what would happen if she allowed herself to be sucked into the vortex of his overpowering personality but somewhere deep inside she had always known that nothing good would come of it.

She didn't want to talk about his women. She wanted to keep things strictly on a polite, harmonious surface level. She didn't want anything confusing to disrupt the calm surface of her life. She'd spent far too many years dealing with chaos and confusion in her own personal life to court yet more of it from another source. She knew that, when it came to James, it would be very easy for the lines between boss and secretary to blur at the edges. He wouldn't notice, but *she* would.

She enjoyed and needed this job. She certainly needed the money and she wasn't about to jeopardise any of that by crossing her own self-imposed boundaries.

'Perhaps you didn't make that clear enough,' Ellie said vaguely.

Naomi had been on the scene for nearly five months, which was something of a record for him. Maybe the poor woman thought that that had constituted the sort of commitment most women sought in a relationship, and therefore that showing up at his workplace wouldn't have resulted in the Spanish Inquisition.

'Of course I made it crystal-clear.' He looked at her with incredulity, as though she'd suddenly started speaking a foreign language, and she returned his gaze coolly, as always. 'Say what you're thinking, Ellie. I can see the cogs whirring, so why don't you spit it out instead of sitting there in fulminating silence?'

Ellie gave up. He could be volatile…energetic in a way that left most people feeling that they were stuck in the slow lane even though they were going as fast as they could. And there were times when she'd had to fade into the background when he had blown a fuse at some hapless person's incompetence.

That said, his moods had always swept past her, leaving her unscathed. He tiptoed around her, respecting the lines between them, and she suspected that, after a string of unsatisfactory secretaries before her, he did his utmost to protect their working relationship. He had curbed his inclination to engage her in discussing her private life. His natural tendency to be provocative and push the barriers had taken a back seat in the face of her quiet resistance.

By nature, Ellie was reserved. It was ironic that she had managed to find herself working in an environment that nurtured exuberance. When it came to recruitment James had chosen carefully, compiling a team of thirty-strong employees who would all coalesce perfectly. Nerdy, yet confident, cutting-edge-clever and not afraid of waging a war to be heard, competitive, yet smart enough to know when to back down. And, of course, however rowdy they became they were all intensely loyal to their brilliant leader. Since she'd been working there, not a single one had come close to quitting.

Amongst this hand-picked crowd, Ellie was the only one who kept herself to herself. She couldn't remember a time when she'd had their free-spirited exuberance. As an only child, she had been loved but cossetted. Her parents had had her late in their lives, after many years of trying for a baby, and she had become the recipient of their reluctance to allow her to do anything that might possibly put her in harm's way.

They had been a unit of three until her father had died when she'd been sixteen, and after that the placid, comfortingly predictable life she had led had come to a crashing halt. Gone were the family days and the quiet holidays to Wales. Gone were the board games in winter and her parents both anxiously waiting up for her to return on the occasional evening out with friends.

Instead, her mother had gone to pieces, and Ellie had had to grow up fast to deal with that. Between the ages of sixteen and twenty, her life had been put on hold. University dreams had been shelved. She had made it through the rest of school, but all her spare time had been taken up saving her mother from herself.

As a couple, her parents had been unbreakable, but when one half of that couple had been removed—in her father's case a mere four months after having been diagnosed with cancer—the structure had catastrophically collapsed. Without Robbie Thompson, her mother had been cast adrift, first retreating into herself and then becoming dependent on alcohol to help herself cope.

Looking back, Ellie marvelled that she had managed to get through school at all, but she had. She had said goodbye to her dream of being an architect, and instead had thrown her energy and talent into absorbing everything there was to know about computer systems. Through it all, she had continued to look after her mother, coaxing her out of her alcohol dependency. They were now at a point where her mother was relatively stable, although after two minor heart attacks she was a shadow of the woman she had once been.

The house had been sold and enough money scraped together to find her somewhere small by the coast, but depression dogged her, and when Ellie thought about it she wanted to burst into tears.

The experience had left her guarded, protective of her privacy and always careful to take nothing for granted. Safety and stability were the two things she craved most because confusion and unpredictability had been terrifying.

Now, James was breaking their unspoken code and was

looking at her, eyes bright and challenging, daring her to open up with what she was thinking. She was tempted, because on this one subject she had strong feelings.

'Like I said,' she repeated quietly, 'I don't have any opinions on what you do outside work.'

'Yes, you do.'

Their eyes met and he grinned and visibly relaxed.

'Was there a reason why she came here?' Ellie eventually asked, and he shrugged and nodded to his private sitting area where he entertained clients or had informal meetings—deep leather chairs, a metal table, and to one side a sofa-bed, because it wasn't unheard of for him to spend the night in the office if things were particularly busy.

'Let's go and relax. Been one hell of a day, and we're not even halfway through it. My head's not in a suitable work space.'

'You're the boss,' Ellie said, and he frowned.

'Yes. I am. You work for me, but once in a while it's okay to take off the professional hat and actually stop hiding away behind that glass wall of yours.'

Ellie blushed. She lowered her eyes, but she could feel a tell-tale pulse jumping in her neck. She was keenly aware of him vaulting to his feet, pushing back the leather chair and heading towards the seating area which was brick-walled and warmly inviting.

'And dump the tablet,' he ordered without glancing round at her, making for the sofa-bed, where he proceeded to lie down with his eyes closed. 'Tell me what you're thinking,' he coaxed. 'Get it off your chest. Trust me, you'll feel better for it.'

Ellie was shrewd enough to realise what was happening here. For once, he had found himself in a situation over which he had had no control. Naomi had shown up out of the blue, blown a hole in his day by creating a scene and had left him edgy and in need of venting. The more she tried to pull back, the more he would goad her into a response. For once, she was in the direct line of fire, and the speediest way to return things to normal would be to give up and go with the flow.

'Maybe Naomi thought you wouldn't hit the roof because she made the mistake of showing up here.' Ellie had taken one of the chairs, and she looked at him sprawled out on the sofa-bed, feet loosely crossed at the ankles, eyes now opened to slits as he looked at her, hands folded behind his head. 'You *have* been going out for quite a long time, after all...'

'A handful of months.'

'That's record-breaking for you,' Ellie said politely, driven to honesty, because he just wouldn't let it go. She felt a surge of annoyance that she had been prodded into going against the grain. Rebellion began to blossom inside her, a little voice telling her that, if he wanted to hear what she thought, then why not give him what he wanted?

James grinned and visibly relaxed. 'So it is. You're a tonic, Eleanor Thompson—five-foot six inches, twenty-four years old and a mystery after three years of working for me. How is it that you know how long I've been seeing Naomi, and yet I don't even know whether you have a boyfriend or not? Have you?' He laughed. 'No need to answer that one, Ellie. I already know that your answer will be that it's none of my business, and of course you'd be absolutely right.'

Ellie stiffened. When she looked down, she saw her neat flats, the smooth navy of her knee-length skirt and the white of her ribbed summer tee shirt.

The amusement in his voice ratcheted up that small rebellious voice. Did he imagine that she had no feelings? That she was as dull as dishwater? When he said that she was a *mystery*, it certainly wasn't in the tone of voice that implied she was intriguing.

'It doesn't matter whether you have a list of dos and don'ts when it comes to women,' she told him evenly. 'Most women don't expect to be hauled in front of a firing squad if they make the mistake of paying a visit to the company where their partner works. I know you must have told her what was and wasn't allowed in a relationship but...'

She stopped in mid-flow. Did she really know anything about relationships? Precious little. Fate had made sure to deny her the chance to have fun with guys in the way every other girl her age did. But she did know what she would and wouldn't want in an ideal world, and she definitely wouldn't want any guy who had a book of instructions of what was allowed.

Her heart sped up as their eyes met and she felt a little burst of satisfaction at having said what was in her mind—toning it down, of course, because the lines of demarcation prevented her from really saying what she thought.

What she really thought was that James Stowe was way too clever, way too good-looking and way too charismatic for his own good. In the cut-throat world of computers and computer software, he ruled the roost and now, as he expanded into the lucrative field of tech start-ups, he was on course for claiming the crown.

Women flocked to him because he was the ultimate catch. Except for the fact that he had no sticking power. Just because he made a big deal of laying all his cards on the table at the start of a relationship, didn't mean that he was the epitome of the gentleman, which it seemed was how he would like to be perceived.

'But...?' he encouraged, eyes bright with interest. 'I'm all ears.'

'But women aren't robots,' Ellie said sharply. 'They're

not always going to do as you tell them. You're confusing them with people you pay to work for you. They're not employees, and if somewhere along the line they think it might be okay to come here for a surprise visit, then I don't think it's very fair for you to let rip because they've gone against your commands.'

She was huffing a little as he slid off the couch to saunter across to the window, where he stood for a couple of seconds, back to her, peering out.

Energised.

'You make me sound like a tyrant,' he mused, turning round and then strolling towards her. 'Have you always felt that way?'

'I...'

'Yes? Now you've started, you can't leave me hanging on. That would be cruel...'

'You did ask me what I thought.' She inwardly winced at the defensive note in her voice. How had this conversation become so derailed? The devil works on idle hands, she thought. For once his hands had been idle, and in she'd walked, perfectly placed for him to have a little Machiavellian fun at her expense.

He perched on the solid, wooden square table in front of her and leant forward, his forearms on his thighs, his fingers loosely linked.

'And I'm very glad that I did,' he murmured soothingly. 'How else would I have known just how much resentment you were stockpiling for me?'

'I haven't been stockpiling resentment, James!' she cried, dismayed. Her cheeks were hectic with colour and she was leaning towards him, every nerve and pulse in her stretched taut with tension.

'She got the wrong idea.'

'What do you mean? What are you talking about?'

Pinned to the spot by incisive blue eyes, Ellie couldn't move a muscle. Her jaw ached from the effort of swallowing and her breathing was shallow and uneven.

Her thoughts were all over the place, because the conversation felt intimate. The gap between them had been breached and she didn't like it.

'Naomi wasn't chucked out of my office. I'm not quite the monster you seem to think I am.'

'I don't think anything of the sort!'

'Sure, she surprised me by coming here and, sure, I don't encourage women to pay impromptu visits to my office. This is where I work. That said, she showed up, and I was perfectly happy to make her a cup of coffee, take time out for fifteen minutes and then escort her out but…' He shrugged. 'The conversation didn't go as expected. It seems that Naomi equated an invite to Max's wedding with a declaration of intent from me. She showed me pictures of the dress she wanted to wear to the wedding and then she hinted one too many times that she wanted more than fun…that she thought it might be time for me to meet the parents. I thought she was kidding and, when I told her that I thought she understood the score, she went ballistic. Women may not be robots, Ellie, but they should be astute enough to know where I stand on the subject of longevity when I've been upfront with them from the start.'

'Poor Naomi…' Ellie could think of nothing worse than actually falling for someone like James Stowe.

'Poor *Naomi*?'

'Her hopes were raised and you dashed them, and I don't suppose you were all that tactful with it.'

He burst out laughing and she threw him a shadow of a smile.

'And just for your information, James, I'm not at all resentful. I love my job. It's challenging and absorbing and, if I don't happen to agree with how you approach relationships, then that's just a personal thing and I don't want you thinking... I wouldn't want that to somehow...'

'It won't.' He waved down her stumbling apology. He looked at her curiously, head tilted to one side. 'Would *you* have thrown a hissy fit if the guy you were dating told you he wasn't into love and marriage?'

'I wouldn't be dating any guy who wasn't prepared to be serious,' Ellis said bluntly. Once again, she was swamped by a feeling of inappropriate intimacy, although she knew that that was on her part. As far as James was concerned, for once they would simply be conversing as two people instead of as boss and employee. He was casual with all his staff and he encouraged them to talk to him about anything and everything. It was all part of his immense charm.

Six months ago, he had spent an hour holed up with her friend Trish, providing her with a shoulder to cry on because she'd broken up with her boyfriend and was finding it hard to concentrate. He had listened, handed out tissues and then offered her one of his houses abroad for a week's vacation with a friend, all paid for by him.

'That's a tall order for a guy.'

'It's a tall order for *you*.' She flushed and then stood up, smoothing down her skirt.

When their eyes met, she could tell that he was amused and sure enough, his eyebrows raised, barely stifling a grin, he said, 'I see the work hat is back on.'

'There's a lot to get through today.'

'I think we've got through quite a bit already,' James mused softly. 'More than could be expected.'

Ellie flinched. He had managed to slide his foot through the door. Not by much, but enough, and she quailed at the prospect of him thinking that a foot through the door somehow gave him permission to introduce a new level to their well-oiled working relationship.

Ellie knew that she was overreacting. When you worked closely with someone, when you were with them day after day, hour upon hour, it was impossible *not* to let them into your life. The fact that she had held him at bay for so long was the very reason for his curiosity about her.

She wished, somewhere deep inside her, that she could be different…that she could be more open. But she'd always been quiet, and that reserved nature had become something more after her dad had died.

Being responsible for her mother had made her independent. She had had no one to help deal with the loss of the person she loved. Her parents had both been only children and, as she was an only child, there had just been her. Her friends had had their own teenage lives to lead. At first they had been sympathetic, but bit by bit the whole business of living had grabbed their attention and, one by one, they had faded away, occasionally glancing back to see how she was doing.

She had coped on her own and she had learned to deal with the problems life threw at her without recourse to anyone and without asking anyone's help. She had learned to be contained to the point where sharing herself felt like a mountain that was too steep to climb.

Certainly, sharing anything about her private life with her boss, her *thoughts and feelings*, had never, ever been an option. Now, it felt as though something had shifted underneath her feet, and she would have to claw back lost ground—get them both back to where they had been.

'Shall I cancel the flights and bookings for Naomi?' Her fingers itched for the safety of her tablet which she had been ordered to abandon. 'Will you still be going to Barbados as planned or would you like me to rearrange that trip and reschedule it for later in the month, when you return from Hawaii?'

'Slow down!' He began heading back towards the working part of his office and, in his wake, Ellie heard the laughter in his voice. She gritted her teeth with frustration. He glanced over his shoulder and, sure enough, his lips were twitching.

'Before I do anything, I'll have to run the gauntlet and face the sea of nosey parkers waiting out here. Wouldn't want to have to bring out the smelling salts because someone's fainted with curiosity. You know as well as I do that some of those computer guys out there can be drama queens...' He paused, one hand on the door. 'And don't despair, Ellie. Give me half an hour, and we'll be back to our usual routine. Boss, secretary...and no lines to be crossed...'

CHAPTER TWO

IT WAS RAINING the following morning when Ellie left her flat for work, a fine, demoralising drizzle that seeped under her lightweight mac and clothes, and settled with clammy persistence on her skin.

She'd had a restless night. The 'back to the usual routine', which James had jauntily flung at her before departing to satisfy the demands of his unashamedly curious staff, had failed to materialise.

At least for her.

The door he'd opened had remained stubbornly open even though she had thrown herself into work for what had remained of the day, barely lifting her eyes from her computer as she'd blitzed all the emails waiting to be dealt with and given ferocious attention to whatever slim backlog of reports there were to go through.

Head bowed, she had still managed to feel the full wattage of his attention on her, however. He'd perched on her desk, rattling off instructions at his usual breakneck speed, and she'd felt his eyes boring into her, felt his curiosity about those titbits he had managed to eke out of her, opinions she had somehow found herself forced into confiding. She had slid her eyes sideways and been confronted with his black jeans pulled taut over a muscular thigh and had hurriedly had to look away.

So now, hurrying against the blowing, fading summer drizzle, the last thing she expected was to hear a woman's voice calling her name from behind. In fact, she ignored the summons for a few seconds, and only stopped when she felt a hand on her shoulder, at which point she swung round sharply, blinking as the wind blew back the hood of her mac and the rain fell lightly against her face.

She peered up, subliminally taking in the high black shoes, the stupidly long, slender legs, the short red burst of skirt and the black top, all partially concealed beneath the distinctive cream and black check of a designer trench coat. The leggy blonde was enviably dry because she'd had the basic common sense to carry an umbrella with her. So, while Ellie pushed her wet hair from her face and grappled with the hood of her mac, which insisted on doing its own thing, the other woman managed to look only slightly and attractively tousled.

'You probably don't remember me.'

Ellie remembered very well. Not many people could forget Naomi. They had met in passing a month ago, purely by chance, when Ellie had been hurrying to cross the road to get to her bus on the other side. Naomi had been in the passenger seat of James's Ferrari and he had screeched to a halt at the kerb to offer Ellie a lift to wherever she was going. Perfunctory introductions had been made, and in five seconds Ellie had been able to commit to memory the bored blue eyes of his companion, the shiny, long, straight blonde hair swept over one shoulder, the pale golden tanned skin flawlessly smooth and the tiny diamond stud in her perfectly straight nose.

No mistaking the blonde standing in front of her now, although the eyes were more desperate than bored.

'Can you please give this to James? He's not picking up any of my calls and he's not answering my text messages... I know I acted out yesterday, but I love him, and I just want to talk to him...'

'Naomi?'

'I've been waiting for ages in the coffee shop over there to catch you.' Her voice wobbled and she breathed in deeply. 'I know he'll go spare if I show up at his office, and it's just not me to lurk by his house waiting for him to get home. Plus, I'd never know when to expect him. I just *need* to talk to him...'

Ellie looked at the outstretched hand clutching an envelope and sighed.

'I'd rather not get involved...'

'Please! Look, it's pouring out here, and we're both getting soaked. You just have to *give him the envelope.* That's *all*.' Desperation had morphed into the natural state of command, which was often the default position of the very beautiful, and Ellie reluctantly took the envelope. In point of fact, *she* was the only one getting soaked and, frankly, she didn't want to stand out in the rain trying to make a point for the next five minutes, getting nowhere.

'Super.' Naomi beamed and stepped back. 'Thanks.'

'I've got to go,' Ellie returned politely. Then she spun round on her heels and bolted for the office with mounting, simmering resentment.

So much for putting behind her the unfortunate business of boundary lines being crossed! So much for returning to the safety of their boss-secretary relationship and relegating that brief lapse of the day before to the past, never again to be revisited!

The slim envelope in her hand was now forcing her to prolong a situation she didn't want, and resentment had turned to fuming anger by the time she entered the converted warehouse that served as James's cutting-edge office.

If she'd had time, she would have been tempted to go

straight to the huge courtyard behind the red-brick building so that she could get her thoughts in order. There, with its rose garden and fountain and benches and abundance of trees and plants and shrubs, all cleverly laid out to provide a peaceful outdoor space for his staff in the middle of buzzy East London, she would have had the opportunity to calm down.

However, at a little after eight-thirty there was no time for calming down, and for the first time since she had joined the company she walked straight into James's office without bothering to knock and without bothering with her usual routine of getting rid of her bag and her mac and readying her computer for the day ahead.

'This is for you.' She slapped the envelope on his desk and then stood back with her arms folded.

In the middle of a phone call, James looked up, and Ellie could see for a few fleeting seconds that he just couldn't believe his eyes.

Where was his well-behaved, dutiful PA? The one who was 'mysterious' yet blatantly dull? She felt a kick of satisfaction as she glared at him narrowly, waiting as he took the envelope and gazed at it, eyebrows raised.

'Going to explain what's going on? Or do you want me to play a guessing game?' he asked, ending his call.

He pushed himself away from his desk and relaxed back to look at her. He'd dumped the envelope on the desk without opening it. Ellie had to take deep breaths, because all she wanted to do just at that moment was wipe the lazy, questioning look from his face.

Like the members of staff, he had no time for the formality of suits, but he had a series of meetings later, and for once was dressed the part. His shirt was crisp and white, although casually rolled to the elbows, and his tailored trousers were charcoal-grey and matched the linen jacket which had been chucked on the walnut unit stand-ing against the brick wall.

He looked incredibly sophisticated, incredibly expen-sive and breathtakingly sexy, but for once her heart didn't skip a beat.

'Guess who I bumped into outside?'

'Ah. So we're going to be going down the guessing game route… How many guesses am I allowed?'

'Naomi.'

He lowered his eyes for a fraction of a second and stilled. 'Ah… And I'm taking it…' he murmured, reach-ing for the envelope and twirling it absently between his fingers, 'That this is a missive from her?'

'She said she'd been waiting in the coffee shop oppo-site to catch me because she didn't want to hand-deliver it to you yourself. Look, I come here to work. I don't come here to get involved in any tiffs you have with your girl-friends.'

'Sit down.'

Ellie hesitated. She had more to say on the subject, but he was still her boss, and how much could she complain before he began drawing lines? He was notoriously lib-eral and open-minded with the people who worked with him. He preferred to get results through nurture rather than wielding a whip. A happy employee, he had told her once, was a productive employee, so he made sure his em-ployees were happy.

But she had seen him with difficult clients and way-ward suppliers. She had seen the cold face of a guy who sat at the top of the pile. There was very much a steel hand within the velvet glove, and there was no way she intended to antagonise him by giving him an earful about what she thought of being dragged into his private dramas.

If he didn't want dramatics, she could have told him,

then he should try and have a straightforward love life. She clamped down hard on the thoughts running wild in her head and did as told.

'I apologise.' He looked at her and for once that easy, watchful charm was missing. 'You're right. You come here to work and everything else is irrelevant. You don't have to tell me that, Ellie. I've had three years to get the message loud and clear. Yesterday, you found yourself forced to share some of your opinions with me, and I expect you're desperate to get the balance back to normal. Am I right?'

Ellie blushed and tore her eyes away from his remarkable face. 'I don't want to be a go-between between you and your girlfriend,' she prevaricated.

'*Ex*-girlfriend. Even if she doesn't want to believe that at the moment, and even though I'm being bombarded with text messages begging for a second chance. You don't need to know any of this because you're absolutely right—being a go-between definitely isn't part of your job description. Believe it or not, the last thing I want is for you or anyone else to get accidentally involved in my private life.'

The blue eyes resting on her were thoughtful and serious. 'The world sees beautiful women on my arm...' He shrugged and smiled wryly. 'The world doesn't get to see what happens between those beautiful women and me. Which is why Naomi's behaviour here yesterday left a sour taste in my mouth. Which is why I am below zero interested to read whatever is in that envelope.'

Ellie hesitated, lured in by the pensive seriousness in his voice, and the feeling that something was being *shared* between them. Which, of course, was an illusion and yet... What he had just said so perfectly dovetailed with what she thought, that she wanted him to expand on it.

'If you don't read it and respond,' she ventured, 'then

you might find that she keeps trying to get in touch until you do.'

'And naturally you don't want to be accosted for a second time by a persistent ex.'

'It's not about that. It's just that…problems don't go away because you want them to.' She flushed. 'At least, that's what I think.' If only they did. If only the problems with her mother had conveniently vanished when she'd been a teenager, leaving her to enjoy her youth without the complications of dealing with situations for which she had been ill-equipped. She felt a shocking urge to cry, and blinked rapidly and with some embarrassment, hoping that he wouldn't notice her crazy reaction.

'Perhaps,' she picked up crisply, 'You'd like me to return when you've dealt with…whatever you need to deal with in reply to…er…whatever is in that envelope?'

'Stay where you are. There's something I need to discuss with you.' He slit open the envelope, scanned the contents and then stuck it to one side. 'I can deal with this later. Now. Tell me what your plans are for the next week or so…'

'My plans?' Ellie looked at him, bewildered.

'I was due to head to Barbados to initiate talks with that start-up company in the expectation of closing the deal a bit further down the line, post a certain wedding ceremony in Hawaii…'

'Yes.' Ellie had no idea where this was leading but she would find out in due course. At least they were no longer skating on the thin ice of personal conversation, although she was still toying with what the contents of that envelope might be.

She had seen the other woman's face, had seen the stark desperation there. It didn't take a genius to figure out that whatever had prompted her outburst of the day before had now given way to horror that she might have blown her relationship with London's most eligible bachelor. That said, bombardment by text message was definitely not the way to go to get a point across. Not to someone like James Stowe.

Poor Naomi. Did she think that James Stowe was the kind of guy to do U-turns? Ellie could have warned her not to hold out hopes for any such thing, but *of course* she would never have done that, because none of this was her business.

Cool reason and the sheer habit of keeping herself to herself fought in vain against stupidly inappropriate curiosity. Was there any side to him that was vulnerable? Could any woman get behind that easy charm to find someone deeper?

She tilted her head to one side and did her best to look engaged with what he was saying, but questions were running around in her head, as though released from a Pandora's box. He was saying something about the start-up company in Barbados and she wondered whether she should be flicking open her tablet at this point to take notes.

'Sorry,' she finally interrupted him. 'Could you please repeat what you just said?'

'Have you been listening to a word I've been saying, Ellie? Or did you temporarily lose touch with Ground Control?'

'Of course I've been listening!'

'Then which bit would you like me to repeat?' He raked his fingers through his hair and flicked her an impatient glance that was tinged with just a shade of disbelief, because not paying attention was something he could never usually accuse her of.

'Forget it. I'll start from the beginning. My plan was to go to Barbados, stay a few days—just long enough to begin the takeover process with the guys over there from Sailstart—and then head over to Hawaii for the wedding at the end of the month. Naomi was going to be in tow, enjoying the hotel she chose, but getting any serious work done with a girlfriend there would have been impossible. So, my plan was to return later in the month for the serious stuff to begin. Following me so far?'

'Please don't be condescending,' Ellie said politely, and he grinned.

'I am very much liking this new version of Eleanor Thompson,' he murmured. 'Can we have a bit more of her?'

His eyes roved over her in leisurely appraisal and Ellie reddened.

Where was the sensible girl with the sensible clothes and the sensible shoes? Why the heck had she been replaced by this outspoken lookalike with rebellious thoughts, a sharp tongue and a devil-may-care attitude that could only land her in trouble?

'But,' he continued briskly, 'getting to the point, I've had a long chat with the boys over there. Did a bit of groundwork on Zoom and everything has been pushed forward. I aim to complete this deal when I'm there, and as you know that will be a critical period, so looks like my trip over there is going to go ahead after all. It'll probably be longer than the original handful of days. The whole circus of lawyers and accountants are going to have to get involved, so it's going to be a couple of weeks rather than a couple of days.'

He frowned. 'No, not a couple of weeks. Scratch that. I need a bit of time to get prepared for Max's big day. Ten days max out there. I'll kill the island-hopping tourist jaunt, so extending the trip shouldn't be a problem.'

'Great.' Ellie plastered a smile on her face. 'I'll make

all the arrangements. Shall I keep the booking at the hotel in Barbados? Or would you like me to change it for somewhere else, now that Naomi won't be going with you?' She paused and wondered whether she had got ahead of herself with that assumption. Did she know the faintest thing about men and U-turns when it came to sex? Lust? She'd read enough articles to know that men were capable of doing extraordinarily idiotic things when they started thinking with the wrong part of their bodies.

Discomfort overwhelmed her as her mind hived off at a tangent and, just for a moment, she had a very graphic image of her boss naked, muscular and aroused.

She felt faint. Her body tingled and she was horrified at the dampness that slowly seeped between her thighs. Her breasts were suddenly hyper-sensitive, wanting to be touched.

'Unless,' she croaked, 'you've changed your mind, in which case…er… At any rate, maybe you could let me know. I wouldn't want to presume anything…'

'You're glowing like a beacon,' he pointed out unhelpfully, and Ellie wanted the ground to open up and swallow her whole. She would be very happy to be disgorged at some later point, after she'd got her act together.

'Am I?'

'Naomi won't be coming along,' he said. 'Although, from what I've glimpsed in that letter of hers, she would like nothing more than just that. I'll keep the room and the hotel, but you'll have to book a separate room as well.'

'A separate room?'

'And an additional flight.'

'Of course. I'll need the details of your companion.' Ellie's imagination leapt into instant overdrive. Another leggy blonde? she wondered. How fast could one man move? At supersonic speed, it would seem. Had Naomi's replacement been waiting in the wings all along? Surely not?

'And,' he countered thoughtfully, 'I really should find out whether your passport's up to date.'

'*My* passport?'

'You'll be coming with me.'

'To Barbados?'

'You'll have to make sure that everything's in place for Trish or Caroline to take over the handling of some of your work, although you should be able to keep on top of most of it remotely, and Higgins will fill in in my absence.'

'Why would I be coming to Barbados with you? I'm afraid that's not going to be possible.'

James frowned. '*Not possible* are two words that have no place in my organisation,' he said coolly. 'I run this ship on the assumption that everything is possible. And the reason you'll be coming with me is simple. I'll need my secretary there because, like I said, I've managed to pull things ahead. And no one else is going to do because you know how I work. Originally, like I *also* said, I hadn't planned on finalising anything on this trip. A few preliminary talks and the rest to be clinched at a later date— probably inviting them here for the sake of convenience. But, as things stand, that option isn't on the cards, so yes, you'll be coming out with me.'

'But…' Ellie breathed in deeply and thought two things at once. The first was that she couldn't imagine being with her boss in a tropical setting, even if work was on the agenda. No. Not at all. And the second thing to cross her mind was her mother, whom she planned to visit at the weekend because the depression seemed to be kicking in once again. After those heart scares, Ellie was determined to do everything in her power to keep her mother on an even keel, and that was to be the weekend's mission. Nice walks, pep talks, home-cooked food.

She took a deep breath and ploughed on. 'I do understand that you might want someone there to keep minutes and do all the usual stuff, but I'm really sorry. I can't take that much time out to go away.'

'Why not?' He leaned forward. 'Boyfriend situation? Sorry, but he'll have to take a back seat for a few days.'

'Won't Caroline do?'

'There's no debate around this, Ellie. Unless you have a water-tight reason for not coming, then I'll expect you to do what you're paid to do.'

And there it was, she thought, the unyielding steel that had got him where he was now. When it came to the crunch, he was hard line, and woe betide if she decided to fight him on this. Aside from which, who in her right mind would fight to avoid an all-expenses luxury trip to sunny climes, when there would be no down side at all, because she would be doing the job she enjoyed doing?

She would have to see her mum, though, and she gritted her teeth and did her utmost to not flinch at standing her ground.

'Of course. But I will need to…have a couple of days off before I go. I'm assuming the timelines will be the same as they were? I mean, leaving on the same day?'

'Why do you need a couple of days off?' He tilted his head to one side and looked at her with a frown. She could see the cogs in his brain whirring, piecing her together, filling out the bits he had started filling out when she'd opened up to him yesterday.

It was annoying, but she was resigned to the fact that it was inevitable, and he would soon get bored with the game. He had a lively mind, so it wasn't surprising that he was happy to push at a door that had opened a bit.

And did it matter? She'd assumed that their working relationship would suffer if those lines between them weren't drawn in cement, but really, would it?

They would rub along—and, yes, he might know a bit more about her—but there was nothing to fear in that.

She shoved aside those uneasy responses she felt when he was around...when he got too close to her...when those sharp blue eyes rested on her for a second longer than they should...

They were where they were. She would just have to deal with it. She hadn't committed a crime in being a little less of a closed book.

'Shopping, I take it?'

Lost in her thoughts, Ellie looked at him in puzzlement for a few seconds.

'Clothes,' he elaborated. 'You'll need one or two reasonably dressy things to wear in hot weather. I'll be wining and dining my soon-to-be clients in style, so you'll have to dress the part. Shop to your heart's content and put it on expenses.'

'I wasn't going to take a couple of days off to go *shopping*,' Ellie retorted vigorously, without giving it much thought, and he burst out laughing.

'No need to sound so affronted. It was a simple assumption.'

'I...'

'I'm sure Romeo won't mind letting you go for a few days. In this day and age, please don't tell me that you have to take time off so that you can stock up the freezer for him.'

Ellie stared at him with such an appalled expression that he burst out laughing again.

'I would *never* be one of those women who felt they had to *stock up the freezer* for some guy because he was too helpless to look after himself for a few days!'

'Didn't think so. All men should know how to look after themselves.'

'And do *you* do much cooking when it comes to looking after yourself?' she heard herself ask, sweetly sarcastic.

'Don't have to,' he responded without batting an eye. 'I have a top chef on speed dial. Whatever he rustles up will always be so much better than any of my attempts. Why do you need time off, in that case? We really won't be away for very long. If you're worried about your place, I can always get someone to swing by every day and make sure no pipes have burst and the milk bottles aren't collecting outside…'

Ellie sighed. 'It's not that.' Was he going to let it go? Not a chance. Letting things go wasn't in his nature. 'It's just that I was planning on going to see my mother at the weekend.'

She saw the confusion on his face and understood where it was coming from. She was a woman in her twenties, surely the business of a family visit wouldn't be sufficient for her to dig in her heels at taking a few days to work abroad? A visit to a mother wasn't in the same league as a visit to hospital to see someone on their last legs, was it?

'She lives in Dorset. I… She's on her own, you see, ever since my father… Ever since Dad died.'

'I'm sorry to hear that, Ellie. You should have said something.' He frowned. 'I don't recall you taking time off for a funeral.'

'My dad died before I joined the company. It's a long story but what it comes down to is that my mother didn't deal with the death very well. In fact, she went to pieces.

I've had to…well… I've had to look after her to some extent because she's…had a few problems.'

'What sort of problems?'

'This is very boring for you.' She shot him a self-deprecating smile and he shook his head.

'I don't want to ever hear you say anything like that again. Talk to me. What sort of problems?'

This is what he did, Ellie thought. It was all part of his huge personal magnetism. His charm wasn't just superficial, it was bone-deep, because it was rooted in genuine interest. When he asked a question and looked you in the eye, he sincerely wanted to hear the answer.

'She couldn't cope.' Ellie tried to inject some crispness into her voice but there was a tell-tale wobble there that she couldn't control. 'She started drinking and the drinking got a little out of hand. It took some time for that to be ironed out, and I'm happy that she's no longer dependent on alcohol, but she's very much prone to depression. She felt like my dad's death took away her reason to live. Since he died, she's had a couple of minor strokes, enough for me to worry about what might happen if another occurred. Right now, she seems to be down again. I could hear it in her voice when I spoke to her at the weekend.

'So there. That's the story. I'd planned on visiting so that I could check the situation for myself—cheer her up, maybe arrange for her to come to London.' She laughed, but it sounded more like a croak, and she ended up clearing her throat.

'Don't you have any other family members who could help you, Ellie?'

'I'm an only child. My parents were only children. There's just me.' She looked down quickly so that he couldn't detect the glimmer of tears in her eyes.

'You must have been…just a kid when your father died.'

'I was sixteen. Old enough to look after Mum.'

'Like I said. Just a kid.'

James looked at her, at the defensive set of her mouth. She was trying so hard to be brave and he imagined she'd spent all those years trying hard to be brave. He knew what it felt like to lose a parent when you were still a teenager. He'd lost both of his. Sometimes in the dead of night thoughts of what that had felt like would surface like eels crawling out of hiding places...dark thoughts about the loss and confusion he had felt all those many years ago.

The truth was that, while Max had taken on the role of caretaker, and while his sister had been swamped with attention from everyone, he had floundered. There had been no one there for him. Not really. No one who could understand the void left. So he had filled the void with friends, activity and a dazzling social life. He had used the tactics of distraction to build a wall around his loss and to seal himself off from dealing with the hurt and sense of helplessness.

James rarely dwelled on a past he couldn't change, but thoughts came at him from nowhere. He remembered that feeling of exclusion, of standing on the outside looking in. He'd been about to go to university, and of course he had, but he had been vulnerable—neither wrapped up in protective cotton wool, as his younger sister Izzy had been, nor fuelled with the necessity to hold things together, which had been his older brother Max's role.

From out of the blue, like a clap of thunder on a cloudless day, he remembered how he had fallen for a ridiculously glamorous older woman who had worked at an art gallery in the centre of Cambridge. She had been bowled over by his accent, by the designer clothes and the fast car—possessions he had always taken for granted. He had been the youthful idiot mistakenly seeking to fill that aching, empty space with the love of a good woman. When he'd told her that he had no idea if he would be able to afford his next meal now that his parents were gone, she'd begun backing away.

He'd been joking, even though he really hadn't known the state of the family finances, only that Max had intimated they weren't as healthy as they should have been. She'd taken him seriously, and even now he wasn't sure just how shocked he'd really been when he'd caught her in bed with his much richer friend. Short, bespectacled, plump Rupert had been over the moon with his conquest.

James had learnt lessons then that had stayed with him for ever. He was very happy to shower money on the women he dated but his heart was something he had no intention of ever giving away. He had rashly given it away once and he wasn't going to make that mistake again. Never again would he allow himself to get emotionally wrapped up with any woman to the extent that he could end up being hurt. No way. *Build your walls*, he had concluded, *and make sure they're impregnable.*

Impatient with his trip down an unpleasant memory lane, he shook his head and focused.

'A lot of responsibility for you at that age,' he mused quietly. 'Especially if you had no one to share the burden with you.'

'I coped.'

'Coping isn't exactly a great way to wile away your teenage years.'

'Some of us don't get given a choice.'

'No truer word has ever been spoken. Yes, of course you can have a couple of days to visit your mother.' He paused and their eyes met. 'If there's anything I can do, I want you to promise me that you'll let me know.'

'Sure.' She stood up and looked at him. 'I'll start sorting out the details now, if you don't mind, and I'll make sure that there's good cover for me when I'm out of the country.'

'Of course you will.'

Letting his guard slip was all well and good in an office in Shoreditch, but no way was it going to happen on a tropical island in the Caribbean…

CHAPTER THREE

ELLIE WAS HIGHLY efficient when it came to James's travel arrangements. She'd had plenty of practice, given his frenetic, country-hopping schedule, and she could book a five-star hotel, in just the right place for whatever meetings he had lined up, with her eyes closed. She knew the kind of thing he wanted wherever he happened to stay. A luxury penthouse, because he liked a lot of space, and nothing near the ground floor because he enjoyed the peace of looking down on a city at night. And wherever in the world he happened to be, he had to have instant access to the double espressos he lived on when he was working flat out.

She didn't know *how* she knew that. She just did. Which meant he must have told her at some point, or perhaps it was just information that had filtered through by osmosis after so long working together.

Barbados was an anomaly, being a business trip as well as a mini-holiday, so the requirements had been rather different. Her job had been made easier because Naomi had chosen the hotel, simply leaving Ellie with the task of securing just the right suite of rooms for them in the eye-wateringly expensive boutique five-star.

Her passport hadn't left the top drawer in years, so looking at images of sand and sea had been a vicarious taste of a paradise she'd thought she'd never get to see with her own eyes.

But now there was no Naomi on the scene. Instead, *she* would be the one staying at the fancy hotel in the tropical paradise, and it felt unnatural to be booking a room for herself in a hotel his ex-girlfriend had picked out. Her needs were infinitesimally less complex than his but that made no difference because the price of even the cheapest room was astronomical. When the booking had been confirmed, she'd actually closed her eyes, breathed in deeply and felt giddy at the thought of staying at a luxury hotel in Barbados.

She'd thought that a couple of days with her mother would bring her back down to earth with a healthy reality check. In fact, she'd expected Angie Thompson to be aghast at the thought of her going away when she was grappling with depression and might have wanted her to be around. But, to Ellie's astonishment, her mother had perked up at the news that her daughter would be heading off to paradise.

'It'll do you good to get some time away,' she'd sighed, before wistfully recalling happy days when she and Robert had had fun saving their pennies and travelling as much as they could. 'You've done nothing but look after me for years. You're a good girl, Ellie, but you need to spread your wings and enjoy yourself, and a little break would do you a power of good. Believe me, I know how much you've sacrificed for me and I'm really happy you're going to have some time out. Don't worry about me. I'll be fine.'

Bewildered, Ellie had wondered whether her mother had been listening to a word she'd said and, if she had, whether something had been lost in translation.

'It's going to be about *work*, Mum,' she'd said firmly.

'But in such a glorious place. Your dad and I always

wanted to go to that part of the world. He'll be smiling down right now to see you getting there...'

'Getting there *to work*. You have *no idea* what a hard taskmaster James is. My nose will be pressed to the grindstone every minute I'm there.'

Could it be that her mother no longer needed her quite like she used to? For a moment Ellie had felt a little disoriented...had wondered whether looking after her mum had become part of her comfort zone. And were that to be ripped away...well, how would she deal with it? She would have to engage emotionally with the outside world for the first time since her father's death. It had felt scary, and a thought best put on ice for the moment.

'How are you going to be able to work when the sun's shining outside and there's a beach a stone's throw away?'

It was a very good question, but Ellie knew better than to give it too much mental air-time. Instead, with all the arrangements in place, she had ducked any uncomfortable speculation and convinced herself that there was no reason why anything should be different simply because of a change of scenery. She'd worked for James every summer for the last three years, hadn't she, when the sun had been shining down? Since when had a little hot weather got in the way of doing a job?

She wasn't going to be marooned with him on a desert island, was she? The hotel would be full of tourists milling about, and when they weren't working she would be able to happily lose herself in that throng, or escape to her room, where she would be able to catch up on her reading. She had a backlog of books to get through. There was also a state-of-the-art gym at the hotel, and she intended to make full use of the lavish facilities.

She suspected that, with work out of the way, she would be left to her own devices while her charming and determined boss wined and dined the young businessmen he intended to add to his stable. Pursuit, when it came to getting what he wanted, was an art form to him. He had perfected it, and he would happily leave her behind once the nitty-gritty had been dealt with. She was his PA, after all, not Naomi, whom he had probably banked on helping him with the client entertaining. Tall, blonde and stunning would have been a definite asset.

Still, her stomach was clenched with nerves as she paused outside the airport terminal for a few seconds to gather herself. She'd seen precious little of James over the past few days, having returned from visiting her mother. On the one hand, that was good, because it put distance between her and the uneasy inroads he had made into her private life, leaving her unsettled and desperate to re-establish the status quo. On the other hand, it was less good, because now her nerves were racing through her like quicksilver as she briskly made her way to the first-class desk where they had arranged to meet.

For all her inner pep talks, Ellie knew that her forbidden attraction was a dangerous weakness. She needed the physical strictures of their working office environment to protect her from…herself and her foolish imagination. It was one thing to begin nurturing thoughts of cutting the apron strings that attached her to her maybe no longer quite so dependent parent, but another to engage emotionally with a guy and finding her feet in a world that had passed her by. It was quite another again to nurture any thoughts about a guy who was utterly inappropriate.

Even from a distance, James Stowe effortlessly stood out. So impossibly good-looking but, more than that, so much in control of his audience. Right now, this consisted of several young, attractive women behind the check-in counter and a pilot, all of whom appeared to be absorbed in whatever he was saying. Lounging against the counter, legs lightly crossed at the ankles, hands shoved into the pockets of his pale, linen trousers, James was talking, half smiling, his head inclined, which gave the appearance of rapt attention.

Which didn't mean that he failed to notice her slow approach, because she could see him straighten fractionally, eyes narrowing as he took in her outfit, which, now that she was in the airport and surrounded by the buzz of excited holiday-goers, felt stiffly uncomfortable.

'What are you wearing?' was the first thing he asked as they headed towards the first-class lounge, having checked in.

'My usual,' Ellie countered. This was the first time she'd been to an airport in for ever, and she had never stepped foot into a first-class lounge before.

She did her best to stop her jaw from dropping to the ground at a world fashioned exclusively for the rich and famous. Uniformed staff were there to await their every command. Would they like something light to eat in the restaurant? Perhaps a late breakfast before taking off? Champagne? Cocktails? They were shown to a buffet sideboard where every type of pastry was there for the choosing. Businessmen sat frowning in front of their computers and, here and there, partners and kids lounged around with plates of half-eaten delicacies in front of them.

James barely seemed to notice their surroundings. 'Ellie, we're going to a hot and humid island. You might find your *usual* a little restricting when we get there.'

'I'll be fine.'

'Breakfast?'

'I grabbed a coffee before I left home…' She glanced at him to find him gazing back at her with amusement. 'But maybe a pastry would be nice. What would you like?'

How did it work here? she wondered, glancing around. Did she summon a waiter across? Head to the breakfast station herself and hope the espresso machine wasn't as terrifying to operate as it looked from where she was? Or, did she do as she was doing now and stare back at him in a welter of indecision, wondering where her work hat had gone?

'I'd like to find somewhere to sit.' He looked around and then nodded towards the window. 'And,' he continued, leading the way, 'you don't have to fetch and carry for me, Ellie. Yes, you're here in a professional capacity, but I'd like you to relax and not stand to attention because you feel you have to.'

'Of course.'

James frowned but resisted the urge to carry the conversation further.

Why on earth was she wearing a knee-length navy-blue skirt and a white top that was destined to crease within five seconds of take off? And were those *tights*?

Of course, he knew exactly what was going on. The second he had seen her he had known *exactly* what was going on. With one hand guiding a wayward wheelie suitcase, the other struggling with her pull-along, and wearing her neat navy and white work-ready ensemble, she looked very similar to the three women behind the counter who had been flirting with him.

Except she wasn't, was she? She wasn't just smart. She wasn't just his valued secretary who was quick enough to actually follow what he was saying and sometimes even pre-empt him. No, she was much *more* than that, as he had discovered a few days earlier.

And *that* was what she was desperately trying to extinguish by showing up at the airport in her impossibly inappropriate gear. She wanted to remind him that his duty was to forget that little interlude when she had shed her starchy veneer and, possibly for the first time ever, had actually *communicated* with him with heart-felt sincerity.

Surely, she should know that a healthy dose of curiosity had got him where he was now? If he hadn't been curious enough to explore outside of the confines of his family dynasty then he would never have discovered the gold mines that lay in the fascinating world of artificial intelligence and all things of a techy nature. He had taught himself coding as a hobby at university and, by the time he'd emerged with his first class degree in Engineering from Cambridge, he'd been equipped not only to help his brother handle the juggernaut of the company he had brought back from the brink, but to develop his own multi-million-pound empire—just as Max had branched out to dabble in the world of boutique hotels and the infrastructure that went with it.

He was curious now, and it had briefly occurred to him, when he had watched her walking towards him pulling those cases, her body language advertising in no uncertain terms the fact that she wasn't here of her own choosing, that he had been curious about her for a while.

Curious in a way he had never really been curious about the many beautiful women he had dated over the years. What was *that* about? She'd walked towards him in the terminal and something inside him had recognised a potent attractiveness that was utterly unembellished and desperate to remain hidden. The graceful sway of her body had momentarily thrown him. Was that the first time? he wondered. Or had that awareness always been there, lurking just beneath the surface?

As fast as that thought entered his head, he banished it back to the hinterland. Had that one and only disastrous relationship, into which he had idiotically flung himself in the wake of his parents' death, severed something in him?

Had that vital curiosity that propelled relationships been killed after his one youthful misadventure?

Yes, he concluded, and a very good thing too. Like Max, he had learned from a young age that emotional investment was destructive, that it left room for nothing else. He'd had a double dose of pain. Losing his parents and making the wrong choice in a woman a million years ago. The first had been infinitely worse than the second, but both had taught him that to turn away from the unrewarding labyrinth of emotional investment was to be master of your own universe. In his eyes, never losing control was a source of strength that enabled him to rise above the haphazard business of getting wrapped up in emotions.

He decided that he was curious about Ellie because he wasn't involved with her on any level other than the purely professional, and that could only be a good thing. As far as he was concerned, knowing the people who worked for him bred loyalty. He needed loyalty from Ellie because he couldn't envisage such a smooth working relationship with anyone else.

'How is your mother doing?' He nodded in the direction of one of the circulating airport employees and within five minutes coffee had been brought to them, along with an array of pastries. His keen eyes spotted her automatically begin to reach for her iPad and he decided to forestall any work talk, at least until they boarded the plane. He reached for the dainty cup of coffee in front of him and sat back and sipped, looking at her over the rim of his cup.

'I'm assuming that, since you're sitting next to me, there was no cause for concern?'

'She…she seemed fine. Better than I thought I'd find her.'

'What were you expecting to find?' He lowered his eyes, shielding his expression, then once again looked at her, this time thoughtfully. 'I'm not prying, Ellie. I'm conversing. Relax.'

She was as stiff as a board. He watched the slow blush, a delicate tinge of colour staining her cheeks. Yes, he thought, she was startlingly pretty. Where did that sex appeal come from? It was unexpected in someone so demure. Except, he mused, *demure* she certainly wasn't once you scratched the surface.

His eyes drifted lazily over her full, perfectly shaped mouth, over the short, straight nose, the sprinkling of freckles which seemed curiously delicate for someone with dark hair. He shifted, suddenly edgy, and glanced away. But he couldn't stop himself from picking up where he had left off with his visual exploration. Her hair was neat and shiny and straight, and he would bet his house that it smelled of flowers. Aside from what looked like some lip gloss, war paint was notably absent. There was a cool intelligence in her eyes that he thought could be damned sexy...

He thought about what she had told him about herself, those little snippets of information, and his curiosity ratcheted up a few notches.

Quite frankly, it was invigorating.

What was wrong in having a little enjoyment? It was called passing the time of day. It wasn't going anywhere. There wouldn't be the usual chase followed by the inevitable boredom.

Within that framework, he felt a surge of intense freedom. He should have been sitting here with Naomi. In fact, he was relieved that he wasn't. He was especially relieved to be leaving the country, because she had continued to text him despite his lack of response, and he had an uncomfortable feeling that she might just try and confront him in an effort to 'patch this silly nonsense up', as she had intimated in one of her messages. The last thing he needed was to be accosted from behind by an ex who wasn't interested in reading the signposts.

'Were you worried that your mother might not want to carry on living?'

'No!' Ellie was shocked at the suggestion, although it mirrored the fear she had felt all those years ago when her mother had sought refuge in the bottle. She'd never verbalised it and no one else had either. It had been a forbidding, frightening thought that had eaten away at her until she had come to realise that her mother would not go down that road.

'I'm sorry,' he said, softly. 'I didn't mean to upset you. When my parents were killed,' he found himself telling her, 'there was some lightweight counselling on offer, largely targeted at my sister, who was much younger. They insisted on a few sessions with me and that was the question they laboured the most.'

'I can't imagine you lying on a couch talking to a counsellor.' Ellie smiled.

'There was no couch in evidence. I think movies have helped create that myth…' He liked the way she smiled—a shy, catch me if you can type of smile. He'd planned on using his time in the first-class lounge to work. It was what he always did. But this beat work hands down. Her fingers stopped instinctively straying to the sanctuary of her tablet, which was in the computer case she had taken out of her pull-along. It sat between them on the little circular table, next to the pastries and their cups, an officious reminder that chit chat shouldn't be happening.

'I went to one session,' he drawled, 'to encourage Izzy to follow suit. But then I headed off to university, where I found far more pleasurable ways of dealing with the situation. Wine, women and song can prove excellent home remedies.' The platitude rolled easily from his tongue as he continued to appreciate an atmosphere that was strangely… *compelling.*

Brought back down to earth by that provocative statement, Ellie's eyes skittered towards the tablet again, and James wasn't surprised when she reached for it, straightened, tucked her hair behind her ears and cleared her throat in a telling signal that time was being called on all informal conversation.

So be it. For the time being.

He was scarcely aware of the drift of his eyes over the crisp, impractical shirt that was tucked into the crisp, impractical skirt. Both were so determined to conceal what lay underneath, but neither could quite hide the jut of her breasts or the slenderness of her waist.

He shifted again, restless, and suddenly needing to move.

'Work.' He slapped his thighs and stood up, abruptly bringing all straying thoughts back to heel. 'Let's work on the Ronson deal. It's picking up pace and maybe we can close on it before the flight gets called…'

He'd been bang on the money about the clothes…

The cool air-conditioning on the plane had insulated her from the reality of the scorching heat that assailed her eight hours later, when the plane touched down at Grantley Adams Airport.

The first-class passengers were off the plane first, and as soon as the heavy door was opened the heat poured in like treacle. She immediately began to perspire.

'Let me,' James murmured, lifting down her pull-along from the overhead locker. 'How did you find the flight?'

'Very relaxing,' Ellie said truthfully, largely because, after half an hour of work-related conversation, James had devoted himself to his backlog of emails and due diligence reports. And because their seats were so spacious, separated by a partition, which he had conveniently chosen to shut so that he could focus exclusively on what he was doing.

She had had the entire flight to herself and she had relished her moment in this unfamiliar world of the uber-rich and famous. It was a world of unashamed luxury where a click of a finger brought you anything you wanted, from champagne to chocolate bars. Her seat was so vast that she'd been able to read her book with her legs tucked underneath her, and the press of a button had turned it into a comfortable bed.

This was how the half a percent lived and this was how James Stowe had always lived. He'd been born into money and, whilst there might have been a brief hiccup within that gilded existence, he had spent his life protected against the harsh realities that most people faced on a daily basis. Even the leggy supermodels he dated, household names who graced the covers of so many magazines, were cosseted and moneyed, thanks to their profession.

She thought of Naomi, with her casual acceptance that attention from everyone around her was her given right. No wonder she had taken it badly when she and James had broken up!

His background couldn't have been more different from Ellie's, and she thought that that might be why she found him so mesmerising...why something in her was stubbornly drawn to him even though she valiantly fought it. He was a shiny bauble. Who could blame her if she was occasionally dazzled by him?

'Slept much?' he enquired, and Ellie looked at him from under lowered lashes. He looked bright-eyed and bushy-tailed and raring to go.

'Not at all. Gosh, it's hot.' This was a different world.

The hot sun beat down over a flawless blue sky. Even the airport staff scurrying around outside seemed to move at a slower pace, taking their time.

'Tights might not have been such a good idea.'

Ellie flushed. Of course he was right, but she had been so keen to return to the safety of being his PA, and re-establishing her hands-off approach, that she just hadn't stopped to think. Yes, she'd known that it was going to be hot, but she hadn't expected this level of stultifying heat.

'I've never been to this part of the world before.'

'I've only been a handful of times. It's worth exploring, so don't think that you've got to bury yourself behind your computer and work twenty-four-seven. A personal driver will be available at all times.'

Ellie interpreted that statement to mean that she would be able to explore on her own, and that went some way to reducing her levels of simmering anxiety.

They moved quickly through customs and were treated like visiting royalty. Once outside the terminal, they were ushered to a long, sleek car which was waiting, doors open, for their arrival.

Thrust into scenery that was nothing like any she'd seen before, Ellie forgot her nerves. She forgot that he was sitting right next to her. She even forgot that her clothes had now stuck to her like cling film. The blast of the tropics was so beautiful that she wanted to drink everything in on the short drive from the airport to the hotel—a scant half an hour, if that. Everything was so different. The foliage, the open fruit and vegetable stalls they passed, manned by one or two people sitting on tin chairs and fanning themselves, the blue, blue skies and the shimmer of heat over everything. She felt hot even inside the cool, air-conditioned car.

It was almost a shame when the car swerved into the

hotel courtyard. She'd seen pictures of the place on the website, and in the flesh it was exactly the same but with people milling around in brightly coloured clothes, stepping into waiting taxis, holding hands and having fun.

Her choice of clothing, worn to remind her that this was *not* a holiday, worn to remind him that this was a *business trip*, felt ridiculous now. It felt prickly and constricting, and for a few wild seconds she felt so out of her depth that she had to stifle a gasp.

She could smell the ocean as she stepped through the archway into the candy-pink hotel, with its bank of coconut trees fanning out over neatly manicured grounds at the front.

'What would you like me to do for the rest of the day?' she asked, turning to him and managing not *quite* to focus on him as he led the way towards the marble reception desk.

'Relax. Go sit by the pool. If you're tired, you can order room service or you can join me in the restaurant. Your choice. At any rate, we meet the guys tomorrow morning.'

'Here?' The thought of room service filled her with delight. She was tired, and spending what remained of the day in her room would give her time to adjust to these new surroundings. It would also give her time to scrutinise her wardrobe and reflect on some of her ill-advised sartorial choices.

'Bridgetown.' He checked them in, then turned to her. 'I don't know about you, but I need a shower.'

'It's so hot,' she agreed.

'You won't be able to wear...' he nodded to her outfit and raised his eyebrows '...any of your suits while we're over here.'

'I... I hadn't expected this amount of humidity. Of course, I'll make sure to dress appropriately.'

'Good, because tomorrow we'll be on a Catamaran for the day.'

'A Catamaran?'

'A twin-hulled sailing boat. My idea. We're dealing with three young guys who live on an island. Seemed a good idea to have the first business meeting on a boat. Besides, I wanted to see the spec.'

'The spec?' Ellie hadn't had to think too hard about the actual venue for the meetings they would be having with the young businessmen. She'd assumed the usual. A conference room in the hotel…a restaurant…maybe one of their houses for an informal dinner. And all with the usual array of lawyers on the side, quills at the ready.

She'd bought an outfit earmarked for each of those scenarios, and a couple of more casual items for exploring the island on her own.

'You remember the super-yacht? We now have it moored in Monaco,' James drawled, not looking at her as he pinged the button to call the lift. 'It's insanely luxurious, but a super-yacht is a super-yacht at the end of the day. Where's the hands-on experience? It has its own speedboat on board if Max or I want to do something a little more adventurous, but at the end of the day it's largely a passive experience. I want to see what a Catamaran has to offer as a hands-on situation. A fleet of them might prove a good investment.'

The brushed steel doors of the lift purred open and they stepped inside. Ellie looked at him and burst out laughing, and he grinned, a slow, lazy smile that sent a bolt of raw awareness racing through her body with the ferocity of an electric shock.

'Can I hear the dulcet voice of reason about to make its appearance?' he purred, lounging against the mirrored panel and staring at her while the smile still played on his lips.

'Someone has to be reasonable on your behalf,' she said primly, but there was a responding smile in her voice and her lips were twitching.

'Why?'

'Because…' He could be so utterly charming that it was easy to have your breath taken away. She was barely aware of the door opening as she followed him out of the lift onto an airy wooden corridor with broad windows overlooking unimpeded views of the sea. 'Because it's crazy to come over here to get hold of a start-up and end up distracted by a fleet of Catamarans.'

'Have you ever known any of my deals to fail?'

'No, but…'

They'd reached her suite without her even realising and now he leant against the door and stared down at her.

'Max was the sensible one,' he murmured, and Ellie's eyes widened as the gap she was trying hard to establish between them started to crumble. 'He took on the responsibility for grabbing the reins and making sure the ship was steered into calm waters. I will be grateful for ever that he allowed me the opportunity to live a little, even if I *have* ended up as part of the sprawling Stowe dynasty.'

He fished a key card out of his pocket, unlocked the door and pushed it open while Ellie stared at him and struggled to come up with a suitable reply to what he had just said.

A sharing of confidences? Or just a passing remark about something that he didn't consider particularly newsworthy? How fragile was the working relationship between them if it could drift off course with a few random, non-work-related remarks?

But, of course, *she* was the one who was obsessed with maintaining distance between them. *She* was the one who was stupidly affected by him because her body remained at odds with her head. She was smart enough to know that nothing in her life had prepared her for a guy like James Stowe. She was certainly smart enough to know that there was a vast difference between being compatible on the work front and compatible on any other front.

'I'm guessing that you won't be joining me for dinner later?'

'I don't think that that's part of my job description while I'm here, is it?'

Ellie had meant to sound light-hearted. Instead she was embarrassed and dismayed at the ungracious, unnecessarily sarcastic tone of her voice.

His lips had thinned and his eyes were suddenly cool. 'You're quite right. It's not.'

'I didn't mean to… What I'm trying to say is that…'

'I can read the writing on the wall as good as the next person,' he said, stepping back so that she felt the sudden drop in temperature between them like a physical barrier. 'I won't force you to socialise out of hours, although naturally, if it's by way of entertaining business contacts, then I will expect you to oblige.'

'Yes, I wouldn't dream…'

'Of course, you'll be paid overtime. I wouldn't want you to think that I'm taking advantage of you because this is not the usual working environment.'

Blushing furiously, Ellie stared down at her feet for a few seconds. There was no point launching into yet another stumbling apology. Where was her much-prized professionalism? She hated the feeling of losing control.

She breathed in deeply, and when she looked at him her grey eyes were clear and calm and she was proud that she had managed to salvage the situation with some dignity.

'Of course. And you didn't allow me to finish. I have no problem entertaining business contacts. I simply meant that this is a first for me, being in a place like this, and I would very much enjoy getting to see a bit of the island in my free time. If I didn't phrase that properly, then I apologise.'

'Now you're beginning to sound as though you're reading from a script. I almost prefer the sniping approach. So, you want time to yourself while you're out here? Not a big deal.' He shrugged, which made her feel foolish for over-reacting to a simple dinner invitation.

'To explore.'

'Naturally. I didn't imagine you'd want nights out to go clubbing.'

Ellie had no intention being drawn into rash self-defence at that provocative generalisation, but holding her tongue was harder than she thought, and she fought to bite back the sharp retort rising inside her.

'What time are things due to kick off tomorrow?'

'Eleven sharp in the conference room on the first floor. We need to brainstorm before we meet the guys at one. Bring your tablet. There's a lot we need to get through before we meet them. They're young and, if there's sailing involved, we'll need to make sure we start laying some foundations down before their attention is distracted.'

'Of course.' Ellie thought that this was more like it. Brainstorming with her tablet and laying down foundations in a workmanlike fashion.

She was smiling, back to her usual unflappable self, as he spun round on his heels to call over his shoulder, 'And don't forget, Ellie…ditch the formal gear. We're going to be sailing the high seas for a couple of hours. You might find a skirt, a blouse and some closed-up shoes get a little restrictive.'

He grinned, mock-saluted and sauntered off before she had time to answer.

CHAPTER FOUR

ELLIE APPROACHED THE hotel boutique and glanced around her. Why on earth did she feel furtive? She wasn't about to rob the store! She was a hotel guest in search of a couple of items of clothing. Couldn't be more straightforward!

But she *did* feel furtive. She felt as though she was sneaking around because she knew what James would do if he spotted her slipping into one of the hotel shops in search of some more appropriate summer stuff. He would laugh, and then he would tilt that handsome head to one side, and he wouldn't have to say anything, because *I told you so* would be emblazoned on his face.

Truth was, he'd been right. In her haste and determination to erase the unfortunate lapses of the past few days, by approaching this trip as nothing but a working arrangement with just a change of scenery to contend with, she had foolishly packed all the wrong stuff. She had thought *office* and had gone for summer suits. She had thought *meetings* and had opted for her neat canvas pumps. She had banked on minimum leisure time with her boss and had stuffed in a couple of pairs of shorts and tee shirts.

In the cool darkness of her palatial bedroom last night, with a view of dark ocean through her window and the sound of night-time tropical insects when she opened the window to breathe in the warm, salty air, she had mentally faced up to her paltry choices. So here she was, at ten in the morning, hovering outside an overpriced boutique where she would now be forced to part with hard-earned cash to buy at least a couple of things that would work for a sailing trip on board a luxury Catamaran and probably a fancy dinner out somewhere.

She cringed when she thought about the cut-off denim shorts buried in one of the hotel drawers and the culottes of two summers back, both of which were absolutely fine if they weren't going to be paraded in front of a guy who was accustomed to the women in his company looking as though they had just hopped off a catwalk. In fairness, many probably had.

Ellie knew that she shouldn't care less what he thought of the clothes she had brought with her. Did it matter? Really? She hadn't been employed because she knew the difference between a Chanel jacket and a Moschino coat. She was here because she was great at her job and he wanted her around to help organise the deal, which was something she was adept at doing without any input from him.

She was here because she was efficient, professional and understood the way he worked, and if she had to accompany him to one or two dinners then she would be required to fade into the background for the remainder of the time.

So what if she showed up in her usual navy summer skirt and another white blouse? So what if he found her bland skirts, and even blander shirts, a source of amusement?

Still, it mattered, and she was cross with herself for *how much* it mattered. Enough for her to have slunk into the boutique the very second it opened and emerge forty minutes later clutching two smart black and gold bags containing a selection of clothes she could ill afford.

She diligently stuck to her usual dress code when she met him twenty minutes later, but he was too focused on what needed to be done to pay her much attention, short of asking her, half an hour after they'd begun poring over the detail of profit and loss columns, whether she wanted anything to eat. Say the word and they would bring whatever she wanted to the conference room.

'I had a huge breakfast.' She politely declined.

'And you slept okay?'

'Brilliantly,' she responded honestly. 'I thought I'd be up, with the time difference, but once my head hit the pillow I was out like a light. The suite is amazing and the bed is fantastic.'

Uninvited, she imagined *him* lying in a king-sized bed very much like the one she had fallen asleep in, and from that diving point she plunged into her newly awakened imagination which was threatening to get completely out of control. She reined it in with effort, inwardly cursing the way three years' worth of self-control around him had been demolished in the space of a few days and a handful of unedited conversations.

She felt the pinch of her nipples against her sensible cotton bra, an unwelcome dampness between her legs, and suddenly the room, which had been perfectly fine moments before, was uncomfortably hot. Too hot. She wanted to fan herself.

Instead, she hastily poured herself a glass of cold water from the jug that had been brought in for them and drank thirstily.

Her eyes slid down to his khaki shorts, just the right length to draw her eye to his muscular thighs and strong calves. His expensive tan designer boat shoes looked well-worn, as did his faded blue and cream polo shirt, and yet as a package deal he looked a million dollars. Money, she thought, bought freedom. And that included freedom from caring what impression you made on other people. It was that very indifference that made him stand out. He wasn't obliged to do anything he didn't want to do and that was all too apparent in his body language. People bent over backwards to please him all the more because he didn't encourage it.

After the stormy break-up, Naomi had bent over backwards to reinstate herself. Ellie knew that because she had taken three calls in the space of a single day before they had left for Barbados, and had, thankfully, been legitimately able to tell the other woman that James wasn't around.

'Believe me,' she had said truthfully, 'If he was in the office, I would transfer you. Perhaps,' she'd added with a twinge of satisfaction, 'You could try his mobile. I'm sure he'd be very happy to take your call.'

She had no idea whether he had taken any calls from his ex, and if he had whether he'd been happy to take them, but that wasn't her concern.

'I have a few calls to put through before I meet our clients,' he said when they'd finally finished fine-combing through the details. 'Unexpected and essential, I'm afraid. Will you be okay making your way to the Catamaran on your own and entertaining the guys for a few minutes if I'm late?'

Ellie watched as he absently looked at something on his phone before helping himself to water, looking at her over the rim of his glass as he drank.

'Of course.' It would be a chance to take in a bit of her glorious surroundings without his stifling presence next to her, consuming all her attention. She smiled. 'Is there anything I should know about our contacts? Aside from the fact that they're young?'

'Nothing.' He grinned back at her and began heading for the door. 'Young computer whizz-kids…probably more brains and energy than common sense. I'm guessing your experience at my company will serve you in excellent stead when it comes to dealing with these three—and don't worry. I won't leave you in the lurch for too long.'

'I'm not worried.' She preceded him through the door and caught a whiff of his woody cologne.

'That's my girl,' he murmured, glancing down at her. 'I can always depend on you.'

Ellie wondered why that sounded ever so slightly patronising rather than complimentary. Dependability was what she was about, so why would she feel *criticised*? Since when had she become so sensitive to every passing remark? How tenable would her job be if she ended up brooding over everything he said and mulling over every expression that crossed his face? Not to mention her imagination suddenly deciding to take flights of fancy at the drop of a hat.

'Thank you,' she returned, drawing back to look at him. 'Will you text and let me know if you're going to be late, and if so how late?'

'I will most certainly do that,' he murmured.

Ellie ignored the lazy amusement in his drawl. 'And should I try and get anything together before I get there?'

'Anything like what—food? Drink? Dancing girls and circus performers?'

'Very funny.' She clicked her tongue with exasperation and his grin broadened. 'Honestly,' she muttered, 'You're impossible sometimes.'

'You're the only one who can do that.' He was looking at her with a veiled expression that was just the right side of serious, and when their eyes met she had to control a shiver of treacherous awareness.

'Do what?'

'Put me in my place.'

A wave of confusion crashed over Ellie and she fidgeted, skewered by the barely readable expression in his eyes. 'And don't tell me that's something you like!' she joked shakily.

'You'd be surprised.' He raised his eyebrows but that lazy intensity was still in his eyes, still sending shivers down her spine. 'Maybe we all need someone who's not scared to put us in our place. Especially powerful men like me.'

He grinned, breaking the spell, and Ellie felt her body sag with relief.

He hadn't meant that. Her imagination was at it again, amplifying his words. So much of what he said was part and parcel of his enormous, unconscious charm, a heady mix of intense focus wedded to light-hearted teasing that got under your skin and gave you goose bumps.

She thought about what he had told her about the aftermath of his parents' death. About Max taking hold of the reins and Izzy finding the warmth of support which had left *him*… Had he dealt with loss by becoming the guy who seemed just fine under the dazzling personal charm?

'I'll make sure what we've discussed this morning is collated and ready to be emailed.' She changed the subject, keen to get away. 'And I'll make sure I'm at the designated spot on time. No need to rush if you're busy. I'm more than capable of handling the situation until you get there.'

She smiled politely and thought that it might be quite relaxing to get used to the businessmen without James lurking in the background, unsettling her.

If the deal came to fruition—and it almost certainly would, because everything he touched turned to gold— then *she* would inevitably be the one most in contact with the new partners, because that was usually the way it worked out. James clinched his massive deals, started the wheels churning, oversaw everything until it was safe to retreat, then left her and his various CEOs to fine-tune the details and handle the after-care. Then all those computer geniuses would move into action, taking the bare bones of the programmes handed to them and expanding them into apps that always captured parts of the market no others had captured before.

It would be worthwhile finding out a little about the guys she would end up dealing with because it always made for an easier relationship.

She thought of the prim and proper clothes she had dragged along with her and breathed a sigh of relief that she had had the chance to blow some of her money on a couple of things that would make a better impression in the casual tropical setting. She had not given sufficient thought to it when she had flung open the doors of her wardrobe in London.

For three years, surrounded by her brainy, wild and whacky colleagues, she had stuck rigidly in the background, had stuck to the persona she had moulded for herself. Years of anxiety, years of looking after her mother, years of sublimating her own grief in the face of bigger concerns, had conferred a serious maturity on young shoulders.

Here, though, under these hot, turquoise skies and velvet, starry nights, she would stop being that careful young woman, risk-averse and taking no chances.

So her boss thought she was Little Miss Efficient and Ever So Slightly Dull?

Well, it would give her a kick to prove to him that there was a bit more to her than knee-length skirts and sensible shoes...

* * *

The short taxi ride from the hotel to the marina, where the Catamaran was waiting for him, was an uncomfortable one because the air-conditioning in the car wasn't working. By the time James had weaved his way through the crowds towards the yacht, he was dripping in perspiration and running thirty minutes behind schedule.

Thank God he could rely on Ellie to hold the fort until he arrived.

Thank God that, whatever stirrings of curiosity he had felt about the solid, dependable woman who had worked for him for the past three years, she was, underneath it all, the mainstay of his working day.

Nothing, he thought as he scanned the marina for the luxury Catamaran he had rented for the day, could ever put a dent in that unflappable personality. She was so adept at keeping a cool grip on whatever situations might occur, such as the one in which he currently found himself.

Annoyingly late.

En passant, he noted the bustle around him, the glitter of the sea, the soporific bobbing of all the yachts moored in the marina, and overhead the dazzling blue of the sky.

For a few seconds, he stopped dead in his tracks, living for the moment. It was not something he often did. Life was busy. Running an empire left little time to look around. He was a man accustomed to life being lived in the fast lane but now… 'Fast' was not what this spectacular island was about, and for a few minutes he savoured the pleasure of the dramatic scenery.

Around him and behind him lay the capital, Bridgetown, awash in sun as dense as treacle. Everyone chatted happily, bustling between buildings that ranged from imposing, older buildings to sleek, modern towers, interspersed with brightly coloured shops and offices. The air smelled of the salty ocean, the burning sun and the aromas of food wafting out from doorways of cafés and little restaurants sprinkled along the promenade that ribboned along the sea front. Along the promenade, with its intricate iron railings, handy to lean against and contemplate the endless ocean, several shops spilled out their stash of brightly coloured clothes, hats and bags for sale, appealing to locals and tourists alike.

He tried to picture Naomi in this setting and was intensely relieved that things had crashed and burned. There was no way he would have been able to devote any quality time to this incredibly satisfying deal, making sure the businessmen he was on the way to meet were kept sweet. He imagined she would have wanted his full, undivided time to escort her to beaches and restaurants where she could be on show.

Ellie, on the other hand...

He headed towards the promenade, moving past little groups sitting at wooden tables, dining out in the sunshine.

He was running late, which was a pain in the neck, but he could rely on Ellie doing everything that needed to be done—from pouring glasses of whatever had been provided by the five-star caterers supplied by the hotel, to taming the young men, and adroitly introducing them to what their roles would be once the company became his. For they would retain some shareholding, with his blessing.

Right now, she would be toeing just the right line between chatty and polite and professional and efficient. He wondered which of her 'dressed for a normal working day' suits she would be wearing, and found himself absently toying with the fascinating notion that she might have leapt out of her comfort zone straight into something that wasn't grey or blue.

In contrast to Naomi, he realised, Ellie, with her quietly unostentatious clothes and neat appearance, didn't *jar*.

Up ahead, he spotted the Catamaran, which he had rented for the day, with a hold on it in case he needed it again. It was in a league of its own, gleaming black, its massive twin hulls holding bedrooms, a dining area and somewhere to relax away from the blistering sun.

Maybe, he mused idly, he should take a break from the high-maintenance woman with all her tiresome needs, and demands which always ended up surfacing sooner or later. Maybe he should opt for *soothing*. He worked all the hours God made and his life was high octane, high stress and high risk. Maybe soothing would work for him. Were there any soothing women in his proverbial little black book? None that he could think of.

Disgruntled mood disappearing with every step closer to the Catamaran, James was in high spirits as he boarded the waiting yacht. No one was on deck, which meant that work was probably under way in the cool, below-deck room which he had specified had to multi-function as a conference area.

He heard voices as he nimbly hopped onto one of the hulls, steadying himself on the railing.

Voices and laughter.

He had no idea what he'd been expecting, but whatever it had been certainly wasn't what greeted him when he ducked down into the spacious living area, with its in-built cherry-wood seating and the matching sideboard groaning under the weight of food and drink, courtesy of the very capable catering staff at the hotel.

The businessmen were there but business didn't appear to be under discussion. Bottles of beer nestled in hands and used plates told a tale of lunch already having been taken.

Unless the business in question involved the uproarious telling of jokes, this was a social gathering, not the work situation he had envisaged.

And Ellie…

He wasn't sure what shocked him more—the fact that she was wearing a colourful sarong and a vest top that advertised a body that had largely been invisible in all the time she'd worked for him, or the fact that she was drinking a bottle of beer.

What the hell was going on here?

Why was she drinking? Of course he'd seen her drink before. But always wine. A civilised glass of premium Sancerre at one of the company get-togethers. He'd never had her down as a beer girl!

And where was the tidy skirt? The neat blouse, top two buttons daringly undone because of the searing heat? Where were the sensible shoes?

And she was *laughing*!

James was taken aback by the depth of his shock when, taken individually, none of the things were in themselves shocking. People wore small clothes in hot weather. People drank beer. People laughed. What was the big deal?

Furthermore, hadn't he encouraged her to dress for the weather? Hadn't he been guilty of gently teasing her about her prim outfits, his tone of voice encouraging her to dare to break the mould?

Well, she had broken the mould, *and then some*. This was a different Ellie. This Ellie was confident and assured, and her covert sexuality was out in the open big time. This Ellie was a woman he had not glimpsed before. She was positively modest in her dress compared to the women he dated and yet she still had the irresistible appeal of a siren. He had to drag his eyes away from her and kill a jealous

suspicion that he was probably not the only one appreci-
ating the assets on view. He didn't do jealousy—never
had, never would!

From where she was sitting, relaxed but still fully in charge
of the three high-spirited young men who were so much
like the guys at the office, Ellie was aware of her boss before he even appeared at the door.

Maybe, Ellie thought, she'd been waiting for him, her
attention riveted to that door, her body laced with tension
underneath the chat and the laughter.

Yes, this was work, but not as she had ever known it.
She had ditched the uniform with a surge of confidence,
spurred on by the fact that all her boss's remarks had somehow made her feel dull and unexciting.

She had felt a thrill of pleasure earlier when she had
stood in front of the hotel mirror and inspected the reflection staring back at her. Indeed, she had had trouble
recognising herself. Had all those years of heavy responsibility really made her forget how young she still was?
She had had to grow up fast to deal with the fallout from
her father's premature death. Had she somehow gone from
teenager to middle-aged woman, skipping all the fun bits
in between?

The brightly coloured sarong and the small turquoise
top were hardly risqué, but she'd *felt* risqué in front of that
mirror. She'd *felt* what she was—a twenty-something girl
with every right to have fun.

Now, as James's eyes swept over her, she refused to be
cowed into thinking that she should have dressed as he'd
no doubt expected.

Antony, Victor and Sol raised their beer bottles in welcome as Ellie gracefully rose to her feet, bottle in her own
hand, and made the introductions.

She moved towards James as he moved towards her, tentatively, to accommodate the faint rocking of the boat as it bobbed on the water.

'Not quite what I was expecting to find,' he murmured truthfully, just low enough for her to hear, but his words spoken in passing because he was already beginning to engage with the young men.

Ellie felt a spurt of unaccustomed anger. Had he expected her to be seated with her notebook and pencil? Slapping down anyone who spoke out of turn? Maybe banishing them to the naughty corner?

Yes, he had! Because she was the efficient PA, never flustered, never out of her depth, always available.

She was swamped with a mixture of simmering rebellion and uncharacteristic recklessness brought on by her slinky clothes and the complimentary looks from the young lads. They were looking at her with the sort of male appreciation of which she had been starved for longer than she cared to remember, and she refused to fade into the background as usual.

She chatted and laughed and helped herself to another bottle of the local lager when it was offered. She knew her stuff and she knew exactly when to focus the minute the conversation turned to work. All the information she had meticulously filed in her head was at her fingertips, and she could deal with facts and figures even after her two beers.

For the first time in ages, Ellie threw herself into having fun. They had hired a skipper for the day, and she felt a burst of freedom as the Catamaran took on the wide blue sea.

A little while later up on deck, with conversation swirling around her, she sat with her knees drawn up and gazed at the limitless horizon. The yacht was moving at a rate of knots and the wind blew her hair around her face. The sky was the purest of dazzling blues and, as the boat left shallow water for deeper ocean, the sea was a dark navy, broken by the white froth of ripples from the wind and the ocean currents.

Victor perched next to her, bare-backed and with no thought whatsoever about sun block, and chatted to her about the turtles you could swim with, and the sting rays you could spot shimmering like pancakes in the sand, if you decided to go snorkelling. He gave her more information about the ins and outs of cricket than her brain could hold, and told her that she had to try Mount Gay rum, which was the best in the world.

At some point, when she had moved on from beer to bottled water, the skipper dropped anchor and everyone except her took the plunge into the bottomless sea.

Antony… Victor… Sol…and James.

Sitting and watching from the deck, hiding behind the sunglasses she had thankfully brought with her, Ellie looked at her boss, so much taller and so much more muscular than the other three. His body was a work of art. Solid packed muscle and a six-pack that was testament to power sessions at the gym. The sun would lighten his hair. It was already deepening his colour.

His trunks, black and halfway down his thighs, were hardly the stuff to fire the imagination, yet she felt weak at the sight of them and the heavy bulge of what was underneath.

The sun was setting by the time the skipper lifted anchor and they began heading back to the marina. Darkness was settling fast. One minute the glare of the sun had mellowed and then the orange orb began to sink on the horizon, turning the skies first indigo, then velvet-black.

High spirits had given way to mellow, serious conversation, and she had taken a lot of notes by the time the yacht drew up to its mooring, working on her iPad and storing up an equal amount to transcribe later.

'I'll take it from here,' James told the skipper. When Ellie made to follow the guys off the yacht, he stretched out one arm, a signal for her to stay put.

'What…what's going on?' she asked as the last of the guys hopped ashore and James, to her consternation, kicked the yacht back into life, nudging it expertly into open water.

Of course he could skipper a yacht, she thought, compulsively looking at his strong, veined forearms as he guided it with one hand. If it came to it, he could probably fly a plane through the eye of a hurricane.

'We need to talk.'

'Perhaps it could wait until tomorrow morning?' She glanced over her shoulder to where the twinkling lights and safety of crowds on the promenade were being left behind.

The pleasant effect of beer was beginning to wear off, and as the yacht picked up speed, heading in the same direction along the west coast as earlier, she felt a shiver of forbidden excitement.

She didn't want this! Hadn't she already made it clear that her time would not be consumed with work-related issues simply because they weren't in an office?

And yet…

There was a sense of simmering danger in the air that made the hairs on the back of her neck stand on end. They were so far away from *normal*. Now, cruising along the shoreline, the panorama was quite different, everything plunged into inky shadows and distant, looming shapes. Yet it was barely any cooler than it had been during the day, with just the faintest of cooling breezes as he slowed the yacht to a soft stop, where it bobbed lazily on the calm water.

When he turned to her, she could only make out his shadowy outline. The angles of his beautiful face were hidden and she couldn't read the expression in his eyes.

'This is a bit dramatic, isn't it?' She laughed a little nervously because it was hard to get a grip on his mood. 'I mean, if you want to talk about what was said about the prospective deal, then we could have…um…caught up in the morning. I may have had a couple of beers, but I remember every word that was said.'

'I would expect nothing less.'

'Then…what's the problem? Why are we out here?'

James thought that that was an excellent question. Unfortunately, he couldn't quite find as excellent an answer, because the hell he knew why he was out here. He just knew that the past few hours on this Catamaran had been a hellish ordeal mentally, trying to channel her back into the predictable box from which she had unexpectedly sprung. Astonishment at what she'd been wearing, at her drinking and at her easy, sexy confidence with those guys had kick-started all sorts of shocking, taboo urges inside him. He had to get it out of his system, and that was frustrating, because he wasn't sure what exactly it was he had to get out of his system.

'You… I wasn't expecting to find you dressed in a sarong and a tiny top,' he opened, and was immediately appalled at the censorious tone of his voice. Since when had he become a feudal overlord?

'Sorry?'

He raked his fingers through his hair and looked uncomfortably at the slight figure in front of him.

The small top curved over her perfectly small, rounded

breasts, the sarong dipping just enough to expose her slim, flat stomach and a glimpse of slender leg every damn time that sarong flared open a little.

Since when had she become the sexiest woman on the planet? Had he registered that before and somehow managed to sublimate it? He had been the victim of a raging libido for the entire time they had spent on the yacht. It had been a mammoth effort not to look at her, and even a long swim in the ocean hadn't been able to douse the sudden fire that had ignited inside him. For once, his formidable will power had not been able to rescue him from feeling like a horny teenager.

'I'm not saying you can't wear whatever you want to wear,' he said in a roughened undertone. 'I'm just saying you caught me by surprise...'

Ellie's mouth fell open. 'You've driven this boat out here so you can tell me *that*?' She glared at him. 'And should I be grateful that you haven't objected to my dress code?'

'Of course...' James tried to rescue the farcical situation with some semblance of rationality. 'It would be an opportune time to consolidate what...has been said...'

'You told me to wear appropriate clothes. I'm wearing appropriate clothes! And, when it comes to work, we could easily discuss that tomorrow! You just *don't approve* of what I've chosen to wear! Which, *incidentally*, is a whole lot less dramatic than what most girls my age would be wearing on a boat in the tropics!'

'Did I say that I didn't approve of what you're wearing?' James retorted with a hint of defensiveness. Where was this coming from? He had no idea, and that lack of control was messing with his head. He couldn't remember a time when he'd actually cared about what clothes any woman chose to wear. Unconvincingly, he tried to tell himself that he was being perfectly reasonable in this instance because she wasn't just any woman, she was *his PA*. She was *paid* to look the part! Her role wasn't to turn him on until he found it impossible to think straight...

'You don't have to,' Ellie said coldly. 'You're accustomed to seeing me one way and one way only.'

'You've hit the nail on the head,' he muttered. He spun round to stare at the dark sky and the even darker sea. He felt hot and uncomfortable in his skin. He felt...*aroused* at the sight of her. He wanted to touch her, and he didn't know what to do with the feeling, so he ground his teeth together and glared at her.

'As of tomorrow, I will return to my normal dress code,' Ellie managed to bite out with such stiff politeness that he knew she was fighting hard not to shout at him. 'And I'll make sure to bring out the *appropriate* stuff when you're not around to disapprove.'

'Don't,' he said brusquely. 'You think I disapprove. Maybe I approve too much.'

His words hung in the air between them, as dangerous as a match being tossed onto dried leaves.

'I don't understand,' Ellie said confusedly.

'Don't you? I couldn't take my eyes off you. Okay, so maybe you're right. Maybe I *have* been accustomed to seeing you in one way and one way only. Maybe I like this break with tradition a little too much for both our good.'

James had never envisaged himself in this position. Had he ever thought about her that way? Maybe. He didn't know. She'd always got under his skin in a strange kind of way. Had it been a simmering attraction he had always refused to acknowledge? At any rate, the words were out and he was unrepentant. In fact, he felt oddly calm.

'I don't know what you're saying,' Ellie whispered.

'Don't you? Then allow me to spell it out. You sat there on this boat, sexy as hell, and I wanted you. It wasn't just the clothes. I saw a different woman and I wanted her. I want her right now. I can't get any clearer than that, can I, Ellie? I want to kiss you. I want to make love to you. Right here, right now, on this boat in the middle of the sea…'

CHAPTER FIVE

ELLIE GASPED HER shock, but through the shock dark excitement coursed with mercurial speed through her veins. She took a couple of steps back, her breathing shallow and rapid, her eyes pinned to the dark shadows of his face.

This wasn't what she'd been expecting. When he'd dispatched everyone and announced that he wanted to take the Catamaran back out to talk to her, she'd put two and two together and come to the vague conclusion that he was keen to discuss what had been agreed during the course of the afternoon on the yacht. That he'd opted to take the boat back out because that was the type of guy he was—he just wanted to have a go sailing it. She suspected that the only reason he'd hired a skipper in the first place was because he hadn't wanted the distraction of being behind the wheel when there was business to get through.

But this…! No! She couldn't possibly! She wasn't built for something like this…she needed *stability* and *boundaries*. Lose those and what next? It would be as perilous as diving head-first into a whirlpool! She needed *control*, yet…

Every bone in her body was melting and she was grateful for the cover of darkness so that he couldn't see the tell-tale trembling of her body. Shameful arousal was a heat pouring through her, and she felt the tingling pool of dampness between her thighs, which made her want to rub them together.

She hugged herself and stared at him.

He was her boss! This shouldn't be happening! Why was it happening? Was he even being serious? She was hardly in the league of all his ex-girlfriends, with their ridiculously long legs and supermodel figures.

A thousand fevered questions raced through her head, but her tongue seemed to be glued to the roof of her mouth and all she could do was stare at him, dumbfounded.

'Tell me about it,' he grated.

'Is this some kind of joke, James?'

'Do I sound as though I'm kidding?'

'But… I work for you! And it's not even as though I'm your *type*!'

'Think I'm not grappling with the same mystery?' He shifted, for once lacking his usual poise. He looked at her, looked away, looked again and then kept looking. 'I'm not a believer in mixing business with pleasure…'

'I know,' Ellie said faintly. Was this conversation really happening? Yes, it was, because there had to be a reason she was finding it hard to breathe. 'You don't like your girlfriends invading your work space, never mind occupying a permanent space in it.'

'All true,' he growled, unconsciously taking a small step towards her, closing the distance. 'and, as an aside, don't think that because I date tall blondes that you're not sexy…'

'We need to stop talking like this,' Ellie whispered shakily. 'We'll head back to shore and pretend this conversation never happened.'

'You think it's going to be that easy?'

'It will be because I'll chuck these clothes to the bottom of my suitcase and return to my boring skirts and tops.'

'And that's why you're sexy.'

'Why? What are you talking about?'

'You say things that make me smile. Do you honestly think that a change of wardrobe is going to quench what I'm feeling? You make me smile and, when you add in a sharp brain, you have a killer combination. I looked at you earlier, poised…confident…at ease with every bit of technical conversation being tossed around… You can't imagine what a turn-on that was.'

He paused and then turned away to grasp the hand rail that ran round the edge of the boat. 'I need to cool off.'

Ellie didn't say anything. Her head was buzzing. She wanted all this nonsense to stop immediately! But she also wanted him to keep on talking, feeding her ego and sending her nervous system into a tailspin.

She *liked* what he was doing to her and that terrified her. The door that had been nudged ajar between them had now been kicked wide open and, whilst she was desperate to get it shut again, whilst she *knew* she had to get it shut again, a wilful part of her couldn't help but toy with the idea of touching him.

She'd wanted to, hadn't she? Hadn't she thought about that in the early hours of the morning, caught in that pleasant place between sleep and wakefulness, when thoughts were allowed to roam free? Yes, *of course* they weren't compatible, not *at all*, but still, acknowledging that did nothing to kill the surge of desire inside her.

'I need to have a swim.'

'You can't!'

But he was already stripping off his tee shirt. After swimming off and on during the day, he had left his swimming trunks on. He was ready to dive into the sea, except this time there was no blue sky above or transparent water lapping the sides of the Catamaran. Now, the sea was threateningly deep, dark and fathomless. Ellie watched in fascinated horror as he moved swiftly to the side of the boat, eschewing the shallow steps on each hull that would have made for a slower adjustment to the coldness of the water.

He dived straight in and disappeared. *Of course he would surface!* She had watched from the sidelines as he had swum earlier on, mesmerised by the graceful fluidity of his lean body slicing through the water, his strokes effortless and powerful at the same time It was so dark that she could barely make out anything. She certainly couldn't make out any surfacing shape and her panic began rising the more she peered into the darkness, hoping to see his silhouette.

The twin-hulled, squat shape of the boat made for a very solid, safe vessel but she now wondered whether he had misjudged the width of it, so much broader than a typical small yacht, and had tried to surface only to find his head bumping against the bottom of the boat. Things could get confusing when you couldn't see clearly and you were in unfamiliar surroundings. What could be more unfamiliar to someone whose stamping ground was the concrete jungle than an ocean, at night, in the middle of the tropics?

Frantically moving from bow to stern and scouring the flat, dark ocean mass, she yelped when she heard his voice behind her. In fact, it took her a couple of seconds to recognise his voice at all, and her heart was in her mouth when she whipped round to see him standing in front of her.

'Where the *heck* have you been?' She was pressed against the railing, gripping it for dear life. The gentlest of night breezes wafted her fine hair around her face and she impatiently pushed her hand through it.

'Swimming.'

He'd fetched a towel from the deck somewhere and was drying himself.

'Yes, I know you've been *swimming*!'

'Then why the rhetorical question? Let's go below deck. I need to get into some dry clothes.'

He spun round on his heels and began heading down to the living and sleeping quarters, ample enough, as she had discovered, for eight people to move around comfortably without getting in one another's way.

'Were you worried?'

The spacious quarters now seemed cramped as he slowly turned to look at her, having flung the towel on the table which nestled in the centre of a fitted L-shaped banquette.

The galley, the saloon and the helm station all flowed into one huge open space in this area. Ellie's legs felt like jelly but, whilst she was desperate to sink onto the padded leather banquette, his dark blue eyes, so dramatic with their lush, dark lashes, skewered her to the spot, making movement impossible.

Down here, the dark, warm night and the inky black ocean were no longer pressing around them. Only the gentle undulating of the boat was a reminder that they were on water.

'I didn't see you surface,' she said thinly. 'Of course I was worried! Anyone would have been in my situation?'

'And what situation is that?'

He'd towel-dried and slung on his dry tee shirt, but the swimming trunks were still on, clinging to his muscular thighs, and she had to steel herself not to look.

One glance and who knew what kind of unwelcome physical responses would be surging through her already heated body?

The electricity between them sizzled and she wasn't going to do anything to ratchet it up further.

He fancied her... He wanted to touch her...to kiss...to make love...

Those words were now lodged in her head and how on earth was she going to get rid of them? There were only so many times she could keep telling herself that they weren't suited. Maybe she had become reliant on her role of carer. Maybe she had hidden behind that role even when her mother had stopped needing her quite so much... Maybe, *just maybe*, she had become fearful of taking all those risks involved with dating guys and just having fun. But, if things had to change, then surely not with a man who had 'heartbreaker' stamped all over his forehead! Her breathing was staccato, uneven, as she continued to flounder helplessly.

'Drink?'

'No!'

He'd moved to the ingenious wine bottle holder that was built into a concealed walnut drawer.

'You're not going to be able to get the boat back...' She followed his movements with avid, treacherous concentration.

James paused, wine glass in one hand, and shot her a slow, lazy smile that made her toes curl. He'd cooled down and was obviously back in control of the situation. Was he sufficiently in control to realise that anything between them, *anything*, would be a disaster?

'Oh, ye of little faith...' He poured himself a glass of red and strolled towards her to sit on the banquette and pat the space next to him. 'You didn't answer my question,' he prompted softly. 'What situation?'

'Huh?' She ignored the space next to him and sidled to sit facing him instead. The soft lapping of water against the side of the boat was a barely discernible noise, more felt than heard. In here, the silence was thick with tension.

'You said that anyone *in your situation* would have been worried sick…'

Ellie noted the way he had tacked the word *sick* onto his sentence, turning it into quite a different emotion.

'Do you mean,' he continued thoughtfully, 'that anyone trapped on a boat would be worried if they ended up on it alone because they might be stranded at sea until someone came along and rescued them?'

'Of course not! I'm not a helpless damsel in distress! If I were on this boat alone, I'm sure I would be able to somehow get it back to shore.'

'Maybe, then,' he mused, sipping his wine and looking at her with the same pensive expression that gave no guidance as to exactly what was going through his head, 'you were concerned that, if your boss disappeared off to that great watery graveyard in the sky, your future as a highly paid worker bee might be on the line. I'll admit there are few companies in London that could rival the working conditions at my place, not to mention the pay…'

'That's a crazy thing to say!' She whitened, thoughts zooming to him involved in any kind of accident, feeling sick at the very thought. 'That's not why I was worried! I was worried because…because…'

'Because,' he murmured, looking at her steadily, his dark eyes boring straight into her, addling her, 'You have feelings for me that go beyond the usual, predictable boss-secretary relationship, don't you…'

It wasn't a question, it was an assumption, and she opened her mouth to deny it but nothing emerged.

'You're attracted to me, whether you want to admit it or not. You're as attracted to me as I am to you. Maybe we might not have said anything before, when we were in London, imprisoned in the routine and normality of my office there, but here we are.'

'No,' Ellie whispered weakly.

'Alone…' he continued with the remorseless determination of a battering ram. 'In this Catamaran, out in the tropics, with nothing but the deep, dark ocean beneath us and the deep, dark skies above us…'

'Stop, please.' She barely recognised her voice. Gone was the no-nonsense firmness which represented the backbone of her relationship with him. In its place as a wavering, pleading hesitancy that exposed all her weaknesses.

He'd said that she had feelings for him.

He'd summed that up as meaning that she was physically attracted to him.

That wasn't the whole story, though, was it? And therein lied the danger. But, sitting here, the danger was sidelined by the tremendous drag on her senses evoked by what he was saying and the way he was looking at her.

'Come sit next to me.'

Ellie hesitated and he smiled, smelling victory, which instantly made her stiffen, even though her heart was pounding and there was a giddy pulsing in her veins.

'We should be getting back.'

'I thought you were concerned about my handling the boat with too much alcohol in my system.'

'James…'

'I've always liked the way you say my name, in that husky voice of yours.'

'Don't.'

'Come sit next to me and then tell me *don't*…' But he didn't leave her wriggle room, instead fluidly vaulting to his feet and before she could take evasive action. He was there, next to her, his body warm and still slightly damp, smelling of the salty sea and something else…

Ellie's breath hitched in her throat and everything in her body seemed to grind to a halt.

When she dropped her gaze, it was to rest on his hand, loose on his thigh.

She could feel his eyes on her, his attention on her, and the silence pressed down until it was suffocating.

When he stroked the soft underside of her wrist with his finger, she closed her eyes and gritted her teeth together.

'Look at me.'

'I... I can't.'

'Why not?'

Ellie glanced sideways but then she couldn't stop herself from feasting her eyes on him.

So beautiful, so dangerous. Up close with him like this felt like the first taste of forbidden fruit and the wetness of her own arousal made her feel faint.

He trailed his thumb over the fullness of her mouth and, when he very gently eased it between her lips, she gave a soft little moan and sucked on it.

What was she doing? How was she ever going to get back from this?

But she was discovering at speed what that little word *lust* was all about and just how useless common sense was as a weapon with which to ward it off.

His mouth found hers and she melted against him with a sigh of pleasure. She clutched at the tee shirt and her body unconsciously curved towards his, seeking his hardness and his heat. His clothes felt like a barrier between them and she wanted to shove her hands under the tee shirt and tear it off him.

He pushed her back and his kiss deepened and hardened hungrily.

She was barely aware of him scooping her up and carrying her through to one of the four bedrooms, somehow managing to maintain his balance on the gently bobbing boat. The sky could have fallen in and Ellie didn't think she would have noticed, so caught up in the moment was she.

During the course of the day, none of the bedrooms had been used. This one, the master bedroom, was spectacular, with a generous queen-sized bed, and hatches and opening portholes which could allow in natural light.

He deposited her on the bed without bothering to switch on the overhead light, for which she was extremely grateful. Heaven only knew, the cold glare of daylight was just around the corner, and with it would come all those horrifying questions she knew she should be asking herself right now, but for the moment she wanted this so badly...

There was no room for questions as she watched him peel away the tee shirt and step out of his swimming trunks.

Ellie groaned aloud and resisted the primal urge to touch herself.

Watching you watching me...

James had never been so turned on before in his life. She lay there, clothed but in disarray, her cheeks hectic with colour and those calm grey eyes hot with the same hunger tearing through him. It was like nothing on earth for him.

It *hurt* taking his time. He was so hard for her. He felt the hugeness of himself, and gritted his teeth and remained still for a few seconds, willing himself to take it easy. Just looking at her was enough to make him want to bring himself to a fast climax and there was no way he was going to do that. But those eyes on him, looking at him as he absently played with himself, touching himself...

Was this what playing with fire felt like? Because this *was* playing with fire. Though temptation had never promised to taste sweeter.

He made sure he had protection at hand and then sank onto the mattress alongside her. Here, the slapping of the water against the sides of the boat was more noticeable because the portholes were open.

He kissed her. He teased his tongue into her mouth and felt her shiver against him. He knew that his hand was not quite as steady as could be expected as he slipped it under the small, stretchy top to find her cotton bra and her small, perfectly shaped breasts. He gently massaged one through the flimsy fabric of her bra.

He'd known she wouldn't wear a swimsuit and she wasn't. What he hadn't expected was how satisfied he'd been that she hadn't frolicked in the sea with the rest of them. He'd had to tear his eyes away from her and it hadn't escaped him that he wasn't the only one. Had she noticed? At any rate, having her remain on deck, dutifully working while they swam, had been just fine with him. He wasn't a jealous guy, but every so often, he'd been honest enough to admit that there was a twinge of something dark that stirred inside him when he caught one of the young guys looking at her.

He baulked at the thought that he might be jealous. He didn't have a jealous bone in his body. To be jealous, you had to invest, and he was over any kind of emotional investment—had been for years.

No. The bottom line was that this sexy creature represented the taste of forbidden fruit, and what could be more succulent?

He eased the bra off her, expertly unclasping it from behind, and groaned as he settled his hand on her bare breast. He raised himself over her, staring down, taking deep breaths as he pulled off the top and bra.

Her skin was soft and smooth, her breasts small and

pert, tipped with glorious, pink, circular discs begging to be licked.

But not yet. First he wanted to savour just the stunning sight of her. See all of her...

He undid the sarong with shaking hands. Underneath she had on a pair of tight shorts, red to match the colours in the sarong, and underneath that her panties.

A voyage of discovery. Heady, sexy, mind-blowing. He'd returned to an adolescent place where he was no longer in control of his reactions. He should have been disconcerted, but instead it was a turn-on. Like taking a white-water ride.

Ellie blossomed under that fierce, appreciative gaze. His nakedness was intensely erotic. When he had clothes on, his good looks were on the killer scale. With him naked, words failed her.

She had never lain like this before, with a man's eyes hungry on her naked body. Her one boyfriend, the guy who should have been her soul mate, because they had known one another for a couple of years before going out, had been a disappointment. It had been a classic case of friends who should never have strayed from the straight and narrow. They had parted company without any bad feelings at all. They followed one another on social media, offering appropriate congratulations as necessary at life's small triumphs, but all that she had taken from it was the firm conviction that, when it came to the physical, she was sorely lacking.

Ben had been pleasant, kind and good-looking. Theoretically, it should have been good between them. Shouldn't it? So this intense reaction now was something she was ill-prepared for and she could feel it sweeping her along with the ferocity of a tidal wave.

The first touch made her moan out loud and she

squirmed as he settled over her and began exploring her breasts with his tongue, with his mouth, with his hands.

Not even in her wildest imaginings had anything felt so good. He suckled on her nipples, drawing them into his mouth while he stroked the soft flesh of her inner thigh. He licked a sensuous path between her breasts and circled her belly button with his finger at the same time. When she squirmed to touch him, he gently propelled her back to tell her that he wanted her to feel like she'd never felt before.

'But…' she protested helplessly and he smiled.

'Don't worry. I'm not a saint. I want you touching me badly and we have all night to indulge… I'm happy to wait.'

'All night?' She'd almost forgotten that they were still on the yacht.

'I have this boat for as long as I want it.'

Ellie sighed. She wriggled as he continued to touch her, stroking her stomach and circling her nipples with his finger. Then his mouth replaced his finger, and she gasped and breathed in sharply as he traced a sensuous path down her stomach with his tongue, inching lower, then parting her thighs with his hands so that she was open to him.

Then he kissed her between her legs, a gentle kiss, blowing softly before inserting his tongue into her wetness. Her instinct at this shocking show of intimacy was to snap her legs together. This was a place to which she had never gone before and an experience she had never had. However, he kept them open and she sank into the most shatteringly exquisite sensations she had ever had.

She squirmed against his questing tongue and groaned uncontrollably as it delved deeper into her, finding the pulsing beat of her clitoris and staying there to tease the swollen bud until she felt the spiral of pleasure soaring out of control. Her orgasm was unstoppable and she arched against his mouth and cried out, her whole body racked with a shuddering, climactic loss of control that blanked everything out of her mind.

Surfacing should have been horribly awkward. Mortification should have been tearing through her as cold reality took grip and made a mockery of her loss of inhibition. Instead, there was no time for searching questions, because now he guided her to pleasing him and, once again, she was lost in the moment and wonderfully *present* for the first time in her life.

Every touch and every sensation exploded in Technicolor. The feel of him and the taste of him as she explored his body the way he had explored hers was an exquisite voyage of discovery, and it felt weirdly *right*, even though a little voice in the back of her mind was telling her that it was anything *but*.

The ripple of muscle under her fingers and the sinewy strength of his body made her giddy with wanting. The sound of his low, urgent groans and the thick shakiness of his voice as he encouraged her where to go, where to touch and how to touch, made her melt.

Swept away on a surge of never-before-felt sensory overload, she only really came back down to earth when at last they lay next to one another on the queen-sized bed, utterly spent. Shyly, she reached for the sheet, but he flipped onto his side to look at her and gently steered her away from covering herself.

'You have an amazing body,' he murmured, sliding one hand along her waist to rest on her hip.

'James...'

'I know exactly what you're going to say.'

'Do you?' She angled herself so that they were facing one another. The silvery light filtering into the cabin made the shadows dance around them and on their faces, but she could see that his eyes were both serious and ever so mildly amused.

His casualness relaxed her. She wasn't sure what she had been expecting post coitus. Maybe horror and embarrassment from him at what had taken place between them. She had steeled herself to deal with his recriminations as well as her own but there was a smile tugging the corners of his mouth.

'You're going to remind me that I'm your boss and that what we just did was the worst thing we could have done...'

'Isn't it?'

'We are two adults who gave in to the chemistry between us. I don't make a habit of sleeping with my employees...in fact, I have *never* been tempted to do anything of that sort...but we slept together and I'm not going to beat myself up over it. Are you?'

'I'd planned on doing that, now that you mention it.'

He laughed and stroked her cheek. 'There's that sense of humour again...don't beat yourself up, Ellie.'

'It's easy for you to say. I don't do this sort of thing.'

'Never?'

'I... Life has always been a serious business for me,' she admitted. 'I've had one boyfriend, but flings? Hopping in and out of bed with strangers? That life belongs to some other girl...'

'We're not strangers to one another.'

'I know but...'

'Shh.' He rested one finger against her lips, silencing her. 'Did you enjoy what we just did? Did you enjoy making love with me?'

His words invoked a rush of heady pleasure and she briefly closed her eyes and breathed in deeply. There was no way she could lie, and she liked his honesty. She nodded, and he laughed softly and told her that she'd have to speak up because he didn't quite catch what she was saying.

'I enjoyed it.' Ellie glared at him, then smiled and tentatively outlined his mouth with her finger.

'So did I. Plenty. Think we should go there again?'

'We can't!' Her grey eyes were confused when they met his. 'How can we? We would never be able to work alongside one another again. It would spoil the relationship we have, and I enjoy my job too much to risk losing it.'

'Don't you think it would be worse if we cut it short now?'

'What do you mean?'

'Think about it, Ellie. We turn our backs on one another and agree to move forward and put this down to a one-off escapade...'

'Yes, exactly!' But there was already a coldness seeping inside her at the prospect of that, even though she knew it made perfect sense.

'Hold on. I'm not finished quite yet.' He sifted his fingers through her hair, twirling a silky strand into a ringlet and then letting it fall, slippery straight again. 'We take that road and how does that play out for us working together, with all that pent-up chemistry still sizzling between us? It would be impossible to relax back into anything approaching a decent working relationship.

'There would also be the danger of everyone eventually sussing that something was going on between us. Some of those employees of mine can trace the scent of something off with the accuracy of a bloodhound. They would see the change between us, and it wouldn't take long for them to put two and two together. And how do you think you would be able to deal with that?'

Ellie could feel tears pricking behind her eyelids but she had no one but herself to blame for this situation. She could have pushed him away. He wouldn't have persisted. Instead, she had allowed curiosity through the front door so that it could kill the proverbial cat.

'You're firing me,' she said bluntly, swinging back and resting one arm across her face.

'Don't be ridiculous. Of course I'm not firing you, Ellie! Why would I do that when you're the best PA I've ever had? Probably the only person on the planet who can put up with me!'

'Then what?' She sneaked a glance at him from under her lashes and her breath caught in her throat as their eyes collided.

'I'm saying we give in to this thing between us…let it run its course as it will. We're here, far away from prying eyes. Let's enjoy this, and trust me, by the time I'm back in London after my brother's wedding this will be nothing more than a pleasant memory which we will be more than happy to relegate to the history books. We'll be able to face one another as we always have done and, if there's an extra added facet to our relationship, then it won't interfere with anything. In fact, it might make what we have even better…'

Ellie's brain seemed to get stuck on the bit about relegating it to the history books, but she swept past that discomfort, because he was right. This was lust, and lust never lasted.

He was also right when he said that to end this prematurely would make things impossible between them because there would be that charge, that *electricity*, waiting to be snuffed out.

Another week here… She thought about this, about the freedom to touch him when she wanted, and she felt faint.

She would return to London ahead of him. He would fly to Hawaii shortly after she left. He had already mentioned drumming up some business there that could dovetail with the Barbados deal. He would have time to explore that before the wedding and then, by the time he was finally back in London, she would be back to her normal self.

She almost laughed because she felt that, once those prim suits were back in place, she would revert to the person she had always been. Her personality was way too ingrained for it to be thrown off-course by a week of giddy passion.

'Maybe…' she whispered, looking down at unknown depths beneath her feet, poised to take a leap. 'Maybe you're right…'

CHAPTER SIX

Ellie looked over the top of her book towards the horizon and James, now just a little dot moving in the blue, blue sea in an apparent bid to reach that invisible point.

Pure bliss.

At a little after four in the afternoon, the sun was still beating down, as golden as honey. The families had started drifting off, but even when the beach had been full, at midday, Ellie and James had still managed to secure a private, quiet spot on the never-ending stretch of powder-white sand. There they had settled down with their lavish picnic, prepared with care by the chefs at the hotel.

What lay round the corner was something she had put on hold, a bridge to be crossed when the time came, and that time wasn't now. What lay round the corner was a little thing called *reality*.

She hadn't been born yesterday. They were in a bubble. In this bubble James was charmed by the novelty of being with a woman who wasn't high maintenance, who didn't come with myriad potential complications and who was fundamentally sensible enough to walk away without kicking up a fuss—unlike his ex. But those were details she had set aside for *tomorrow*.

Now was…*this*. A beach, a book, the sun and that disappearing dot… James… *Her lover*…

Yes, the days were going by, but slowly. This was day three and it felt as though time was standing still, everything moving with a casual lack of urgency. This was an island where no one saw the need to rush, and it was incredible how quickly both of them had adapted. The deal was just about there, going through the last-stage formalities where lawyers swarmed all over documents like flies. But there was no sense of speed because the guys all took the stance of, 'Hey, it's going to happen, so why the rush? Enjoy the island first!'

So plans had changed accordingly, with James's trip to Hawaii being put back by several days to accommodate their easy going business partners. He would be cutting it a bit fine, but he would still have time to spare before the wedding.

Ellie had been overjoyed, but she had concealed it well, because he had made it very clear that this was all about living for the moment and that was a concept she was eager to embrace. 'Living for the moment' didn't involve any dangerous, unstable waters, any currents that could drag her under.

'You understand me,' he had told her only the day before as they had lain on the deck of the Catamaran, out in the middle of the deep blue sea, with nothing on and pleasurably sated from making love.

The compliment had been a double-edged sword, though, because he had continued, smiling, lying on one side so that he could tease her nipple with a finger. 'You know I don't believe in permanence so there's no chance you would ever get the wrong idea about this, about what we have.'

He'd been lying back, squinting at the azure sky for a few seconds, his hands behind his head. 'I made a mistake with Naomi,' he had mused. 'I believed her when she told me that she was into her career, that she was on the same page as I was, that what we had was fun.'

When he'd looked at her again, his dark blue eyes had been serious and yet lazily appreciative. 'You and I...' he'd grinned crookedly '...have been together long enough for you to know just where I stand on that subject.'

So, yes, Ellie knew just what the limits of this relationship were. She had realised very quickly that a display of *anything* that might be interpreted as her looking for more than what was on the table would be a very bad idea indeed.

But was she looking for anything more than what was on the table? She told herself not, but was she being completely truthful?

It was a question that had lodged itself at the back of her mind and exploring that would open a Pandora's box which she might find impossible to shut once the lid had been lifted.

She knew that as instinctively as she knew that he would be able to put this brief distraction behind him without any difficulty. He knew how to compartmentalise. It was what made it impossible for his emotions to take the lead. In so many ways, he had imparted that information to her without her even really realising it. In so many ways, his values were the polar opposite of hers...so wasn't that protection enough against anything...dangerous?

When they were with their business contacts, James was all business. He didn't try and pretend that there was nothing going on between them, but she knew that his focus was elsewhere, on the deal finally waiting to be sealed, with signatures on all the right lines. Work was his priority and all else was pushed into the background next to it.

It was why he could operate a constantly revolving door situation with the women he dated. He gave them one hundred percent of his undivided attention while the romance was running hot, but the second he began walking away was the second they became part and parcel of his past.

She was in a different category, because she would still be working with him, but she knew that the same principle would be applied. Once back in London, she would revert to being his PA, and if there was an added dimension to their relationship then that was something he would find amusing but certainly not a distraction.

And for her that worked...*didn't it?*

Like he'd said, she thought, with just the faintest stirrings of unease as that distant dot began to head back to shore, once this was out of their system normality would return. The electricity would fizzle out. That was how it had always been for him and for her...

She might have had next to no experience but she certainly knew what her head told her. He fundamentally wasn't her type, which meant that what she felt was purely lust, and everyone knew that lust and longevity were not things that went hand in hand. Lust wore thin very quickly. The fact that he would set the example by switching off would help their working relationship. She would simply follow his lead and it would be fine.

Of course it would!

She sat up, drawing her knees to her chest, watching as he swam back to shore. Next to her was the camera he had bought at huge cost two days ago. She would never have guessed that he was a spectacularly adventurous photographer, but it was a hobby that somehow fitted his unpredictable, highly creative yet incredibly driven personality.

It also gave an insight into someone who enjoyed a sense of solitude, which no one would ever have guessed, given the charming, extrovert nature of his personality. Those glimpses of his complexities had fired up her curiosity and imagination, but she knew that that too was a dangerous response, because it sucked her in, dismantling the necessary distance she was trying to maintain between them.

But, good heavens, keeping him at arm's length was tough to maintain when he made her body soar, her mouth run dry and scrambled her brain so that thinking straight felt like an effort demanding huge will power.

She watched as he stood up, shook the water off, raked his fingers through his hair and began walking towards her, every movement poetry in action.

Behind him, the backdrop of crystalline, azure water and the deepening blue of the late-afternoon sky was so picture-perfect that she wanted to grab the camera and capture it before it was lost to time and memory.

His wet swimming trunks clung to his muscular thighs and dipped down below his belly button, perfectly emphasising his six pack. Hiding behind her sunglasses, Ellie watched, mesmerised by his sheer animal beauty.

He was grinning when he stopped in front of her and held out his hand for her to grab.

'I can't see the expression on your face when you're hiding behind those things,' he teased. 'But I'm hoping that it's unfettered joy at the thought of us heading back to the bedroom...'

Ellie shielded her face and allowed herself to be pulled to her feet.

The modest black swimsuit she had brought with her had been replaced with a racier number in the sort of bright colours she would previously have avoided.

Shopping for non-essentials, that enjoyable leisure activity beloved by most twenty-somethings, was something she'd had neither the time nor the inclination to indulge. Here in this lazy heat, and basking in the open appreciation of the least suitable guy on the planet, she had discovered that it was something she rather enjoyed.

She glanced down at his long fingers entwined with hers and shivered, because there was something so intimate about the simple gesture. It was as though they were two lovers holding hands, maybe with a future stretching out in front of them.

She quickly whipped her straying thoughts away from any such cosy notion. There was no 'maybe' future for them on any romantic level. What they had was the here and now, and that was a good thing, because he could break a girl's heart. *Her heart, were she to be foolish enough to give it to him.*

'I forgot to mention,' he said, scooping up the remains of their picnic and stuffing it all into the basket provided by the hotel. 'I had a text from Izzy.'

'Your sister?' Ellie had met Izzy in passing a couple of times and had liked what she had seen. She was a stunning blonde girl who clearly adored her slightly older brother.

'She doesn't want to ruin Max and Mia's big day, but she said she couldn't keep the secret to herself any longer...'

'She's getting married?'

'To the guy of her dreams, it would seem,' James drawled, eyebrows raised with amusement. 'It seems my family are falling like ninepins.'

'Are they waiting for it to be your turn next?' Ellie said lightly. Staring straight ahead, with swaying coconut trees on one side and the gently rolling blue water on the other, her bare feet leaving footprints on the powdery, pale sand, she wondered what it would feel like to have the love of the guy holding her hand.

'Not if they're in their right minds,' he returned wryly.

'I've only met your brother once, but he didn't strike me as the sort who was keen to walk down the aisle...' She remembered a striking, dark-haired guy with scarily forbidding features, as tough as James, but without the easy charm that made his brother so accessible.

'I hope this isn't the sound of you thinking that I'm the sort of guy to be seduced by family peer pressure...'

His voice was still teasing but there was an undercurrent of coolness running through it that set off a warning bell in Ellie's head.

'I hope you're not,' she returned swiftly, and she felt his sidelong glance, although he didn't break stride.

'Intriguing remark. Want to expand?'

Ellie felt the hot tingle of perspiration on her face. This was a forceful reminder of the limits of what they had, and he was reminding her that that was something she would do well not to forget.

Pride stiffened her. The last thing she needed was for him to get the idea that she was somehow morphing into one of those women who ended up hanging onto his every word, weeping, wailing and falling apart when he decided that it was time to move on.

He laid down parameters. Well, she, for one, would be following them!

'You don't have to worry that I would ever get the wrong idea about...*this*...' she said, with an equal amount of coolness in her voice. 'I won't. What we have stays here, and that suits me very well, not just because anything else would interfere with my working relationship with you but because you're the last kind of guy I would go for. In fact, I would say that you've done me a favour...'

'How so?'

'You've reminded me that I'm still young,' Ellie told him, and that was the truth. 'That there are guys out there, and that falling in love is still something that is waiting for me. You've given me back my confidence.'

'I'm very glad to be of service,' James murmured.

Everything she had just said should be exactly what he wanted to hear because it all made sense.

For a second, when she'd hinted that he might be inclined to follow in his siblings' footsteps, he had thought she might be dropping hints.

Nothing had given him any suspicion that she might be following in Naomi's footsteps, tempted to barge past the Keep Out signs, refusing to give up even after the door had been slammed shut, but could he be sure? She remained as professional as she always was when they were in the company of their business partners, even fractionally moving off if he got too close.

To his surprise, he found her evasive measures irritating. He had perversely wanted to touch her, to remind their potential business partners that she was his. He hadn't. Possessiveness was something he personally had no time for as a trait and, if fleetingly he had wanted to stake his claim, then that had to do with a perfectly gentlemanly desire to protect her from any developing situations she might not have been able to handle. The guys were exuberant and open in their appreciation of what they saw.

Good job the deal was practically done.

A few more days here and they would go their separate ways and, when they next met, normality would once again be resumed.

It was exactly what he wanted, and the fact that she had reassured him that she wasn't about to get any ideas about where this was going should have made him feel better than it did.

Disgruntled, he wondered whether it would be appropriate to point out that not many men liked seeing themselves as a trial run for other guys!

That was the only reason her remarks had made him

feel edgy. Truth was, he had timelines when it came to women, and she was no different, even though she might have known him better than most. Possibly better than anyone else did. Inevitable, given that she worked for him and saw him more than most men saw their wives.

What they had would run its course. Every involvement with every woman always ran its course in the end. It was the way he liked it. Nothing deep and so no messy, painful aftermath. So why the hell was he ever so slightly irked at what she'd just said?

He dropped her hand and moved a little away, creating necessary distance between them, searching for his self-control, wondering whether the sun and forty minutes worth of swimming in open ocean had done something to him—made him a bit light-headed, made him think that she'd got under his skin a little too much for his liking.

'I've completed the last bits of paperwork for the deal here.' Ellie noted the way he had stopped holding hands and stepped just fractionally away.

Did he think that he had to further remind her that this meant nothing to him but a bit of fun?

Had she somehow communicated something to him... done something to make him think otherwise...?

Anxiously, Ellie tried to think back. The mere fact that she felt she might have somehow signalled to him that she was in deeper than she'd ever expected, despite the very sensible mantras she kept repeating to herself, sent a chill of apprehension racing up and down her spine.

Bring it back to work...

In the thick, suddenly uncomfortable silence, she chatted about everything she had managed to get through earlier while he had been in front of his laptop. Legal technicalities had been ironed out! Patents sorted! Signatures were awaited but she didn't foresee any problems...

Eventually, her voice tapered off and she stared straight ahead. For the first time she was blind to the exotic beauty of their surroundings, to the hum of distant insects, the sound of the lapping ocean, the stunning riot of colour of all the flowers, the people and the infectious sound of laughter.

She felt the loss of his touch like a physical blow, and that scared her, making her doubly determined to keep her feelings under wraps.

Their dedicated chauffeur was waiting to take them back to the hotel. She slid into the back seat and closed her eyes for a few seconds, enjoying the cool air-conditioning after the scorching heat outside.

What was going on? Was this the prelude to the good-bye speech? Only now that it was imminent did she realise how much she had been looking forward to really enjoying the last few days with him.

Did that make her seem clingy? The very thought was mortifying. She thought of poor Naomi and felt a twinge of intense sympathy.

She clasped her hands together on her lap and stared through the tinted windows, wondering what line of conversation to take to break the increasingly uncomfortable silence between them.

'You've gone quiet on me,' James murmured. Ellie slid her gaze across and breathed a mental sigh of relief because the sudden coolness between them had filled her with horror, disproportionately so.

'Have I? I thought I'd been talking quite a bit about closing this deal we've come here to do.'

'Less work and more play...'

'If you say so...you're the boss, after all...' He tugged gently and she shuffled closer to him. He closed the privacy partition, separating them from their driver, and tilted her face to his.

'I am,' he agreed, tracking the outline of her mouth with his finger and sending a thousand little electrical impulses reverberating through her body. 'I've spent the whole day wanting to touch you. In fact, if it weren't for the fact that we'll be at the hotel in under twenty minutes, I would be doing a lot more than I'm doing now...'

'Really?' Ellie queried huskily. 'Like what?'

'I'd quite like to pay some attention to your breasts... Have I mentioned that you have beautiful ones?'

'James, stop!' But she was laughing as her whole body went up in flames at his evocative words and the searing hunger in his dark eyes.

'Tell me I'm not turning you on...'

'Maybe you are.'

'Just *maybe*? Maybe you'll get a little more turned on if I tell you that I'm looking forward to taking that bikini off you very, very slowly and then, once I've devoted sufficient attention to your breasts, I intend to get between your legs and taste you down there until you're begging me not to stop...'

'Shh...'

'Are you wet for me yet?'

'You know I am.'

'Would you like to come against my mouth? I know you enjoy that...'

'Not as much as I enjoy feeling you inside me.' Looking at herself from a distance, looking at the woman now saying what she had just said, Ellie could scarcely believe her ears. She had never thought she could be so uninhibited and she had to acknowledge that that had been his great gift to her.

She had opened up with him, against all odds, and she had blossomed in ways she could never have imagined.

She was in such desperate need of being touched, after

that hot conversation in the back of the car, that she practically leapt out of her seat before the driver had had a chance to pull to a stop.

And James was in as much of a hurry as she was.

They were holding hands, and neither of them had expected to be greeted by a woman. Indeed, they barely realised that they were on a collision course with the towering blonde until she was suddenly *there*, right in front of them, her expression more shock than fury.

James gathered himself at speed and stood back, expression closed, concealing his shock as he looked at his ex for a few stunned seconds.

'Naomi. What the hell are you doing here?'

'I came...to see whether we could patch things up. I know you never answered my texts but... I know how proud you are...' She was talking to James. She was staring at Ellie. Her cool, assessing eyes glittered as hard as diamonds.

'I told you it was over.' His voice was tight and controlled.

He had managed to pull them all to one side. Ellie was hardly aware of being manoeuvred out of the main stream of traffic along with Naomi, who was wearing the briefest of shorts, the tiniest of cropped tops and carrying a hold-all bearing a well-known logo.

'So what's going on between the two of you?'

Her voice had risen. Ellie could feel curious eyes on them. Hardly surprising, given the fact that Naomi was clearly a supermodel, James was clearly incredibly important and incredibly wealthy and the altercation between them was clearly going south.

A cabaret of sorts was about to commence and who wouldn't be interested in taking a ringside to witness the event?

She thought of Naomi kicking off at the office in her absence and wondered whether a repeat performance was on the cards, this time with a far more judgemental audience.

'This was supposed to be *our* holiday, James! I even *chose this hotel*!'

'I am *not* going to get into this with you again, Naomi. This was not a trip for you to make. I don't want a scene in a public place but I'm warning you—if you don't leave, I'll have no option but to call the manager to have you discreetly escorted out of the hotel.'

'You can't do that! This is a public place! Besides, you wouldn't *dare* risk a scene!'

'Want to try me?'

'Were you involved with your little secretary before we broke up, James?'

Everything in Ellie wanted to rage against the sweeping insult behind that accusation, but tact made her hold back the words begging to be delivered.

She was on the periphery of this, and besides, whatever the rights or wrongs of Naomi showing up on the island in the hope that her physical charms might achieve what texts and phone calls presumably hadn't, Ellie felt a twinge of sympathy for the other woman.

She was uneasily aware of just how effortlessly you could get blinded to the reality of a situation. James was just so persuasive, so charming, so incredibly dynamic, sharp, clever and unexpectedly thoughtful in ways you could never have predicted.

Just as well she knew the parameters of this game being played, but even so…

Naomi had wanted more. Without those parameters really in place, was it any wonder she had been tempted to show up here…?

'Okay. I think I've had enough of this.' He looked around, searching for one of the members of staff.

Ellie stepped in to say quietly, 'That's insulting to James and it's insulting to me, what you're inferring.'

'Well, it's obvious that you two are an item,' Naomi bit back without hesitating. 'It's obvious you're *all loved up.* Do you honestly think you're going to get anywhere with him when *I* couldn't?'

Out of the corner of her eye, Ellie could see the worried face of the hotel manager as he scuttled at pace across the marble foyer.

'You won't!' Naomi leaned in to Ellie.

'You don't understand…' Ellie began, distraught at what was happening, and keen to eliminate herself from a scenario in which she didn't feel she truly belonged.

How dared this perfect stranger think that she, Ellie, was so lacking in principles that she would have hopped into bed with her boss while he was seeing another woman?

Yet, she *had* hopped into bed with him, hadn't she? And the time lag between Ellie doing that and him breaking up with the stupendously beautiful blonde looking at her with ice-cold eyes *had* been shamelessly brief, hadn't it?

So Naomi had flown over here, desperate to effect a reconciliation…

And Ellie? Was clinging to these last few days just as desperate—even if her desperation was hidden behind a veneer of self-control and nonchalant acceptance of the ground rules laid down?

When she thought of their relationship coming to an end, to returning to London where she would plaster a bright, beaming smile on her face and pretend nothing had happened, there was a feeling of terrifying *emptiness* underneath all the bracing assumptions that this was something that would fade in no time at all.

How different was she really from the woman who had crossed the Atlantic to reconnect with a guy who no longer wanted her? How vulnerable would *she* find herself when things resumed between them professionally, with this brief interlude relegated to the history books?

Had anything in her life prepared her for this? No. Too many years living a sheltered life had allowed James, with his larger-than-life personality, to roar through her with the force of an all-consuming tidal wave, battering down the door she had spent so many years keeping firmly shut between them.

Suddenly exposed to thoughts she had managed to wilfully avoid, Ellie felt her heart begin to race.

Low, urgent words were being exchanged between James and Naomi, but it was all just background noise, eclipsed by a weird thundering in her ears and a sickening realisation that she had managed to lose all control over what was happening in her life.

Having been immersed in her thoughts, she resurfaced to Naomi hissing under her breath that she would be sorry.

Sorry for what?

She looked at James in confusion, feeling as though she'd fallen asleep during the middle of a play only to wake up to an ending that made no sense.

'James may have told you that he's serious about you, but he's not. Word to the wise: don't get your hopes up. *There won't be a wedding ring on that finger any time soon!*'

She spun on her heels, sweeping past the hotel manager who had halted in his tracks at some point, no doubt having been given an invisible signal by James. Eyes followed her, avidly curious. One or two phones were recording the whole episode but Ellie had too much on her mind to pay a blind bit of notice to any of that.

Instead, she scrambled behind James as he summoned the lift with a thunderous expression which he couldn't quite manage to conceal.

As with the snapping smartphones, Ellie ignored the thunderous expression and said bluntly, just as soon as the doors had snapped shut behind them, 'What did she mean by that?'

'By what?'

'Fingers and wedding rings! Did you tell her that we were some kind of *item*?'

'It would have been difficult for her to have escaped that conclusion.'

'No, it would have been very easy to have set her straight!'

The lift doors pinged open and she hurried after him, eager to have the privacy of a room with no chance of wagging ears or eyes on stalks.

'We were holding hands when we entered the lobby,' he reminded her with a level of calm that got on her nerves. 'You were flushed with wanting me. We couldn't wait to get back to the bedroom. A fool with poor eyesight would have been able to put two and two together.'

He was stripping off as he spoke, prowling the elegant sitting area that adjoined the massive bedroom.

All that startling masculine beauty. It had got right to her, demolished her defences, but she refused to allow it to leave her helpless. She wasn't going to drift along until things fizzled out between them in a few days' time.

In some way, Naomi's appearance had put things into miserable perspective, and if she didn't take hold of the reins now then when would she?

'So now she thinks that this is serious? Now she thinks that you broke up with her so that you could bring me here to take her place?'

'Do either of us care what Naomi thinks?'

His eyes were cool, already distant. Ellie wondered whether, down the line, he would care what *she* thought. No chance. He was impervious to emotion, which was why it was so easy for him to take what he wanted when it came to women and then discard them when they began to bore him.

'I care,' Ellie said quietly. '*I* care, James. I'm not like you. I can't just do whatever I want to do and to heck what other people think.'

He flushed darkly and raked his fingers through his hair. He'd stripped off the shirt, unbuttoning the shorts that hung low on lean hips. She had to look away so that her body didn't begin misbehaving. With an unconscious gesture of self-defence, she hugged herself and stared at him, not having moved from the door, having remained standing while he had powered into the room.

'Who says we aren't an item?'

'You let her think that this was serious, and it's not, and I know why you did that. You did it because you wanted to get rid of her and that was the most efficient way of doing it.'

'She was going to believe what she wanted to believe,' James countered, but he hadn't breached the distance between them, and the air shimmered with antagonism.

'I think we need to call it day.'

'Oh, for God's sake, Ellie. Isn't that something of an overreaction? Why? Because an ex huffed and puffed and thought she could blow the house down?'

Because I think I'm falling in love with you.

It was a shattering realisation, one that had crept up and ambushed her when she hadn't been looking. She *should* have been looking. Instead, she had been busily telling herself that she couldn't possibly fall for him because she was *too sensible.* As if being sensible made her invincible.

She breathed in deeply, taking her time to think, knowing that hysteria on any level just wasn't going to work.

'Because I stepped back, had a good, long look at myself and I didn't like what I saw.'

'Which was what?'

Which was a complete fool with cotton wool for a brain.

'I wasn't raised to have flings. It's not what I do, and it's especially horrible to know that someone might actually think I'm the kind of person who doesn't mind sleeping around with some guy who's involved with someone else. I was brought up with a lot of principles, and I guess I thought I could dump them for a while, but I was wrong. I can't. We could carry on with what we have but, now that I've come to my senses, it would be hard for me to return to where we were...'

She sighed and looked away. She wished she could read what he was thinking but, for a guy who was apparently so open, he was adept when it came to revealing only what he wanted to reveal. Right now, she had no idea what was going through his head.

'In that case,' he said coolly, 'you're probably right. I'm not looking for involvement, Ellie. Not me. Never will be.'

A dagger had just shot through her heart but she only had herself to blame. She nodded and managed a smile. 'I'll move myself back to my bedroom...'

And what happens next?

He answered that unspoken question without her having to try and find a subtle way of asking it.

'I anticipate,' he drawled, 'that all signatures will be in place tomorrow. There's no more schmoozing to be done. The deal will have been done. To avoid any potential awkwardness, you are free to arrange a flight back for yourself, and I will see you when I return to London in a couple of weeks.' He inclined his head to one side and gave her a half mocking salute. 'That suit you?'

'Yes.' Ellie nodded, her face as blank as his. 'That would be for the best…'

CHAPTER SEVEN

JAMES GAZED OUT from the balcony of his suite at a view that was incomparable.

Sprawled on the hand-made bamboo chair, long legs stretched out on the matching footstool and hands folded behind his head, he let his eyes feast on a tapestry of navy blue sea and a sky that was ablaze with all the vibrant colours of sunset. Russet and burnt orange against a backdrop of deepest indigo and midnight-blue. No painter could have captured the natural beauty.

However, as he nursed a rum, the only persistent image in his head was that of his recently departed personal assistant.

For the first time since they had touched down on the island, his bed was empty. In a fitful sleep, he had rolled onto his side at a little after three in the morning, automatically reaching out for her warmth, but had jerked awake, uncomfortable at the thought that he didn't care for the sudden emptiness of his sleeping arrangements.

Since when had he had a problem sleeping on his own? Indeed, that was something he had always actively encouraged. It was rare for any woman to occupy his bed overnight, and certainly never for nights on end, as though some kind of habit was being nurtured.

He had been interested to see how breakfast together

would go, following what he still considered to be an overly dramatic and premature ending to what they had going on. He'd imagined that he might have to deal with her embarrassment.

Understandable.

She lacked his considerable experience in these matters. In fact, when he thought about her, which he had done for most of the night, it was to conclude that she was strangely innocent and touchingly disingenuous, despite the outward image of a cool, controlled and utterly unflappable professional.

It tickled him pink to think that he was the one-in-a-million guy who had seen right into that very private part of her.

So he had been surprised and a little disgruntled, several hours earlier, when he had sat down to breakfast with a woman who was once again metaphorically dressed in her London work uniform.

Every time he had tried to steer the conversation in a more personal direction, she had blanked over and looked at him with polite, ever so amused grey eyes and then promptly returned the conversation right back to work. Deals that were brewing on the side lines... An email from a company he had casually approached six months previously that was now interested in doing business with him... The sudden absence of one of the CEOs whose mother had been rushed to hospital following a car accident...

She had been thoroughly and admirably in control, and *naturally* he had been immensely grateful to be spared the awkwardness of having to get things back on track in preparation for a resumption of their normal working relationship.

He had reminded himself of the continuing nightmare

of the ex who couldn't go away. Another lingering ex was the last thing he needed.

Still… Was there any reason for her politely but firmly to decline his suggestion that he accompany her to the airport?

'Good Lord! That's very sweet of you but of course I don't want you coming with me to the airport!' She had knocked back his offer with incredulous laughter and then followed up by wryly informing him that she was perfectly capable of checking in at an airport, even if it *had* been ages since she'd had a chance to go abroad before this.

He had gritted his teeth and smiled when she had earnestly thanked him then for the opportunity to visit such a wonderful island. And when he had tilted his head to the side and asked her whether that was all she wanted to thank him for, she hadn't been in the slightest bit coy.

'Oh, the sex was lovely,' she had said warmly, but her eyes had glazed over, and it had been perfectly clear that the *lovely sex* was something she was already in the process of putting behind her.

Who was he to complain? She'd made it easy for him. She had pulled back from dwelling on the fact that she *didn't do casual*, saving him the necessity of gently reminding her that emotional relationships were a beast he steered clear of.

He drained his glass. It was a little after six and he would spend the remainder of the evening working. He'd signed off on the deal he had come to finalise, and in the blink of an eye he would be boarding a plane for Hawaii, no doubt in the mood for some distraction.

Dwelling was a much-overrated pastime. There would be no time to *dwell* when he was working by day and playing by night. It was a tried and tested formula that had always stood him in good stead. It had worked when his parents had died, and it had worked in the aftermath of his juvenile crush on a woman who had only been good for warming his bed. It would damn well work now.

He stood up, stretched and absently appreciated the rapidly sinking ball of fire disappearing over the horizon. Give it three days and he would probably be hard pressed to remember just how intense the past few days on this island had been...

Ellie gazed at her mobile phone, which had not stopped ringing for the past eight hours.

The trip back had been uneventful enough, and she had almost managed to convince herself that putting distance between them would work wonders when it came to clearing her head.

She'd fallen hook, line and sinker for her boss, and so of course it was going to be a towering mountain to climb for that brief liaison to be erased from her memory bank, but erased it would be. She had no choice in the matter, at least not until she managed to find another job that paid as well.

She had managed to get through the nightmare of their last breakfast together in one piece. Her jaw had ached from the discomfort of the phoney smile she had plastered to her face, but she had got through it, and that was the main thing.

It had been a pointer that overcoming this suffocating misery was achievable.

She landed at Gatwick Airport and took a taxi back to her flat. The idea of trudging on public transport seemed way too depressing and arduous.

She knew that one of the things she would have to become accustomed to was going to be the drudgery of normal life.

She'd always taken great pride in being the sort of person who wasn't easily impressed by the trappings of wealth. She'd worked with James Stowe and seen first-hand the amount of money he lavished on the women he dated, because she often found the receipts for ludicrously expensive items kicking around on his desk, and had privately smirked at the superficiality of those women who were actually impressed by all that sort of stuff.

And yet, she now found herself swelling their numbers, seduced by the pleasure of all those comforts that went hand in hand with great wealth. She had gazed at the perfect splendour of a pristine beach, dipping into a picnic prepared by a top chef, and she had felt so blissfully happy.

Did that make her superficial? No. Worse than that, she had to acknowledge that she would have felt just as blissfully happy had they been tucking into chicken and chips eaten out of plastic baskets, because James had been the reason for her happiness.

Nevertheless, she would have to come right back down to earth, and fast. And for the first twenty-four hours, she actually believed that that was on the cards. She unpacked, stuffing her newly acquired clothes to the back of her wardrobe, where she anticipated them spending a few years hibernating before she gave them to a charity shop. She could never entertain the notion of wearing all those brightly coloured items of clothing again, not when they would always remind her of a time that had come and gone in the blink of an eye.

Then she had an early night and tried to plan her return to work the following Monday without a broken heart stamped all over her face. The last thing she felt she could deal with was sheepish, embarrassed, inquisitive looks from concerned colleagues.

* * *

Fate had other ideas when it came to giving her a break, and now here she was…

What on earth was she going to do?

The phone had been ringing off the hook. There were two men with cameras outside her house, lounging by a car, smoking and waiting for her to emerge from where she had now been in hiding for the past day.

She felt as if she was suddenly under attack on all sides, and she had no idea what she was going to do.

The first call, from one of her colleagues at work, had alerted her to the fact that she was suddenly in the spotlight and *newsworthy*.

'Hey, girl, what's going on?'

Ellie had heard Trish's sing-song voice but, before she'd been able to fill her in on the successful outcome of her trip to Barbados, she had been pinned to the spot by a series of good-natured questions that had left her reeling.

The second she had hung up, she had found the tabloid headlines on her phone and had watched her whole life begin to unravel with sickening horror.

Of course, Ellie had known that James was the darling of the tabloid press. A billionaire, ridiculously good-looking, and with the gravitas and money that came from the complex and cut-throat world of business.

He was also courteous towards reporters. He always seemed to recognise that they were doing a job and, as long as they didn't go anywhere he didn't want them to go, he was unfailingly co-operative. Hence he graced the covers of magazines and newspapers with predictable regularity because of the transitory nature of his relationships and the high profiles of most of his exes.

But now…

Now *she* was the woman…the one who had finally

'snared the country's most eligible bachelor'... The quiet little secretary who had 'worked her magic from the side lines'... The one who had 'managed to get the ring on her finger and the date set for a walk down the aisle'...

Of course, in a week's time this would all be history, and the reporters would be busily finding someone else to pin to the wall, but for now...

For now, she was trapped in her own house and when she did emerge, which she would have to in the next day or two to return to work, she would have to hope and pray that the furore would have died down.

Usually, Ellie would have taken a deep breath and cheerfully told the lot of them that it was all just a ridiculous mistake. If you ploughed your way through a problem, it was usually the fastest way of dealing with it, but there was now the added complication of her mother.

Every problem seemed to open a door to a new one. She cradled a cup of tea, frantically trying to work out how on earth she was going to deal with the accumulated lot of problems.

Her train of thought was interrupted by the frantic ringing of the doorbell. At six thirty in the evening this was the last thing she wanted and she ignored the piercing summons until her mobile phone began ringing as well, and up popped his number.

James.

Her heart stopped and she sank back against the chair and closed her eyes for a second.

Through all this, she hadn't stopped thinking of him. Would news of this have reached him in Barbados? He only read the broadsheets, but the gossip grapevine that did the rounds at work would surely have reached him?

She reluctantly took the call and braced herself to be

upbeat when all she wanted to do was hide away until the whole mess blew over.

'Open the door, Ellie!'

'James…' Her voice petered off.

'Open the door! I'm outside.'

'Outside?'

'Standing on your doorstep, to be precise.'

'I don't want to go outside. There are people there.' She heard the sound of tears in her voice and cleared her throat.

'I've got rid of them.'

'You have?' Relief washed over her, and for the first time in her life she weakly discovered what it felt like to have someone there to have her back and pick up the pieces.

Taking no chances and not stopping to be concerned that she was clad in nothing more than an old tee shirt, a pair of tight leggings and some gaily patterned bedroom slippers, Ellie went to the front door and unlocked it just enough to make sure that he was really there.

He was.

The breath whipped out of her and she stared for a few seconds, drinking him in with such shameless compulsion that she forgot the horror of her current situation.

He was in a pair of dark jeans and a dark polo shirt, with a battered tan bomber jacket hooked over one shoulder. He looked so utterly unfazed that she could only stare, mesmerised.

'Shouldn't you be on your way to Hawaii?'

'Open the door and let me in. I've sent the two reporters on their way, but I can't guarantee they won't be back, and an argument on the doorstep when we're due to be married any day soon is going to send them into a feeding frenzy…'

Ellie promptly undid the chain and fell back as he

brushed past her into her tiny hallway before spinning round on his heels to look at her.

'Why didn't you call me?' he demanded, staring at her.

How could he be so controlled? So calm, beautiful and utterly unruffled?

It didn't seem fair. She pulled herself up, stiffened her shoulders and glared at him.

'Call about what?' she asked with cool defiance.

Frozen to the spot by the laser sharpness of his eyes, it was an effort to unglue herself from her rigid position and head towards the kitchen, making sure to circle round him. She felt his eyes on her back as she walked ahead of him and into the small kitchen with its weathered pine table and mismatched, colourful chairs she had bought from a car boot sale a few months ago.

Only a handful of days ago, this man had been her lover, but that was then and this was now and Ellie was not going to let him think that she couldn't cope with what was being thrown at her.

Still…

She was glad that he was here. Somehow, his very presence felt like a guarantee that peace and order would be re-established.

'Can I get you some coffee?'

'Can you stop acting as though I'm a stranger? You should have called to tell me that the paparazzi were camping on your doorstep. How long have they been there? Since that bloody article hit the headlines? I'm guessing you've been bombarded with phone calls as well. It's easy for these people to get hold of a mobile number if certain security measures aren't in place.'

Bombarded with information and swept along by his instant dominance over the situation, Ellie could only subside weakly into one of the chairs, where she proceeded to rest her chin in her hands. She looked at him.

Coffee would have to wait. She felt she needed something a lot stronger. Scotch, maybe. A double. Except, there was none in the house. Her phone buzzed and she looked at it but didn't pick up.

'You have my apologies,' James murmured in a low voice. 'You look as though you could use a drink, and I don't blame you. What have you got?'

'There's a bottle of wine in the fridge…' She wanted to be strong and in charge, because they were no longer involved with one another, but it felt so good for him to take charge that she waited and then sighed with barely concealed relief when a glass of wine was placed in front of her.

'Talk to me.'

'Why are you here?' was what came out of her mouth, and he frowned.

'Did you expect me to read all that nonsense emblazoned across the tabloids and then head off to Hawaii, leaving you to deal with the mess?'

'I'm not your problem.'

'Let's put pride to one side just for the moment,' James said neutrally. 'Have you left the house? Spoken to anyone?'

'No and no.' Ellie sighed. 'I've been avoiding the phone. And it's not just the reporters…it's everyone at work. I…' Tears welled up and she hurriedly looked away, stared at her hands on her lap and breathed in deeply. 'It's pretty awful,' she whispered.

Guilt rammed into him with the force of a runaway train. The look on her face…

He'd got on that plane without any internal debate.

He'd read what had been unleashed in the gossip columns on the opposite side of the Atlantic and *not* getting on a plane and heading back hadn't been an option. Not when he'd been furious with his ex and even more furious with himself for putting Ellie in the situation in which she had found herself. *You made the mess and it was up to you to clear it up.*

He raked his fingers through his hair now and had to force himself to remain seated when what he wanted to do was vault upright and stride restlessly through the tiny kitchen, unless he brought his mind back under control.

Naomi. Bloody Naomi. Nothing like a woman scorned. She had taken stock of the situation when she had descended unannounced at the hotel in Barbados. She had seen with her own eyes exactly what was happening, and she had reacted with a vengeance, returning to London and running to the newspapers as fast as she could.

And why? Because her ego had taken a battering and she had known the best way she could get her revenge. He was a commitment-phobe? Then why not dump him in his own worst nightmare, publicly engaged to be married to someone, she must have assumed, who would be the last woman on earth he'd be attracted to long term, given his well-publicised penchant for leggy beauties...

Now Ellie was here. He could see that she could barely keep herself together and he couldn't blame her. So guarded, so incredibly private, and now thrust into the limelight in ways that she would find horrifying.

He thought of her returning to work, braving those first steps in and knowing that the gossip mill would have been working overtime, and he inwardly winced.

No point dwelling on it, he decided. A self-pity fest wasn't going to get either of them anywhere.

'A united front and point-blank denial from both of us

will kill this rumour dead,' he promised. 'I could have contacted people I know in that field and put the record straight, but I had to find out what was going on over here. I also baulk at having to justify anything to anyone,' he admitted. 'I'm assuming you know who is behind this?'

Ellie nodded. She didn't trust herself to speak.

'I don't have to tell you that my ex has chosen to wage war on the wrong man.' His face hardened. 'She will find out that my influence extends much further than she could ever expect. I suggest we face the press together and laugh this whole thing off. It will be an easy enough job to put the blame where it rightfully belongs—on the shoulders of an ex with an axe to grind.'

'It's…it's not as simple as that.'

James frowned. What could more complex?

'Have your family…? Has it reached them over there?'

'Izzy has a fondness for tabloids and all things gossip.' He half smiled wryly. 'She probably knew before the print on the paper had time to dry.'

'And have you…told them anything? Have they been in touch?'

'I thought it best to say nothing until I had spoken to you.'

This was why she had crossed that line, Ellie thought. It had nothing to do with how he looked, the reach of his wealth and influence or even the fact that he was far and away the most dynamic, intelligent, forward-thinking, downright *fascinating* person she had ever met.

It was because he was a decent guy.

She'd somehow managed to convince herself that the sort of man she would eventually go for would be a stereotype, as though decent guys all came wrapped up in the same packaging. But James Stowe, on the surface just the sort she couldn't possibly fall for, ticked every single box when it came to being one of the good guys. And that, she knew now, was why sleeping with him had felt so *right*.

He might not love her, or even care about her the way she loved and cared about him, but he had still thought to consider her amidst all of this, to hear what she had to say.

'My mother has been in touch with me,' Ellie said flatly. 'Several times.' She sipped the wine and felt the rush of alcohol to her head.

He said nothing but his sudden stillness was telling, as was the way he was looking at her, eyes narrowed thoughtfully, head tilted to one side.

'And?' he prompted softly when she lapsed into awkward silence.

'And she's very excited.'

'Ah...'

'I never thought she indulged in gossip mags, but it seems that that's her secret vice.' Ellie smiled wanly. 'It seems that it's the secret vice of her entire book club.' She sighed and looked at him steadily. 'When she phoned me, I honestly had no idea she would have been phoning to tell me how pleased she was for me.'

'Go on,' he encouraged quietly.

'It was the happiest I'd heard her sound in a long time. In fact, just before I flew over to Barbados, I was actually beginning to worry that she was going to give in to her depression again. It's plagued her over the years and, although the doctor would never confirm in so many words, I think that her depression and all the associated stress had something to do with her strokes. She was pleased that I was going to Barbados... Maybe she doesn't need me as she once did, but underneath it all I still worry that she could so easily slide back down that hill. She called...she called and she was so pleased for me.'

'I see.'

Ellie didn't have to read the expression on his face to know what was going through his head.

He'd banked on a swift explanation to the press, probably a couple of phone calls and a joint statement from them both, shrugging off the whole sorry saga.

Yes, Naomi had exaggerated everything wildly out of context, but a woman scorned, he would doubtless insinuate, would be capable of any number of things from slashing tyres to fabricating ruinous stories.

He rightfully assumed that, if you gave too much airtime to gossip, you breathed life into it.

But now…

Now, behind that carefully guarded expression, he would be livid and she felt terrible about that.

'I'm afraid that if I laugh it all off my mum will be distraught, even if she did a job of hiding it, and I'm afraid for her health—both mentally and physically.'

'And for good reason, from what you've told me.'

'I'm very sorry about this,' she said in as controlled a voice as she could muster. 'I'll have to… Of course, things will be sorted and the truth told…'

'Well, not entirely the truth.'

'What do you mean?'

'There may have been some colourful exaggeration as to the gravity of our relationship, but we *were* lovers.'

Ellie reddened. Heat coursed through her body, setting every nerve ending alight and rousing a vivid imagination she had spent the past couple of days trying to extinguish.

She squirmed, the breath catching in her throat, and once again she was helplessly aware of the thoughts leaving her head in a rush while her body kicked in with gusto.

'Yes, well, I obviously won't… I mean, that's all over now, so there would be no point… The fact is that I wanted to go and see Mum so that I could explain everything face to face.' She took a deep breath and exhaled slowly. 'I know this must be just awful for you,' she said quietly. 'If you would wait just a bit before you say anything to the press, then I would be so grateful. Mum would be so confused if she were to be let down by reading another gaudy headline.' She sighed. 'I can't bear to imagine what's going through her head now. What must she think of me?'

'Why would she think anything differently of you?'

'She knows that this…this *person* who went off and had some fling with her boss on a tropical island isn't the girl she brought up. If you knew my mother, you'd under-stand what I'm saying.'

She had never been a risk taker. She had been brought up in a loving and careful way. You could never have a guarantee when it came to matters of the heart, but with James there was only ever going to be one outcome. Sleep-ing with her boss had been like jumping from an aeroplane without a parachute. In a life where Ellie had had to deal with pain, she had foolishly courted yet more of it with-out meaning to, and now this horribly contorted situation had come down to this—a situation where it wasn't just *she* who was affected.

James looked at that soft, vulnerable face, a face she had always been so careful to conceal, and something twisted painfully inside him.

She would suddenly have found herself besieged by slings and arrows on every front. He marvelled that, not only had she not jumped on the phone and demanded he sort things out, but she was here, clearly upset and yet still trying hard to put a brave face on it.

'You could be wrong.'

'I'm not. Trust me.' She smiled wanly. 'I was an only child. You wouldn't believe how protective they were of me, both my parents. They worried all the time when I wasn't around.'

'You're very lucky,' James heard himself say, to his surprise. 'My parents were largely noticeable by their absence. Perhaps not with Izzy. She got the best of them because she was so much younger, but certainly Max had no real idea who they were, and neither, to a large extent, did I.'

He shot her a crooked smile, slightly embarrassed at that confession, and even more astonished that he rather liked that she had been the recipient. 'When you have all the money in the world, and the freedom to do whatever you want with it, without any parental control or discipline or interest, you'd be surprised how pointless it all seems.' He paused. 'Your mother has never met me. What she knows about me is what she's read in those lurid gossip articles…'

'I know. Again, I'm very sorry this isn't going to be as straightforward as you'd probably predicted.'

He waved down her apology. 'Stop telling me how sorry you are. You shouldn't be. If you're afraid that your mother will be disillusioned when she finds out what happened, then don't you think it's important that she meets me?'

'Meets you?' Ellie's mouth dropped open. Meet James Stowe? She tried to picture her anxious, diminutive mother, thrust into the presence of this over-the-top dynamic guy with the sharp, restless brain and the ridiculous good looks, and she visibly shuddered. 'Why would that help anything?'

'Think about it,' James murmured, one hundred percent of his attention focused on her. 'If you tell her that it was all a complete fabrication, then chances are she's not going to believe you. Even if she pretends to. You know what they say about no smoke without fire. Then she'll wonder why you might be lying and, whatever conclusion she reaches, she'll be disappointed.'

'Yes, well…' Ellie looked at him, a little flustered, because she had no great urge to give him a minute-by-minute rendition of what she intended to say to her mother, largely because the conversation was still a work in progress in her head.

'If you tell her the truth…that you and I were lovers… then from what she will have read in the gutter press, from what Naomi has managed to convey, she will assume that you were taken advantage of by me. How do you think she will feel about that?'

He didn't give her time to formulate an opinion on what he had just said, but seamlessly moved on. 'She'll either be heartbroken that her baby girl has let herself be seduced by a big, bad wolf, or else she'll be worried that your taste in men might be heading in the wrong direction. Or both.'

'I hadn't actually got as far as considering what…'

'You don't want any unintentional stress being put on her shoulders, do you?'

'Of course not!' The wretched man had a point, and it wasn't one she had considered. Her mother worried. Would she end up more worried after a frazzled explanation about what had actually happened? Disappointment that there would be no wedding bells after all was one thing. The fear that she, Ellie, might somehow have decided to abandon the moral code she had always lived by would be something altogether more difficult for her to deal with. Wouldn't it?

'Then here's what I suggest.'

His voice was softly bewitching, lulling and mesmerising her. He'd finished his glass of wine and she realised she had too. She'd barely been aware of drinking it! Part of her knew that she should deal with her mother on her own, that any suggestion that her boss climb into the picture would just be an added layer of complication she could do without, and yet…

She was seduced by his voice, by the certainty he conveyed that somehow everything was going to be all right… that if he came along the business with her mother would be sorted to a far more satisfactory degree. It was in his nature to take charge and he was good at it, and right now she *wanted* someone to take charge. She had been going out of her mind ever since her private life had been splattered across the tabloids.

'What's that?' She opened the door to whatever he was about to suggest.

'We both go to see your mother. We can fill her in on what happened, and at least she'll have a chance to see that I'm not the guy portrayed in those articles—the guy who messes around with women for his own enjoyment and was happy to do the same with you. We had a relationship, but it was consensual and enjoyable, and was our mutual choice to bring it to a close. Meeting me will take the drama out of the situation. And, when we've explained that to her, then we can see about filling in the rest of the world…'

CHAPTER EIGHT

Waiting by the window, peering out into the still grey light of a dull, rainy morning that hadn't quite broken, because it wasn't yet six, Ellie wondered how she had managed to be coaxed into this so easily.

But he had come through that front door behind which she had been hiding, he had taken control and she had been grateful.

She was also guiltily aware of feeling a sense of relief that someone else would be there when she broke the news to her mother that she wouldn't, after all, be walking down the aisle, followed swiftly by a trip to the hospital to give birth to those long-awaited grandchildren.

Ellie had known that her mum wanted her to settle down. It was almost as if she didn't think her job as a mother had been done well unless Ellie got married, had kids and lived happily ever after. Or at least, it would seem, *had a bit of fun*. Maybe that was part of the reason why she had been happy to see her go to Barbados. Maybe, when Ellie had had her back turned, worrying about her mother had changed into her mother worrying about *her*.

How was she to know that having fun would come at painful cost?

Did it make sense that James come with her? Overnight, she'd managed to justify it to herself. Yes, even though her mother would find out that any hat buying expeditions would have to be put on ice, at least she would see that the love affair had been a lovely time out, with neither one taking advantage of the other. She would see that there had been nothing sordid about it.

She wouldn't see the pain because Ellie would keep that to herself. She would be relieved that her daughter was finding her feet and stretching her wings, getting ready to fly.

A mature, adult fling. She felt giddy when she thought about her mother finding out that her baby was capable of a meaningless fling, even if it was with a guy she might actually approve of—because when James laid on the charm he was as close to irresistible as any human being could get.

James showed up on time, his sleek, black low-slung Porsche pulling up outside her house just as daylight was tentatively beginning to make an appearance. She watched for a few spellbound seconds as he vaulted smoothly out of the car, dressed entirely in black, and bounded up to her front door, which she pulled open before he could ring the doorbell.

'You're ready,' he said appreciatively. 'I wondered whether I'd get here to find you'd bolted your front door because you had a change of mind.' He bent to sweep up the small overnight bag she had packed and looked at her quizzically. 'Is this it?'

'I keep clothes at Mum's. I'm just taking a few essentials.' They'd agreed that he would come for one night because the trip was too long to go there and back in a day. She would stay on for a week or more while he returned to work and doused the flames of curiosity that would be blazing on the office floor. By the time she was ready to return, he had assured her with breezy confidence, everything would be entirely back to normal.

She believed him. It was one more nightmare he'd promised to sort out and she was willing to put her faith in that promise. Having always considered herself to be built of very stern stuff, given all the responsibilities she had taken on her shoulders from such a young age, she was amazed at just how pliable she was when it came to leaning on someone else.

'No nuisance calls overnight? No lurking men with cameras on the pavement this morning?'

They were walking towards his car and she slipped into the low, leather seat as he opened the boot of the car and slung in her bag.

'Nothing.' She felt a familiar tingle as he slid into the driver seat and briefly turned to look at her, one hand resting on the steering wheel, the other on his thigh.

In the barely there half-light his eyes glittered, boring straight into her. Since he'd descended on her, taking her by surprise, he had made no move whatsoever to touch her. In no way at all had he shown any interest in picking up where they had abruptly left off.

Yes, he had mentioned their relationship in passing, almost as an afterthought, and *of course* Ellie told herself that she was profoundly grateful for that closure.

The last thing she wanted was for him to put her in an impossible situation. No way under the sun would she welcome those sexy dark blue eyes on her, assessing, speculating, *encouraging* thoughts she knew were too close to the surface for her own good.

He had no idea what she felt, what was going on in her head, and she meant to keep it that way. He had no idea that his very lack of interest would be her source of strength when it came to recovering from her own foolish love.

And then, just as soon as her feet were back under the desk, she would start casually casting around for another job. She would explain, when the time came, that Barbados had opened her eyes to the possibility of a job where going abroad would feature more. She'd think of something to say, because she couldn't see a way of working alongside him indefinitely. Not feeling the way she did.

He switched on the engine and was manoeuvring along the narrow road, having programmed her mother's address into his satnav.

Now, she slanted disobedient eyes to the hand resting lightly on the gear stick and shivered. She despised the way she still wanted those hands to touch her, wanted those supple fingers to trail a burning path along her skin, to slip into the cleft between her legs, into her.

With the searing force of a branding iron, images of him were scored into her head, lodged so impossibly tightly that the tipping point between containment and despair, when she was with him now, felt as flimsy as a whisker.

'Good,' James returned with a note of smug satisfaction. 'I made a couple of calls. When you're in the public arena, it always pays to be cosy with a couple of the more senior of the paparazzi. There's a hierarchy there, and if you know how to use it it can come in useful. I let the word go out that they can have their story in a couple of days' time. Pursue, and they'll find connections they never knew they needed slamming the door on them.'

'Really?' Ellie was impressed.

'Really.' He half smiled. 'Most people know that getting on the wrong side of me isn't always the best way forward.'

'Well, thank you. It certainly helped with my sleeping last night.' She paused, and then continued in an awkward rush, 'I just want to thank you for making things easier for me. All of this…it's neither your fault nor mine. It's just something unexpected that happened, but you really have made dealing with the consequences…um…easier. You know—letting me have a week off work while you deal with the fallout there.'

'You're not accustomed to asking for help, are you?' he enquired softly and Ellie blushed, not looking at him, but staring straight ahead as he threaded through the narrow streets towards the motorway.

That was the sort of personal question he would never have asked her before they'd become involved, and it was just another reason why she knew she would have to quit her job just as soon as she could.

From passionate lover, he was now making his way to that awful place known as good friend…except he wasn't, was he? She didn't want him to adopt the role of being a shoulder she could cry on simply because he'd managed to get under her skin, just because they'd slept together, but she knew he would. He already was!

That would be the added dimension he had referred to, the one that would exist between them once their affair had run its course.

She projected to a point in the future when she would have to watch him hop back into the dating scene, return-ing to his normal luxury diet of catwalk models, as far as he was concerned, knowing she had returned to her quiet spot in the corner of the office—dutiful, efficient and once again background.

'Are you?' She threw the question back at him and he burst out laughing.

'Touché,' he said drily. 'Although, in fairness, why would I ever ask for help when I can handle pretty much everything myself?'

'You're so arrogant,' Ellie heard herself say, and then could have kicked herself for falling into the same trap he had…for going back to that place where they were intimate and where intimate things could be said without raising an eyebrow.

'So you've told me before. You wouldn't want me any other way.'

Ellie fidgeted, suddenly uncomfortable in the tight confines of his sports car.

Casting about for something inoffensive to say, he was the first to break the silence. 'So, tell me about your mother.'

'My mother?'

'What should I expect?'

'Does it matter? I mean, we're going there so that we can tell her face to face that this is all a storm in a teacup. I don't think you need to know what she's like, do you?'

'What's the point of my presence in that case? You want to smooth over anxieties your mother might have about this whole messy situation? Then I suggest you tell me about her so that I can emerge a sympathetic character as opposed to a serial womaniser who's used you for his own nefarious purposes and can barely show an interest in your only living relative. In which case, she might question my presence in her house in the first place.'

James could feel her tension. She was wired. Poor sleep, nervous tension. A strong person suddenly catapulted into uncertain, stormy seas without a lifebelt. It was pleasing to think that he was able to throw her that vital lifebelt. Having never seen himself in the role of knight in shining armour, primed to save damsels in distress, he was quietly pleased with himself now.

So much so that it overrode what he knew he should be feeling, namely intense rage that Naomi had dumped him from a very great height into the one situation she knew he would deeply resent. For the inveterate bachelor, widespread and incorrect rumours about getting married constituted a nightmare. On a personal level, it was a huge nuisance, and when the woman in question was someone like Ellie then it took on a whole new dimension.

Of course, Naomi was shrewd enough to have clocked that immediately. He would see that he returned the favour in due course, but for the moment he couldn't say that he was unhappy to find himself at the wheel of his Porsche, driving to Devon in the early hours of a grey autumn morning with his PA next to him. Nor did he harbour any regret about doing what he was doing for the sake of her mother, a woman he had never met and didn't know from Adam. He knew that her mother was mentally fragile and to help remove that one worry from her shoulders was the least he could do.

He slid a sideways glance at the small figure hunched in the deep leather seat, face averted as she stared through the window at nothing in particular. She was chewing her lower lip and he didn't have to see her face to know exactly what expression she would be wearing—the one of someone suddenly carrying the weight of the world on her shoulders.

A wave of protectiveness washed over him and he determined that when she returned to work it would be to find all her colleagues suitably silent on the matter of their publicised affair. Anyone who dared make her life uncomfortable would face his wrath. It was the least he could do.

He could handle a situation like this. Rumour…gossip…malice. He could handle them because he had become emotionally untouchable. But for the first time that was something that failed to soothe. Was it that laudable to make a habit of avoiding anything that smacked of involvement? It was a question that had never bothered him before but for some reason it bothered him now. He brushed his unease aside.

'So you were telling me about your mother...?'

Ellie sighed and gave up. What was the point in being tight-lipped on the subject anyway?

When she looked back at herself as she'd used to be—working for him, aloof, professional, utterly private—it was like looking at a stranger from a distance. He had managed to invade every nook and cranny of her life and this trip to Devon would be the final battering down of everything she had kept so closely guarded, whether through habit or design.

'My mum's not old. In her mid-sixties. My parents had me when they were quite old, which is probably why they were always so protective. They'd tried and had just about given up when I came along. When I think about it, they were a unit for such a long time, just the pair of them, that they were both very dependent on one another. And my mum's always been quite gentle, with Dad the one taking the lead.'

'So when he died...'

'It was so unexpected. Barely any time to adjust. Yes, when my dad died, my mum's frailty really came to the fore. Since then, she's found a niche where she lives. She has her book club, and she gardens and bakes cakes for the local Women's Institute. But what worries me is that it's almost as if she's been waiting all this time for something like this to happen—for me to find a guy and get married and settle down. I mean, I *knew* she hankered after grandchildren. She always makes a point of faithfully reporting each and every friend whose son or daughter had a baby...'

James burst out laughing. 'Not very subtle, in other words!'

Ellie grinned, relaxed a little, looked at him and felt that swoop of bursting love and affection inside her, however unwelcome the sensation might be.

'Not very. The point is that I would have told her immediately that this was all a load of nonsense, would have explained the situation on the phone, but I didn't want to take any chances with her getting stressed out and worried.'

'Maybe she's not quite as delicate as you think.'

'You could be right,' Ellie mused, a little startled at that shrewd observation, which was one she had slowly begun to reach for herself. Yet she wasn't certain enough of her mother's strength to take chances. 'Who knows? You might change your mind when you meet her.'

And, James thought, *I am meeting her...*

And he realised that he was looking forward to the prospect...

The skies were grey when the sleek sports car finally began the winding conclusion of the trip from London. They had driven through a series of towns and hamlets of varying sizes, passing silent churches and small open markets that were beginning to bustle into life as the day took shape.

Finally James pulled up in front of a small cottage that formed part of a cluster, all nestled with their own perfectly groomed gardens, tucked away in the maze of lanes and tiny tree-lined streets skittering in the foothills of the mighty Exmoor.

They had driven through a small village just big enough to house essentials for a small community, dominated by a picturesque church that sat squarely in a rectangle of perfectly manicured lawns, its doors wide open to welcome whoever wanted to enter.

This couldn't have been more out of James's comfort zone. A life of privilege and access to everything money could buy had never provided him with any insight into the life of someone living in a tiny rural community.

He took a few seconds to look at the house in front of him. It was small and cream with a path to the front door that resembled something a child might have drawn, winding and cobbled and bordered by a bank on either side of neat grass, which was in turn fringed by equally neat hedges.

James breathed in deeply and shot a look at the girl next to him as she hesitated briefly. On the spur of the moment, he grasped her hand and, somewhere inside him, was gratified when she didn't let it go.

Ellie felt the warmth of his fingers curling into hers and didn't think twice about curling her fingers right back into his, even after they left the car.

But she dropped her hand the second her mother opened the front door before the knocker had had time stop reverberating through the cottage.

'Mum!'

'Ellie! Darling!'

Angela Thompson was a small, thin woman with a face that would have been quite striking had it been plumper and less careworn. Her eyes were large and dark, her hair just touching her shoulders, as straight as her daughter's but threaded with grey. She had the look of someone who had spent far too much time crying.

Just at the moment she was beaming, however, and for the very first time Ellie remembered the carefree woman her mother used to be. The hug she received was warm and long, then her mother stepped back and eyed James, assessing him.

'Very nice,' she said approvingly.

Ellie's mouth fell open. 'Mum, this is…er…'

'I know. I've read all about you.' She stepped back to

allow them both to brush past her, and *en passant* James inclined his head to kiss her on each cheek, French-style.

The cottage smelled of fresh bread and everywhere was sparkling. Cleaned in honour of the prospective son-in-law, Ellie thought with dismay... And *fresh bread*? Once upon a million years ago her mother had loved baking, but that had all been put on hold for so many years that it was a struggle to remember just when her mum had last baked anything at all.

With increasing alarm, she pondered this development while absently recognising that somehow James had managed to take control of the conversation, chatting about the drive down, answering questions about Barbados, all this as they were guided into the airy kitchen where ingredients were arranged for a hearty breakfast.

'You must be exhausted after your long drive...maybe you'd like to head up to your bedroom for a quick freshen-up?'

'Bedroom?' Ellie parroted weakly, surfacing slowly to the fact that dismantling her mother's misconception was going to be a more uphill task than she had first thought. Yes, her mother had sounded pleased and happy down the disembodied cell phone, but now, here in the flesh, Ellie was shocked at just how *alive* Angela Thompson was, just how *animated*.

'Of course. I've made up the guest room for the both of you.' She smiled and *winked*. 'Darling, your room just has that silly single bed, which wouldn't do at all. Now, why don't you both take your bags up? In the meantime, I'll start breakfast. Bacon fine for the pair of you? Eggs? I've got the most wonderful free-range eggs from Joan's chickens.'

'This is *awful*,' was the first thing Ellie said just as soon as the bedroom door was shut. She stared at James and tried to ignore the double bed dominating the small room and the vase of freshly picked flowers on the old-fashioned dressing table with the triple mirror. 'Are you *listening*?' she hissed, as he calmly peered through the window to the back garden and the acres of open countryside beyond.

'I'm listening.'

Ellie advanced a couple of steps into the bedroom. She'd dumped her small holdall on the bed and only now noticed that he had deposited his black leather overnight bag next to hers. They sat there, touching, like a couple of mocking reminders of the time they had spent in bed together.

Annoyed, she snatched hers and dumped it on the chair by the dressing table.

'What are we going to do?'

'I'm confused by your use of the plural. Haven't I already done my bit?'

'You've done more than just *your bit*.' Ellie thought of her mother preening and gazing at him, clearly mentally uploading photos of him as her future son-in-law about whom she would be able to boast to all the neighbours.

'Explain.'

'You…you… There was no need to go overboard with the charm!' Ellie exclaimed despairingly.

'I thought we'd agreed that it would be a good idea for me not to be cast in the role of ruthless, womanising cad? I thought…'

He paused and looked at her with his head tilted to one side. 'I thought we'd come to the conclusion that if you didn't want your mother unduly worrying it would be a good idea for her to at least understand that what we shared did not involve you being taken advantage of. Or, worse, didn't involve you losing all sense of good judgement— at which point she might imagine that you were setting a precedent for making up for lost time by having random sex with guys who were no good for you?'

'Yes, but…'

'But nothing, Ellie. I'm here because you've been thrown into the deep end by Naomi and, believe it or not, I accept a great deal of responsibility for that. I'm willing to do what I can to level the playing field, but don't forget that my presence here is for your benefit.' He shrugged. 'Left to me, I would brush off the inconvenient rumours without thinking too hard about it.'

'I know.' Ellie sighed. Could she blame him for being himself? He charmed. Could she blame her mother for warming to his charm? No.

She'd always had the choice to do what he would have done—to shrug off the inconvenient rumours without going into a tailspin. She could have explained everything to her mother over the telephone. She could have braved out the curiosity and gossip at work, knowing that everything faded in the fullness of time.

She hadn't, so here she was, and she surely couldn't start laying into him for just playing the part she'd asked him to play?

Which didn't mean that she didn't despair of the situation.

'I'll sort it out,' she assured him. 'You stay put here. Unpack. Have a shower. No *en suite* bathroom, but there's one at the end of the landing. Mum's probably put towels in there for us.' She tried to conceal a treacherous shiver at the thought of him standing naked under the shower, face upturned, eyes closed as the water poured over his impressive body. 'I don't care what you do but let me have half an hour or so to fill her in. The scenery outside is amazing. You can…er…stare through the window and appreciate it.'

Ellie didn't give him time to muse on the joys of doing what she'd just told him to do. She raced down to the kitchen to find her mother busily setting the pine table. In the centre there was bunch of freshly picked flowers in a vase. The bread was out of the oven and Ellie's mouth watered.

Her mother was pottering, humming something under her breath, and for a just a second Ellie was catapulted back in time to when her dad had still been alive...when *this* was what life had been like...when life for her mother had been a place where humming took place and baking was a thing of pleasure.

She breathed in deeply and stepped forward with a smile pinned to her face.

James gave her half an hour. Picturesque though the scenery was, indeed as beautiful in its own grey majesty as the blistering blue skies on the opposite side of the world, there was only so much he could stare at when his mind was busy trying to project to whatever scene was taking place in the kitchen downstairs.

He couldn't even focus on his laptop, which said something. For the first time, he felt as though he had walked, eyes wide open, into a situation the likes of which he had never dealt with before. He didn't do personal dramas when it came to women. He had never allowed himself to fall victim to the one thing he loathed, namely the idiocy of getting so wrapped up with a woman that you ended up straying into her dilemmas, having views on problems that had nothing to do with him...

He was discomforted by the realisation that this wasn't his comfort zone, and he could only placate his feverish brain by reminding himself that this was a temporary break in proceedings and that normal life would resume in no time at all.

In fact, he mused, pulling open the bedroom door and resisting the urge to take the stairs two at a time, he wouldn't be here at all were it not for Naomi and her mischief-making. He would be in Hawaii, soaking up more sun, doing the whole work, women and song thing and catching up with his brother pre-wedding. He would be relishing some healthy distraction! He enjoyed women. Women enjoyed him. But, when he thought about enjoying the joys of *anything* with another woman, his mind went blank and he felt as though he was staring into a fog.

He heard Angela's voice through the kitchen door which was ajar, and he paused, not so much trying to hear what was being said as wondering how he should approach this situation, given Ellie would have broken the disappointing news to her mother that they were not the couple she had been led to believe. He barely recognised the alien sensation that momentarily swept through him as indecision, so accustomed was he to having complete control of whatever situation he happened to find himself in…

He pushed aside the unfamiliar feeling and nudged open the door. The first thing he saw was Ellie smiling, smiling and smiling, as though her face might crack at any second.

And, in that instant, he knew exactly what was going on.

How much deeper could this hole get? Ellie thought, wrung out at the end of a day that seemed to have stretched to infinity and beyond.

Aside from escaping briefly just before their early six o'clock dinner, so that she could finally get to the shower and have some tormented down-time to herself, she had been on the go. Fending off questions, feeling the incisive boring of James's eyes on her, wherever she went, trying hard not to stare down at the calamitous abyss opening up at her feet. And, of course, silently thanking her boss for not cornering her so that he could ask the one question that must surely be on the tip of his tongue…

What the hell is going on?

She owed him an explanation but she was dreading what she foresaw as a showdown. He'd done her a favour in returning to London to rescue her from her own inexperience in dealing with the nightmare that had landed in her lap. He owed her. That would have been his take on things. Even if they hadn't slept together, he would have seen her as *his* responsibility in any kind of awkward situation that might have been generated by him, because, put simply, he was one of the good guys, however tough and uncompromising he might be in the work arena.

Her mother retired early, at a little after eight, to read and have a bath and absorb the day's events.

Kitchen clean and counters wiped, Ellie finally allowed herself to be cornered. Rather, barricaded in, because James positioned himself at the door of the kitchen, arms folded, eyebrows raised, and looked at her for a few seconds in silence.

Like her, he had escaped to have a shower earlier on, after their hearty breakfast at almost midday and tea in the garden at four. He was in a pair of faded jeans, a grey long-sleeved tee shirt that lovingly and unfairly emphasised his lean muscularity and some tan loafers that would have cost the earth.

'So…' he drawled. 'Help me out here, Ellie. I thought, after I'd spent half an hour staring out at the great British scenery, that I would come down to the kitchen to find your mother semi-tearful but resigned, in front of a cup of tea, having received the disappointing news that there wasn't going to be any happy-ever-after...'

'I know.' Ellie shot him a guilty look from under her lashes. She indicated one of the chairs by the table, thought better of it and then moved to the back door that led out into the garden. She needed some fresh air, even if the air was a little too fresh for what she was wearing. Leading the way, she unhooked her old mac from the door and stepped into a pair of wellies, even though it wasn't raining.

Her mother's garden was small and manageable but gave the illusion of being absolutely enormous because it backed onto open fields. With just the light from the kitchen behind them, the garden was shrouded in darkness, and beyond the fields rose and fell with dark uniformity, much like the ocean at night, the very ocean they had left behind.

Ellie didn't look at him as she straightened one of the garden chairs and curled up into it, tucking her legs under her, covering them with the mac. She felt the brush of his arm against hers as he adopted a similar position, both of them staring out at the vast landscape.

Her skin tingled from that accidental brush, making her shiver with that unwelcome sexual awareness that had dogged her all day.

He'd been the perfect gentleman. He'd charmed her mother and had been unfailingly considerate towards her, and Ellie had hated every second of it, because it wasn't what she wanted from him. *Not any more.* She wanted passion and fire and craving, and all that hunger that had flared in his eyes every time he'd looked at her a million years ago in Barbados...

The wretched hopelessness of it engulfed her. She could no longer summon up any enthusiasm for the prospect of slowly weaning herself off him. All she could see was a guy who didn't love her and anguished days spent working alongside him, watching him carry on with his life while she was cruelly rooted in the past, desperately trying to move on but condemned to become a spectator to other women taking her place in his bed.

'I couldn't do it,' she said sadly. 'I really tried, but I just couldn't bring myself to do it…'

CHAPTER NINE

'I REALISE YOU'RE probably quite annoyed…' *Livid*, she mentally amended. 'I prepared my speech. I was going to be light-hearted about it, tell Mum that it was all just a silly mistake…that that's what happens when a vindictive ex is in the picture…'

She sighed.

'But then she rushed into telling me about how happy she was…overjoyed… How long she'd spent worrying that life was passing me by… I was hell-bent on taking care of her, and didn't see that somewhere along the line she really just wanted me to take care of myself. Now she thinks that I'm finally happy, that I've found the one for me.'

'I understand,' James murmured.

'She started crying, but in a quiet way. Said how lost she'd felt after Dad died, that she'd been a burden to me and that it was so wonderful to finally see me happy, and actually living life the way it should be lived. I think those were her exact words.'

What Ellie failed to mention were the other things Angela Thompson had said. She had spotted them holding hands through the window, before she'd answered the door. She could see how much love there was between them. She'd been feeling so low, but now she felt as though she'd been given a new lease of life…

Every smiling confidence had plunged the dagger deeper into Ellie's heart. No longer could glib explanations gloss over what had happened, yet how on earth could she go into the detail of how she *really* felt about her emotionally unavailable boss? How could she make sense for her mother of the way she had meandered, eyes wide open, into an emotional quagmire, where she was now stuck loving him while he turned his back and walked away? How could she tell her mum that what had started between them had only started because she had just been so different from his glamorous ex? From *all* his glamorous exes? That she had been the new and different toy with which he had enjoyed playing for a while but was never going to hold on to for very long?

Every joyous utterance from her mother had been a cruel reminder of just how far from the truth she was. In the end, Ellie had cravenly backed away from the confession she had been intent on making.

'I... She knows you won't be staying beyond tomorrow. I told her you had urgent business to see to in London. You'll be leaving first thing.'

'You're upset,' James murmured, eyes shielded.

'Of course I'm upset!' Ellie burst out in angry frustration. She strode towards the bed and flung herself on it, utterly exhausted and angry with him for being so calm. But then what was at stake for him, really? After this interlude, life would return to normal quickly. She would be the one left picking up pieces. She would be the one having to deal with her mother's bitter disappointment after he'd swanned off, having done his bit. And that didn't even begin to cover the horror of dealing with her broken heart.

She rested her arm over her eyes, banking down a desire to cry. She knew he had joined her on the bed when his weight depressed the mattress. She tensed, wanting him so badly that it hurt, yet refusing to yield to the fierce physical pull he had over her. She kept her arm draped over her face.

She didn't expect him to scoop her up, but he did, and she didn't struggle when he enfolded her in his arms and rested her head against his shoulder.

A kind and caring gesture, she thought as her body began to stir into heated response.

He stroked her back and she was dimly aware of him murmuring soothing things under his breath. She began to relax. She didn't want to make love. She *knew* that that was a place she no longer had a right to revisit. Yet they did, slowly and tenderly, and it felt as though everything was happening in a dream. He held her for a long time, coaxing her anxieties out of her, stroking her hair until she was melting against him, eyes closed, her breathing evening out.

Thoughts flew out of her head as fast as her anxieties. Her mind went a complete blank and familiar sensations settled in to replace the arousal of her body, her breasts becoming tender, her nipples pinching and then hardening into tight buds as his hand slipped under her top to caress her. He knew her body so well, could strum it with the dexterity of a maestro.

She didn't open her eyes. She allowed herself to be seduced into trance-like pleasure, opening up to him with the hunger of someone deprived of sustenance for too long.

Her clothes were removed. She felt the coolness of the night on her naked skin and his silent, caressing fingers on her, touching her in places she had come to love being touched and sending her body up in flames.

Neither of them spoke and it felt as if they were both in the same place, contemplative and aware that there would be a situation to deal with when this brief interlude was over. But, for the moment, Ellie *needed* this, whether it made sense or not.

He nuzzled her breasts and explored her body, gently caressing her between her legs and feeling the wetness of her arousal, and she did the same for him, pleasuring him with her hands and her mouth until he was groaning, low, husky and urgent. They were moving in slow motion, languorous and fluid. He went between her legs, tasting her with his mouth and his tongue, flicking and teasing her clitoris while she coiled her fingers into his hair, clinging like someone needing anchorage in a storm.

He didn't stop. He wanted her to come against his questing mouth and she wanted it as well. It felt right. She moved against him, squirming, her breathing fast and shallow, and then she came in a spasm, arching up while he continued to probe her most intimate place with his tongue. His hand rested on her belly, tugging so that the sensations were so powerful that she had to stifle the urge to cry out loud with pleasure.

She breathed him in as he rose up to straddle her, and opened her eyes only once to see him take his manhood in his hand, circling it firmly but gently, pleasuring himself while she cupped him in her hands and rose to delicately lick the veined hardness.

He came on her, a hot splash that she rose to greet with her mouth, savouring its saltiness while the sadness she had kept at bay began permeating back into her.

Exhausted, she could barely utter a word when, after what felt like dreamy hours, he lay next to her. She curled against him, fighting sleep but unable to resist it, and the next time she opened her eyes a thin, grey light was seeping through the curtains into the bedroom.

She struggled into a sitting position, disoriented for

a few seconds, then registering what had happened the night before.

Also registering that the space next to her was empty and, glancing at her phone at the side of the bed, that it was a little after six in the morning.

Early.

While the thoughts were still foggy in her head, the bedroom door opened and in he walked, as stealthy as a big cat, not bothering to turn on the light, instead making for the bed and perching on the side. Aside from a towel wrapped round his lower half, he was naked, and she closed her eyes and breathed in deeply as she tried to get her thoughts into some kind of order.

'How long have you been awake?' she asked, heart thundering inside her, reacting all over again to the intense pull of his masculinity.

'Not long. Long enough to have a shower and do some thinking.'

He looked at her, pink and sleepy-eyed, her hair tousled, just the slope of her narrow shoulders visible because she had pulled the duvet up to her chin, which she rested on her knees. There were instances, thoughts that flashed through his head, that made it impossible to remember her as his dutiful PA.

None of this had gone according to plan. He had anticipated something clear cut, possibly a bit uncomfortable but largely sanitised. He had anticipated a situation he would walk away from, dusting his hands free of complications that he had told himself he could do without. They had slept together but there had been a finite time limit imposed on what they'd had, and at no point had it really occurred to him that that time limit might end up going off-piste so accustomed was he to exercising complete control over all aspects of his life.

He'd done the right thing in returning to London once the story had hit the press and he had done the right thing in suggesting they faced her mother. He had accepted responsibility for the fact that none of this would have happened had he not dumped his ex and then turned his attentions to the one woman he should never have contemplated going anywhere near, whatever her hidden attractions.

Had he planned to sleep with her again?

He honestly didn't know.

Common sense had prevailed once, but he was honest enough to acknowledge that it had flown out of the window the minute he had returned from Barbados to find her holed up in her house, like a prisoner terrified of a firing squad positioned outside the front door. Every protective instinct he'd never known he had had kicked in with stupendous force.

Was that what had reawakened the attraction he had been confident of putting to bed? Had the novelty of new sensations propelled him into wanting to light that fire all over again?

Yet he had managed to hang on to his common sense, had managed to look at the bigger picture and take on board the role he knew he had to play to assuage her mother's fears and doubts.

He had chatted to her mother but, all the while, his eyes had strayed to Ellie, who'd been as nervous as a kitten. He had noted her interaction with her mother, had seen the concern and love there. He intuited the pain she would feel at the thought of crushing her mother's optimistic, romantic dreams. He knew what pain felt like, how it could sear a hole right through you until you were dazed with it, and something inside him had twisted.

Guilt? A conscience?

Was that why he had been driven to sleep with her again? Because his conscience had been pricked? Because he had seen her tremulous fear of letting her mother down and had recognised, guiltily, that he had put her in that position?

Or was it just a case of something started that had ended prematurely?

James did not underestimate the power of sexual attraction. He'd still wanted her, whatever label he chose to put on it, and she still wanted him. Their relationship had not behaved according to the rules he had laid down, but weren't there always exceptions to rules?

He had been adamant that things would need to stop so that normal working relations between them could resume after he returned from Max's wedding. He'd always kept his working life very separate from his love life. However, the two had merged, and maybe this was just something they both needed to finish. It wasn't about emotions, it was about finishing a chapter that had been started. They were both adults and she had her head screwed on. Why should it interfere with the excellent working relationship they both had?

Her grey eyes, locked on him, were wary. He raked his fingers through his hair and noted the way she swallowed, all too aware of him just as he was all too aware of her.

'Last night...' he murmured.

'I know. Shouldn't have happened.' Ellie looked at him defensively.

'But it did,' he said gently.

'I was in a poor place. Things hadn't worked out the way I thought they would...' She glared at him accusingly. Why couldn't he just leave it be? she wondered fiercely. Why did he have to drag everything out in the open for an early-morning post-mortem?

The way she had succumbed to him, given herself to him, was a cruel reminder of just how much she loved him and how much she had so foolishly invested in him.

'No,' he agreed. 'And, trust me, I can understand your dilemma.' She failed to fill in the gaps so he continued, his voice soothing and sinfully seductive. 'Your mother is fully invested in this business about us being an item. She's spent the past few years despairing of you ever meeting someone.'

'That's a massive overstatement!'

'And now here we are. She likes me...'

'There was no need to go overboard with the James Stowe charm.'

'I had no idea that that was what I was doing.'

'I had hoped that she might see us together and realise how ill-suited we were to one another, but you had to lay it on thick.'

'You can't blame me for being myself—'

'I tried to point out the glaring differences between us,' Ellie interjected bitterly, thinking of her valiant, doomed attempts to get things back on track. 'I told her the sort of background you came from, the life you were accustomed to leading. I reminded her that, once reality kicks in, things begin to fade...'

'And she wasn't buying any of it?'

Ellie shook her head curtly. She decided not to mention her mother's response to all those genuine and true observations. She had listened, her head tilted to one side, a smile tugging at her lips, and philosophically had told her that she recognised what love looked like.

Besides, she had added, hitting below the belt with the unerring accuracy only a devoted parent could bring to the table, 'I know you and I know you would never hop into bed with a man just for the sake of it. You're just not that type of girl and you never have been.'

'Maybe she needs to see first-hand that things don't always go according to plan,' he said thoughtfully, and Ellie frowned.

'What are you talking about?'

'Last night happened for a reason,' he ruminated. 'And that reason had nothing to do with the fact that you were in need of comfort...'

Ellie reddened. Outside the sounds of the day beginning infiltrated the bedroom, the early-morning greyness gradually turning into weak sunshine and trying its best to get past the curtains.

'You still want me,' he forced out into the open, just what she didn't want to acknowledge, and she closed her eyes for a few seconds, her breathing quickening while she desperately wished that she was somewhere else. 'It's nothing to be ashamed of,' he murmured, trailing his finger along her jaw with such devastating effect that her breath hitched in her throat and her eyes fluttered open.

'It's mutual. I still want you. I never saw this coming,' he admitted with roughened honesty. 'I never thought any of this would happen, but it did. When we were in Barbados, I saw this as unexpected but temporary. Fun for a few days until fate decided otherwise. I still want you, so why not continue what we have? You can't bring yourself to tell your mother that this isn't going to end up in marriage, and she can't see it because we only ever see what we want to see, and what your mother wants to see is you with me.

'Maybe she needs to see us have this relationship and then, when it inevitably fizzles out, she'll accept that it was something that wasn't meant to be, with all the best intentions in the world. Maybe, that's what the hungry paparazzi needs to see... Instead of mounting a defence, maybe we just need to go with the flow and let what we have run its course...'

Ellie listened to all of this in stunned silence. She knew exactly where he was going with this. When it came to women, James liked to be the one who called the shots. He was always the one who ended things. Like a toddler with a never-ending supply of brand-new toys, he enjoyed the freedom to dispose of one toy exactly when he wanted before moving on to the next.

He was being perfectly honest when he told her that he hadn't foreseen things happening the way they had. Even when they *had* ended up in bed together, he had still not foreseen wanting to continue what had started against all the odds.

It would fizzle out. It was, in his words, *inevitable*. She wasn't one of his drop-dead gorgeous supermodels. She was his efficient, very ordinary-looking personal assistant. He had been charmed by the novelty, but he had always assumed that the novelty would wear thin very quickly. It hadn't and, because it hadn't, he now saw no reason why they shouldn't continue what they had until it did.

On every level, he was a sensualist.

Into the lengthening silence, he continued without hesitation, his self-assurance growing by the second. 'You're speechless,' he said with satisfaction. 'I get it. It's not a solution either of us ever thought of because we were both sold on the notion that everything had to be neatly wrapped up before start of play. We broke up because… I suppose I got a little spooked. I got the sense that you might have been reaching out for some kind of emotional involvement. We broke up, but it doesn't mean that what we had was *broken*. We wanted each other then and we still want each other.'

'Sorry?' Ellie felt as though she had suddenly been plunged into an alternate universe where perfectly understandable words and sentences were reaching her as unintelligible mutterings in a foreign language.

Yes, she knew where he was going with this, but she couldn't credit his massive misinterpretation of her expression and her silence. How could someone so smart and so perceptive be so dense?

'We both thought that a few days in Barbados would get this out of our system. We both knew that it was a flash-in-the-pan situation. Still is, but the fire under the pan is taking a little longer than we anticipated to die out...that's the power of lust.'

'I don't think you understand...' Ellie said slowly.

He raised his eyebrows and smiled with the smooth confidence of a guy who had never been wrong-footed by a woman before in his life. He smiled with the utter confidence of a guy in complete control of his life and the outcome of the decisions he made. Right now he had decided that he wanted to carry on with what they had, and on the surface Ellie knew that every aspect of what he was suggesting made sense.

To him.

Because he wasn't involved. Because the ending was inevitable. Because as far as he was concerned they were on the same page...just two adults who had had a bit of fun...so why not drift into having a bit more fun until the whole thing became boring and petered out? Sure, he'd been *spooked*, but he was willing to overlook that, was willing to write that off as a by-product of their mutual physical attraction.

And suddenly she realised that returning to work and pretending that nothing had happened while she hunted around for another job wasn't going to do. Nor would she be able to return to work while trying to masquerade as the perfect PA she'd used to be, keeping her emotions in check while she was in front of her computer and at her desk, simmering in anticipation until they could sneak out, at separate times, to reunite in a blaze of passion somewhere.

It all felt overwhelming and seedy, and she was terrified of being tempted into a situation that would end up destroying her.

How easy it would be to mentally shut the door behind which the inevitable would be waiting for her. How easy it had been to jump into bed with him in the first place and then to stay there, living in an unreal bubble which she had known all along was going to burst. How easy it had been to kid herself that everything would be fine because she couldn't possibly fall in love with someone like James Stowe.

'How long do you think it would last?' she asked, her voice curious and conversational 'You know...the sleeping together...until the inevitable happens?'

Taken aback, he was silent for a few seconds, frowning and then giving her question bemused house room.

'How long is a piece of string?' he said eventually, and shrugged. 'Does it matter? It's not something we can put a timeline on...'

'No, I don't suppose it would be,' Ellie intoned coolly.

'We tried the timeline before,' he dismissed impatiently, 'and it didn't work. Why bother trying to pin things down this time round?'

'Why indeed?'

'What's going on here?' He looked at her, eyes narrowed, trying to get inside her head. She could see that, could sense it, could sense his growing bewilderment that the plan he had decided upon was not quite going in the direction he had anticipated.

'Us carrying on? It's not going to happen, James.'

'Your reason being…?' He smiled slowly, eyes darkening, and she fought to combat the swirl of hot sensation that slow smile so effortlessly unleashed inside her.

'You're right when you say that I didn't expect…what happened between us to happen.' Ellie inhaled deeply and stared down at a dizzying abyss yawning open beneath her.

'Neither of us did, believe me…'

'I have always been serious when it comes to guys and relationships. I said as much to you.' She smiled sadly. 'Which is probably why I have so little experience.'

'When did you ever have time for relationships? You were responsible from a young age for the well-being of your mother.'

Ellie ignored the genuine empathy in his voice because that was just what had got her into hot water in the first place. His easy ability to empathise…a personality that was tuned in to those around him in ways that were instinctive and seductive.

He didn't have women running around behind him, weeping and wailing when things crashed and burned, because he was rich and good-looking. His charms lay way beyond those narrow parameters and she had been short sighted not to have clocked that earlier on, when her heart had still been intact.

'I guess,' she said, 'I absorbed how close my parents were, and knew deep down that that was the sort of relationship I wanted for myself. I wasn't brought up to indulge in wild flings and one-night stands but, James, that's pretty much what happened, isn't it?'

'It was certainly wild, but a one-night stand it most definitely wasn't.'

'I thought I would be able to enjoy what we had, and walk away from it with only a bit of a dusting down necessary before everything returned to normal, but I was wrong.'

'What do you mean?'

There was a guarded edge to his voice that Ellie couldn't miss.

'I should have asked myself how it was that it turned out being so easy to just fall into bed with you.'

'Sometimes, when the atmosphere is just right...' A sudden wicked grin chased away the wariness that had been there before. 'Hot sun...white sand...blue sea... It's a recipe for sex between two consenting adults who're attracted to one another.'

'James, I never thought I could fall for a guy like you, but I did.'

Ellie watched as the lingering smile on his face disappeared. Comprehension followed swiftly. He was adding up and making sense of all those things that should have been a giveaway but which he had ignored, missed or misinterpreted.

'I don't get what you're trying to say.'

'You do, James,' Ellie told him gently.

She wondered whether he was thinking that this was a Naomi moment all over again. Another romp in the hay with someone he'd assumed was as casual as he was. She almost felt sorry for him.

'I could pretend,' she continued, watching as the colour drained from his face. 'That I don't feel the way I do. I know it would make life a lot easier for you but, when I walk away from this, I don't want to walk away with things left unsaid. I don't regret what happened between us, but I would regret *that*. I *would* regret thinking that I hadn't told you how I felt.'

Looking at her, James was aware of the cogs in his head working way below their usual optimum, whirring efficiency. His thoughts were blurry, even though he knew exactly what she was saying, just as he knew exactly how he should be reacting.

With horror. He hadn't signed up for this. He'd signed up for a few days of fun. Uppermost in his mind, however, was one overriding thought... *What's wrong with a bit of pretence? Whoever said that honesty was always the best policy needs to have a major rethink...*

'Of course,' he heard her continue calmly, 'I realise that this puts us in an untenable position, so I do have a suggestion.'

'You have a suggestion...'

How could they possibly be having this conversation here? In a bedroom? Barely dressed? Was that why he was finding it so difficult to focus? Why his thoughts were all over the place?

'My mum knows that you're due to leave today, that you could only pop down for an overnight stay because of work. You can get dressed and leave now, before she's up and moving about. She takes her time in the morning. I know you're probably going to think that I'm leaving you in the lurch workwise, but I won't, and you have my word on that.'

'Work hadn't yet crossed my mind.' James gritted his teeth.

Ellie ignored the barely audible interruption.

'I will remain here for a few days and this time, without you around, I can begin to lay the foundations for why things won't work out between us.'

'Fill me in, Ellie. I'm all ears.'

'First and foremost,' she said slowly, 'the hours you work. Too long. The very fact you had to dash off early in the morning because of business. I've worked for you, so I know how dedicated you are to your work, to the exclusion of everything else. Maybe I thought I could deal with that, but I was wrong. You go to Hawaii in a couple of days and, once you leave, I will return to the office and start sourcing my replacement.'

'You'll have to brace yourself for the wagging tongues…'

'I know,' Ellie told him quietly. 'But I will, because I intend to take responsibility for this, and not cower and hide away. When everything first blew up, I literally felt like a rabbit caught in the headlights, but that's not me.'

'No. It's not.'

'I've faced up to this situation, faced up to the fact that I made a terrible mistake in falling for you. But I guess…' she smiled wistfully '…that's something you're used to.'

She paused and aired the thought that had earlier crossed her mind. 'Poor Naomi was guilty of the same breach of the rules, but you don't have to worry that there will be any "kiss and tell" revelations. I intend to stay below the radar and, if anyone decides to camp out on the doorstep, then they'll be treated to such a diet of "no comment" that they'll give up in boredom.'

Accustomed as he was to taking complete charge of any situation involving women, James stared at her for a few silent seconds, digesting what she had just said.

She had spared him the discomfort of having to end things and he decided that he was grateful for that reprieve. Naturally, he would have had to sever all ties in the end, despite his initial suggestion that they let what they had play out until it had reached a natural conclusion. He didn't do emotional commitment and she had always known that.

Where she had lived with the calamitous effects of what happened when love didn't work out the way you expected it to, she had still clung to the romance of falling in love, to relationships that stayed the course, sailing towards happy-ever-after endings. Perhaps because, unlike his parents, hers had been devoted to her. For him, unheard and barely visible to both his parents, love equalled pain. So, while she still had faith in its existence, he had none. That was just the way it was.

She had read the situation perfectly. It was a relief, he determined. Now was his cue to take his leave, yet he remained pinned to the spot, frowning, then finally said, 'Forget about the replacement or coming into the office and facing down whatever gossip is sure to be circulating.'

He thought of her discomfort, of her putting on a brave face and battling through it, head down, betraying nothing of her inner turmoil. His brilliant PA would be back in place, calm and unflappable, though this time in the face of a nightmarish twist of fate.

She'd been right when she'd said that she had reacted emotionally to the sudden onslaught of paparazzi and their vulture-like curiosity. She would have done, he thought, because she wasn't battle-hardened as he was.

She was also head over heels in love with him and that wouldn't have helped matters...

He thought back to those amazing eyes lazy on him, intent veiled... He thought of the slow, low murmurs as she'd moved under his exploring hands...the feathery whisper of her fingers trailing along his body, touching him in a way that had never failed to set his body ablaze with an insane craving... It shook him.

'Take as long as you want when it comes to letting your mother down gently.' He took the lead from her but his voice was unsteady as he killed wayward thoughts and focused on moving forward. Habits of a lifetime took over. When it came to women, moving forward was what he did.

'I can make a list of potential candidates to replace me,' Ellie said stiffly.

He was relieved that she was walking away. He couldn't wait to be rid of her now that she had told him how she felt.

Under her stony expression, her heart was breaking in two, but she would not regret the confession that had left her lips. It was called walking away with a clean slate. Unfortunately, the clean slate opened up the reality that she would have to find another job, and the chances of it being as well paid, not to mention satisfying, were slim.

'No need.' He began moving off, gathering belongings and chucking them into the hold-all he had brought with him.

'And don't worry about pay.' He glanced over his shoulder. 'I'll make sure you remain paid in full until you find another job, whenever that may be.'

They stared at one another in heated silence for a few electrifying seconds, and he was the first to spin round on his heels, his body rigid with furious tension.

She could barely watch as he got dressed, his back to her. What else was left to say when he was at the bedroom door, bag in hand, ready to go?

Nothing.

She lay down and rolled onto her side, turning away, waiting until she heard the soft click of the bedroom door being shut behind him.

CHAPTER TEN

No comment!

Sprawled in his expensive leather chair in front of his wood and steel desk, James glared at the computer screen winking at him, demanding a level of attention he was incapable of giving.

No comment had been his catchphrase ever since he had returned to London a day and a half ago.

No comment to the reporters eager to get a scoop. *No comment* to his employees, who had backed away as soon as they had recognised the warning intent in his eyes should they choose to pursue their curiosity.

Thus far, he had fielded three phone calls from an excitable Izzy, demanding to know what was going on and asking when the big day was going to be, because she would have to start shopping for a hat. He had done his best to quell her ridiculous enthusiasm but for once he was discovering that there were situations in life he could not readily cope with.

He impatiently pushed himself back from the desk and swivelled the chair to stare out of the window. For once, his door was closed. No one dared knock on it. He had been like a bear with a sore head and they all knew better than to disturb him.

Ellie.

He'd texted her. Obviously, that had been perfectly reasonable, because he had to know when 'no comment' could morph into 'things didn't work out as expected'. Today's hot-off-the press news would, he knew, be history within days, but still, he needed to know how to play things out, and he had given his word to her that he would wait until she was comfortable telling her mother the truth.

She'd replied to his embarrassingly long-winded text quite simply.

All's fine here, thanks. Will keep you in the loop. I will tell Mum it's off by the end of next week.

He'd be in Hawaii by then.

He would be facing curious family members and he would not be able to shut himself inside an office, having pinned a metaphorical *Enter at your own risk* sign on the door.

He would…

What would he do? Say? *Think?*

For a few seconds he was swamped by a suffocating sensation of powerlessness. It was like a blanket over him, stifling his ability to think straight. All he could see in his mind's eye was Ellie, with her smooth, calm face, her intelligent grey eyes and, behind that calm intelligence, all that fiery, sexy passion that had energised him a way he would never have imagined possible.

Walking away had made sense, but for once doing what *made sense* had not worked in his favour. Because, if anything, she was in his head more than she had ever been.

Why? He was conditioned to run the minute things started getting heavy with a woman. So why was he dragging his heels now? Especially when Ellie had been the

one to fire the starting gun. Was it because, for all his illusion of control, the simple truth was that he had always
ambushed all chance of getting serious with anyone by
choosing women he'd subconsciously known would end
up boring him? Until Ellie had entered his life, leaving
him here, not knowing what to do...

He frowned, absently reached for his phone, recognising that initial one-second flare of anticipation that there
might be a missed call or a text waiting to be read from
her, then opening up the photos he had taken in Barbados.

Yet again, he was surprised at just how many he had
taken. There were pictures of her laughing, looking at him
over her shoulder, sitting on the beach, making funny faces
because she didn't want him pointing the lens at her, even
though the provocative flare in her eyes told another story.

Suddenly suffused with restless energy, thoughts previously sluggish accelerating with astonishing speed towards
conclusions that now poured out from behind carefully
sealed doors, he vaulted to his feet and strode to grab the
trench coat draped over the back of a chair.

Ellie heard the sound of the doorbell with a grunt of dis-
pleasure.

It was a little after nine-thirty in the evening. Her
mother was asleep and she was staring at a book on her
lap, masochistically enjoying the pain of replaying images of James in her head and speculating on a future that
held no joy at all.

At this very moment in time, she was staring down the
barrel of no job, no desire to return to London, a deadline
within which the stories she had started spinning to her
mother about her break-up would have to accelerate and a
bottomless pit of memories that promised sleepless nights
wracked with misery.

The last thing she needed was one of her mother's friends popping by to drop something off. From experience, she knew that many of her mother's friends, all of them dog owners, thought nothing of having that last dog-walk late at night, using it as an excuse to deliver something or other, or nip in for a cup of coffee and a quick chat.

She opened the door with her polite expression at the ready…and for a few electrifying seconds felt the blood drain from her face as she stared up at the last person she expected to see standing outside her mother's house.

A feeling of *déjà vu* slammed into her with the force of a sledgehammer and it was all she could do to remain standing in the doorway, as rigid as a block of marble.

What the heck was *he* doing here?

How many times did he have to walk away before he realised that *walking away* should remove the option of suddenly materialising on her doorstep?

She thought back to their last conversation, to her admission that she had fallen in love with him… She'd never seen a guy back away so fast. He'd seen the conflagration ahead, and had run in the opposite direction just as fast as his legs could take him. Even though she'd expected nothing less, she'd still been devastated at his response.

Mortification surged through her, as well as mounting anger. 'What do you want?' she demanded bluntly. 'What are you doing here?'

'Let me in.'

'Over my dead body.' But she couldn't help but sneak a glance towards the staircase behind her, because if her mother ventured out of her bedroom getting rid of James would not be possible.

Yes, Ellie had begun the process of cementing all the differences between her and James. All those niggling things that were already bricks in the wall that would eventually separate them.

With a timeline set for herself of a mere week, she knew the process would have to be ratcheted up. But at this point in time, a mere couple of days since James had returned to London, the foundations she had begun to lay would be blown out of the water should her mother clap eyes on the guy shamelessly standing at the front door.

She was infuriated that, despite everything she was feeling, she could still tune into his over-the-top sexuality with such effortless ease. The guy had practically had a seizure when she had admitted her true feelings for him, yet here she was, *still* fighting to ward off the spool of vibrant images unravelling in her head.

'Where is your mother?'

'Asleep,' Ellie said sharply. 'And I don't want you coming in because I don't want her to know that you're here.'

She loved him.

She'd closed her eyes, gritted her teeth and admitted how she felt, because that was the sort of person she was. Honest, upfront and straightforward. But what had he done? He'd run faster than a sprinter at the sound of the starting gun.

Now, with her foot poised to nudge the door shut in his face, he felt a sickening sense of panic that he might have left things too late, because the truth was that love when it fell on barren ground, was quick to turn to hate...

What would he do without her in his life?

He felt giddy at the flashbacks that poured into his head—watching her down-bent head as she fiddled on her iPad, searching for just the thing he had asked for, her calm amusement at all his rowdy employees, who always seemed to do as she asked whenever she asked, the way she had guarded her private life and then shared it with him, handing him the gift of her confidences…

'I was a complete fool.' There was no point trying to preserve his dignity or play games in which he might emerge the winner. There was just this moment in time and his one chance to try and fix what he had wilfully broken.

'I don't want to have this conversation. I want you to go before Mum hears someone at the door. She might be a sound sleeper, but doorbells can wake people up. I don't want her seeing you. You're not getting it, James. *Don't just stand there staring at me!*'

'I'm getting that you opened your heart to me and I—'

'Now I *really* want you to go!' The last thing Ellie needed to hear was a minute-by-minute recap of her soul-baring confession. When she had admitted to him how she felt, she hadn't expected to clap eyes on him again, but now he was here, larger than life, and it was agony.

'You love me.' He breathed urgently, his voice lacking its usual self-assurance. 'And it's mutual.' He said that very fast, to forestall her slamming the door on him.

On the verge of shutting the door very firmly on his well-heeled loafer, Ellie paused and looked at him suspiciously.

She'd been down this road before, hadn't she? *Let's carry on*, he'd urged. *Where's the harm? Let's get what we have out of our systems and then we can break up… why not?*

But surely he wouldn't be so cruel as to use her own declaration of love against her in some stupid quest to take what he still wanted? Did he think that her loving him made her a dead cert for a replay, using the same reasoning he had used before? Was he arrogant enough to think that he would be doing her a favour by inviting her back into his bed, and would use whatever verbal tools he wanted, knowing that she was vulnerable to them all?

'I hate you,' she whispered, already in full defence mode at her own internal line of reasoning. It had leap frogged from assumption to assumption until she had managed to convince herself that she could not possibly believe anything he had come to say. Least of all some crazy, mumbled admission of love which he had pulled out of a hat like the proverbial rabbit.

She heard the shuffle of footsteps overhead and stifled a groan of frustration.

'Just go! Mum's waking up…'

'Let me in. She doesn't have to know that I'm here. I want to talk to you. When I'm done talking, I'll leave and she will never know that I've been in the first place.'

'Ellie? Did the doorbell just ring?'

Her mother's thin voice quavered from the bedroom door which was just up the narrow stairs and mercifully out of sight.

'Get in,' she snapped at James, channelling him past her and towards the sitting room, into which he obediently vanished, leaving her to take the stairs two at a time, just preventing her mother from trundling down to see what the fuss was all about.

Five minutes later, she was in the sitting room, door closed, heart beating so fast she felt it was going to burst right out of her chest. She didn't know what he was there for. He'd mentioned something about love, but it was clear and always had been that he hadn't the faintest idea what *love* was.

The bottom line was that she had settled her mother back to bed after mumbling vaguely that nothing was happening, there was no need to come down—*nothing to see here*. But her mother's eyes had been curious, and Ellie would have to dispatch James before curiosity got the better of sleep. Because, if her mother decided to see for herself what was going on, then all the hard work she had done building up stories of incompatibility, would have been for nothing.

In her mother's mind, the very essence of *love* would be a guy racing hundreds of miles to be with the person he loved because he couldn't bear to be apart from her.

She remained by the closed door, leaning against it, arms folded and eyes narrowed as she looked at him for a few seconds in stony, unforgiving silence.

'Speak, and make it quick, James. I don't want Mum coming downstairs and finding you sitting here.'

'I can't say what I've come here to say with you standing there by the door, like a prison warden waiting to escort a criminal from the building.'

Ellie sourly interpreted that to mean that he wanted her close, close enough to reach out and touch her. If he had come here hoping to scratch an itch that hadn't conveniently disappeared as he'd hoped, then he would surely suspect that one touch and she'd be right back in his arms?

After all, she loved him, and love made idiots of everyone. Look at poor, deluded Naomi!

For the sake of voices not being heard, because noise had an irritating habit of travelling to all sorts of nooks and crannies in the small cottage, she edged closer. But, instead of perching on the sofa next to him, she adopted a stiff position on one of the chairs, from which she continued to look at him with jaundiced suspicion. It was an effort to keep memories at bay. She could feel them just there, waiting to surge forward to undermine all her barely-there resistance.

'I've begun to explain things to Mum,' she burst out fiercely, leaning forward. 'I've begun to tell her that we're very different people, too different for things to work out between us. I've begun to let her down, and it's not *fair* of you to just show up here so you can ruin *everything*.'

'We're barely engaged. How can our differences be rising to the surface so fast?'

'I *know* you!' Bright patches of colour scored her cheeks. 'Of course you were never going to fall in love with me. Do you think I haven't seen the way you are with all those women you dated in the past?' She looked away and her voice was low, bitter and honest. 'No matter what they looked like, when it comes to women there's only so much you're capable of giving, and all of it can be summed up in two words. *Good sex.*'

'Just *good*?'

'I'm glad you think this is funny,' Ellie said sharply.

'I don't.' He raked his fingers through his hair and leant forward, arms resting loosely on his thighs.

'I'm not climbing back into bed with you, and if I was stupid enough to fall for you then I'm also smart enough to know how the ground lies.'

James gazed at the mutinous set of her mouth, the defiant glitter in her eyes, and marvelled that he hadn't recognised what he felt for her sooner than he had. Surely he should have clocked that so much more had pulled him to her than some passing attraction?

She fired him up on every front. She was demanding, smart and had spent three years making him adapt to her without him really realising it. It was crazy that he hadn't seen that for what it was—a slow drift to an emotion he only now recognised and accepted.

'I don't want you falling back into bed with me,' he countered softly, and a shadow of bewilderment flashed across her features for a barely perceptible second or two.

He winced, thinking that those were the tramlines her thoughts were travelling down—that the only thing he could possibly have come for was sex. He honestly couldn't blame her.

'Good!' Ellie said stiffly. 'Because there's no way I intend to do that.'

'I wouldn't ask you to, unless there was a ring on your finger.'

'I beg your pardon?'

'I love you.'

Ellie stared. Her mouth fell open. Her brain moved back sluggishly half an hour, to recall his opening words when she had greeted him at the front door.

Had he meant what he'd said? *That he loved her?*

'I don't understand…' She managed to breathe while her heart picked up frantic speed and her mouth dried up so that she could barely swallow. Joined up thinking was proving difficult.

'When we went to Barbados…' He sighed heavily, channelling his thoughts. 'Falling into bed with you… I didn't look beyond a straightforward situation of two people who had discovered their mutual attraction to one another, recognised it and decided to follow where it led. Under a tropical sun, things blossomed, and it was all very black and white.

'I look back on my life and I see that it was always very black and white when it came to relationships. I knew what loss was about, and in my mind it was always associated with the emotional freefall that came from loving someone and then being let down by them. If you never loved, then you could never be let down.'

'And what began in Barbados was going to stay in Barbados,' Ellie said softly, remembering just how clear he had been on the rules of the game, at which point she had blithely deferred thinking about tomorrow because today was too much fun.

'Come and sit next to me,' he murmured, patting the space beside him on the sofa. Ellie hesitantly shifted over to the spot and curled up, feet tucked underneath her, still too suspicious to go too close but already opening up to the roughened honesty of his voice and what he was saying to her.

He covered her hand with his but respected the small distance she had made to maintain between them.

'That was the plan,' he said gravely.

'Until Naomi appeared and blew everything out of the water.'

'Everything had been blown out of the water long before then,' he mused thoughtfully. 'I always assumed that I was immune to emotional involvement with any woman. Like I said, I lost both lost parents when I was young, but you lost a parent devoted to you. I lost parents who were devoted to one another. Money bought them freedom from any kind of conscience. They dipped in and out of our lives. They were spectators, you could say, although in Izzy's case perhaps that would be an exaggeration. She got the brunt of their attention. For me...'

He shook his head ruefully. 'Not so much. You'd think, that being the case, that their loss would have been felt less, but not so. It felt like questions I had yet to ask could then never be answered.'

Ellie shifted closer to him so that her knee was touching his thigh and she could feel the spread of warmth from his body, enfolding her like a safety blanket.

It struck her that there was something about him that had always made her feel safe, even when she had just been his dutiful secretary. She had always known that he had her back. When she thought about it, all the time he'd been *telling* her that he didn't do emotional investment, he had been *showing* her that he did. And that had culminated in him trekking across the Atlantic to hold her hand and support her because he had known that she would need him, even without her having to tell him. He *knew* her, just as she knew him.

'I had an ill-fated relationship shortly after the death of our parents,' he admitted heavily. 'I would say that that was the nail in the coffin of any inclination I might have had to test the waters of emotional involvement.'

'What happened?'

'I sought refuge in the wrong woman. I was lost, and I foolishly thought that I needed someone to help me find my way. It was a learning curve. After that, I closed myself off, and I liked it that way. I liked knowing that I was in control of everything and everyone. No unpleasant surprises. Women came and went and there was no attachment. If any of them started thinking outside the box, well, I guess, looking back, I was pretty ruthless, but it was a ruthlessness I never questioned.'

Mesmerised by this outpouring of heartfelt admissions, Ellie could only stare at him, round-eyed.

'I always knew the score, so when we became lovers I assumed you did as well, because you knew me as well as I knew myself. No attachments. Three years working with someone...' He smiled wryly. 'You were all but my wife without the ring on your finger.'

'That's hardly true.' Ellie flushed and lowered her eyes.

'Maybe not then but certainly once we became lovers.' He stared broodingly at her, then smiled again—a lazy, rueful smile that sent a tingle racing through her. 'I'd never felt so comfortable with anyone before. Of course, now I know why. I was in love with you, and everything was different. The lights had been switched on, only I didn't realise it. I just knew that I wasn't ready for things between us to end.'

'And yet when I...when I told you how I felt...'

'I did what I was programmed to do,' he admitted ruefully. 'I fled, but there was only so far I could run and for only so long. The last day and a half have been hell, and there was no way I could contemplate going to Hawaii and pretending that my life wasn't in freefall without you in it.'

Every word he said was music to her ears. She had bared her soul and now he was baring his.

'So,' he concluded, reaching towards her to tangle his fingers in her hair, eyes pinned to her face. 'I can't live without you. I love you and I need you and I was a fool for not recognising the symptoms of love sooner. I told you that I wouldn't expect you to sleep with me without a ring on your finger...so, will you marry me?'

'I think...' Ellie smiled and looked at him with all the love she was now free to express. 'I think you know the answer to that...'

Ellie slipped her hand into James's, looked up at him and smiled.

She couldn't have been happier. Yet now, a mere couple of days after his proposal, she found that she was nervous as they walked towards the private function room in the five-star hotel where she would meet his assembled family.

'You look radiant,' he murmured, tipping her chin so that their eyes met. 'And it's not as though congratulations haven't already been flying across the airwaves.' He grinned. 'Izzy has texted a hundred times. They can't wait to get to know you.'

Ellie glanced down at her dress, jade-green and softly falling from thin spaghetti straps to just above her knees.

She had angsted over what to wear and, concluded, with precious little time to choose, that the outfit would be fine for a lunchtime do, bearing in mind that many more would be joining them for an early supper—including, she had gathered, Max's fiancée Mia's sprawling family. She took a deep breath and met his reassuring grin with a smile.

'Seems unfair that Max and Mia's big day is just round the corner and we've gate-crashed it with an announcement of our engagement…'

'We didn't do that,' James pointed out. 'A certain malevolent ex did…'

He thought back to the text he had received from Naomi a couple of days ago. She hadn't been able to resist getting in touch so that she could rub his nose in it, pleased with herself for landing him in a place she'd figured he'd loathe. It had given him huge satisfaction to inform her of the aisle he would be walking down with the woman he loved right there by his side. No need to block her number, because he knew that he wouldn't be hearing from her again any time soon.

'Besides,' he added thoughtfully, 'I think Max is only too pleased that he's not the only die-hard bachelor to find himself hopelessly in love. I spoke to him just before we flew, and he actually crowed that yet again big brother is leading the way…'

'You always manage to say the right things,' Ellie murmured, and raised her eyebrows when he replied without batting an eyelid,

'Is that the sound of you admitting that you'll be marrying the perfect man?' He burst out laughing, pushing open the imposing door in front of them at the same time, 'No…don't answer that. Your expression speaks louder than words and, my darling, I wouldn't have it any other way. Now…time to brave the lion's den…'

Ellie had no time for her nerves to flourish. They opened the door to a quiet gathering. Max and Mia, and Izzy and her fiancé Gabriel, and a little child with long, dark hair and bright, curious eyes.

The room had been adorned with flair, a picture-book story of everything Hawaii had to offer. Beautiful plants dotted the huge space and stunning local paintings adorned the walls. Ellie took it all in and smiled, relaxing as the women leapt to their feet and came towards her while James, smiling, moved to kiss his sister in passing before joining the guys.

A quiet segregation of the sexes, soon to be remedied, but just for the moment Ellie was enfolded by Izzy and Mia, with Rosa bobbing around and clamouring to join the club, just the thing to set her at ease.

'I can't believe James is getting married!' Izzy squealed. 'Mind you, the real shock was Max.' She hugged Mia, a striking olive-skinned girl with skin as smooth as satin and long, brown hair pinned to one side with a deep red hibiscus flower, and kept her arm slung affectionately round the other woman's shoulders. They both looked at Ellie, eyes lively and warm.

'We girls have to tame these guys,' Mia confided, grinning. 'And that includes Gabriel!'

'Can I tame someone?' Rosa demanded, which was the cue for the guys to burst out laughing as Max asked what plots were being concocted. And then Ellie was being shepherded to the table, where champagne was waiting to be drunk and a mouth-watering array of local dishes were set out, with two waiters standing stiffly by the doors, ready to be summoned to serve the food and pour the drinks.

In one sweeping glance, she took them all in—her new family. She was barely aware of champagne corks popping but she *was* aware of glasses being raised for a toast to Max and Mia.

'To Max and Mia!' she said on cue.

Her turn would soon be coming and she couldn't wait…

* * * * *

COMING SOON!

We really hope you enjoyed reading this book.
If you're looking for more romance, be sure to
head to the shops when new books are
available on

Thursday 5th August

To see which titles are coming soon, please visit

millsandboon.co.uk/nextmonth

MILLS & BOON

THE HEART OF ROMANCE

A ROMANCE FOR EVERY READER

MODERN
Prepare to be swept off your feet by sophisticated, sexy and seductive heroes, in some of the world's most glamourous and romantic locations, where power and passion collide.

HISTORICAL
Escape with historical heroes from time gone by. Whether your passion is for wicked Regency Rakes, muscled Vikings or rugged Highlanders, awaken the romance of the past.

MEDICAL
Set your pulse racing with dedicated, delectable doctors in the high-pressure world of medicine, where emotions run high and passion, comfort and love are the best medicine.

True Love
Celebrate true love with tender stories of heartfelt romance, from the rush of falling in love to the joy a new baby can bring, and a focus on the emotional heart of a relationship.

Desire
Indulge in secrets and scandal, intense drama and plenty of sizzling hot action with powerful and passionate heroes who have it all: wealth, status, good looks…everything but the right woman.

HEROES
Experience all the excitement of a gripping thriller, with an intense romance at its heart. Resourceful, true-to-life women and strong, fearless men face danger and desire - a killer combination!

To see which titles are coming soon, please visit

millsandboon.co.uk/nextmonth

MILLS & BOON

Coming next month

THE SICILIAN'S FORGOTTEN WIFE
Caitlin Crews

"I wish only to kiss my wife," Cenzo growled. "On this, the first day of the rest of our life together."

"You don't want to kiss me," she threw at him, and he thought the way she trembled now was her temper taking hold. "You want to start what you think will be my downward spiral, until all I can do is fling myself prostrate before you and cringe about at your feet. Guess what? I would rather die."

"Let us test that theory," he suggested, and kissed her.

And this time, it had nothing at all to do with punishment. Though it was no less a claiming.

This time, it was a seduction.

Pleasure and dark promise.

He took her face in his hands, and he tasted her as he wanted at last. He teased her lips until she sighed, melting against him, and opened to let him in.

He kissed her and he kissed her, until all that fury, all that need, hummed there between them. He kissed her, losing himself in the sheer wonder of her taste and the way that sweet sea scent of hers teased at him, as if she was bewitching him despite his best efforts to seize control.

Cenzo kissed her like a man drowning and she met each thrust of his tongue, then moved closer as if she was as greedy as he was.

As if she knew how much he wanted her and wanted him, too, with that very same intensity.

And there were so many things he wanted to do with her. But kissing her felt like a gift, like sheer magic, and for once in his life, Cenzo lost track of his own ulterior motives. His own grand plan.

There was only her taste. Her heat.

Her hair that he gripped in his hands, and the way she pressed against him.

There was only Josselyn. His wife.

He kissed her again and again, and then he shifted, meaning to lift her in his arms—

But she pushed away from him, enough to brace herself against his chest. He found his hands on her upper arms.

"I agreed to marry you," she managed to pant out at him, her lips faintly swollen and her brown eyes wild. "I refuse to be a pawn in your game."

"You can be any piece on the board that you like," he replied, trying to gather himself. "But it will still be my board, Josselyn."

He let her go, lifting up his hands theatrically. "By all means, little wife. Run and hide if that makes you feel more powerful."

He kept his hands in the air, his mock surrender, and laughed at her as he stepped back.

Because he'd forgotten, entirely, that they stood on those narrow stairs.

It was his own mocking laughter that stayed with him as he fell, a seeming slow-motion slide backward when his foot encountered only air. He saw her face as the world fell out from beneath him.

Continue reading
THE SICILIAN'S FORGOTTEN WIFE
Caitlin Crews

Available next month
www.millsandboon.co.uk

JOIN US ON SOCIAL MEDIA!

Stay up to date with our latest releases, author news and gossip, special offers and discounts, and all the behind-the-scenes action from Mills & Boon...

 millsandboon

 millsandboonuk

 millsandboon

It might just be true love...

MILLS & BOON
Desire

Indulge in secrets and scandal, intense drama and plenty of sizzling hot action with powerful and passionate heroes who have it all: wealth, status, good looks…everything but the right woman.

MILLS & BOON
MEDICAL
Pulse-Racing Passion

Set your pulse racing with dedicated, delectable doctors in the high-pressure world of medicine, where emotions run high and passion, comfort and love are the best medicine.